Christian turned from the view outside and fiddled with the seam of the curtain, watching the men, waiting for their reaction.

'They're bonny, but what of them?' Rab said at last, his brow knotted with puzzlement.

'I want to make shawls like that.'

Both men looked astonished, then Benjamin Selbie said, 'You're not serious!'

'Why not?'

For a moment he floundered, looking from one to the other of the cousins. 'The Paisley folk don't weave materials like that.'

She took the shawl from Rab and ran it through her hands, her fingertips relishing the cool firm feel of woven silk. 'I'm my father's daughter, Benjamin, and I'm not afraid to take risks. In five or ten or twenty years,' said Christian, stabbing the air with a slender finger for emphasis, 'someone right here in Paisley'll be making a lot of silver out of weaving those shawls. I want it to be me.'

Benjamin Selbie's eyes widened, then his face became expressionless . . .

DAMASK DAYS

Evelyn Hood

SPHERE

First published in Great Britain in 1990 by Headline Book Publishing PLC
This paperback edition published in 1998 by Warner Books
Reprinted 1999
Reissued in 2010 by Sphere

A CIP catalogue record for this book
is available from the British Library.

ISBN 978-0-7515-4506-7

Printed and bound in Great Britain by
Clays Ltd, St Ives plc

Papers used by Sphere are natural, renewable and
recyclable products sourced from well-managed forests and certified
in accordance with the rules of the Forest Stewardship Council.

Mixed Sources
Product group from well-managed
forests and other controlled sources
www.fsc.org Cert no. SGS-COC-004081
© 1996 Forest Stewardship Council

Sphere
An imprint of
Little, Brown Book Group
100 Victoria Embankment
London EC4Y 0DY

An Hachette UK Company
www.hachette.co.uk

www.littlebrown.co.uk

To my husband,
Jim Hood,
With love

And to the staff of Paisley Central Library
And Paisley Museum
With grateful thanks

Acknowledgement

I am indebted to *The Paisley Shawl* by M. Blair, *The History and Romance of the Paisley Shawl* by A.M. Stewart, and to Mrs I. Crawford of Kilbarchan for research material used in this book.

E.H.

Chapter One

Sunlight glittered on the trimming of the big drum that led the procession, and on the pikes carried by the militia marching behind the drummer. Its brilliance made a brave show of the red coats worn by the bailies and burgesses marching in the main body of the procession.

It seemed, that June day of 1784, to be anxious to make up for the long bitter winter that had killed off a considerable number of Paisley's old folk, and a fair sprinkling of new-born infants as well.

'There he is – there goes Uncle Robert!' Christian Knox released her cousin Rab's arm and waved vigorously at Robert Montgomery, marching with the other new bailies.

'He's awful red in the face, is he not?' Rab asked anxiously as his father strode by, looking neither to right nor to left.

'So would you be if they'd just taken you by the arms and legs and douped your rump on the Doupin' Stane,' said Christian on a splutter of mirth.

Her cousin looked at her with reproach. 'It's a great honour to be appointed a bailie and to take part in the Lonimers Day parade.'

'Mebbe,' said Christian, unrepentant, 'but it seems to me to be a daft, unmanly thing to do to mark the dignified occasion – bouncing a man's backside off a stone!'

1

'It's tradition.'

'That doesn't make it any the less daft.' Then as the last of the procession passed by and the crowd about them began to break up and flock to the town centre for the speechifying she flapped her hands before her face in a vain attempt to ward off the day's heat and added, low voiced: 'You've not forgotten about tonight, have you?'

'No, but . . .' Rab hesitated, gnawing on his lower lip.

'Och, Rab! You're not going to let me down?'

'I'm not happy about it at all. You'd be best to forget the whole business.'

'Why should the laddies be the ones to get all the fun? All my life I've wanted to swim in the Hammills – and you promised to go with me.'

'Aye, but – why can't Daniel be the one to take you?' demanded Rab. 'He's your brother – not me.'

'If I asked Daniel to take me he'd only take fright at the thought and go running to Mother and Father with his tongue wagging. Please, Rab,' she coaxed as only Christian could, adding when he hesitated: 'If you don't want to accompany me I'll go swimming by myself.'

'You can't do that! It'll be dark, and if anything happens there'll be nobody to help you.'

Christian whisked about and joined the throng easing their way along the footpath, making towards the town centre, where her mother and father and young brother would be waiting for her. 'Nothing'll happen,' she threw over her shoulder. 'So I'm going, whether or not I have to go alone.'

For a moment she thought that Rab had decided to stick to his own decision, and refuse her. For a moment she thought that her hoped-for swim in the pleasantly cool waters of the River Cart was lost.

Foolish and impetuous though she may be at times she

had more sense than to go to the Hammills alone at night.

Then to her great relief she heard the patter of feet behind her and he caught up with her.

'I suppose someone has to make sure your daft ideas don't lead you into trouble, Christian Knox.'

She beamed at him and slipped her hand into his. 'An hour before midnight, then, down at the Hammills?'

He caught at one final straw. 'You've got nothing to wear.'

'I've filched a pair of Daniel's breeches. And one of his shirts. An hour before midnight, then?'

'Aye,' said her cousin with resignation. 'An hour before midnight.'

Christian heaved a great sigh of pleasure, and, rounding the corner of High Street, plunged into the seething, holiday-minded mass of folk, towing Rab behind her, in search of their families.

It was the custom in Paisley for the folk to go to bed early and rise early. After dark, the only people in the streets were revellers, beggars with no place to call home, and the Town Watch, made up of local men who took it in turns to patrol the streets during the dark hours.

So everything was quiet when Christian crept down the staircase of her father's fine home on Oakshawhill. She made for the rear of the house, tiptoed through the kitchen, and let herself quietly out of the back door, leaving it on the latch so that she could slip back in when she came home.

All during the hot bright day she had been looking forward to her first swim in the Hammills. Although the sun had long gone the night was warm and airless, and her skin tingled at the thought of contact with cool water.

There was a pleasant freedom, too, in the clothes she

was wearing. Her slim legs, unhampered for once by skirts and petticoats, were clad in a pair of her brother's breeches and hose, and she had donned his linen shirt and bundled her dark hair beneath one of his caps for good measure, just in case she met anyone on the way.

Down the brae she went, out into the High Street at the Almshouse corner, then turned left, swinging confidently along the street and covering the ground fast.

In no time at all she had reached the Old Bridge in the town centre, left the road, and was clambering down the river bank to where the water foamed over the Hammills, a small natural weir on the River Cart. The river itself ran through the heart of the town, by the open market place. It was in the deep pool immediately below the Hammills that the town's boys swam in the summer.

Down here, away from the street, pockets of warm dark shadow were cast by the banking, although the Hammills themselves glowed with a silvery light, patched here and there with black as the water foamed over the rocky lip. The pool below the weir was a smooth, dark, cool, inviting mirror beneath the starry sky.

There were no lights in the houses huddled along the opposite bank, or in the back windows of the houses and shops skirting the bridge.

Christian surveyed the scene and drew in a deep breath of satisfaction. For years, ever since she was a small child, she had longed to join the boys scrambling over the rocks and diving joyously into the water amid great bursts of spray. But it wasn't done for girls to swim with the lads, and until now she had yearned in vain.

A hand reached out from the sleeping town behind her and took hold of her shoulder. She spun round with a gasp of fright that was hastily swallowed and disguised

4

as a fit of coughing as she saw that it was only Rab.

'Wheesht, will you!' he said in panic, thumping her on the back. 'D'you want the Town Watch about our ears?'

'What did you have to fright me like that for?' she hissed back indignantly, then: 'What's that you're carrying?'

He released the bundle beneath his arm and let it drop to the ground between their feet. 'A cloth to dry ourselves with.'

'Oh.' She hadn't thought about bringing a cloth with her. Rab surveyed her pityingly, and shook his head.

'It's big enough for both of us. Unless,' he added hopefully, 'you've changed your mind?'

'Would I be here if I had?' She pulled Daniel's cap off and let her hair spill free, then kicked off her shoes and turned towards the water. 'Come on, then!'

With a shrug of resignation Rab unfastened his shirt and let it drop to the ground.

In the moonlight the upper part of his body had a golden glimmer to it. He was broad-chested and slim-waisted, lithe and easy in his movements, free now of childish plumpness and hovering, at fifteen years of age, on the verge of manhood.

'Can you swim?'

'Of course I can!' Christian's voice was scathing. 'My father used to take us to a wee loch up the braes. I learned to swim there.'

She didn't tell him that it had only been the once, and that her father had kept a firm grip of her all the time, refusing to let her go beyond the shallows.

Instead, she made for the water, grimacing with pain as the stones underfoot stabbed into her instep.

Once again her cousin's hand grabbed her. 'Not so near the weir! Here, where it's shallow.'

She followed him, then gave a suppressed squeal as her foot splashed into the water. 'It's cold!'

'Of course it's cold – it's running water, and it's come all the way down from the braes. Come on.' Rab kept a firm grip on her wrist, drawing her into the pool.

She ploughed after him, setting her teeth against further squeaks and squeals as the deepening water clasped her ankles, calves, knees and thighs in its icy grip.

'Now,' said Rab when they were waist deep and the water was eddying round them. He released her hand, then suddenly ducked forward. With a back-kick that splashed water over her face and breast, he was gone.

She stared wildly about the dark stretch of the pool; it seemed to take a long time before his head broke surface a few yards away.

'What are you waiting for?' he asked, and turned away from her to swim towards the opposite bank. Christian lunged into the water, the breath going from her at its chill.

All during the hot day she had thought longingly of the pool's cooling kiss. But she hadn't realised that it would be so cold. Unable to swim well, numbed and confused, she almost panicked when the stony river bed seemed to drop away from beneath her feet. Then she saw a rocky outcrop nearby and managed to flounder clumsily over to clutch at it. Her bare feet sought and found the stony bed and she stood up, pushing long wet hair from her face, then scrambled from the water to perch on the rock.

Rab came back across the pool with enviably easy, graceful strokes, and halted a few yards away, treading water.

'Are you all right?'

'Of c-course!' Christian's jaw had taken on a life of its

own. It was vibrating with cold, and it was hard to speak clearly.

'Are you sure?'

She found that if she took in a long deep breath her voice sounded better. And when she relaxed her tense muscles, the chill eased and a tingle of well-being and exultation began to spread through her. She had done it! She was swimming in the Hammills!

She drew her feet up on the rock, hugging her knees. 'I'm quite sure!' Then, as he said nothing, but stayed where he was, staring at her, she asked tartly, 'Have I grown two heads?'

'No, I just . . . I . . .' Rab said, and continued to gape.

Christian was quite unaware of the picture she presented in the moonlight. Her small face, with its sleek cap of wet hair, revealed the promise of a rich mature beauty to come; Daniel's soaked shirt and breeches moulded the sweet youthful curves of her body; her slim ankles and bare feet were snowy white against the dark rock, each perfect toenail gleaming like a tiny pearl in the moonlight.

'I . . . I . . .' said Rab, and Christian, suddenly and unaccountably embarrassed by his look, got to her feet, balancing on the slippery uneven rock.

'Out of the way – I'm going to dive in.'

'No!'

She had often seen the lads diving off the rocks, and envied them the feeling of swooping through the air like a bird. She knew that the pool was deep enough to be safe.

'It's easy,' she said, and swung her arms up, just as she had seen the lads do. Rab, realising only just in time that there was to be no stopping her, threw himself to one side to avoid a collision.

Somehow, in spite of her belief that she was going to arc through the air, dividing the surface of the pool neatly, like a leaping fish, Christian's entire body hit the water with a resounding crash that knocked the breath from her.

There was an explosive noise in her ears, as though the entire town had fallen apart, and she was dimly aware of a great burst of spray.

All at once the water had become as hard as the ground; diving into it felt like the time she had fallen out of the apple tree at home on to the hard bruising earth.

She opened her mouth in an automatic squawk of protest and choked on black water. She wasn't at all certain whether she was going down towards the river bed or up towards the surface. She was in a world of water, with no floor or ceiling, no north or south.

Rab's hands clutched at her and pulled strongly. She felt Daniel's shirt rip, and even in her panic had time to realise that her mother was going to be furious about it.

Then her head broke the surface and she spluttered and choked, drew in a long bubbly breath and choked again as she was bundled to the bank and deposited in shallow water, where she sat and gasped like a stranded fish.

When she lifted her head, pushing her soaking hair from her face, Rab was standing over her like an avenging angel, his eyes dark pools of horror at the thought of what might have been.

'Ye daft fool, ye! Telling me that ye could swim when ye couldnae!'

'I can!' she said feebly, then, gaining energy now that the crisis was over: 'If you'd left me alone instead of gripping at me like that—'

'If I'd left you alone you'd have drowned! D'you realise

that, Christian Knox?' He stooped and took her by the shoulders, shaking her. She heard the shirt tear again, in the region of her shoulder blades.

'Let go of me!'

'That's the last time I—'

In their anger with each other they had completely forgotten the need for caution. By the time they heard feet scrambling towards them down the banking it was too late to hide.

A lamp that had been hidden behind a sturdy body was suddenly brought into view, illuminating the pair that struggled and squabbled in the shallows.

'What's afoot here, then?' a man's voice wanted to know. Rab released his cousin and stepped back, his hands falling to his sides. Christian scrambled up to stand by him, her hair streaming water over her shoulders and back.

'By God,' the man behind the lamp said in astonishment. 'It's a lassie!' Then he raised his voice. 'Come and see the bonny pair of fish I've caught in the river tonight.'

Rab's gaze smouldered accusingly at Christian in the lamplight as the second watchman slithered down the banking to add the glow from his own lamp to the scene.

'What is it, Fraser?' He stepped into the golden pool of light – a tall man with a head of thick dark hair gleaming silver at the temples, and a strong square face marked by a smallpox scar on the right side, from the corner of his mouth to the lobe of his ear.

His hazel eyes took in the scene with one sweep, then blinked and widened, staring.

Christian and Rab looked back at him in horror. They

hadn't realised that this man, of all men, was on the Town Watch tonight.

There was a long, tense silence, then: 'Well, Christian?' Gavin Knox asked his daughter coolly. 'What d'you mean by this, madam?'

Chapter Two

'Well?' Gavin asked as his wife came into the kitchen.

Margaret Knox closed the door behind her and laid the empty cup on the table. 'She drank it all down, and she was almost asleep when I left her.' She looked at the wet clothes her husband had been trying to arrange before the range. 'Look at Daniel's shirt – ripped almost clean from waist to collar! I'll have to sew—'

'You'll do nothing of the sort. It was Christian who damaged it, and Christian will repair it.'

'If she doesn't catch the pneumonia first, and die.'

'Not her. Not Christian,' said Gavin with calm assurance, leaving the soaking shirt and breeches and putting one arm around his wife. 'The good Lord meant her for a long and colourful life, I'm certain of that. Come on, it's time we were getting to our own bed.'

In the privacy of their bedchamber Margaret said wistfully. 'I wish Christian was as biddable and as easy to raise as Daniel. If you ask me, he should have been the lassie, and her the laddie, the way their natures lie. What's going to become of her, Gavin? One of those days her wildness is going to be the death of her.'

He blew the candle out and slid into bed beside her, settling his big body into the mattress with a sigh of contentment. 'Don't fret yourself. She's your daughter, Margaret, and always was. Now you know what heartaches you must have given your own mother in your younger days.'

'I was never like that. For one thing, I would never have thought up a daft notion like swimming in the Hammills. She could have drowned!'

'But she didn't drown, so there's no sense in fretting yourself over what might have been. Rab's a sensible laddie – he looked after her.'

'Sensible! Letting her coax him into mischief isn't my idea of being sensible! He's too soft with Christian altogether. She can wrap him round her little finger. I'll have something to say to Robert and Annie about that son of theirs tomorrow!'

'You'll do nothing of the sort. He's a young man now, a full weaver with his own loom. I'll not have you carrying tales to your brother about Rab – pay heed to me now, Margaret.'

She subsided, recognising the tone in his voice and knowing that there was no sense in arguing with it. Then after a while, she lifted herself on one elbow.

'Gavin,' she said, 'I can't help worrying about the lassie.'

'I've noticed,' said her husband dryly.

'She belongs neither to one world or the other. She's got no need to go out and earn her living, as I had to do – and yet, she's altogether too intelligent and too wilful to settle down as some man's wife. What's to become of her?'

'No doubt Christian'll decide that for herself. Now that she's coaxed me into paying for extra lessons when she's finished with her schooling next month, she might end up as a teacher herself.'

'I can't see Christian as a teacher. If she'd had the inclination she could have been helping me in the Poors'

Hospital schoolroom,' mused Margaret, who managed to do other things as well as run her surgeon husband's home and see to their children.

Gavin gave an almighty yawn and turned over. 'Go to sleep, Margaret. Christian'll make her own way in the world, never fret.'

'You'll talk to her in the morning, before you go out of the house?'

'I'll do that.'

'And be firm with her,' said his wife. 'She's gone too far this time. You mind what I'm saying, Gavin Knox.'

'I hear you,' Gavin's voice mumbled from the darkness. 'And I'll be firm, I promise you. I'll promise you anything, if you'll just go to sleep, and let me do likewise!'

Rab arrived at the house the next morning before the surgeon and his family had finished breaking their fast. The maidservant led him into the empty parlour, where he paced the floor nervously, jumping when the door opened.

'No need to loup like a flea, for it's only myself,' his cousin Daniel said cheerfully. 'I've just come to get my schoolbooks.'

'How's Christian this morning?'

Daniel grinned. 'Her hair's standing on end after its soaking, and her nose is red. She's going to have a right chill.' Then his blue eyes sobered. 'Man, what possessed you to go along with her mad scheme?'

'It was my idea, not hers.'

Daniel gathered up the books lying on the table by the window and fastened a leather strap round them deftly. 'I doubt if it was. But it's brave of you to take . . .' He broke off as the rest of his family came into the room.

'Is it not time you were away to the school, Daniel?' his father asked curtly.

'I'm just going.'

'Well, Rab?' Gavin said when the door had closed behind his son.

Daniel was right. Christian's eyes were shadowed with want of sleep and her hair, which hadn't been properly brushed after its soaking, had dried to a frizzy mop round her pale face. Her nose was pink-rimmed. Rab's heart went out to her. He wrenched his gaze away from her, and faced his uncle.

'I came to tell that last night was all my doing.'

Gavin, dressed and ready to set off to Glasgow, where he was due to attend to patients in one of the city's infirmaries, gave him a steely glance.

He was in no mood to be forgiving, for when he had finally slept the night before he had dreamed about his daughter's body washing to and fro beneath the Hammills, her pale dead face turned up to the moon.

The picture was still with him, and as a result he had come to the confrontation in a tense frame of mind.

'Indeed? And have you no brains at all in that thick-skulled head of yours? D'you not realise what could have happened to my daughter if your foolish idea had got out of hand?'

Christian went to stand by her cousin. 'It wasn't Rab's fault at all, so don't listen to him.'

'But—'

'It was mine, and I don't know,' she said, glaring at Rab over her shoulder 'why *he's* here at all. It was me who asked him to go to the Hammills last night. It was me,' she went on, quickly and loudly, as Rab opened his mouth to protest, 'who dived off the rocks.'

'Diving?' Margaret, horrified, caught at her

husband's sleeve. 'What's this about diving from the rocks?'

'I knew what I was about! Only Rab didn't know that and he caught hold of me and that's when Daniel's shirt tore, and—'

'I don't know what got into your head, lassie,' her father thundered. 'Diving from the rocks, indeed – and you scarce able to swim!'

'I can swim well enough.'

'That you can't, milady. Thirteen years of age, and you don't have the sense you were born with!'

'Rab, you're two years older than Christian – you should have had more idea of the dangers,' Margaret chimed in, and the boy's face went dusky red.

'Mebbe it's as well he was there,' Gavin said. 'If Christian had gone alone she might have been killed.'

'I tell you, I knew what I was about!'

'Not,' her father said icily, 'when I saw you. You were like a drowned rat – and don't deny it.'

She opened her mouth to do just that, and spoiled her argument by sneezing instead.

'There!' Margaret pounced. 'You've caught a chill!'

'I haven't,' Christian protested, and sneezed again.

'It seems that you've decided on your own punishment, lass,' Gavin said, a hint of amused sympathy warming his eyes. 'You'll stay indoors today.'

'And mend your brother's shirt,' Margaret added.

If Christian had let matters lie there, the business might have been over and forgotten. She knew full well that she had been in the wrong and deserved her punishment. But the horror of missing a day from school went straight to her tongue.

'I'll mend the shirt – but I'll not keep to the house, Father.'

Groaning inwardly, Rab tugged at her sleeve, but she rushed on, unthinking in her panic. 'I've only another few weeks at the school, and I must go today!'

Gavin, on his way to the door to fetch his hat, stopped and swung round, the half-smile leaving his face.

'You'll do as I say.'

'I'll not!' Then, seeing the storm clouds gathering on his brow again, she added hurriedly: 'Please, Father – anything but staying away from the school when I've only got a little while left there as it is!'

Father and daughter faced each other. Two pairs of hazel eyes clashed and held. Then Gavin gave the merest hint of a shrug.

'Very well. Go to school, if you must,' he said. 'But you'll have to accept another punishment.'

'I will.'

'Then I withdraw my agreement to pay for those extra lessons you've been pestering me for.'

Her mouth dropped open with shock. 'But—'

'You said you'd accept another punishment, and you'll not get a third chance. The matter's ended, Christian. There's no more to be said!'

Colour flooded into her face, then receded as quickly. With a muffled sob she caught up her skirts and fled from the room, pushing past her father.

'Uncle Gavin—'

'I said the matter's ended, Rab. As far as your part in last night's madness goes, I've no doubt your father's dealt with you, so we'll leave it at that. Margaret, I'll be home in good time for my supper.'

He walked out, leaving Rab dumb with misery. He knew, as they all knew, how desperately Christian wanted to continue with her education. Her younger brother, Daniel, was a scholar at the Grammar School on School Wynd, but to her chagrin his sister, who attended a ladies' school, was coming to the end of her formal education. She had been overjoyed when her father had agreed to pay for special tuition for her in Latin and arithmetic and geography.

Margaret, as appalled as her daughter and Rab at the severity of the punishment, caught up with her husband in the hall and said low-voiced, 'Gavin – you surely don't mean it?'

He settled his tricorne hat firmly into place on his dark head. 'I've said it, Margaret, and I'll not go back on it now.'

'You're being too hard on her!'

'Confound it, woman, you were the one who hectored me about being firm!'

'I know, but—'

Gavin kissed her on the cheek and opened the front door. 'I've said it, and there's no going back. Christian must learn the meaning of discipline. The matter's settled, and there it must rest. She's only got herself to blame,' he said, and left the house.

Margaret Knox had been born in a weaver's cottage, and was the daughter and sister of weavers.

All her life Christian had loved the sound of the looms, and whenever she could she spent hours watching the weavers at work. Scarcely a day passed when she didn't visit the cottage in Townhead where Rab worked with his father.

As he had expected – as he had hoped – she came to the weaving shop later that day for sympathy and consolation.

Rab's drawboy, a child employed to work the overhead harness of the draw-loom, was sitting on the footpath

17

in the afternoon sun, his bare toes, used to standing for long hours on a cold earthen floor, wriggling ecstatically in the heat. His small grubby fingers were busily plaiting and twisting yarn into a 'simple', the cords the drawboys pulled on to set the harness in action.

Stepping down from the door to the earth floor of the shop, blinking in the sudden dimness after the bright sunlight, she found Rab alone.

There were only two looms in the small shop, one a hand-loom worked by Robert Montgomery, the other a draw-loom worked by his son.

Rab had recently finished his apprenticeship with red-headed Jamie Todd, a close friend of the Montgomery family, and he was proud of his skill with the draw-loom, a fairly new innovation in Paisley. Unlike the hand-loom, the draw-loom could weave curved, intricate patterns.

When Christian came in with storm clouds still darkening her brow, he was busily rubbing two long hand-brushes together to work a solution of flour paste well into them. The smell of the paste hung in the air.

'I thought you might look in.'

'It's not fair!' Christian burst out, close to tears.

'I'm vexed for you, Christian, but does it really matter if you never have the way of Latin and figuring?' Rab asked sensibly. 'You know enough now to see you through life.'

'It's not life I'm thinking of, it's the learning itself!' Christian sneezed, and dug irritably in her pocket for a handkerchief, which she swatted at her nose.

Rab passed her on the way to his loom, where he swept the brushes, one in either hand, over the warp threads stretched between the back beam of the loom and the intricate wooden harness above. 'I never studied these extra things, and I don't feel the lack.'

18

'You already knew what you wanted to do with your life. Daniel's getting the chance to study all manner of things, and he's no more clever than me.'

'Aye, well, Daniel's probably going to take up some sort of trade that needs a lot of knowledge,' Rab tossed the words over his shoulder, then put the brushes down and peered closely at the warp, testing a strand between finger and thumb. The paste strengthened the yarn. With a nod of satisfaction he picked up a big square goose-quill fan and began to waft it close to the warp to dry the paste.

Christian returned to the real bone of contention. 'My father promised me those lessons, and he's gone back on his word!'

'Only because you wouldn't accept the first punishment he came up with.'

Christian was silent, nibbling at her lower lip. She would have given everything she possessed to be able to turn the clock back, to bow her head meekly and stay away from school for the day as her father had commanded. But knowing that she had been in the wrong didn't help matters now.

'You should have taken his tongue-lashing and kept your own tongue between your teeth,' Rab went on remorselessly. 'The way I did when the Town Watch hauled me home last night and woke my own father.'

'I've got more smeddum in me than that,' Christian returned, with a flash of spirit.

Rab put the fan aside and tested the warp again, shrugging the criticism off with one movement of his broadening shoulders. 'At least it got the scolding over with, and no more loss on either side,' he said. 'Anyway, you should have kenned that your own father was with the Town Watch last night.'

'How was I to know he was taking on someone else's turn as a favour?'

They glared at each other, then Rab said uncomfortably, 'You'd best go – my father'll be back at any minute, for he's only taken some muslin to the tambourers. I'll get into more bother if he thinks I've been chattering to you instead of getting on with my work.'

Christian, working on suppressing another sneeze, nodded absently. Robert Montgomery was one of the local weavers who had taken up the weaving of fine muslins as well as linen. He himself was a hand-loom weaver, and after the muslin was woven the designs had to be tamboured – sewn on by hand.

'Rab, I must have those lessons, even if I have to steal the silver to pay for them!'

'Don't be daft!'

'How else can I get it?' She threw her hands out. 'I can't work for it – I don't know how.'

Looking at her, arms outspread, her back to the sunlit window, the light from behind her piercing the loose bodice of her gown and picking out the shadowy outline of her slender body, Rab was suddenly, disconcertingly reminded of the vision she had made the night before. Then, her breasts and waist had been outlined by the wet shirt, her skin like alabaster in the moonlight, her face almost that of a stranger, a woman.

His pulses leapt, then throbbed, and he swallowed to clear a thickened throat, averting his eyes, going to the window that looked out on to the street and thumping on the glass to let the drawboy know that he was wanted.

'You'd best go,' he said again, almost pleadingly. 'Away home and stitch Daniel's torn shirt!'

'It's already done.' Christian dropped her arms to her

sides and walked to the other window-sill to run a finger over the bars of the birdcage that sat there. Its inhabitants were two young sparrows that Rab's drawboy had taken from the nest and raised by hand. Perky and cheerful, falling over each other to investigate the finger that had been poked between the bars of their temporary home, they were almost old enough and strong enough to be taken to the braes and set free.

The boy came scurrying in and took up his position by the loom, grasping the simples in his two hands. Rab slid on to the 'saytree' – the long weaving bench.

'And it's as good as new,' Christian said over her shoulder. 'He'll scarce be able to tell which shirt I took. Stitching's the only useful thing I've learned in that dame's school. But it's not going to—'

Then she stopped as Rab's earlier words burst into her mind like a shower of sparks from a fire. She left the fledglings to their own devices and swung back to confront her cousin, her face glowing.

'That's it, Rab! That's the answer! I'll earn the money to pay for my own lessons!'

'How?' he asked warily. The drawboy, impatient to be at work now that he had been called in from the sunshine, let go of the cord and plunged his fingers into his thick, dirty fair hair, nails clawing at his scalp, keeping one wary eye on Rab.

'Tambouring, of course,' Christian carolled joyfully. 'Tambouring for the weavers!'

Chapter Three

Robert Montgomery stretched booted feet across his sister's hearthrug, took an appreciative swig from the glass in his hand, and completed his tale: 'So I thought I'd best come and see what the two of you said before I agreed to take the lass on.'

Margaret eyed her husband apprehensively, and was glad to see that Gavin, resting one shoulder comfortably against the mantelshelf, was grinning.

'I've no objection. In fact,' he added, 'I'm pleased to know that she's going to fill up her time with some useful work instead of getting into more mischief. Does she know you're here?'

'I told her I'd feel happier if I spoke to you first.'

'And what did she say to that?'

Robert hesitated, then laughed and admitted, 'She said I was welcome to do as I wished, but she was going to take on tambouring anyway – for someone else if not for me. And to tell you the truth, I'd as soon it was for me, for I'm badly in need of some good seamstresses.'

'You'll find Christian one of the best. She's a fine hand with a needle.' Margaret allowed herself that brief moment to boast about her daughter, then got down to more serious business. 'Now – tell me how Annie's getting on, for it's been a week or two since I last spoke to her.'

Robert accepted another glass of claret and settled himself deeper into his chair. He seldom came to his sister's fine house, and it gave Margaret pleasure to see him sitting in her parlour. Pleasure – and a little pain, because with every day that passed Robert grew more like their father, Duncan Montgomery, who had died just over a year before.

Meg, Duncan's wife, had decided to spend her remaining years in Ayrshire, on the farm where she had been raised, looking after her two brothers, both widowers now.

Robert and Annie had moved their brood into the house in Townhead, on the western side of the town, that Duncan and Meg had built when their own children were small.

'Annie's fine. As busy as ever, for all that the two lads are grown now.' Then he said proudly, 'Duncan's started his apprenticeship with Jamie Todd.'

'You'll be hoping he'll do as well on the loom as Rab.'

Robert shook his head. 'I doubt that. Annie says that in every two, there's a rebel. That's our Duncan – and your Christian, mebbe. And look at our own brother Thomas, taking up medicine instead of following in Father's trade as I did. No, Rab's the natural weaver of the two. But that doesnae mean that Duncan can't do well for himself once he puts his mind to it and stops stravagin' off with his friends whenever he gets the chance.'

When Robert finally took his leave Margaret closed the door behind him and went back into the parlour.

'It's sad, the way families break up. There's my mother down in Ayrshire, and Thomas a physician in Dunfermline – and for all that Robert's close by I see so little of him.'

'It happens with families.' There was a curt note in Gavin's voice. His parents had long since died, and the short visit his wanderlust brother had paid to Paisley several years before had ended in trouble and bitterness.

'Did you know about this latest escapade of Christian's?' he went on, anxious to divert his wife's mind from the past.

'She mentioned it to me as a way of earning the money for her lessons, but I thought that—'

'You thought I'd put my foot down?' He raised an eyebrow at her.

'To tell the truth, I did.'

Gavin shook his head. 'I said I'd not pay for them, but I didn't forbid her to find the silver herself. I'm proud of the lassie, Margaret. She's got determination. Although,' he added thoughtfully, 'I'm not certain she'll keep at it.'

'I think she will.'

'We'll see,' said Gavin. 'We'll see.'

Normally Christian hurried eagerly to school, but on the morning of her final day she walked slowly, beneath a cloud of despair. It would be some time before she earned enough to pay for additional tuition. In the meantime she must study as best she could, using her own carefully preserved schoolbooks and borrowing books from Daniel.

Sometimes, in her darker moments, she had begun to wonder if her nimble fingers would ever earn the sum she needed. But she kept her doubts to herself. To voice them would be to recognise them openly, and to admit defeat before she had even entered the battle.

As she turned into Sneddon Street her feet seemed to tap out a dirge: 'the last time, the last time . . .'

This was the last time she would walk to the building that housed Miss Glen's school for young ladies, the last time she would turn in at that particular door, the last time she would climb these particular stairs, the last time she would take her seat at the shabby wooden table.

The other pupils, excited at the prospect of the summer holidays and, for some, the end of their schooldays, were in a festive mood throughout the day. Christian ignored them, working hard, trying to prolong the last precious moments of her education for as long as she could.

When Miss Glen finally rapped on her desk and dismissed the class the others fled, scurrying down the stairs and out into the sunshine in a giggling, chattering bunch. Christian slowly picked up her books, a lump gathering in her throat.

'Come along, lassie, I've got plenty to do if you haven't,' Miss Glen urged, adding as she waited at the door: 'And what d'you intend to do with yourself, now that your schooldays are over?'

'I'm tambouring for my uncle.'

'Indeed? You'll do well enough at it, for you were always one of my best needlework pupils. But I'd have thought you'd have gone in for teaching. You've got the ability.'

'Mebbe – one day. First I must earn some money. I've more learning to do.'

The woman gave an exasperated click of the tongue. 'Lassie, you're not still on about that, are you? I've told you before – reading and writing and needlework are all that a young woman needs. You've done well, and there's no sense in wanting the moon.'

There was no sense in arguing with her, either. Christian had tried it often enough, without success. So she kept her rebellious eyes on the floor and said, 'Yes, Miss Glen.'

'Well, I suppose tambouring's as good an occupation as any for the time being. It'll keep you out of mischief until the right man comes along and gives you a house to look after.'

The lump disappeared in a great gulp of outraged frustration. Christian bounced out of the door and down the stairs, completely forgetting to record the last time her foot touched each familiar tread, and shot out into the sunshine like a cork freed from a bottle.

'I'll show her!' she vowed behind compressed lips as she marched homeward, her precious books tucked beneath her elbow. 'I'll show them all, I don't care how long it takes!'

The vow, and the anger that had prompted it, made her feel a little better.

The summer unfolded like a rich, colourful carpet. It was a beautiful summer, a summer for walking and playing bowls and swimming. The Paisley weavers, working from home and free to plan their own hours as long as the work was done, started their looms early in the mornings and had finished the day's work by noon, enabling them to make the most of the warm afternoons.

To Rab's annoyance Christian was far too busy with her tambouring to climb the braes around Paisley with him, or to wander along the river banks.

True, she made a pretty sight sitting in the garden behind her father's house, her downbent dark head framed by the mass of honeysuckle at her back, but he soon grew tired of lying on the grass, watching her.

'You're going to ruin your eyes and turn into an old woman before your time,' he said gloomily. Christian's

27

gaze lifted to his for a moment, then returned to the muslin cloth stretched tightly between the wooden rings in her hands. Her needle continued on its flashing way through a floral pattern.

'Och, Christian – come for a walk.'

'Later, mebbe. I must get this finished.'

After a while Rab got up and wandered to the gate that led round the side of the house to the road. He looked back once, but her head was still bent over her work. Sulkily, he left.

Throughout the summer, Christian stitched busily. Muslin after muslin flowed through her hands, reams of coloured thread blossomed into pattern upon pattern, but although her uncle seemed pleased with her work and was always ready to give her more, the supply of coins she was storing carefully in a wooden box in her room still seemed pitifully small. Counting it over one day she realised that if she wanted to earn enough, she must do more than sew. After a day or two spent in thought, she laid her sewing aside and went purposefully out of the house and down the hill to visit Robert Montgomery.

He eyed her warily as she marched into the weaving shed. There was something about the set of her shoulders, the glow in her eyes, that he had come to recognise as a sign that his niece had thought of another idea.

She didn't keep him in suspense for long. 'Uncle Robert, would it not be a good idea if your tambourers were to work together?'

'Under the one roof, you mean? Lassie, if you're thinking of gathering a crowd of chattering women in this weaving shop, let me tell you—' he began with mounting alarm, but a small upraised hand stopped him in mid-sentence.

'Indeed I am not – that's a daft idea if ever I heard

one,' she said sweepingly. 'What I mean is, would it not be better to have one person responsible for taking the work round the women and bringing it back to you, instead of you having to spend time on it, or them coming here and taking up time that you need for your loom? It seems to me that if I was to see to it for you and guarantee to get the work back to you when you needed it I could save you a lot of bother.'

The beat of Rab's loom slowed and stopped. His head appeared round the edge of the wooden frame. 'Christian, what mad notion have you got in your head now?' he wanted to know.

'Nothing that concerns you,' Robert snapped across the shop at him.

'But Father—'

'Get on with your work and leave me to attend to mine!'

Rab's crimsoning face disappeared. His loom started again, the shuttle crashing from side to side as he wrenched savagely on the cord.

'And how much extra would this – service of yours cost me?'

Christian met his eyes boldly. 'A wee bit more than you pay now – but only a wee bit, and for that you can leave the worrying to me. If I let you down you can take the money off what you're due me,' she added quickly, and saw that the suggestion had hit home.

'Have you asked the women if they'd be agreeable to this?'

'I thought it best to speak to you first. If you're willing, I'll have a word with them.'

'They'll never agree to it.'

'They might. Can I talk to them?'

Robert hesitated, gnawing on his lower lip. He had

little patience with the business of tramping around the town delivering cloth to the tambourers and collecting it again when it was sewn. But the alternative was to have the women coming to him, cluttering up the passageway and the street outside with their bairns, chattering and laughing outside his door and window. It would be a relief to let someone else deal with that side of things.

'Speak to them, then,' he said at last. 'But if they're not happy with the idea—'

'I'll never mention it again,' she finished the sentence, already on her way to the door. 'Thank you, Uncle Robert – you'll not be sorry!'

When she had whisked out, letting the door clap to behind her, Rab said 'It'll never work! They'll never take notice of a wee lass like her.'

'If they do I'll be well rid of the responsibility of these women.'

'I don't know why you let her talk you into these daft ideas,' his son objected.

'Mebbe it's because there's times when I think your cousin Christian has more sense in the tip o' one finger than you have in your entire skull,' his father rapped back, his voice roughening with sudden irritation at Rab's moodiness. 'Now – will you get on with your work or do I have to take the back o' my hand tae ye?'

Three women besides Christian worked at embroidering cloth for Robert Montgomery. By the time the day was out she had managed to gather them together in the kitchen of the oldest tambourer, Marion Bruce.

The women listened to Christian's plans in silence, giving each other sidelong glances from time to time. There was a full minute's pause when she finally finished speaking, and she had the sense to say no more, leaving it to the others.

Finally Marion, the widowed mother of a large brood ranging from a married daughter to a toddler son, said 'Will it mak' ony difference tae the money we make? Mister Montgomery's no' goin' tae cut it back, is he?'

'It'll not make any difference at all. But if we can turn out more work – and that might happen when you don't have to spend time taking the finished work to Townhead or collecting the new cloth – it could mean more money.'

'I'm a' for givin' up the tramp tae the weavin' shop,' Marion said. She was a huge woman, often troubled by breathlessness, although her chubby fingers were among the most skilful in Paisley when it came to fine needlework.

One of the others, a woman Christian only knew as Wee Mag, nodded, but the third, a thin, sharp-eyed woman with a mouth that looked as though it had just tasted vinegar, disagreed.

'I see no reason why we should let a lassie like this start orderin' us around.'

'I'm not ordering you, I'm just offering to bring the cloth to you and take it back and share out the money as fairly as it was ever done.'

'It sounds fine tae me, Trina,' Wee Mag ventured, but Trina sniffed.

'Listen – would it not make sense for us to work together? My Uncle Robert's a fair man, but there are others that take advantage of women trying to earn their own keep,' Christian urged.

'Ye're right there,' Wee Mag chimed in. 'My neighbour wis jist tellin' me the other day that Alexander Semple doon by St Mirren Brae tried tae get her tae tak' a sack o' potatoes in place o' the money she'd earned – an' her wi' three bairns an' a sick man tae feed an' clothe, an' rent tae pay, forbye.'

'She didnae agree tae it, surely?'

'She'd nae choice, poor body. She doesnae keep well hersel', an' she couldnae afford tae anger the man. She worries hersel' near tae death as it is when she's too ill tae work, in case he tak's on someone better an' turns her awa' when she goes back tae his door.'

There was an immediate clatter of tongues, each rising above the other in a crescendo of indignation. Christian had to wait until it had subsided before she said, 'All the more reason for us to work together, then. And if one of us fell sick the others could share out her work until she was better so that she'd not lose her place.'

Marion wagged her head. 'Ye cannae argue wi' a promise like that, Trina, surely?'

'I cannae – but I don't see why it should be her that takes charge,' Trina said waspishly. 'She's only just started tambouring. Why shouldn't it be yin o' us?'

Exasperation put a whiplash into Christian's voice. 'Because it was my idea, that's why!'

Marion rumbled and wheezed with laughter. 'That's telt ye, Trina! Are ye with us or are ye no'?'

Trina's mouth writhed for a moment before she said reluctantly, 'I suppose I'll hae tae join ye. But mind this' – she added, glaring at Christian – 'one penny less in my hand an' I'm oot o' it!'

'You an' the rest o' us, Trina,' Wee Mag assured her, and Marion nodded in agreement.

'You'll not be sorry,' Christian promised, resisting the impulse to cross her fingers for luck as she spoke.

'She's what?' Gavin asked explosively two days later.

'She's arranged to take responsibility for all of Robert's tambouring,' Margaret repeated patiently. 'You have to admit that it makes sense, Gavin.' She herself had once employed a number of women weaving tapes on small inkle looms, and had built up a thriving little business. It had been taken over by her brother Robert a few years earlier, when Margaret finally decided that running her home and teaching the children at the Poors' Hospital was enough for any woman. 'There was a woman at the door this very morning asking to speak to her. She's heard of Christian's scheme and she wanted to know if she could get into it.'

'Dear Lord! Are you telling me, woman, that my daughter's going to follow in your footsteps?'

Margaret smiled a trifle smugly. 'It looks like it.'

'God help Paisley then, for it'll probably not know what's hit it once she gets going!'

By the time autumn had begun to spread its flame-red cloak over the braes Christian's growing band of tambourers needed more than the work Robert Montgomery could give them.

Unable to bring herself to turn down the women who wanted to join the group, she tramped around the town talking to the manufacturers until she found one who could use her tambourers' services.

Martin Campbell, once apprentice to Duncan Montgomery, Christian's grandfather, had, in his turn, become the owner of a number of looms. But drink had got the better of Martin, and his hard-working wife, determined not to see her home sold from under her and her children turned into the street, had wrenched the reins from her husband's hand and now saw to the weavers herself. She kept Martin supplied with money and he was content to drink it away with his cronies in the local howff and leave her to her own devices.

'I'd be glad to let you see to the tambouring for me, lassie,' the woman said when Christian approached her. 'It's one worry less for myself and, from what Robert Montgomery tells me, you'll make a good job of it.'

With a team of women working for her Christian was at last freed from the burden of continuous sewing. 'But I'm still not making enough money to pay a tutor,' she mourned to her mother as they worked together in the garden, gathering in the clothes that had been spread over the bushes to dry. 'By the time I pay the lassies their wages there's not enough left over. Mister McKechnie in Storie Street charges more than I've got.'

Margaret's sleeves had been rolled up to beyond the elbow. The afternoon sun touched her arms with gold as she shook out one of Gavin's shirts and folded it. 'I'm certain your father would be willing to pay the rest, for you've worked hard this year.'

Christian shook her head.' No, I'll not ask him. I said I'd do it on my own, and I will. And I'll not take it from you either,' she added as Margaret opened her mouth to speak. 'I'll just have to wait longer, that's all.'

'Och, Christian, what good will extra learning do you anyway?' Margaret said in sudden exasperation. 'Being a scholar doesn't mean that life's going to be good to you. Here, give me a hand with this sheet.

'I was speaking to a poor old soul last time I was at the Poors' Hospital,' she went on as they spread the sheet out between them, arms stretched wide, then took a firm hold of the corners and began to fold it. 'From what he says he was a scholar in his youth but he's had nothing but hard times throughout his life. What good has learning done him?'

Christian looked up from her task, her eyes bright with interest. 'What's his name?'

Margaret dug into the recesses of her memory, then said 'Mally. Mally Bruce.'

'I wonder if there's still enough of the scholar in him to teach me? I doubt if he'd charge as much as Mister McKechnie!'

Margaret dropped the tamed and folded sheet into the basket at her feet. 'By the look of his nose, like as not his brain's addled by drink.'

Christian dropped another clean dry shirt into the basket and beamed on her mother. 'I'll go and see him tomorrow. You never know – he might suit me very well.'

'He's in the garden. But you'll be fortunate if you get one civil word out of the man,' the Hospital Mistress said when Christian marched in and asked for Mally Bruce. 'He's a bad-tempered old—'

She stopped, folding her mouth firmly over the word that had almost spilled out, then said primly. 'He'll have to change his ways if he wants to stay here, I can tell you that.'

Mally Bruce was easy to find. He was on his own in a distant corner, fork in hand, attacking a vegetable bed as though it had done him a personal wrong. He was a scarecrow of a man, tall and thin and long-boned, his nobbly wrists and ankles protruding from the shabby clothes he wore.

When Christian said, 'Are you Mister Bruce?' he whirled about, the prongs of the fork held before him like a weapon. They were no sharper than the piercing black eyes set between bushy grey brows and a shiny red hooked nose that spoke, as her mother had said, of a history of drinking.

The man's mouth was quite lost between that nose and a jutting, aggressive chin. Atop his face a great untamed bush of grey hair escaped in all directions from beneath a shabby tricorne hat.

'Who wants tae ken?' he asked suspiciously.

'My name's Christian Knox. My mother teaches the children here.'

'Whit's that got tae dae wi' me?'

Someone with less courage would have turned and fled, but Christian, who had been intrigued by unusual characters since babyhood, stood her ground and said, 'My mother tells me you were a scholar.'

'Well?'

'Is is true?'

'Are ye doubtin' me?' He took a step forward, the prongs of the fork glittering in the sun as he moved from the shadow of the wall.

Christian swallowed hard. 'I'm looking for a tutor who knows the way of Latin and arithmetic and geography – and history.'

The fork prongs were lowered slightly. 'A tutor, is it?'

She could tell by the way he shaped the words that the man was almost toothless, as were most of the poor and elderly folk in the town. Even so, her sharp ear heard a certain elegance in the way he used words. This man could indeed have been a scholar once.

'For your brother, mebbe?'

'For me.'

'You?' The thick shaggy brows knotted together so fiercely that she was afraid that they might tangle together and stay that way. 'Ye're a lassie!'

'I know,' said Christian patiently.

'Lassies dinna learn Latin an' arithmetic,' said Mally Bruce scathingly, and turned back to his work.

Her patience began to wear thin. 'If I want to learn, I've as much right as anyone. All I'm asking is, will you teach me?'

There was amazement in his black eyes when he looked back at her. 'Me?'

'Mebbe you've forgotten it all.'

'I've no' forgotten nothin'!' Then he said slyly, 'What'll ye gie me in return?'

'I could manage a penny a week.'

He spat on the ground. 'Oh aye? An' if they' – his shaggy head indicated the Hospital building and the people in authority within its walls—'didnae tak' it aff me I'd nae doot spend it on drink an' get mysel' throwed oot ontae the street.'

Exasperation sharpened her voice. 'What d'you want, then?'

'A turney lay, that's whit I want. A turney lay so that I can earn my ain keep, an' get oot o' this place. But the likes o' you,' he finished contemptuously, 'could never get me such a thing. So be off wi' ye an' leave me tae my work!'

This time the back presented to Christian was implacable. The conversation was over. She walked slowly towards the Hospital, her mind working feverishly.

A turney lay, a knife-grinding machine, would cost far more than she could afford. It would take her months, perhaps a year, to save up enough money. She couldn't bear the thought of waiting for so long before starting her lessons.

She had already thought of Daniel as a tutor. He might well be willing, but the two of them knew each other too well. They would probably end up squabbling.

But there was a way . . .

She turned and ran back to where the old man was

driving the fork viciously into the earth, grunting with each push.

'If I get you a turney lay, will you tutor me?'

'I telt ye tae go awa' an' stop botherin' me, lassie! Ye'll never get yin!'

'But if I did,' she persisted, 'would you tutor me?'

He pushed his hat back on his head and stared down on her for a long moment. Then he said slowly, 'Lassie, you get me a turney lay an' I'll teach ye everythin' I know under the sun.'

'I'll be back,' said Christian, and ran from the garden.

'What nonsense is this you're on about now, Christian Knox?' Mistress Mary MacLeod demanded of her great-niece. 'Knife grinding indeed. I thought you'd become a tambourer?'

'It's not for me, Aunt Mary. It's for an old man at the Poors' Hospital who'll teach me arithmetic and Latin and the like if I can give him a turney lay so that he can earn his own living again.'

The words spilled over each other in Christian's haste. 'Only I can't buy one for a long time yet – unless you lend the money to me.'

'So it's silver you're after.' Mary sniffed, and expertly tossed a round of pastry over on the floured kitchen table. 'Make yourself useful, lassie – cut up that rhubarb nice and small. Kirsty's got the toothache so I've packed her off to her bed with some cloves and a hot cloth about her face, and I've got all the running of the house to see to.'

Christian obediently set to work on the firm juicy stalks of rhubarb, fresh from her aunt's kitchen garden.

'Just a loan, Aunt Mary,' she said as she chopped. 'I'll pay it back as soon as I can, I promise you.'

Great-aunt and great-niece eyed each other. One was rheumaticky, wizened as an apple, most of her life behind her; the other was fresh and lovely, poised on the threshold of the future. But both of them were filled to the brim with the business of existing, of living and being and doing.

Mary ran the roller over the pastry once more, then cut out a circle with an expert sweep of the knife and lined a pie dish with it. It was, of course, just the right size.

Now that she had finally given up the millinery business she had started as a young woman Mary MacLeod was a lady of leisure, mistress of a big house, comfortably off in her own right, and downright wealthy because she was the widow and sole beneficiary of a well-to-do man. Even so she remained true to her beginnings as a farmer's daughter, and she was happier working than idle.

'That you will, my girl,' she said, gathering the cut pastry together neatly and re-rolling it. 'Only a fool gives money away and expects nothing back. You mind that – it'll stand you in good stead through the years to come.'

'You mean you'll give it to me? I mean – lend it to me?'

'Has it not occurred to you, Christian, that if you're going to have to borrow the money to buy the turney lay you might as well borrow it to pay Mister McKechnie and get yourself educated properly?'

'Aye, it has. But there's more to it than that, Aunt Mary. There's Mally Bruce to think of now, you see. I promised him – and he's desperate to get out of the Hospital, you can see it in his eyes.' Christian's brow was knotted with the need to explain a difficult point properly. 'I couldn't just go to Mister McKechnie now and leave the old soul where he is. Not now!'

Mary nodded, well satisfied with the answer to her question.

'I suppose there's times when folk must come before silver. Though not often. You shall have your money,' she said.

Within two weeks Mally Bruce had left the Poors' Hospital and had set himself up as a street knife grinder. He settled in a room in a shabby tenement building at the bottom of St Mirren Brae, close to the river bank, and here Christian visited him twice a week for tuition.

'Gavin—' Margaret Knox said nervously when she discovered that her daughter intended to go to the fearsome old man's house unaccompanied.

Her husband put a reassuring hand on her arm. 'I said we'd let Christian go her own way, and it seems to me that she's doing better than most. There's no harm in the old man, and she'll get tired of this business about learning, you wait and see.'

On that count, he was wrong. Within days Christian had discovered that Mally Bruce's bark was much worse than his bite, and he, despite himself, was impressed by her thirst for knowledge.

No matter what the weather was like or how busy she was, Christian never missed a lesson. Often, if there was a lot of tambouring work to do, she would take her sewing to Mally's house and work away at it while memorising Latin verbs or reciting the names of the countries of the world, her mind and her tongue as quick and as sharp as her needle.

The girl's great desire to learn unlocked memories that had been buried deep inside the old man for many years.

Memories of past times when he had been able to hold his head up and walk the streets proudly in the knowledge of his own worth. He became a willing tutor, though a hard taskmaster, and he found himself with a willing pupil, eager to be driven and nagged. Through Christian, Mally Bruce began to appreciate knowledge once again.

Christian luxuriated in the pleasure of learning once more, of opening textbooks and setting herself to master their contents, of taking quill in hand and facing the challenge of a blank sheet of paper – a moment as exciting as those of her childhood winters, when she would advance with small booted feet towards a stretch of fresh, untouched snow, preparing to tramp her own personality on to its pristine perfection.

The only problem was Mally's fondness for ale. At first, he kept well away from the howffs, knowing his own weakness only too well. But the jingle of one coin against another in his pocket, and the lamplit, noisy, warm friendliness of the howffs when work was over for the day, proved to be too much of a temptation.

The first time Christian arrived for a lesson to find the old man staggering round his lodgings, singing loudly, was the last. Tight-lipped, she stood by the door, her eyes fixed on him. The singing faltered, slowed, stopped.

'Wass'ma'er?'

'You are, Mally Bruce. I'm shamed of you, so I am!'

'Leave a man alane an' min' ye're ain business.' He collapsed on to the bed.

'I am minding my own business. You're supposed to be learning me Latin, and look at you!'

He gave a surly grunt and watched from beneath lowered brows as she whisked round the room, hanging up the few pieces of clothing he had.

She rinsed out his mug and plate, then made tea in the battered tin pot.

'I dinnae want that,' he said when she held out the steaming mug of tea.

'Drink it.'

'Where's my fee?'

'In my pocket, and it'll stay there till you've earned it.'

'I need it now.'

'So's you can go back down to the howff? Listen to me, Mally' – she thrust the mug into his unwilling hands – 'if you'd as soon drink as teach me, I can find someone else – someone pleased to take my penny.'

He glowered at her, and she glowered back. He was still glaring over the rim of the mug as he drank the tea.

'All of it. That's better,' she said when it was done. 'Now lie down and have a sleep.'

'Wha' about my money?'

'What about my lesson? Anyway, it seems to me,' Christian said ruthlessly from the doorway 'that you owe me a lesson, for the work I've put in for you today.'

'You're a hard bitch, Christian Knox!'

'I am that, Mally Bruce. And I'm glad you've found out, for it'll mebbe put an end to your drinking when I'm due for a lesson,' she shot back at him, and slammed the door behind her.

Just when it seemed that everything had come together for Christian, just when she was standing on her own feet and earning the money for her tuition, she lost one of her clients. Martin Campbell, staggering back home one night after being thrown out of the howff where he had been drinking, fell down the outside staircase leading to his home and broke his neck.

His widow, free at last, sold off his looms and took

herself and her children off to her brother's house in Kilwinning.

The woman's decision to stop manufacturing cloth left Christian's small group with a problem. The anxious tambourers crowded round Christian at the meeting called in Marion's kitchen, Trina's voice rising above their worried babble.

'Well, milady, an' what d'ye plan tae dae noo? There's no' near enough work for the eight o' us. And as far as I'm concerned,' she added, eyeing the women who had come into the group after its formation, 'those that were here first get whatever work's going. It's only right.'

There was an immediate outcry. One of the new-comers, a woman as formidable as Trina herself, stepped forward, fingers clawed. 'Listen, you – it's the folk that need the work that should come first. Those of us that dinnae hae men tae help share the burden!'

'Ye think so?' Trina's mouth took on a dangerous, square shape. Her own fingers began to curve into hooks that could tangle themselves in hair and reach for eyes.

'Here, youse two – nae fightin' in my kitchen!' Marion stepped between the women, her bulky body all but hiding them from each other.

'Listen to me!' Christian seized a wooden ladle and rapped hard on the side of a soup pot. The noise brought eight heads swinging round towards her.

'There's no need for folk to be put out of work. I'll find another manufacturer.'

'An' who'll ye find?' Trina wanted to know. 'Work's no' that easy come by.'

'There must be somebody – anybody. Wherever he is, I'll find him,' Christian said firmly, and was out in the street before she fully realised what she had let herself in for.

That night, while the rest of the household slept peace-fully, she tossed and turned in her bed, a list of Paisley manufacturers wending its way backwards and forwards through her head. Every one of them, she knew well enough, already had his own tambourers.

She wished, briefly, that she had never thought of getting the women together in a group. But the thought was dismissed almost at once. What was done was done; she had set her foot upon a certain road and she must continue to follow that road, even if it meant looking as far afield as Glasgow for an employer to take on the women's work.

The clock in the hall downstairs struck three. As the melodious echoes of the third chime died away it suddenly came to Christian that perhaps she should search among the manufacturers who didn't as yet employ tambourers. And hard on the heels of the thought came one name.

Angus Fraser of Forbes Place, the man who had been on the Town Watch with her father the night she and Rab had gone swimming in the Hammills, was one of the town's best-known manufacturers. As far as Christian knew, he only sold plain cloth, with no patterning to it.

Perhaps he could be persuaded to try his hand at tamboured muslin. She smiled into the darkness, then was surprised by a yawn that almost made her jaws ache. Ten minutes later, her problem solved for the moment, she was asleep.

Time was getting on, and Angus Fraser was beginning to think that the dark-haired snippet of a girl sitting in his office was never going to go away and leave him in peace.

'As I said when you first came in, Mistress Knox,' he said for the third or perhaps the fourth time, 'I've never felt the need to have my cloth patterned. The buyers are quite content to take it as it is.'

'You'll not deny that my women do fine work.' She pushed the sample material across the desk towards him.

'I'll grant you that, but—'

Her eyes, long-lashed and the same colour, he suddenly realised, as a particularly beautiful smoky quartz brooch his late wife had owned, held his firmly.

'It's all very well saying that your customers have never asked for figured muslin,' she said, 'but if you offered it to them they might well be pleased.'

'*If*' – he emphasised the word – 'I decided to offer figured cloth to my customers, my weavers could no doubt find their own tambourers.'

She pounced on the words. 'And charge you more for the finished cloth? And mebbe not produce such good work as this?'

'You were intending to provide tambouring free of charge, then?'

Her cheeks reddened at the mild irony in his voice, and her chin lifted to a higher angle. 'No, of course not. But I'd charge a fair rate, and you'd get good reliable service for your money.'

'Tell me, Mistress Knox, what do your parents have to say to their only daughter going into business for herself?'

Taken aback by the unexpected change of subject, Christian blinked at him, then rallied. 'They don't object. You think they should?'

'You're very young.'

He saw anger burnish the girl's eyes to an even more striking, jewel-like brilliance. 'I know that many folk consider youth to be a crime, Mister Fraser,' she said coldly, 'but it's one we must all commit at some time or another, like it or not. And it's something I'll be able to overcome one day.'

A small hand reached out and gathered up the rejected cloth. At last the girl got to her feet. 'Thank you for giving me a hearing, Mister Fraser,' she said with angry politeness. 'I'm sorry to have wasted your time – and my own.'

He watched her move, straight-backed, to the office door, then surprised himself by saying abruptly, 'Just a moment.'

She turned, waited. He reached out for the sample cloth, and she surrendered it. The figuring was, as she had said, among the best work he had seen. The stitches were neat and precise.

'Are all your women as good as this?'

'They are, sir.'

'Mebbe I'll give them a trial,' he said almost harshly, half annoyed with himself for having given in to this determined child. 'Call tomorrow and I'll arrange to have some cloth set aside for you. But it's only a trial, mind you.'

As he watched, the anger smoothed out of her face. Her eyes took on a radiance, her small neat teeth sparkled in a smile that seemed to light up the whole room and brush him with its warmth. He found himself responding to it without effort.

'Oh – thank you, Mister Fraser!' Her youthfulness gave itself away in the breathless way the words burst out. 'You'll not regret it, I promise you!'

Then she was gone, and he was alone, the neatly figured cloth still in his hands and the golden haze of her gratitude still in the air around him.

Before the summer was out a strong friendship had sprung up between Christian and Mally Bruce; a friendship that set Rab, closer to Christian than anyone else until then, afire with jealousy.

'I never see you now,' he grumbled.

'You do so. I come to the weaving shop at least twice a week.'

'Aye – bringing tamboured muslins back and collecting more cloth. But we don't talk the way we did, or go out walking as often.'

'Och, Rab – I must earn the money to pay Aunt Mary back. Now that we're tambouring for Mister Fraser as well there's an awful lot for me to do. And the learning doesn't come easy. There's a deal of work in it. Though the other day Daniel tested me out,' she went on, her eyes brightening, 'and he says I've nearly caught up with him.'

Rab groaned. Slowly and surely, it seemed to him, he was losing Christian. Losing her just when he had begun to realise how much she meant to him.

Chapter Four

Outside Angus Fraser's warehouse in Forbes Place a great crowd of folk was clustered; weavers waiting to return completed webs and collect new ones, spinsters and winders and pirn-makers and travelling chapmen and representatives from the English cotton mills eager to display samples of their wares.

Inside, seated on a chair in Fraser's small, untidy office, Christian Knox was saying with shocked disbelief, 'Me? Oversee your warehouse for you?'

The man on the opposite side of the desk smiled, his good-looking features breaking easily into humour. 'I'll admit to being as surprised as you are, Mistress Knox. Two years ago, when you managed to persuade me to take on your tambourers I was sceptical about your ability. But damn me, you've got more brains and more common sense than most, even though you're so young.'

'I'm nineteen!'

He bowed his head in amused apology. 'Your pardon, mistress. I forgot that you're of an age with my own son. Young still, but old enough in wit, at least, to make a good overseer.'

'Should your son not be offered the position?'

'Alexander,' said Angus Fraser with a slight edge to his voice, 'isn't as interested in the warehouse as I'd like.

I need someone altogether more . . . conscious of responsibility. What d'you say?'

Then, as she floundered for words, he added penitently: 'Forgive me, I'm hurrying you along far too fast. Bring your parents to my house for supper tomorrow evening. I can talk to them about it then.'

'No need to ask their permission, for I've made up my mind to accept – if you think I can do the work.'

'As to that I've no doubt at all. I've been watching you closely, Mistress Knox, and you've got a good head for business on your shoulders. But even so' – he stood up and offered her his hand – 'the supper invitation stands. Give yourself time to think about my offer.'

She stepped outside in a daze, threading her way through the waiting crowd without seeing any of them.

Angus Fraser had started off as a chapman, travelling on horseback between Scotland and the manufactories in England with yarn and cloth in his saddlebag, peddling his wares to all and sundry. Later, he had brought his family to Paisley and settled in the town, dealing as a middleman between the weavers and the Lancashire cotton mills.

Gradually, using a good mixture of common sense and shrewdness well laced with honesty, he had developed his business until he now owned some five hundred looms in the town and the surrounding district.

He had become one of the most respected 'corks' – the local word for a manufacturer – in Paisley. His warehouse was one of the centres of the weaving industry, now that the local weavers obtained a great deal of their yarn from south of the Border. To be overseer in the Fraser warehouse was something of an honour.

Christian sped along the riverside and up through the

Cross without noticing her surroundings.

She almost skipped up Oakshawhill, and once she was on the flat again she gathered her skirts up and began to run, bursting into the house, through the hall and in at the kitchen door to demand breathlessly of the little maid, 'Where's my mother?'

'Where else would she be at this time on a Monday but in the wash-house?'

Margaret Knox, busily plunging sheets beneath the steaming water in the big wash-tub with a pair of long wooden tongs, gave a small scream as she was seized from behind and enveloped in an unexpected hug.

'Christian – for any favour, watch what you're doing! The tongs were nearly in the tub then!' Then she took a proper look at her daughter, and with a change of tone asked anxiously, 'What's happened?'

'I'm to be a warehouse overseer – working for Mister Angus Fraser!'

'Mercy!' said Margaret, too stunned to notice the tongs slide into the soapy water.

Angus Fraser, a widower, lived with his son and daughter in a handsome house on Paisley's High Street. At the back was a long yard; the front of the house gave directly on to the pavement.

The long dining room windows were curtained against the inquisitive gaze of passers-by, but the sounds from outside – the occasional cry of a late vendor, the creak and rattle of carriage or wagon wheels, the jingle of harnesses, voices raised in merriment or song or argument now and then – reached the ears of the six people seated at the table.

Fraser had deliberately refrained from talking about business while his family and guests ate. Instead, he introduced a variety of subjects, and kept the conversation going with practised ease.

Although she had been dealing with him for two years, Christian had never really looked hard at the man before. To her, he had simply been a manufacturer, a cork, someone who supplied work for her tambourers. Now, eyeing him across the handsome oval table with its starched white linen and its silver candlesticks and fine plates, she saw a man who had recently entered his forties, but still retained the enthusiasm and interest of youth: a tall, broad-shouldered man, neatly made and free of the slightest suggestion of a paunch. His face was long, with twinkling grey eyes and a firm mouth that nevertheless smiled easily.

His hair was still fair enough to disguise any grey that might have crept into it, and was unpowdered, drawn back and tied with a dark blue bow. She noted he was tastefully and expensively dressed, in a blue jacket over a white shirt and pale brown embroidered waistcoat, with buff-coloured breeches.

He was, she decided, a most likeable man, a man she would enjoy working for. At that moment he happened to turn his head and their eyes met. His were faintly amused; he raised his brows at her, as though asking whether her study of him had resulted in a good or a bad opinion. Flushing, and hating herself for it, Christian turned away hastily and found Alexander Fraser, by her side, eager to engage her in conversation.

Despite the younger Fraser's charm and his obvious interest in her, it took only a few sentences for Christian to decide that although he shared his father's good looks he was as yet a pale imitation of the older man. His talk was all of society in Edinburgh, and in London, where he hoped to go as soon as possible.

His dislike of Paisley and its provincial attitude irked Christian from the first. She understood why his father was looking outwith the family for a good overseer; Alexander's obvious lack of concern for the affairs of the town and its people would have done little to further the interests of the warehouse.

His sister Rachel, five years younger than Christian, was dark instead of fair, and presumably resembled the mother who had died many years ago. She was talking vivaciously at the other side of the table to Margaret.

Within five minutes of entering the house Christian had decided that Rachel was spoiled by her father, and altogether too childish. At her age, Christian had gone swimming in the Hammills and started earning money as a tambourer. She doubted Rachel had ever made a decision for herself.

When the meal ended Angus led them all into a pleasant parlour on the opposite side of the hall. Rachel settled by the fire with her embroidery, while Alexander, to Christian's annoyance, seated himself by her side.

The conversation that had been started at the table continued for a while. It was a subject that could be heard wherever folk congregated, one that held everyone enthralled. Across the water, Britain's nearest neighbour, France, was in turmoil. The peasantry had rebelled against the nobility, and the whole of France, it seemed, was ablaze with class hatred. The British watched uneasily, fearing that a spark from that blaze might fly across the sea and ignite the torch of rebellion in their own midst.

Angus Fraser was of the opinion that the British folk, and more particularly the Scottish, were not of a rebellious nature.

'I'd not be too complacent if I was you,' Gavin Knox disagreed mildly.

'They're better treated than the French were, from what I hear.'

'Some of them. If you were a surgeon, sir, you'd know that for every man with work and silver in his pocket to feed and clothe his family there's one or two or mebbe more with nothing. Not knowing where his next meal's coming from, or where he might lay his head from one night to another causes great fear in a man. And frightened folk can be dangerous folk. Even more so if they've got wives and bairns to worry about too. What have they got to lose if they rebel?'

'Their lives,' Alexander Fraser said crisply.

'They'll lose their lives anyway, if there's no food and no shelter for them. And by rebelling they just might win – the way the French peasants seem to be winning.'

'So you support the overthrow of the rich? That's a dangerous philosophy, sir,' Angus pointed out, and Gavin shot him a slightly irritated look.

'No, no! I'm explaining how rebellions start, and saying that we're not much better protected from them than the French were.'

'I think we help our poor more than they did.'

'A little,' Gavin admitted. 'But not enough.' Then, perhaps noticing the way his daughter had begun to fidget, he went on smoothly: 'But we're not gathered together tonight to discuss the French revolution.'

'No, indeed.' Angus smiled warmly on Christian, then turned to her parents. 'I take it that your daughter's told you of my offer?'

'She has. I must say, Mister Fraser, it seems strange that a man of your standing should think of offering work of that nature to a lassie not yet twenty.'

Christian flushed, and shot her father an angry look. Angus gave a rich, amused chuckle.

'I share your surprise, Mister Knox. But my warehouse overseer's had to give up work due to a bad lung condition. I need someone I can trust, someone with a quick eye and a sensible mind to oversee the place. My first choice would, of course, be Alexander—'

'You know fine that I've no wish to stay in Paisley,' his son said swiftly.

'Exactly. And there's little point in trying to get him to change his views, for they're well settled – and often expressed,' his father said dryly, and the young man reddened. 'I've been watching your daughter go about her business for some time, Mister Knox, and it seems to me that she could well make an ideal overseer.'

'D'ye tell me?' Gavin asked in some surprise. To him, Christian was still a child toying with the idea of growing up.

'I do indeed. If,' Fraser added swiftly, 'the plan met with your approval. I'd not take her on otherwise.'

Christian, unable to stay silent any longer, twisted anxiously in her chair. 'But I've already said—'

'I'd not,' Angus Fraser repeated, fixing her with a firm eye, 'take you on otherwise.'

She glared, and he returned the look with a twitch of the lips. Defeated, she turned her eyes to her father's face.

'It scarce seems fitting work for a surgeon's daughter,' Gavin said slowly, and her heart sank.

'But Father, I'm of weaving stock too, don't forget that.'

'Margaret? What do you have to say in this matter?'

'I say that Christian's not one to sit back and wait for marriage to come along, so she's as well kept busy. Why shouldn't she work in a warehouse if that's what she wants to do?'

Gavin pursed his lips, then suddenly gave way and smiled at his daughter. 'Very well, let's see what sort of job you'll make of it.'

'Oh!' She almost rose to fly across the room to kiss him, then realising where she was she sank back into her chair and said demurely, 'Thank you, Father.'

'I second that.' Angus Fraser held out a hand and Gavin shook it. 'I'll take good care of her, I can promise you that.'

For all the world, thought Christian, half-amused, half-embarrassed, as though he'd just been given a wife instead of an employee.

'It's not Christian I'm concerned about,' her father was saying wryly. 'It's the poor souls under her supervision.'

'Surely not,' Alexander protested. 'I can't imagine Mistress Christian being anything but charming.'

'You don't know me well, sir.' Christian's voice was dry, and her father's smile broadened at its tone.

'I would hope,' Alexander murmured later, when the others were talking and he got the opportunity to speak unheard by anyone but Christian, 'to know you better one day.'

'Difficult, sir, if you persist in going to London. I,' said Christian, nose in the air, 'am very happy to stay here, for I don't think London has anything to offer me.'

In the privacy of her own bedchamber a few hours later Margaret said thoughtfully, 'That's a fine-looking boy Angus Fraser has.'

Gavin, stripping off his jacket and waistcoat, gave her a long look. 'Don't you start any blackfooting, Margaret Knox. The lassie's not begun working in the warehouse yet, and by the sound of it young Fraser's not going to be around Paisley much in the future.'

'I'm not blackfooting,' she protested from the comfort of her pillow. 'It's just that he seemed interested in Christian, and I wondered if perhaps one day . . .'

'Perhaps – and perhaps not. Let the lassie get the measure of the work first, for I'm thinking that it'll take up all of her time for a year or two. I doubt marriage will be in her mind for a good while yet.'

In her own small room across the upper landing Christian was already in bed, wide awake, going over the visit that had just ended.

For her own part, she hadn't given Alexander Fraser another thought. Her mind was filled by his father.

He was, Christian thought contentedly, a man she would enjoy working for. She recalled the level gaze of his grey eyes, his faith in her ability, the way his mouth quirked at the corners when he was amused.

She snuggled deeper into the bed and wondered what his wife had been like. She must have been a very special kind of woman. A man like Angus Fraser would be most selective in choosing his mate.

He was a man she greatly admired.

A man it was very easy to admire.

Chapter Five

Now that she was to take up her duties at the warehouse Christian no longer had the time to see to the group of tambourers.

'But I can't just walk away from them,' she said to Mally on the morning after Angus Fraser's dinner party. Her brow was wrinkled with worry. 'It was my idea to have us all working together, and they've come to depend on it.'

'Surely there's yin o' them wi' the brains tae tak' ower,' the knife grinder grunted. He was never at his best in the mornings.

'There's Marion – but she's got enough to do, what with her bad lungs and her children to see to. I'd not like to ask her.'

'Is Trina Walker no' yin o' yer tambourers?' he asked, and when she nodded he said with the air of someone who has just solved the problems of the world: 'Ask her, then.'

'Trina? I could never ask her! She grudges the time to say a few civil words to me when I deliver the cloth to her. She's never liked the idea of us working in a group.'

'Only because she's no' the high heid yin,' Mally said shrewdly. 'D'ye think she could dae it right – see tae the siller an' a' that?'

'I think so. She's sharp as a pin.'

'Then ask her. She can only say no, an' I doot if she will. That man o' hers is a right waster – never in work an' forever drinkin' in the howffs.'

'I suppose you see him there, do you?'

'A' the time,' said Mally, without realising that he was giving himself away. 'It's a shame, so it is. The woman works hard for him an' his bairns – an' his auld mither an' faither forbye. It's nae wonder she's got a sour way wi' folk, workin' the way she does tae keep them a'. A wee bit o' self-respect might be the very makin' o' her – an' takin' on the tambourers could be jist the thing.'

When she left him Christian drew in a deep breath, squared her shoulders, and walked along the High Street to Orr Street, where she found Trina sewing diligently, alone for once in the single room she shared with her children, her husband and his elderly parents.

'The cloth's no' finished yet. It's no' supposed tae be ready till the morn,' she said ungraciously when she saw who her visitor was. She shuffled back into the room and picked up her work, seating herself on a stool by the window where she could catch the daylight. At once her needle began to flash in and out of the muslin held taut in the round wooden tambours.

Christian closed the door behind her. 'I'm not here for the cloth, Trina. I've come to tell you that I'm going to work in the Fraser warehouse as the overseer.'

Trina's head came up sharply. Her nostrils flared. 'The warehoose? An' whit's tae become o' the rest o' us noo that you're set up wi' a braw position?' Her voice was heavy with accusation.

'You can all go on as you are, tambouring for my Uncle Robert and Mister Fraser. But I'll not have the time to fetch the cloth and see to the money. I thought you'd mebbe take that on.'

The woman's needle slowed and stopped. Her jaw sagged with astonishment. 'Me?'

'Why not? You've got a good head on your shoulders. You could do well for the rest of the women, and for yourself too.'

'But . . .' For once, Trina was lost for words. When she did find her tongue again, it was to say feebly, 'Surely Marion's the yin ye should be askin'?'

'You'd be the best one to deal with the money and with the manufacturers. And you'll know where to find me if you should need my help. But I don't think you will. You'll take on the work, then?'

She watched the woman's face as amazement gave way to consideration and then to excitement and a faint flush of pleasure. For the first time since they had met Trina smiled. The bitter lines etched deep into her face melted away, and with a jolt of surprise Christian realised that once, before life had laid its intolerable burden on her narrow shoulders, Trina had been a lovely young girl.

'Aye,' Trina said. Then, her voice strengthening, she repeated, 'Aye – I'll dae it!'

When she first took up her new duties Christian found herself facing some opposition from the men and women who already worked in the warehouse, as well as those who visited it. Other warehouses in the town had had women as overseers, but not this one, and it came hard to some folk to have to take orders from a woman, or consult a woman on business.

But she gritted her teeth and worked hard, and most of them began to accept her as the days and weeks and months flew by.

There was no denying her ability. As overseer she had

to know how much yarn there was in the warehouse, and how much finished cloth. She had to know where the yarn came from, which weavers it was to go to, who among the weavers working for Angus Fraser were reliable and who needed watching.

She had to deal with the chapmen and the weavers, the women who spun the hanks of yarn on to pirns for the looms, the carters and loom dressers and the tambourers. The textile trade was complex, and the task of each person involved in the spinning of yarn and weaving of cloth had to be dealt with individually.

Six months after Christian became overseer Alexander Fraser left for London. His father went with him to see him settled, and left her in charge.

He came back to find the work going on calmly, and his pretty little overseer sitting in her small office, frowning and murmuring under her breath as she added up figures.

For a moment he stood unnoticed in the doorway, looking at her, remembering the first time he had set eyes on her, when he and Gavin Knox, sharing the Town Watch, had come upon Christian and her cousin Rab Montgomery down by the Hammills.

It was strange to think that the half-drowned, defiant slip of a child they had confronted then was the same creature as this elegant young woman, the curls of her dark hair resting against a rounded cheek, her thick lashes lowered as she studied the book on the desk in front of her.

A wave of tenderness swept over him. Alarmed and embarrassed by his own feelings, he cleared his throat, and Christian looked up then smiled, laying down her quill pen and slipping from the high stool she sat on.

'You're back, Mister Fraser. Did you have a good journey?'

'Well enough. I saw Alexander settled, and made a few

good business contacts. My son's idea of setting up a London establishment for the Fraser house may well turn out to be a good move. I found a buyer for the extra bales we have in stock, and an order for more, besides. I'll give you the letters and agreements when my trunk's unpacked.'

He unbuttoned his coat. 'Did anything happen while I was away?'

'I'd to speak sharply to Tam Logan, for his web was late coming in again, and the work wasn't as good as it should have been.'

'How did he take it?'

'Not well, but he's got no choice. I told him that we'd seek another weaver elsewhere if it happened again.'

'You did the right thing.'

'And that new warehouse man you brought in last month, the Highlander . . .'

She paused, frowning.

'Gregor MacEwan? What of him?'

'There's something about the man. Oh, he's good enough at his work, but . . .'

She hesitated. How could she describe her feelings about the dark young Highlander? It was as though there was an air of brooding trouble about him, like a cloak clinging to the lines of his rangy body.

'If he's been worrying you, then rid yourself of him.' Fraser's voice was brisk and matter-of-fact. 'You know that I trust your judgement.'

'I'd not want to take a man's livelihood away from him without good reason. And he's neither said nor done anything wrong. But he's got the ears of the other men, and it wouldn't take more than a few words from him to discontent them if he so pleased.'

'Then let him go and be done with it.'

'No.' She was sorry she'd spoken. 'Leave things as they are for the moment.'

He was frowning, reluctant to drop the matter.

'I'll not hesitate to send him away if I think it's necessary,' she said quickly, then, to divert his thoughts, 'Now – look at this.' She opened a box and took out a wooden pirn with some yarn wound round it, picking at the end of the yarn and drawing it out between finger and thumb. 'A packman brought it in. I liked the feel of it, but I told him I'd have to see what you thought. He's coming back the next time he's in Paisley.'

Angus took the yarn, rolled it between thumb and forefinger, held it up to the light that came in through the windows, then pulled hard against the pirn. The yarn was strong and true, without any of the lumpiness that spoke of shoddy material or poor spinning.

'Aye, it's fine.' She noted with relief that his mind had left the subject of the Highlander. 'You've got an eye for good work, Christian. I should take you with me on my next trip to the Lancashire mills, where most of our cotton's spun.'

Her eyes lit up – just the way Rachel's did when he brought a present back from his travels, he noted indulgently.

'I'd like that fine!' she said.

'Then we must see to it,' said Angus Fraser, smiling down on his young overseer.

The day was as clear as spun glass, the air sharp and exhilarating. Christian and Rab tumbled off the cart that had brought them and others to the small frozen loch cupped in the braes, their booted feet crunching into white untrodden snow.

'I feel as though it's been years since I last skated!'

Christian brushed the snow from a rock and sat down to put her skates on.

'I'll see to them for you.'

'I can do it myself. I'm not handless!'

But he insisted, kneeling in the snow before her, fitting the skates carefully on to her small feet.

As he worked, Christian looked about her contentedly, drawing in great, sharp, searing lungfuls of the chill air. The familiar hills and hollows and clumps of whins had taken on a completely new look beneath a glittering coat of snow and ice, and smoke writhing from the town chimneys far below promised warmth and comfort for the skaters when the day was over.

'There you are. Wait until I've got my own skates on,' Rab added hurriedly as she stood up.

She laughed at him over her shoulder, but waited by the edge of the lake until he was ready. About a dozen people were already on the ice. At the far side of the little loch someone with the foresight to bring some unwanted timber along had started a fire.

'Scared to go on to the ice on your lone?' Christian asked when her cousin joined her.

'You never know – I'm a year older than the last time. Mebbe I've lost the ability.'

She wound her arm about his waist. 'Poor old man! I'll look after you.'

Above her head, Rab beamed. These days opportunities to be with Christian were few and far between, for as her father had predicted, she had become completely absorbed in her work over the past year.

But for now the warehouse was out of her mind as she wobbled uncertainly on to the ice, then leaned forward into the rhythm and felt her skates biting into the frozen loch and knew that her sense of balance hadn't forsaken her after all.

'You've not lost the art. Well, not quite,' Rab added as she stumbled over a rough patch and almost fell against him. She regained her balance, but Rab, who had tightened his grip about her slim waist, didn't loosen it.

Holding her like this, her bonneted head close to his shoulder, the smoke of their breath mingling in the cold air, he was happy. He wished that this day, this moment, could go on for ever.

In the past year maturity had fitted itself naturally about Christian's shoulders without her noticing it. She was too busy to realise that her neat-featured face with its large long-lashed hazel eyes and its frame of silky dark hair had become beautiful.

Rab, hurtingly aware of the change in her, and of the changes in himself, had been watching and waiting with rapidly dwindling patience for her to notice him as something other than a cousin and a childhood friend.

Carefully, casually, he guided her to the part of the loch furthest away from the other skaters.

'I'll race you to the far bank.' She twisted from his grasp like a fish, moving away from him, faster and faster.

'Be careful, the ice there might not be strong.' His words were blown back in his face by the wind, and he realised that she couldn't hear him, that she was speeding now towards an area that hadn't been tested.

'Christian!' His heart in his mouth, Rab leaned all his weight on his skates, willing them to speed over the ice. He waited to hear the first ominous creaks, to see Christian slipping into deep, dark water, out of his reach. He could almost see the small mittened hand reach out to him in vain hope, then slip beneath the surface.

'Christian!'

He was so intent on the terrible pictures in his mind that when she halted and turned towards him, unharmed, saying, 'Och, the ice is too rough here for skating!' he didn't have time to stop himself.

He caught a brief glimpse of her astonished face, eyes bright and nose pink with cold, as he swept past, then one of his skates caught on a raised piece of ice and with a yell he soared into the air, arms wheeling frantically.

Somehow, he turned himself round in mid-air. White snow and blue sky whirled crazily then, with a painful crash that swept the breath from his lungs, he landed on the banking.

The first thing he heard, when the world had steadied itself again, was Christian's laughter, peal after helpless peal. Raising his head and squinting beneath his lashes he saw her on the ice, mittened hands to her face, her shoulders shuddering. He let his head fall back on the snow, and concentrated on getting his lungs to work properly.

'Rab, get up – you'll catch your death of cold lying there,' she spluttered when the laughing fit was over. Then, as he lay motionless, her voice began to sharpen with alarm: 'Rab?'

Rab lay still. Christian's skates clattered towards him, then darkness fell over his closed eyes as she knelt by his side.

'Rab? Oh dear God – Rab, speak to me!' Her hand, wrested from its mitten, was warm and soft on his face. Her breath touched his lips.

'I'll fetch the others.' She was getting up when his hand shot out and caught at her arm.

'Never mind the others!'

'But you – oh, Rab Montgomery, there's nothing wrong with you at all!' Half laughing, half crying, she punched at his shoulder. 'You frighted me to death, you great daft lump! Get up at once!'

'I think I've bruised my back.' He held a hand out. 'Help me up.'

She took the hand, then gave a muted shriek as she was pulled down into his arms.

'Rab,' she managed to say, then he claimed her mouth and the rest of the protest was muffled against his lips. For a moment Christian struggled, then gave in to his superior strength and, though she would never have admitted it, to her own impulse.

Locked in each other's embrace, rolling in the snow, they kissed and kissed again, each kiss becoming longer and more intense. Rab's cap had fallen off when he fell; Christian's bonnet came adrift now, and strands of her soft hair fell across Rab's cheek.

Finally she pulled herself free and sat up, breathless. 'Look at the two of us – covered with snow. Come on over to the fire.'

'Christian.' He tried to draw her into his arms again.

She shook her head, backing away from him, getting to her feet. There was something in his blue eyes that worried her, an intensity that she wasn't yet ready to acknowledge and handle.

'We'll catch the pneumonia, sitting here. Come on.'

She walked the few steps to the ice, balancing carefully on the blades of her skates, and held her hand out to him. 'We'll have to be careful for the first yard or two. The ice is rough here.'

'I noticed,' said Rab wryly, and got up. The moment was over. He had held her and kissed her, but the time to talk to her seriously was gone, and he would have to wait for another opportunity.

As they skated towards the figures gathering round the fire, he whistled cheerfully.

Mally Bruce had taught Christian all he knew of Latin and geography, history and arithmetic. The arithmetic in particular stood her in good stead in the warehouse, and her ever-eager mind was content to turn its attention to the manufacturing trade.

The ending of her lessons, something she had once dreaded, didn't trouble her after all. At some time during the transition from school-pupil to tambourer to overseer her great hunger for knowledge had become a hunger for business. Every day in the warehouse she was seeking and learning and storing new information away in her avid brain. At last, she was content.

The loan from her great-aunt Mary MacLeod had long been repaid, and Mally was now a familiar figure in Paisley's streets, energetically cranking the handle of his turney lay, the machine that had given him his self-respect back. But although the lessons were over he and Christian remained fast friends. She often visited him in his shabby little room, where the two of them pored over the latest news-sheets and talked of every subject under the sun.

Christian counted him as one of her dearest friends, and there was little in her life that Mally, well able to keep a secret, didn't know.

During 1792 trade began to fall off and many of the weavers found themselves without work. With difficulty, Angus and Christian between them managed to keep the warehouse and the people dependent on it busy. Christian saw to it that the tambourers were kept on and Trina, who had proved to be an excellent choice as their new leader, used her quick wits to make sure that the women under her care managed to go on earning a living.

But many of the town's young men, disheartened by the lack of work, enlisted in the Army.

Duncan Montgomery, Rab's younger brother, set off one day for Falkirk with a friend who was going there to enlist, and didn't come back.

His distraught mother came running to Oakshawhill the next day with a hastily scrawled letter in her hand.

'Look at that,' she wailed, thrusting the single page into Margaret Knox's hand. 'It's from our Duncan, the daft gowk!' Then she collapsed into a chair in a flood of tears.

' "Dear Father and Mother," ' Margaret read aloud for Christian's benefit. ' "I take this opportunity of letting you know that I am in good health and hoping that this will find you all the same. I am very sorry to inform you that I am volunteered." '

She lifted her head and stared at her sister-in-law. 'What's the laddie talking about? He'd no notion of volunteering, surely?'

Annie, gasping, pointed a trembling finger at the letter, and Margaret turned her attention back to it.

' "I had no intention of doing this, but Tam that was to volunteer got me filled with drink and when I got sober I had enlisted and they would not let me off." '

Annie's sobs redoubled.

'Christian, for any favour pour out some of your father's brandy for your aunt.'

'It was d-drink that did for my laddie,' Annie wailed. 'I d-don't want it!'

'Nonetheless you'll take it, for you need something to steady you.' Margaret took the glass from her daughter

70

and almost poured the small drop of brandy down Annie's throat.

'Don't worry, Aunt Annie, we'll not let you lose your head and volunteer,' Christian said, and earned a furious glare from her mother.

'He'll be fine, Annie. See, he says further on in the letter that it's only for seven years and mebbe it'll be less. And he's mebbe coming home for a visit soon.'

'A visit?' Annie Montgomery almost shrieked. 'A visit – and him with a loom with a web on it, waiting for his return from Falkirk! Finish the letter!'

' "I'm with the eleventh regiment of the Scots Guards and I only got six pounds of bounty for signing – one half of it in hand and the other half when we join with the regiment. This is all at present from your loving son Duncan Montgomery." '

'God love the laddie, he didnae even get a decent bounty! Duncan never was any good with money – or with drink,' said his mother, and started weeping once more.

Over her bent head, Margaret and Christian exchanged helpless glances.

Annie wept again when Duncan arrived home a few weeks later, self-consciously proud of his new uniform, and cautiously pleased with himself now that he had had time to get used to the idea of being a soldier instead of a weaver.

'Uniform or not, my mother gave him a right clout on the ear when he walked in,' Rab told Christian, 'and before he could get over the ringing in his head, she was hugging and crying over him. Ach, it'll do the laddie good. He'll get to see the world, and it'll mebbe make a man out of him. Duncan aye had too much of a conceit of himself to be a good weaver.'

'Since you think it's going to do him so much good I'm surprised you're not marching along with him when he goes.'

Rab shook his head, his gaze intent on her.

'I've got my reasons for staying in Paisley,' he said. 'Good reasons. I'm not leaving, not for anything.'

'I am – for a wee while. Mister Fraser's going down to the cotton mills in Lancashire soon, and he's promised to take me with him.'

'You – going away with that man?'

'What's wrong with it?'

'Everything's wrong with it!' Rab said explosively, his face reddening. 'A lassie going off with a man of his age!'

For a moment she stared, bewildered, then she grasped his meaning and her own face crimsoned.

'For any favour, Rab Montgomery, I'm not eloping with the man, I'm only going down to see the manu-factories and buy yarn for the looms!'

'I'll not allow it!'

'It's got nothing to do with you!'

Rab's mouth opened and shut once or twice, then he said lamely, 'Your parents'll never agree.'

'Of course they will,' Christian said scathingly. 'Any-way, I'm old enough to please myself.'

'Have you told them?'

'Not yet. I'll speak to them tonight.'

'They'll be against it.'

'They won't.'

'They will,' said Rab, with quiet, stubborn despera-tion in his voice.

Chapter Six

As Rab had hoped, Gavin Knox and his wife were reluctant to agree to their daughter's proposed trip with her employer.

'I know that it's only a matter of business and that there's no foolishness or harm in it,' Margaret explained patiently to Christian. 'But I'm thinking of what folks'll say – an unmarried young woman and a widower going off together like that.'

'If folks have nothing better to do than tattle, let them!'

Gavin's face hardened. 'Christian, I'll not have you speaking to your mother like that. She's not happy about you going off to Lancashire with Angus Fraser on your lone and neither am I, and that's an end to it.'

'I can't blame them,' Angus Fraser said when Christian, furious and humiliated, reported the conversation to him. 'I'd not be over fond of the idea if it was my Rachel that was going off with some man, even if he was old enough to be her father.'

'You're not old enough to be my father – don't say that!' The heated words had tumbled out of her mouth before she could stop them. She felt herself turning poppy red, just like an empty-headed lassie – in front of Mister Fraser, too!

But when she glanced from under her lashes at her

employer she saw that he was looking everywhere but at her, and that he, too, had a hint of warm colour in his cheeks.

'Whether I am or not it was quite wrong of me to suggest such a ploy,' he said. 'I didn't think what I was about – I just thought it would be a good thing for my overseer to see the mills at work.'

'But I want to see them!'

'Would your parents agree to the trip if I took Rachel along with me and asked you to come as her companion as well as my employee?' he suggested.

The news that Rachel Fraser was to go to Lancashire as well made all the difference, and in April Gavin and Margaret Knox delivered their excited daughter and her luggage to Waingaitend, where she and the Frasers were to take the morning stage coach to Glasgow on the first step of their journey to Lancashire.

'I hope we're doing the right thing, letting her go,' Margaret said to her husband as the coach lumbered off with Christian's gloved hand waving from the window.

'Christian's a woman now. Letting her go,' he said shrewdly, "may be the only way to keep her. Come on home and stop fretting, Margaret. You've still got Daniel to look after – for a little longer.'

In Glasgow Christian and the Frasers changed from the small local coach to the fine new vehicle that was to take them to Bolton. Fraser, who would have made the journey in half the time on horseback if he hadn't had two excited young women with him, took his place on top while Christian and Rachel settled inside with four other women.

By the time they had lurched and jolted down through the rolling benevolent Border hills and reached England

Rachel had forgotten her initial excitement over the journey and become fretful and uncomfortable, but Christian, determined to make the most of her first long trip away from home, relished every mile.

'Travelling far, lass?' one of the older women in the coach asked with friendly curiosity. Her accent held the rich savour of northern England, heard often enough on Paisley's streets these days. The Lancashire spinning mills produced more yarn than their own weavers could use, and agents from the various manufactories often went north to offer their wares for the hungry Paisley looms.

'To Bolton, ma'am.'

'Bowlton, is it? A grand place, Bowlton!'

Bowlton! Christian rolled the local pronunciation round in her mind, shaping it with her lips. She liked it.

They had to make two night stops, with the girls sharing a room with the other women from the coach. Not even the discomfort of lying on a narrow lumpy bed, the snoring of her room-mates, or Rachel's repeated whispered insistence that she could hear beetles scurrying over the floorboards towards her could reduce Christian's high spirits.

She had been fortunate enough to gain a seat by the window, and watched, fascinated, as the wild, beautiful Lancashire moors and hills gave way on one side to the flat plain by Morecambe Bay, with the sea's shimmer just discernible in the distance.

Then there were more hills, like home and yet, in some strange way, not like home at all. English hills. A turnpike road jostled and bounced the carriage along from rut to rut before, on the evening of the third day, they reached the end of their journey and came upon Bolton, a place of manufactories and streets and houses.

* * *

Angus Fraser had booked accommodation for himself and his two young companions in a large and prosperous inn not far from the mill where he was to do business.

Rachel, exhausted and peevish after the long journey, examined the spacious, spotless bedchamber thoroughly, but was unable to find a trace of beetles, mice, or any other nocturnal menaces. She tested the large and comfortable bed, then promptly removed her clothes, letting them lie where they may, and crawled between the sheets, unable to face the evening meal. Christian changed out of her travelling clothes, washed herself thoroughly, brushed her hair until it shone, and put on a blue cambric dress.

'D'you think it'll do, Rachel?'

Rachel roused herself, but scarcely gave it a glance before closing her eyes again. 'There's nothing wrong with it.'

Christian gnawed at her lower lip. 'It doesn't look as grand as I'd first thought. It's my best gown, too.'

'If it's your best,' said Rachel peevishly, wanting only to be left in peace, 'then it'll have to do, won't it?'

Christian twisted and turned before the spotted, flawed looking-glass, trying to see the dress from every angle.

'My great-aunt Mary says that it doesn't matter what you're wearing, it's the way you wear it.'

'Then think of yourself in silks and lace and be done with it,' the voice from the bed was taking on a distinctly irritable note. 'My father'll be waiting for you, and he hates to be kept waiting for his meal.'

'Mercy, I forgot about him!' She flew out of the room and down the narrow twisting staircase. But Angus Fraser, waiting for her as his daughter had predicted, didn't seem to be in the least impatient. His eyes flared as he studied her from top to toe, and he nodded approvingly before leading her to the room where their meal was to be served.

At first, during supper, they were awkward with each other, for it was the first time they had been alone together other than in the warehouse office, and talk about business soon ran out.

But gradually the ice began to thaw, and by the time the meal was over Christian was telling Angus all about Mally and the extra tutoring the old man had given her.

'I think I've seen him about the streets. He's a fearsome-looking old man.'

'He's not fearsome at all. When next you see him near your house tell your servants to give him your household knives and scissors to grind, for he's in need of the work.'

'You still visit him, although he no longer tutors you?'

'Oh course. He's a good friend.'

'But that hovel where he lives – there must be all manner of folk there.'

'Some honest, some dishonest, all of them poor souls with nowhere better to go.'

'Are you not afraid in case they might harm you?'

'I've visited the houses by the river all my life, with my mother and on my lone, and never come to harm.'

She smothered a yawn, for she didn't want the evening to end. There were still some crumbs of sweet pastry scattered over the empty plate before her. She kept her head bent, concentrating on gathering the little flakes together with her finger, until the yawn was under control.

'I must admit,' Angus Fraser was saying, 'that I'd be concerned if Rachel took it into her head to visit such a place.'

'Ah, but Rachel and I are very different,' Christian said

blithely, her attention more on the crumbs than the conversation. She had managed to get them into a tiny sugary mountain; she pressed the ball of one finger against it to gather up as much as she could. 'I was always allowed to stand on my own two feet, whereas she's been coddled all her life.'

Deftly, she transferred the sweetness to her lips. Then she suddenly realised what she had just said, and looked up at her employer with shocked eyes, her finger still in her mouth.

'Indeed? So you think I coddle my daughter?'

There was a coolness in his voice and the indulgent smile had faded. But it was too late to retract what she had said. And anyway, it was the truth.

'I do, Mister Fraser. Rachel's a young woman, near enough, but it seems to me that you treat her as a child. I can see why you might want to go on thinking of her as your little daughter, but it'll not do her any good. You're just fashioning a stick for your own back.'

There was a short silence while she stared down at the table and waited for the storm to break about her head.

Then a loud voice said from the doorway: 'Damn me if it's not Angus Fraser himself!'

A man and woman, both well-fleshed but most elegantly dressed, bore down on their table.

'Aye, it's Fraser all right. What brings thee to Bowlton?'

There was a flurry of introductions; it transpired that the newcomer was a Mister George Blake, one of the mill owners who dealt with the Fraser company.

'We were just taking some dinner in the next room before going home,' he said, the words aimed at Angus Fraser, but his small blue eyes fixed on Christian. 'It's fortunate that I happened to glance in through the door

78

while we were passing on our way out, and saw you. Two more chairs here,' he bawled imperiously at a servant, who ran to obey him.

Then he turned his attention to Christian again. 'Warehouse overseer, eh? By God, Fraser, I'd give my right arm to have such pretty employees in my warehouse!'

His wife, in an elaborate embroidered brocade dress with the skirt caught up at the back with a bunch of ribbons so that the frilled, beribboned petticoat could be seen, gave him a vicious look as she settled into her chair, and he cleared his throat nervously and called for something to drink.

'We were just about to retire for the night,' Angus Fraser began, and Mistress Blake gave a sudden loud titter behind her hand. Her hair was elaborately upswept beneath a hat massed with feathers that waved and bobbed each time she moved. Beside her, Christian felt like a peasant in her best blue cambric.

Angus Fraser's face tightened at the woman's amusement, the strong bones standing out beneath the skin. All at once Christian realised why her parents had stubbornly refused to give their blessing to the trip when it had only involved herself and Angus.

Gratefully, she remembered Rachel, no doubt sound asleep by now in the upstairs bedchamber.

'What a pity Rachel's unwell and unable to meet your friends,' she said swiftly to her employer, then explained to the woman by her side: 'Mister Fraser's daughter came to Lancashire with him. I agreed to act as her companion. I'm afraid that the journey upset her.'

'Indeed?' There was disappointment in the round face only inches from her own. 'The poor child,' Mistress Blake said, uninterested.

The evening wore on. Christian, who had wanted to stay up for hours on this first night away from home, found herself longing for her bed.

Mistress Blake's flow of malicious gossip about people Christian had never met, and her husband's bright inquisitive eyes, studying every inch of her over and over again, boring into her flesh until she began to feel as though he was touching her, became extremely tedious.

She could tell that Angus Fraser, drinking steadily, disliked the intruders as much as she did. It was a relief when he drained his glass for the last time and got to his feet.

'It's time to retire. We have a long and busy day ahead of us.'

The Blakes, thwarted, called for their carriage and disappeared into the night with one last leer on his part, one last barbed remark on hers.

Light-headed with relief at their going, Christian accepted a lit candle from the inn-keeper and went up the staircase ahead of Angus Fraser.

At the top of the stairs they paused; the room Christian was to share with Rachel was on the left, along the corridor. Angus Fraser had another flight of stairs to climb.

'Is it Mister Blake's mill we visit tomorrow?'

It was a relief when he shook his head. 'No, thank God. I've never liked the man, and now that I've met his wife, I like him less.'

'They thought—'

'I know what they thought, damn their midden minds!' His voice was savage, each word forced out between set teeth. 'I'm sorry, Christian. I never wanted you to be exposed to such – such crass vulgar ignorance.'

'Och, don't worry about me. Bad thoughts can't hurt anyone but the folk that think them. Besides, we know the true way of things.'

His hand reached out and touched her hair, then cupped her cheek. 'You're a sensible lassie, Christian Knox.'

'I'm not a lassie!'

He held his candle up so that her face was illuminated in its soft glow. His other palm was still warm against her face. Suddenly, desperately, she wanted to turn so that her mouth was against it, but she didn't dare.

'You're right,' he said, low-voiced. 'You're a woman – and right now I'd give everything I have to lose twenty years from my age.'

The lamplight wove a golden cage about them. There was a murmur of voices from down below, but up here there was only silence, and the two of them, locked together, yet apart – too far apart for Christian's comfort.

'You've – you've no need to wish that,' she whispered, willing him to sway towards her, to put his arms about her.

'Aye, I have.' His words were so low that she only just caught them. For a long moment they stared at each other, and she tried hard to let him see in her eyes the words she couldn't say out loud. Not yet.

But instead of drawing her near Angus Fraser stepped back, pulling away from her, leaving her alone.

'Good night, Christian,' he said abruptly, harshly, and turned towards the stairs.

The shadows of the candle he carried danced ahead of him as he began to ascend them. Slowly, dazed with what had just happened to her, Christian moved towards her own room.

Mercifully, Rachel was fast asleep, her face a pale blur on the pillow. Christian undressed, put on her nightshift, blew the candle out and slid into the bed without disturbing the younger girl.

All that day she had expected to be thinking as she courted sleep: 'Tomorrow I'll see the mills.'

Instead, she found herself thinking: 'Tomorrow, I'll see him again. Tomorrow I'll spend the whole day with him. Tomorrow . . .'

She drifted into sleep with the memory of his hand warm against her face.

On the following morning Christian woke early to the sound of clogs in the street beneath her window, carrying their owners off to shops and manufactories. Rachel was still asleep, and she was content to lie still, listening to the Bolton folk outside, thinking with a mixture of astonishment and delight about her new feelings for Angus Fraser. She longed to see him again, but there was also a sense of embarrassment at the thought of meeting him face to face.

Someone rapped on the door, and Rachel woke, fully recovered from her travel sickness of the evening before. The new day had begun.

It was Rachel who eased Christian's first meeting with Angus. He was waiting downstairs for them to join him for breakfast, and his daughter ran into the room ahead of Christian and threw herself into his arms.

Over her shoulder he said: 'Good morning, Christian. Did you sleep well?'

'Quite well, thank you.' His face was pale after his drinking of the night before, and there were shadows under his eyes. He looked as though he had been lying awake half the night, she thought with loving compassion.

Then the food was carried in, and they all sat at the table, and somehow it became possible to meet Angus Fraser's eyes and to behave as though everything was the way it had been before last night.

By the time they emerged from the hotel the footpath outside was clear of people going to work, though the narrow street was busy enough, mainly with carts carrying cloth, yarn, or unworked cotton on the last stage of its long journey to the mills from the Americas, by way of Liverpool docks.

Bolton and the great Lancashire mills were a revelation to Christian. Paisley's spinning and weaving was still carried on in cottages, and few of the workers were expected to travel from their homes to manufactories and mills.

In Bolton, it seemed, all the men, women and children were employed in huge buildings that thundered and vibrated to the beat of machinery and the clank and rattle of horsewheels and waterwheels.

Christian had assumed without question that Paisley was the centre of the textile world. But on that day she was forced to think again, for the amount of cotton she saw being carded and spun, from its raw beginnings to the finished product, ready to be shipped off to the weaving communities, was quite beyond belief.

At Angus's request, the mill owner they were visiting led the little party through the entire place himself. Rachel, her nose wrinkling at the smell of oil and the stuffiness of the building, cast only a brief glance at each department they visited, but Christian lingered as long as she could, asking questions all the time, so fascinated by what she saw that she forgot everything else.

Angus watched her and listened to her with surprise and respect. When the owner said, at the end of the tour, 'By God, Mester Fraser, tha's got an overseer there as quick-witted as any man,' he nodded.

'I think you're right, sir.'

Christian blushed with pleasure.

'If I were thee I'd keep hold o' her.'

'I intend to, Mister Dickson,' said Angus Fraser. 'I intend to.'

Christian returned to Paisley ready to talk about the Lancashire mills to anyone willing to listen.

'You surely don't want that sort of thing here in Paisley, do you?' Rab asked at last, tired of hearing about the impressive manufactories in England. They were alone in his father's weaving shop, and Christian had been chattering on for a good half-hour.

'No, of course not. There's the bad side to them as well. The smell of oil, and the noise, and the fluff in the air catching at your breath – and the children.'

Her eyes darkened at the memory of the children, many of them little more than babies, with their tiny pale faces and eyes huge with lack of sleep, thin little limbs sticking out of frayed sleeves and trouser legs. Most of them were paupers, with nobody to care what happened to them.

'I know that they can't work the mills without them, but it's no way for wee ones to live, crawling about under machinery and dragging great baskets around, with never the time to run and play and breathe good country air. But the size of the place, Rab – and if you'd just seen the bales of yarn piled up in the store, waiting to be taken away—'

'You're off again,' he said dourly.

'I can't help it – oh, Rab, d'you know what a pleasure it is to be working at something you really care about? For the first time I'm not envious of Daniel. Let him go to his precious university. Thanks to Mally I've got the Latin and thanks to Mister Fraser I've got work enough to keep me busy.'

'For how long?'

'For as long as I choose.'

She went to where he sat on the saytree of his loom and earnestly cupped his face in her hands.

'D'you realise, Rab, that in two or three years' time I could be travelling down to Lancashire and mebbe even to London on my own, buying and selling for the Fraser warehouse?'

'Christian, see sense! You're a lassie, not a man. In two or three years' time you'll be wed, with a home and bairns and a man of your own.'

The precious memory of those few minutes alone with Angus Fraser jumped into her mind, and was pushed back out again. She let Rab go and turned away, her chin jutting.

'Not,' she said, 'until I want it.'

'You will want it.'

'I'm happy enough with the way things are. I'm happier than I've ever been before.'

'Aye, you look it,' he said slowly, suspiciously. 'You look as if a lamp's been lighted inside you. Has something happened – something you've said nothing about?'

'It's just – liking what I'm doing. It's being happy with the way things are, that's all.'

'Will you stop using that word!' He scowled at her, then said wretchedly. 'Can you not see how unhappy you're making me, with your constant talk of Angus Fraser and your work in his confounded warehouse?'

'You're never jealous!'

'Jealous? Are you blind, woman, that you can't see that I'm sick with love for you, and sick with the fear of losing you?'

Christian's amusement faded away; Rab looked anxiously for a softening in her face, only to see her expression freeze in shock.

'Rab,' she said uncertainly, 'you're teasing.'

He got to his feet. 'Christian, look at me!'

She did, and saw that in the past few years her friend and playmate had become a man. Saw, too, that he looked stark with misery, his eyes afire with the feelings he was at last letting free.

'Marry me, Christian. Marry me and forget all this nonsense about the warehouse and the mills and all the rest of it.'

'No Rab, I can't do that.'

There was no kinder way to put it. If she had tried to let him down gently, she knew, he would have taken it for a sign that he had a chance. And that would have been even more cruel.

Even so, he persisted. 'Why not?'

'Because I don't want to be your wife. I've got other things to do with my life.'

He took a step towards her and caught her shoulders. 'A weaver's not good enough for you, is that it?'

'That's not it at all, and you should be ashamed of yourself for thinking that it is. A woman's got the right to decide against marriage if she chooses. And I so choose!'

'Christian—' he said, then pulled her to him and kissed her, his mouth bruising hers mercilessly, his arms crushing her until she felt her ribs creak. There was no love in the kiss, none of the easy familiarity and quickening, youthful passion she had known when they had kissed in the snow up by the little loch.

For a moment she was frightened, for a moment she tensed, and began to struggle free.

Then she made herself stand still in the tight circle of his arms, unresisting and unresponding, until the embrace relaxed and eased and he stepped back, a mixture of anger and loss and shame darkening his face and making him look older than his years.

She wondered, in that moment, why she had never noticed that Rab had grown up.

'You'd best get out of here and leave me be. My father'll be back any minute,' he said eventually, gruffly, turning to his loom.

The kindest thing to do was to leave him without another word. Christian walked from the loom shop, closing the door gently behind her, and went home.

Margaret Knox, busy with her needlework in her comfortable parlour, had the sense to hold her tongue until her daughter had finished speaking. Then she said, 'The self-same thing happened to me when I was much the same age as you.'

'Who was the man?'

'Jamie Todd.'

'Jamie?' Christian's tone was incredulous, and Margaret laughed.

'Aye, Jamie. No need to sound so surprised. I'd my admirers the same as you have, milady.'

Christian had the grace to flush. 'I didn't mean that. It's just that – I can't see you as a weaver's wife.'

'Neither could I. My whole life was in front of me, and I'd no notion of marrying – until I met your father. I told Jamie he was daft.' Margaret smiled over the memory.

'What did he say to that?'

'He went off to be a soldier. Then he came back to the loom, and now he's happier with Islay and their son than he'd ever have been with me.'

'I wish,' said Christian in a sudden spurt of anger, 'that the daft fool had kept his mouth shut!'

'He said what he had to say.'

'I'm sorry for him, Mother. But that's no reason to marry him, is it?'

'Mebbe,' said Margaret, ignoring her husband's advice about blackfooting, 'there's someone else in your mind?'

Christian felt her face growing hot, and turned away, pretending to look for a book. 'Who could there be?'

'I was thinking of Mister Fraser.'

Christian spun round. 'What put such a daft notion into your head?'

'Just a thought,' said Margaret, certain that her guess had been right. 'After all, you're a bonny lass, and clever into the bargain. And he's no doubt looking for a wife.'

'What makes you think that, when he's been content to be a widower for all these past years?'

There was a sudden, tense silence. Margaret laid her sewing down in her lap and stared at her daughter.

'I meant Mister Alexander Fraser,' she said at last, slowly. 'The son, not the father.'

'Oh.' Christian's high colour, which had begun to fade, returned. She snatched up the first book her fingers closed on, muttered something, and hurried from the room, bringing the conversation to an abrupt close.

Left alone, Margaret stared at the door for a long time, her delicate brows knotted between her eyes.

Chapter Seven

To Christian's disappointment, Angus Fraser didn't refer again to the episode in the English hotel. His manner towards her continued to be that of employer to employee. If anything, he was more aloof than before.

At first, in her usual impetuous way, she thought of bringing the matter up, facing him with her love for him and the feeling she was certain he had for her. But then she decided, on reflection, to let matters lie for the moment.

She was content enough to work for him and with him – it would perhaps be unwise to do or say anything that might endanger the relationship that they already had.

The Christian of two years ago would have thought nothing of making her feelings known, of tossing a stone into the pool to see what happened. The more mature Christian was half afraid of the ripples that would be caused.

To her great sorrow, but not to her surprise, an awkwardness came between herself and Rab after his declaration of love in the weaving shop. Rab made certain that they were never alone together, and if they did happen to meet he was abrupt with her, spurning her attempts to be friendly.

The days passed. Annie Montgomery called in on Margaret Knox in a more cheerful frame of mind, bringing with her the latest letter from Duncan, the reluctant soldier. After a miserable journey by sea from Leith to the Thames, during which he and most of his companions had been badly affected by sea-sickness, he had arrived in London and was enjoying life as a soldier after all.

The Army had been reduced after the American war, but with France in turmoil, and working-class folk beginning to mutter about conditions in Britain, there was a move to recruit more soldiers from the ranks of the unemployed.

Recruiting parties were billeted in the grain store at George Place, military music was heard in the town on the Sabbath for the first time, and the local people became used to the sight of soldiers, brave and bright in their tartan plaids, with feathers in their blue bonnets, on their streets.

Stepping out of the Almshouse pend on to the High Street one day, Christian almost collided with Rab. His face crimsoned as he recognised her, and the hand he had put out to steady her fell from her arm as though his fingers had been burned. He began to walk on, but she caught up with him, determined to put an end to the coldness between them.

'We seem to be going in the same direction. You'll not object if I walk with you?'

'I can't stop you,' he said gruffly, without looking down at her. She strode along, matching him step for step, trying to think of something to say.

They passed two soldiers, then a group of three more.

'It seems as though the town's full of the militia,' Christian offered, and to her surprise she got a reply.

'If they think to keep the working folk down by force of arms, they're fools.'

'Working folk? It's against France they're recruiting, in case the people's army there should take it into their head to invade their neighbours.'

He met her eyes for the first time in weeks, looking down at her pityingly. 'You believe that tale, do you?'

'Why should I not?'

'They're recruiting soldiers in order to guard the Government and the rich folks like your Mister Angus Fraser against the rest of us. They're growing frightened – and well they might.'

The chill in his voice struck through her like a winter wind. She stopped short on the pavement, clutching his arm in both hands, fear for his safety bridging the chasm that had opened between them.

'Rab, you've not joined one of those Friends of the People societies, have you?'

'What makes you think they've got such a society in Paisley?' he countered evasively.

'The Paisley folk were never slow when it came to politics. There's almost certain to be one, at least. Answer me, Rab – have you joined with them?'

A slow, secretive smile came over his face. 'If I had, I'd not be likely to tell you, for it could mean the jail for me.'

'You've not,' she said, in hope. 'You'd have more sense than to get yourself into that sort of trouble.'

'You're speaking like one of the masters now, Christian.'

'Nonsense! I just don't want to see you in the jail, or sent off to Botany Bay in one of those terrible convict ships.'

The panic in her face gave him a warm glow of

pleasure. She cared – she must care! He put his hand over hers, and at the contact the ache in his heart quietened. 'Don't you worry, lass. I'll not let anything happen to me.'

'That's not an answer,' she started to say, then Rachel Fraser came out of a shop just ahead of them, her pretty face brimming with her pleasure at seeing them there, and no more could be said on the matter.

The feeling of unease that Christian knew whenever Gregor MacEwan, the Highland warehouseman, was around was proved to be justified when one of the warehouse girls came to her to report that some yarn was missing.

Angus Fraser was in Edinburgh, and the task of looking into the matter fell to Christian. When she had completed her enquiries she had no doubt of the name of the culprit. All the evidence pointed to the Highlander.

Sent for, he denied the charge; not with horror and indignation, as Christian would have expected from an innocent man, but blandly, with a slight smile on his lips and a mocking light in his eyes.

When she told him flatly that she didn't believe him, the man became insolent, openly defying her, confidently testing her authority to the limit.

The smile only disappeared when Christian met his bluff and told him coldly to take the money owed to him and leave the warehouse. He started to bluster, to threaten, his soft voice suddenly hard and menacing.

She held her ground, faced him down. Muttering something that she took to be an oath in Gaelic, he snatched up the coins and left, turning at the door to give her a look that chilled her to the bone.

Alone in the little office, Christian sank on to the stool

behind the high desk, her hands clasped tightly together to stop the tremor that ran through them. She wished that Angus Fraser was there to advise her. At that moment, she missed him more than she had ever missed him before.

When he returned on the following day he heard the whole story in silence, then said, 'I would have called out the militia and had his house searched.'

'The yarn's probably on some loom by now – and a loom in one of the villages outside Paisley, not in the town.'

'Even so—'

'If the yarn had been found the man would have faced a flogging at the very least.'

'And deserved it for stealing from his employer!' Angus Fraser said harshly.

'I couldn't have had that on my conscience! It was bad enough having to turn the man away . . .' Her voice shook, then broke. She bent her head hurriedly and busied herself with the books and papers lying on the desk.

'Christian?' A finger tucked itself below her chin and raised her face. She blinked hard to chase the tears away, and firmed her lips.

'What's amiss now?' he asked in amazement.

'I've – I've never put anyone out of work before.'

'Tush, lassie – you'll have worse to do before you're done. No need to weep over a thief. Here—'

He produced a handkerchief and gently dabbed at each eye in turn, smoothing away the moisture that was tangling her long lashes. His face was only inches away from hers, his eyes intent on his work.

The strength and confidence of the man filled the little room. His nearness set Christian's fingers and toes tingling. Unable to stop herself, she put a hand up and laid it against his cheek.

He paused, handkerchief in hand. For a moment they were both motionless, then he drew back.

'Christian—'

'I love you.'

'No!'

'I do,' she said stormily. 'I love you, and I think that you love me.'

A mixture of expressions fled across the face close to hers. He straightened, replaced the handkerchief in his pocket and said, after a clearing of the throat, 'You're the same age as my son. How could there be anything between us?'

'What has age got to do with caring for someone? It just happens – it's happened with both of us. You'll surely not deny it?'

He moistened his lips, then said slowly, 'No, I'll not deny it to you, for that would be foolish. But nothing can come of it.'

'Why not?' It was an anguished, angry cry straight from her heart.

'Because I'm too old for you, Christian. You deserve someone – better than me. Someone young and at the beginning of life, like you yourself.'

'Angus—' It was the first time she had called him by his given name. 'I know what I want!'

'Aye, and I know that I care for you too much to let you do the wrong thing,' he said wryly, and for just one moment she was warmed by the deep feeling in his eyes. Then his expression went carefully blank and he said, 'Heed my words, Christian – nothing can come of it. I'll not allow anything to come of it. Mebbe it would be better if we didn't see so much of each other

– if you found work somewhere else.'

Dismay caught at her heart, squeezing it painfully, 'D'you want me to go?'

He smiled, a twisting of the lips that didn't reach his eyes. 'Indeed I don't, for you're the best overseer I've ever employed. But now that we – know—'

'If you're so set on having your own way,' she said through stiff, cold lips, 'we'll say no more about it, ever again. But don't turn me away altogether, Angus. Please. I couldn't bear that.'

'Neither could I,' he said huskily.

'It's settled, then?' She gathered some papers together busily, dazed with grief and longing for him. 'We'll say no more about the matter.'

'Aye.' There was relief in his voice. 'I'm glad you're willing, lass. You'll see – it's for the best.'

'Yes,' she said.

But deep inside, she continued to hope.

Alexander Fraser came home from London to attend the gathering held to celebrate his sister's birthday. He had matured, just as Christian had matured. Now he dressed far more elegantly than a Paisley man, and there was even a trace of the southern English drawl in his speech.

'You must persuade my father to send you down to London soon, and I'll introduce you to the merchants who buy our cloth,' he told Christian, his eyes openly admiring her. 'Believe me, Mistress Knox, you would delight in the social life there – and they would take a great delight in you.'

'I'd like fine to see the place, and the markets there.' She smiled at him.

Just then, Angus Fraser came into the room, Rachel on his arm, and watching him, it seemed to Christian that, beside Angus, Alexander and Rab and Daniel were callow youths.

The wind that had risen in the late afternoon swirled down St Mirren Brae and howled round the warehouse, setting its timbers creaking and groaning. Drafts, finding their way in through a hundred cracks, set the candle on Christian's desk a-dance, so that shadows circled the walls like ghostly birds.

She turned the page of the big ledger and carefully began another row of figures, paying little heed to the noises outside and inside the place.

The warehouse was as familiar to her as her own home now, and even though everyone had gone and she was alone in the place, with night gathering outside, she didn't feel in the least lonely. She had had a busy day with little time to bring the book-work up to date. When that happened, she preferred to stay behind for a while; as often as not on these late evenings Mally or Rab looked in on her, and walked home with her when she had locked the warehouse up for the night.

She was in the place strictly against Angus Fraser's orders. When he first discovered that on occasions she stayed behind when the others had gone, he had forbidden it.

'I don't like the thought of you in the place alone,' he had said. 'There's not many folk around this part of the town at night. Besides, you put in enough time during the day. The work can always wait until the next morning, surely.'

But Angus had left the warehouse early that afternoon, with no intention of returning before morning, so what he didn't know wouldn't hurt him, in Christian's view. She preferred to know, when she went home, that everything was well in hand for the following day.

Before she was done Mally came slipping in through the double doors, his lanky body only needing an opening of a few inches.

'I'll not be long—' she began, looking up, then stopped when she saw the expression on his face. 'What's amiss?'

He stared into the shadows beyond the small office. 'Is there naebody else here?'

'I'm on my lone.'

'Where's Mister Fraser?'

'He'd to go to Elderslie to see a weaver. He'll be back in his own house by now.'

In the candlelight Mally's face was uneasy, and his eyes flickered around the place in a way that made Christian feel as though cold water was trickling down her spine. She put her quill down.

'I was in Bessie Lawson's howff a few minutes since—'

'Mally, you've not spent all your hard-earned silver on drink again, have you?'

'Will you wheesht an' let a man finish what he's got tae tell ye! There was a lad in the howff, a Highlander, talkin' over loud about how you'd turned him oot o' his place o' employment.'

'Gregor MacEwan,' she said without hesitation.

'I've no knowledge o' his name, only o' his intent. He was drinkin' hard, and talkin' tae his friends o' burning this place doon.'

She felt the blood in her veins slowing down and chilling. 'When?'

'I'd say it's tonight. I came at yince tae mak' sure you were oot o' the place. Come on, lassie, the sooner we're well away frae here the better.'

His hand locked on to her wrist, but she shook it off, her mind racing. 'Mally, run to Mister Fraser's house and tell him – quickly now!'

'I'll no' leave here withoot ye.'

Christian picked up her cloak and turned to blow the candle out. The place was plunged into darkness as she led Mally to the door and fumbled with the catch.

'I'll be along at your back. I must get the ledgers and the money together in case anything happens. I'll be all right. Go on, now!'

The door was open, and Mally, still mouthing protests, was pushed out. To her relief he took to his heels and fled, arms flapping by his sides, across the street and into the darkness.

Christian glanced quickly round. There was nobody to be seen, not even a passer-by. The wind rustled and rattled among the rubbish in the gutter.

She ducked back into the warehouse, fumbling for the desk, the ledgers, the small tin box where Angus Fraser kept the money needed to pay the weavers and spinsters.

There was too much for her to carry. She took her cloak off, spread it on the floor, put the books and the money-box into it, and gathered the cloth up to make a bundle.

On the way back to the door, she stopped, lifted her head, and listened intently.

The new sound came from the back of the warehouse, not the doorway. Gently, Christian laid down her load just inside the closed doors and made her way, hands feeling into the darkness before her, towards the fumbling, scratching noises. As her groping fingers encountered the first of the bales of finished cloth piled against the building's rear wall there came the sound of wood splintering, and a sudden waft of cold air touched her cheek.

Someone was outside the warehouse, at the rear wall, which gave on to the yard then the river bank. There would be nobody about at the back to see what was going on. They had chosen their spot well.

The warehouse was old, and in some places the wood was beginning to rot. Whoever was outside had pulled away a piece of rotted planking and was, by the sound of it, pushing kindling into the gap, hard against the bales of cloth inside. Gregor MacEwan, thought Christian, would know that finished cloth, readily inflammable, was stacked on the other side of that wall. The wind was blowing hardest against the rear wall; once the kindling and cloth were ignited it would fan the flames, forcing them inward towards the heart of the building, where the yarn and the wooden pirns would feed it.

Slowly, step by step, Christian retreated, thankful that at least nobody had discovered that the door was unlocked. Nobody had tried to get into the warehouse. Nobody was there to see her slipping out.

She was wrong. The creak of the door as she eased it open must have alerted the man set to watch the street and warn his friends if anyone was seen. Christian had scarcely slipped out into the night when there was a surprised, muffled oath behind her, and groping fingers scrabbled at her shoulder then took firm hold.

With a gasp of fright she twisted frantically. The stuff of her gown gave with a rending sound, and she was free. Knowing that she would only manage a few steps before being caught again, she swung round, arms stretched out before her, letting the weight of the bundle she carried pull her about.

A man loomed at her from the shadow of the warehouse.

The cloak, weighted with books and with the sharp-edged money-box, struck him in the midriff, and he gasped and doubled up just as the first leaping glow of flame showed from within the building.

Christian dropped the books and began to flee, but a hand reached up from the ground and wrapped itself about her ankle, pulling her off-balance. As she went down her nose caught the acrid smell of burning cloth.

She had time to realise that the fire had caught well, then something hit her hard on the side of the head and she tumbled into darkness.

She recovered her wits to find herself in the middle of noise and confusion. Opening her eyes, she realised that she was on the ground, before the open warehouse doors. Inside was a dull red glow. All about her men were running and shouting. Mally knelt beside her, his lined face haggard with worry.

'Are ye a' right, lassie?'

She tried to get up, but something was holding her back. 'Mally,' she said groggily. 'I told you to run and fetch Mister Fraser!'

'I did – I did. An' the Toon Watch tae. But the scoundrels got awa',' he said regretfully. 'Are ye hurt bad?'

'I'm fine.' She tried to get up again, and a familiar voice by her ear commanded: 'Be still!'

She turned her head away from the warehouse and from Mally, and realised that her shoulders were being supported by Angus Fraser, who was kneeling beside her. He had taken his jacket off and wrapped it about her, and she could feel the hard muscular warmth of his shoulder beneath her cheek, through the material of his shirt.

'The fire—'

'Hush, now. It's not had time to get a hold. There's a chain of men pouring water on it from the river. It's you I'm worried about.' His fingers touched her hair lightly, and she winced. 'You've had a blow to the head. Your father's been sent for. Just lie still till he comes.'

She leaned back against him, heedless of the mud and the dirt that was ruining her gown, heedless of the slow trickle of blood that ran from the side of her head to stain his shirt, content to rest where she was for ever.

Mally, having satisfied himself that she was going to live, loped off to help the fire-fighters, his long gawky limbs giving him the look of an animated scarecrow in the light from the lamps that had been brought to the scene.

'Lassie, what were you doing, working in the place on your lone? Did I not tell you not to do it?' Angus Fraser was demanding harshly.

'It's as well that I was. If I'd not been here for Mally to find, the warehouse might have been burned to the ground.'

'Damnation to the warehouse, and to everything in it,' he said, his voice shaking as he gathered her closer. 'Let it burn to the ground. It's you I care about – you!'

Chapter Eight

The news that Mister Angus Fraser was to marry with
Christian Knox raised more than a few eyebrows in the
Paisley parlours and kitchens, and caused far more
excitement than news of the attempt to burn down the
Fraser warehouse.

The warehouse was saved, with only a little damage
done to it or its contents. The culprits weren't caught,
and although Gregor MacEwan was closely questioned
by the militia, there wasn't enough proof to make an
arrest.

So the fire was dismissed in a few sentences, and the
gossips settled down to the more interesting news about
Christian and Angus.

'You can't blame them,' Margaret said to her Aunt
Mary MacLeod. 'The lassie's the same age as his own
children. I wondered if that bump she got on the head
had deranged her, but Gavin says it hasn't.'

'Tuts, Margaret, there's nothing wrong with the lassie
except love. You told me yourself a while back that you
thought she was interested in the man.'

'Aye – in the way that lassies sometimes fancy themselves in love with men who've got more experience of
the world. But I never for a minute thought it would
come to marriage!'

'I married a man years older than myself, and I never

regretted it,' Mary said complacently, then glared when her niece pointed out:

'But Aunt Mary, you were a lot older than Christian at the time.'

'From what I can see, he's as daft on her as she is on him. And he's an honest, respectable soul who'll do everything in his power to make Christian happy.'

'Gavin says it was downright embarrassing, having a man near enough to his own age asking for his daughter's hand in marriage.'

'Margaret, Christian's not going to have any of the bother of setting up a home and starting a new life that most lassies have. She'll be going into a fine house, with everything she could want in it, including the love of a good man.'

'And two step-children – one of them her own age.'

'Ach, she'll not let that fret her – not Christian. The laddie's in London, and she and the lassie get on well enough together, from what I've seen.'

'But one day Christian might well meet a younger man, and what'll happen then?'

'I hope you'd more sense than to say that to her face.'

'I did say it to her face, and she just laughed and said there'd never be anybody but Angus.'

'If you want my advice,' said Mary with an air of finality, 'you'd be well advised to give the two of them your blessing and be done with it, for they're set on taking the same path side by side, whatever you have to say about it.'

Margaret nodded. 'You're right. But I'm mortally sorry for poor Rab. He's had a fancy for Christian since they were bairns together. And now he's lost all hope of winning her.'

*   *   *

Christian had hoped to tell Rab her news before it reached him from other sources, but as soon as she walked into the weaving shop and saw him she knew that the gossips had reached him first.

His father's loom was still, but Rab was working hard, his little bare-footed drawboy dragging on the lashes with all his might, pulling at the high harness so that groups of warp threads lifted to allow the shuttle to fly beneath them.

'Can I have a word with you?'

Rab's sturdy body didn't cease its swaying dance as he worked the loom. 'I'm listening.'

So was the drawboy, his eyes round with curiosity in his small dirty face. Christian glanced at him, then at her cousin.

'You've heard.'

'Aye, I've heard. Were you hoping to keep it a secret from me?' The words were ground out between set teeth. His face was drawn with misery, his eyes dark. The sight of him wrenched at her heart.

'I wanted you to hear it from me. I wanted to explain—'

'There's nothing to explain. And there's nothing to say. If you want me to wish you well,' said Rab above the steady click-clack of the loom, 'then I do. But only you. Not him.'

For a moment she hovered uncertainly, then anger at his stubborness began to take hold of her. Why should she tell him she was sorry, when her whole being was on fire with happiness? Why should she feel guilty because she loved Angus instead of Rab?

She could only go away, leaving him with his loom and his misery.

Rab Montgomery left his parents' house and walked restlessly, aimlessly, through the town streets. Outside the house where Angus Fraser lived he stopped, then crossed the rutted muddy street, ducking between a cart and a man on horseback, and loitered in a doorway, watching the house.

Late though it was, there was a great deal of coming and going, for there was to be a wedding on the following day. Rab's mouth twisted downward into a sneer as he watched. The lamps had been lit in the house, and he could see folk coming and going in the rooms inside. Once or twice he caught sight of Angus Fraser himself.

He had been there for almost an hour when the door opened again and Rachel Fraser came out. Before Rab realised what was happening, before he could move away, the girl had crossed the street, and stood before him.

'I thought it was you standing over here. If you're looking for Christian, she's not with us tonight.'

'I'm not looking for her. I was . . . I . . .' He fumbled for some excuse, found none, and shut his mouth, glowering down on her, furious with himself at having been seen.

Understanding and then sympathy flowed into her pretty little face, and she put a hand on his arm.

'Rab, I'm sorry.'

'What for?'

'I've seen the way you looked at Christian. I'm sorry you're losing her.'

'Mebbe I'm sorry for you, too – getting a new step-mother.' The words were like hot coals in his mouth.

'Och, that doesn't bother me at all,' Rachel said blithely, adding with a grin that showed a dimple in one cheek, 'though Alexander's in a bit of a taking about that. Come on over to the house for a glass of ale,' she coaxed when he said nothing.

He couldn't trust himself to speak. He wanted to lash

out, to hit at someone. And he didn't want it to be Rachel, who was too young to know anything of the way love hurt. Roughly, he dragged himself free of her clasp and strode off down the street.

His main purpose, when he left home, had been to try to see Christian, to make one last attempt to talk her out of this marriage. They hadn't spoken to each other since the day she visited the loom shop to tell him that she was to wed Angus Fraser.

But now he realised that it was too late, that she was lost to him for all time.

So instead of turning left, through the pend at the Almshouse then up the winding lane to Oakshawhill, he went to the right, plunging down narrow New Street towards the river, with no thought in his mind but to walk until he was too tired to think.

As he emerged on to Causeyside, near to the Fraser warehouse, his ears pricked to a muffled throbbing, like the far-off beating of a big heart.

'It's the weavers, lad.' An old man stumping past with the aid of a stout stick volunteered the information. 'They wild rascals from Espedair. They're sayin' that a cork out at Carriagehill's been cheatin' them, so they've made his effigy.'

He skirted a stinking puddle and shuffled on about his own business. Rab paused for a moment, then his pulses seemed to fall into the rhythm of the distant beat of the drum and, without stopping to think what he was about, he began to run in the direction of the sound.

Traditionally, the weavers all kept to their own areas within Paisley as well as in the little communities scattered all about the boundaries. Weavers from the west of the town rarely mingled with those from the north, south or east.

The men who lived and worked in the vicinity of the Espedair Burn, near the River Cart, were particularly fiery by nature, proud and independent, hard-working and quick to repay a slight or an injustice to one of their people. It was their habit, when they felt that a manufacturer had treated them badly, to make up his likeness with straw and cloth, carry it through the streets to the beat of a big drum, and hang it in full sight of his windows – and those of his neighbours. The cork who was treated in this way usually repented quickly and came to a mutually acceptable agreement with his weavers.

Normally, Rab would have kept well out of the way, for this dispute had nothing to do with him. But tonight there was fire in his blood and rage in his heart. So he ran, and at Carriagehill, where the town's streets gave way to lush green countryside and the small shops and dwelling-houses dwindled out and were replaced by fine big houses built by manufacturers, he caught up with the vengeful weavers.

The effigy, plump and bald-headed, with a twist of yarn about its ears to denote a fringe of hair, rode high on the shoulders of two men who strode purposefully behind the man thumping on the big drum. After them, in a close-packed group, walked the rest of the weavers, grim-faced, each man wearing the long apron of his profession.

The rest of the procession was made up of excited, noisy drawboys and younger children, most of them bare-footed, hopping nimbly around the stones in the road. There were a few older stragglers like Rab himself, mainly young men who had gone along to see the fun.

Just after Rab had joined it, the procession halted at the gates of a square, comfortable stone house set in its own neat garden. Faces danced in agitation behind the window panes as the men carrying the effigy selected a sturdy tree opposite the house, in full view of the neighbouring buildings.

A drawboy went shinning up the trunk with one end of a rope in his hand. The other end was attached to the effigy's thick neck. The rope was secured, and amid cheers the figure was drawn up and up, to dangle above their heads in the soft evening breeze.

The lad in the tree dropped deftly to the ground, grinning from ear to ear. The effigy twisted slowly on the rope, dancing to the relentless beat of the drum.

After a moment the house door opened and a man came out on to the top step. There was a sudden silence. Rab saw at a glance that this was the cork. The effigy hanging by its neck from the tree was a cruel, but excellent, likeness.

The weavers who had carried the effigy, together with two of the men who had walked just behind them, advanced into the garden to talk to the manufacturer while the others waited, shuffling their feet, talking amongst themselves.

Almost at once it seemed as though the manufacturer, red-faced and visibly shaken, was about to strike a bargain with his workers. The effigy would be taken down and given to the youngsters to burn, and the weavers would retire to a howff to drink to their success.

But this time there was an unexpected break from tradition. As the cork nodded, apparently agreeing to something the group of men at the steps said, a dark-haired, poorly dressed young man standing near Rab bent swiftly, scrabbled at the ground, straightened, and swung his arm.

There came the crash of breaking glass, and a woman's

scream from inside the house. A hole flowered in the middle of a ground-floor window pane.

As the two or three people with him stooped to pick up stones the man gave an exultant whoop. His arm swung back again. Another stone flew, and struck sparks from one of the two stone pillars by the front door. Rab saw blood spreading on the forehead of one of the weavers by the steps as a splinter of stone struck him.

The cork and the deputation dodged to the side and then scattered, the cork leaping back into the house and slamming the door, the others lunging down the path, arms flailing in a futile attempt to stop the hail of stones that was now bombarding the house.

The children had joined in, screeching hoarsely with excitement, hurling pebbles, sticks, clods of mud – whatever came to hand. Without realising how it happened, caught up in the growing hysteria of the crowd, Rab joined in, and knew a surge of warm satisfaction when a jagged stone left his palm and smashed through an upper window, sending sparkling splinters of glass on to the gravel path below.

The march had turned into a riot. The weavers who had sought only to air their grievances were struggling to regain order. The men who had thrown the first stones were lifting and throwing as fast as they could, while the children scrambled excitedly about and got in everyone's way.

'Come on, man – before the militia get here!' A hand caught at Rab's shoulder, spinning him away from the house. Common sense and reason had completely deserted him. Caught up in the exhilaration of the moment he took to his heels and followed the ring-leader and his friends, running away from the road, crashing through undergrowth and bushes, the blood racing through his veins.

They didn't stop until they had reached the river bank near Causeyside. Then at last they halted, dragging air into their lungs, listening for sounds of pursuit, laughing and slapping each other on the back when they realised that they were safe.

Rab, suddenly aware that he was the only stranger, stood awkwardly apart for a moment before the leader of the group turned to study him with bright, interested eyes.

'You'll have a drink with us?' The man's voice, like the voices of two of his three friends, carried a soft Highland lilt.

Rab hesitated for only a moment. 'Aye, I'll drink with you.'

'Good!' The man gave him a friendly slap on the shoulder. 'And what do we call you?'

'Rab. Rab Montgomery.'

His new friend nodded. 'Rab Montgomery. And I,' he said, holding out a hand, 'am Gregor MacEwan.'

Chapter Nine

Alexander Fraser had sulked and pouted all through the marriage ceremony, throwing Christian hurt glances whenever he could.

But during the reception in the High Street house afterwards, she noticed that he cheered up remarkably quickly when Angus told him that he wanted him to set up a warehouse in London.

Thinking of the young man's sudden change of mood as she sat alone in the bedchamber, brushing her hair before the mirror, Christian smiled to herself, then wished ruefully that Rab's wounded pride could be cured as quickly as Alexander's. Her cousin hadn't attended her wedding.

Even so, it had been the best day of Christian's life. But now it was late in the evening, and the guests who had thronged the house earlier were gone. Although his room had been made ready for him, Alexander had decided to spend the night with friends, remembering, as he left, to cast one final soulful look at his father's new wife.

Rachel had been invited to Oakshawhill, and had gone off happily with Margaret and Gavin. Like her brother, Rachel fell in love easily, and at the moment Daniel, now in his final year of studying law at Glasgow University, was the centre of her universe. Not that he had noticed it, for Daniel rarely lifted his head from his books.

Apart from the two maids downstairs, the master of the house and his bride had been left alone to start their married life. Christian had stripped off her yellow figured silk gown, her red petticoat and the white petticoat beneath it, and her silk stockings. Now, in the new nightshift that she had made and embroidered herself, she was waiting for her husband.

The brush ran through her long tresses from crown to tip, over and over again until the hair crackled and shone with life. She gave one last sweep, then put the brush down and let her hair fall like a glossy curtain down both sides of her small face. Then she rose, and went across the room, and climbed into the large high bed to wait impatiently for her husband, who was putting on his sleeping attire in the adjoining room.

He kept her waiting for another four minutes. Then he came slowly to the bedside, his eyes fixed on her as she leaned forward and drew the coverlet aside so that he could join her.

The bed creaked as he climbed into it. Christian moved eagerly into his arms, and he kissed her, then held her back.

'Christian, are you certain?'

She laughed up at him. 'It's late to ask me that, when the minister's spoken over us and your ring's on my finger.'

'Not too late—'

'Oh, but it is, Angus Fraser. You're saddled with me for ever.'

He took a handful of soft hair and let it run through his fingers, like cool silk. 'You look so young. Like a child.'

'Angus, put out the candle,' she commanded, and he did so.

In the darkness, she moved back into his arms, thrilling

to their strength and to the sudden quickening of the hard male body so close to hers, only two thicknesses of material away.

'There,' she whispered against his throat. 'In the dark, nobody's any younger or any older than anybody else. In the dark, my love, there's only you and me and our loving.'

With a low moan, he lowered her to the pillows, and took her mouth in a long slow kiss.

Marriage to Angus Fraser was the best thing that had ever happened to Christian. He was a loving and considerate husband, intent only on making her happy. Christian moved into her new role as mistress of her own home with ease.

There was only one flaw in her happiness, a flaw that became apparent a month after the wedding, when she announced that it was time she was returning to the warehouse.

'But I've appointed another overseer,' her husband protested.

'Only until I was ready to go back.'

'My darling, there's no need for you to work in the warehouse now. You've got other duties to fulfil.'

'Angus, Rachel and me between us can run the house perfectly well, and I still have time for the warehouse.'

He drew her into his arms and kissed the tip of her nose. 'It wouldn't be seemly for Mistress Fraser to work in the warehouse.'

She looked at him in dismay. 'What else am I to do with my time, then?'

'What do other wives do? There's the servants to see to, and folk to entertain and to visit.'

'But—'

'Christian,' said Angus, the smile still on his face, but a hint of exasperation creeping into his voice. 'I'll not have the whole town laughing at me because my own wife's working in my warehouse. See reason!'

She bit her lip, then nodded. But when he had left the house she prowled restlessly from room to room, suddenly feeling as though she was in a cage. Finally, stifled, she put on her cloak and went off to visit her great-aunt.

'That's what marriage is all about, lassie,' Mary MacLeod said briskly when Christian had poured out her grievances. 'You surely didn't expect things to go on as before, did you?'

'You kept your millinery shop on after you were married, and my mother taught the children in the Poors' Hospital and employed women on the inkle looms.'

'That,' said Mary sweepingly, 'was different. I was working for myself, and your mother was employed by the management of the Poors' Hospital. We were neither of us working for the men we married. As for the inkle looms – you'd be too young to mind it, but when Margaret first took them up it caused such trouble between her and Gavin that they nearly parted company. You'd not wish that on yourself, would you?'

'No, but—'

'Be content, Christian. Hold your tongue and bide your time,' Mary advised. 'Angus Fraser's a good kind man. But he's like any other man – he needs to be handled the right way. You'll get your nose back into the business if you just have the sense to wait till the right time comes along. Besides,' she added, 'there'll no doubt be bairns to take your mind off the warehouse and suchlike.'

* * *

116

It was hard advice for a nature as impetuous as Christian's to follow. But she loved Angus dearly, and for his sake she managed to content herself.

Gradually, her patience bore fruit. Although she didn't return to the warehouse, Angus frequently talked over his business problems with her, and more often than not took her advice, as well as taking her on trips to the Lancashire mills, and to Edinburgh.

But it was galling, during these visits, to have to sit with the womenfolk and listen to social gossip when she would much rather have been with the men, talking business. Nonetheless, in her own way, Christian managed to keep in touch with the textile trade.

To her disappointment, she remained childless. Daniel, who had married a fellow student's sister as soon as he left university, was now practising law in Glasgow, and became the father of a baby girl within a year of his marriage; a second daughter was born ten months later. And still Christian waited for a child.

Angus, who already had a son and a daughter, was unperturbed.

'It's not for the want of loving, sweet,' he pointed out. 'Perhaps the good Lord's just decided that we must wait – or do without.'

'Perhaps,' Christian said tartly, 'the good Lord's decided that I'd be better fitted working by your side than bearing your children.'

But Angus only laughed, and told her that there was plenty of time yet.

She saw little of Rab now. He was never present at any family gatherings, and his mother reported, furrowing her brow with concern, that he was rarely at home.

Poor Annie Montgomery had more than her fair share of worries. The French troubles had erupted into war, and Duncan's regiment had been sent abroad. There had been no word from him for several months, and between fretting over whether or not her younger son was still alive, and fretting over the change in her elder son, Annie was at her wit's end.

Mally, who remained a firm friend, although he and Angus – each possessive over Christian, each a little jealous of the other – never really took to each other, told Christian that her cousin had taken up with Gregor MacEwan, and was believed to be a member of one of the illicit societies that had sprung up in the town.

At first, Christian grieved for the friendship that had died. But gradually her new life as a married woman covered and obliterated the sadness.

There were always beggars sleeping against the house-walls; shapeless, ragged bundles huddled in the shadows. But there was something about one particular bundle – a long-fingered hand lying palm up on the pavement by the man's head – that caught Christian's attention as she hurried across the Old Bridge one night after visiting friends in the New Town across the river.

It was a bitterly cold night in early winter. With the early going down of the sun a chill had gripped the air.

Christian bent over the sleeping man, her nose wrinkling at the strong smell of drink, and prodded gently at him with one toe. He obligingly stirred, turning his head so that the light from a nearby window fell across his face.

'Mally! Mally Bruce, you promised me that you'd not go drinking again!'

In her vexation, she stooped and caught hold of the lapels of his coat, shaking him. The back of her hand touched his stubbled cheek and she recoiled at the chill of the old man's skin. Her anger ebbed as she realised that he was in danger of dying if he was left there for much longer.

'Mally! Wake up, Mally!' She crouched beside him, shaking him hard.

He opened one bleary eye and, after a lot of effort, focused it on her.

'Mist'ss Chis – Chir – my wee pet,' he said, on a waft of alcoholic breath, then his eye rolled up until she could only see the white, and the lid fell over it again.

'I'll "wee pet" you when I get you home, Mally Bruce,' she promised between set teeth, trying to pull him to his feet.

For a man who was all skin and bone he was surprisingly heavy. She managed to get him to sit up, but when she tried to ease him to his feet the task was beyond her.

Still kneeling on the ground by his side, she looked around. There was nobody to be seen. The folk with homes to go to had long since scurried indoors, and the beggars had sought early shelter for the night.

'Mally, you've got to try to get up! You'll die if you don't get home!'

He mumbled something, then snored. Christian, at her wits' end, slapped his face hard. Mally jerked awake, a stream of oaths flooding from his lips.

'Och, hold your tongue, you old fool! It's me, Christian. Get to your feet. Go on now, do as you're told!'

Grumbling, he managed, with her help, to stand up, though he was swaying like a young sapling in a gale.

Christian put one of his arms about her shoulders, but when she tried to lead him along the footpath his feet seemed to be glued to the ground, although the rest of him accompanied her.

She stopped, supporting his weight. 'You'll have to walk. I can't carry you!'

He snored again, and his head fell forward and pillowed itself on her shoulder.

'Oh, Mally!' She was near to tears with exasperation and worry, unable to make him move, unable to ease him gently down again so that she could go to seek help.

Then, to her relief, she heard someone coming along the footpath with brisk strides.

She strained her eyes into the near-darkness. 'Can you help me?'

'Hello?' It was a man's voice. A second later he appeared from the night. He halted, took one look at the scene before him, then advanced purposefully, the cane he carried flipping deftly from one hand to the other, transformed from a support into a formidable weapon.

'Let the lady go.' He reached out to pluck Christian aside, the cane arching back over his head, ready to strike.

With a yelp of horror she released Mally and jumped forward to catch at the arm holding the stick.

'No! He's a friend of mine!'

The blow halted in mid-air as Mally, instead of crashing down on to the path and hurting himself, folded, joint by joint, into a neat bundle on the footpath by Christian's skirts and finally toppled over on to his side, snoring again.

'A friend?' the man said, puzzled. 'Surely, ma'am, this vagabond was attacking you?'

'Not at all. And he's not a vagabond!'

'But you cried out.'

'I needed your help. He's had too much to drink and if I don't get him home he'll die of the cold. Will you not help me?' she added imploringly as he lowered the cane.

He looked from her to the slumbering creature at her feet, then shrugged and stooped to grip Mally's arms and hoist him upright with one effortless movement.

'If I take one arm and you take the other we can walk him between us,' Christian explained. 'He's got a room not far from here.' But when they tried it, Mally's feet trailed helplessly behind him.

'I'll have to carry him,' the man said. 'Here, take this.' The cane was thrust into Christian's hand, then its owner slung Mally over his shoulder, took a firm grip on the old man's legs, and said: 'If you'll lead the way, ma'am.'

Silently, Christian obeyed. When they reached the room she found and lit the candle that always sat on a shelf just inside the door.

'Put him on the bed there,' she instructed, stirring the ashes in the hearth. There was still some heat in them, and a faint glow in the core. Working quickly, she managed to coax the fire into life again, and fed it from the small pile of kindling wood stacked by the hearth. There was a box with some coal in it too, she noted with relief.

The man who had carried the knife grinder home was kneeling by the bed, rubbing one of the old man's hands. Christian brushed by him and began to unfasten Mally's coat, then his tattered shirt. He began to mumble feeble protests, but she ignored him.

'What are you doing?'

'His clothes are wet. I must get him out of them or he'll be ill.'

'I can do that for you.' There was embarrassment in his voice.

'I'm not handless.'

'But—'

'If you want to make yourself useful you can pour

121

some water from the kettle into a bowl, so that I can wash him.'

'Where—'

'The kettle's by the hearth, keeping warm. You'll find a bowl somewhere. You've got eyes in your head, haven't you?' She threw the words over her shoulder, anxious for the old man's sake. His entire body was chilled. Another hour out on the footpath, and it would have been too late.

Hands closed about her shoulders. To her surprise, she found herself firmly but gently drawn away from the bed.

'You can pour the water into the bowl,' the man said levelly. 'I will see to getting his clothes off.'

She opened her mouth to argue, but he had already started work, his back to her, and there was nothing to do but obey him.

She had filled the bowl and was looking for a cloth when Mally's mumbling and grumbling rose to a sudden roar. She turned to see his long shirt-sleeved arms wrap themselves round the rescuer, who was pulled off his feet and landed heavily on the floor, Mally on top of him.

'Rob a poor old sowl, wid ye?' the knife grinder snarled breathlessly as Christian flew to the rescue, dragging at his thin shoulder.

'Leave the man alone, Mally! Get off him this minute, you daft old fool!'

'Eh?' He looked up at her with bleary, blood-shot eyes. 'Mistress Christian – whit are you doin' here?'

'Looking after you – not that you deserve it.' She hauled him to his feet, pushed him on to the bed. 'Sit there and behave yourself!' Then she turned to his victim. 'Are you all right, sir?'

He got to his feet, brushing his coat down. 'I think so.'

'He's too full of drink to know what he's doing. Mally—'

She was answered by a snore. Mally had fallen sideways on to the bed and was sound asleep once more. Christian looked at him in despair, then at the stranger.

He grinned broadly. 'I think, ma'am, that we should continue with our good work.'

Together, they washed Mally as best they could, ignoring his mumbled curses and the hands that beat feebly at them from time to time, then dried him with a rough cloth, scrubbing hard at his skin to bring some warmth into it.

Finally, satisfied, Christian drew the coverings over the old man, tucked them in securely, and stood up.

'I think he'll do now.' She turned to look at the stranger for the first time. 'I'm grateful to you, sir.'

'Ma'am.' He sketched a bow, then looked around the shabby little room and asked hesitantly: 'Do you live here as well?'

'Me? I do not.'

'I thought you might be his daughter.'

The thought made her laugh. 'He's just a good friend of mine. I'd not want any harm to come to him.'

In the candle-light the man's hair was a golden cap about his head. He was a head taller than Christian, dressed in a good russet-coloured coat. His mouth was wide and mobile, with a pleasing upturn at the corners, and the planes and shadows of his face in the dim light spoke of a good strong bone-structure beneath the skin. It was difficult, in the dim light, to tell what colour his eyes were, but the winged brows above them were, like his mouth, pleasing to look at.

She realised that they were staring at each other, and

hastily turned towards the bed. 'I think we can leave him now.'

'Perhaps I can escort you home?' From his accent, he wasn't a Paisley man. There was a lilt to the way he spoke that reminded her a little of the Edinburgh folk.

'It's kind of you, sir, but I can manage very well on my own.'

'At this time of night?'

'I know the town and its folk well. Besides, I've not far to go.'

She cast a final look round the room then opened the door and blew out the candle.

'Even so,' his voice said from the darkness as he followed her down the stairs.

'Keep one hand on the wall, for the stairs are treacherous in the middle, and follow close behind me,' she instructed crisply.

When she had led him out of the close and back to the Old Bridge she paused.

'I think our paths divide here. I go this way, while you were walking towards the New Town when we first met.'

'I have lodgings there. Am I not even to know your name?'

'Christian Fraser.'

He bowed over her hand. 'Benjamin Selbie.'

'I'll bid you good night, Mister Selbie – and thank you for your assistance,' said Christian, and left him.

Angus came into the hall as she opened the street door. 'I thought I would have to come and look for you!' He fussed around her, taking the cloak from her shoulders.

'I found Mally in the street on my way home. He'd been drinking, the fool. I had to get him to his own house.'

'I don't like the thought of you walking in the streets at night, in the dark.'

'I can see to myself.'

'Even so, I worry about you.' He drew her into his arms, kissed her. 'Upstairs with you. The servants and Rachel went to bed long since.'

She waited at the bend of the stairs, looking down at him as he bolted the street door against the night and extinguished the lamps one by one.

Then, candle in hand, he joined her, and she settled easily into the circle of his arm.

'I was thinking,' he said as they climbed the rest of the stairs together, 'of holding a gathering next week. We've not had one for some time. There are some folk I've met in the way of business that I'd like to invite – and there's our friends too, of course. What d'you say?'

'I'd like that.'

'Grand,' said Angus as they reached the top of the stairs and went to their bedchamber.

As soon as Angus had left the house on the following morning Christian went along to see Mally.

He was up and about, and, she was glad to note, none the worse for his sleep on the wet footpath, although she could tell by the careful way he moved that his head ached.

'There wis a man here,' he said as soon as she walked into his room. His eyes refused to meet hers, roving instead round the walls. Guilt was written large on his seamed face.

'Never mind the man – Mally Bruce, I'm shamed of you. Drinking until you fell asleep on the footpath like any common beggar!'

'It wis only a glass o' ale,' he protested feebly.

'Three glasses, more like. Or four, or five. Who were you with?'

He furrowed his brow. He looked owl-eyed today, moving slowly and stiffly about the room. His turney lay stood in its corner, neglected.

'Cannae mind,' he admitted at last, shame-faced.

'Mally, you promised to keep away from drink.'

'I will, lass, I will, from now on!'

'You mind that you do.' Then she said: 'What man's this you're talking about?'

'Some stranger, never seed him afore in my life.'

'A young gentleman with fair hair?'

He ducked his head in assent, then winced and put his hand to his forehead. 'Wanted tae ken aboot ye.'

'It'll be the man who helped me to get you home last night. D'you not remember?'

He started to shake his head, then thought the better of it. 'I've never seed him afore. He wanted tae ken who you was an' where he might find ye.'

'Did you tell him?'

' 'Deed I did no',' said Mally at once. 'Offered me silver, he did, but a' the same I'd say nothin'. Wouldnae be seemly, you bein' anither man's wife.'

'Did he tell you anything about himself?'

'If he did, I didnae tak' note o' it,' said Mally.

Going home, she wondered about Benjamin Selbie, who had offered Mally money in return for information about her. His interest was flattering.

On the other hand, she was a married woman and, as Mally had rightly said, a further meeting wouldn't be seemly.

All the same, she was on the lookout for him as she went through the streets later, on her way to the market with Rachel.

She didn't see him until three days later, when, at Angus's invitation, he visited the Fraser's High Street house.

The gathering was in full swing. The house was thronged and Christian was kept busy moving among her guests, making sure that their needs were met.

'My dear,' Angus said by her side, 'allow me to present Benjamin Selbie from Falkirk, who recently took up a position with the Union Bank.'

Alerted by the name that had lingered in her memory she turned swiftly and found herself looking up into brown eyes that widened in astonishment as they met hers.

'Welcome to our home, Mister Selbie. And to Paisley.'

'Mistress Fraser.' He bowed over her hand, straightened, saw that Angus had moved away to greet someone else, and said, 'I'd hoped to meet with you again, but not here.'

'Why not?'

'Not as the wife of my host,' he said, low-voiced. 'I'd thought – hoped – that perhaps—'

'Well, Mister Selbie?'

He hesitated, then said ruefully, 'I'd hoped you might be his daughter.'

'I see. Angus does have a daughter, Rachel. She's over there. A very charming girl. My step-daughter. You must meet her.'

He didn't turn to look at the corner she was indicating. Instead, he glowered down at her, his brows knotting.

'You're making mock of me, Mistress Fraser.'

'And you, Mister Selbie, were talking out of turn,' she reminded him gently.

He shrugged, then his brow cleared and he smiled. 'Forgive me, ma'am, I deserved the reprimand. My tongue tends to run away with me at times, as my mother never tires of telling me. How's your friend the knife grinder?'

'None the worse for his sleep on the footpath.'

The smile deepened to a grin. 'He was a sorry sight when I called on him on the following morning. His head, I think, was troubling him.'

'Mally's used to an aching head,' Christian said dryly. 'Are you to stay long in Paisley, Mister Selbie?'

'I'm hoping to settle here, for I like fine what I've seen of it so far.'

'Where are you lodging?'

'I've rented a house in Silk Street, near the bank. Since I'm to be in Paisley for some time at least, I wanted somewhere with a yard at the back. Although I'm a banker by profession I'm a horticulturist by inclination.'

'Indeed? We have a good Society in the town.'

'I've already become a member. My interest lies in roses,' he began, then Angus brought someone else over to meet him. The talk turned to business, and Christian moved on to another group.

'That's a fine young man – Benjamin Selbie,' Angus said when the guests had departed and he and his wife were alone in their parlour. 'A man with a good head on his shoulders, and a good future before him.'

'He tells me that he's rented a house with a yard so that he can grow roses.'

Angus settled comfortably into the cushions of his favourite chair.

'We must invite him here again, Christian. Perhaps,' he added thoughtfully, 'he and Rachel might come to enjoy each other's company.'

Chapter Ten

Rab Montgomery, forging his way along the crowded footpath, eyes on the ground, looked up with a start. A gloved hand had touched his arm, and when he saw his cousin standing before him colour flooded into his face.

'It's yourself, Christian.'

'How are you, Rab?'

'Well enough,' he said reluctantly, longing to move on but not quite able to walk away from her. She was dressed in a green silk gown beneath a short russet jacket and there were feathers on her bonnet. She looked prosperous, and very lovely.

'You never call on me.'

'I've got other things to do.'

Her eyes darkened. 'Aye, I've heard that you're seeing a lot of Gregor MacEwan. Rab—'

'Well?'

She hesitated. 'I'd not make a great friend of the man if I was you. He's nothing but trouble.'

'Damnation, Christian, will you mind your own business!'

'Rab!'

The sudden hurt in her face was more than he could bear.

'I must go,' he said, and pushed past, leaving her

standing alone. What right had she to lecture him? What right had she, after her betrayal, to choose his friends?

He was carried on the wings of his anger to Gregor's house, one of a close clutter of buildings on the Old Bridge that linked Paisley's old and new towns.

The Highlander shared two tiny rooms with his widowed mother, his younger brother and three sisters. Small and gloomy, old and damp, the house had become familiar to Rab.

Arriving at the door, he rapped on it, using the signal that had been agreed among the young members of the Friends of the People Society. After a moment it was opened by Breda, the eldest of Gregor's three sisters.

'They're all here, and waiting for you.'

She stepped back to let him in. The passage was narrow: as Rab drew his hat off and went by the girl the back of his hand brushed against her blouse, and tingled to the rounded softness beneath the material.

Startled, he glanced at her, and met dark eyes that sparkled back at him from a small pointed face.

'They're waiting,' said Breda again, with a faint smile. Confused, he ducked his head and went before her into the room where his friends were crowded round a table scattered with books and pamphlets that had been taken out of their hiding places for the meeting.

'Where have you been?' Gregor asked at once. 'We thought the militia had stopped you.'

'I was just held back.' Rab couldn't tell them that his mother had insisted on reading to him and his father, over and over again, the letter she had received at last from Duncan, who had survived a campaign in Hanover in which hundreds of his companions had been killed, both in battle and during a forced march through bitter weather afterwards. Now, to Annie's relief, Duncan was safely back in London, none the worse for his ordeal.

'You're here now. Sit down, and let me tell you what they said in Glasgow.'

Rab took his place at the table. Gregor had been at a Glasgow meeting of representatives from all the local societies, and had his report to make. Afterwards, they talked far into the night, a group of restless young men, their blood thrilling to the knowledge that their words, if reported to the wrong people, could land them in the town jail. It was all a matter of words as yet, but one day, they were certain, words would give way to action.

When the French had stopped many of their British admirers in their tracks by executing their King, Rab and his friends had secretly toasted the rebels. While his own soldier brother went to war with France, Rab talked endlessly about his hopes for a revolution in Britain.

His parents didn't know it, but when he was with his friends Rab was ashamed of his brother. But Gregor and his fiery speeches filled a void that had been left in his life by Christian's desertion.

The young weaver's sunny nature had changed. The life and the future that had contented him before had turned sour. His daily work at the loom was now only something to be endured so that his evenings could be spent with Gregor and the other members of the Friends of the People Society.

But on this particular evening a new element had been added.

Now and again, while Gregor's eloquent voice flowed on, Rab looked up, beyond the table, to where Mistress MacEwan and her daughters huddled round the tiny fire, talking quietly in their own Gaelic tongue.

As often as not, his gaze caught Breda's eyes like dark jewels staring boldly back at him.

Rab looked, and looked again, and the warmth in his blood grew to a heat that knotted deep within him.

Christian's chance meeting with Rab plunged her into gloom. The change in her cousin frightened and worried her.

Mally had told her that he often saw Rab and Gregor MacEwan together in the town howffs. As far as Christian was concerned the Highlander was a dangerous man, and by keeping company with him Rab was in peril.

But there seemed to be little she could do about it. Rab was a grown man, free to follow his own inclinations. She kept telling herself that. And she kept worrying.

She went in at her own front door, her mind filled with thoughts of Rab, to be greeted by the sound of laughter from the parlour – Rachel's familiar musical trill, Angus's voice, and another, deeper voice. When she opened the door Benjamin Selbie, seated on the couch beside Rachel, got to his feet, his attractive young face still alight with amusement.

'There you are, Christian. Selbie looked in on us in the passing,' Angus said comfortably.

'And look what he brought!' Rachel held out a pale pink rosebud, soft and silky within its cloak of green leaves, trembling on the threshold of its bloom.

'The first of the season. And this is for you, Mistress Fraser.' Selbie lifted another long-stemmed rose from a table by his chair and presented it with a bow.

The second rose was a knot of deep-red furled velvet. Christian lifted it to her face, and caught a trace of the scent still hidden within its tight petals.

'If you put them in water and stand them where they can catch the light they should open in the next few days,' Selbie said. 'Roses are my particular preference. Once I was well settled here I sent to my father for cuttings and roots and set about making my own garden. I'd be honoured if you would come to see it. All of you,' he added hurriedly, turning to Angus and his daughter.

'We must – we will,' said Rachel. 'Tomorrow?'

'Why not?' Angus said. 'I've got more than enough to keep me busy, but I'm sure my wife and daughter would enjoy seeing your garden.'

'Christian?' Rachel looked anxiously at her stepmother. Christian laughed and nodded, the fragrance of the roses all about her.

'Tomorrow would do very well, Mister Selbie.'

'Good,' he said with satisfaction. 'Tomorrow it shall be.'

Benjamin Selbie had rented a little two-storey house in Silk Street. Although the summer was in its infancy yet the small yard behind the house was a mass of colour, thanks to his careful tending.

Small, tight, white and crimson roses clung to the red brick walls that enclosed the yard, while bushes loaded with pink, scarlet, and gold blossoms filled the centre. The air was heavy and sweet with the perfume of the flowers and the busy humming of the fat bees who gathered pollen from the golden heart of each rose.

When he had escorted his guests round the garden Benjamin took them indoors to where tea waited in a cool shady parlour.

'I can't imagine why you bother yourself with such a dull business as banking instead of setting up as a gardener,' Rachel announced.

'It's because my head likes to busy itself with calculations and figures and business. I'd soon tire of digging and pruning and planting if my brains had nothing to occupy them. There was never any doubt in my mind,' said Benjamin Selbie, 'about what I would do when I was full-grown. Banking attracted me like—'

'Like a bee to a rose?' Christian suggested gently.

He threw back his head and gave a peal of warm, infectious laughter. His hair, she decided, looked as though it had drawn its colour from the sun itself. Angus and Alexander Fraser both had pale, almost flaxen hair, but there was a pleasing warm, golden-red tinge to Benjamin Selbie's head that seemed to light up any room he was in.

'Well put, Mistress Fraser. Yes, banking is my life. But roses are my dearest love.'

'The ladies must be sorry to hear that,' Rachel said pertly, and he grinned at her.

For a banker, Christian thought, he was a remarkably cheerful young man. Her limited experience of men in his profession had led her to think of them as sombre and humourless.

'Perhaps I should say that roses are my dearest love at the moment. One day, perhaps, they will take second place to a stronger passion.'

His eyes surveyed them both, lingering rather longer than they should on Christian. Rachel got to her feet suddenly, with a rustle of petticoats.

'I think it's time for us to go,' she announced.

'I can't think why you invited him to call next week,' Rachel said shortly as the two of them walked back home.

'It was your father's idea.'

'Indeed? Perhaps he thinks that Mister Selbie might make a good match for me.'

'Perhaps.'

'If so, then he's wrong,' said Rachel in a sudden flurry of temper, scowling fiercely at a small pig that was rooting about among some rubbish in the gutter.

Christian was used to her step-daughter's bouts of petulance; it was all part of Angus's spoiling of the girl.

'Don't you care for Mister Selbie?' she asked blandly, refusing to let the girl's childish ways irritate her.

'Not particularly. And even if I did,' said Rachel, her mouth tight, her eyes hostile, 'it's you he likes, not me.'

'Rachel!'

'It's true,' the girl said stormily. 'I could tell it by the way he looked at you. Why is it always you the men like, and never me?'

And she flounced ahead of Christian, skirts swinging, thrusting her way through groups of people and scattering them indiscriminately.

It was a relief to Christian when Angus suggested in the early autumn that he and his wife and daughter should visit London, where they could inspect the new Fraser warehouse and meet Alexander's bride.

Throughout the summer months Rachel had been quite impossible, and she and her father had quarrelled on more than one occasion.

'I don't understand what's wrong with the lassie,' he said to his wife one morning when they were dressing for the day ahead. 'She was never like this before. And before you say it, Christian, I've no wish to be told again that it's my fault for treating her as a child.'

Christian, brushing her hair, bit back the words that had sprung to her lips. Angus was worried enough about Rachel without having words with his wife as well. But she was quite certain, all the same, that Rachel's tempers were solely due to her father's spoiling.

'Mebbe a visit to London would be good for Rachel,' she said instead. He came over to her, his shirt half-fastened, and put his hands on her shoulders, smiling at her in the mirror.

'It'd be good for us all. I'd like fine to see the new warehouse. Alexander's come up with some scheme whereby we could ship some of our cloth overseas ourselves instead of selling it to the merchants first, and I must find out more about that. And I'd ike to see what sort of a wife my son's found for himself.'

It was the noise that Christian first noticed when they arrived in London. The clatter of coach and cart wheels and hooves on the cobbles, a cacophony of voices ringing up from the crowded streets and footpaths, the chiming of bells from one or other of the great churches.

The next impression she gained, as the coach moved deeper into the city, was the smell – rotting vegetables, new-baked bread, fish, the sweet, mouth-watering scent of fresh strawberries on a barrow, coffee, wafts of alcohol from the open doorway of a public house.

She and Rachel, in window seats, openly gawped at the comings and goings. The street vendors bawled their wares, some of them armed with bells or clappers to draw the crowd's attention. There were sedan chairs, serving-lassies and housewives with their covered baskets over their arms.

Servants in livery, many of them with black faces, loped before some of the carriages and chairs, clearing the way for their masters and mistresses. Ladies and gentlemen, magnificently attired, alighted from their carriages or sat high above the noise and clutter, looking down on it from upper storey windows.

Angus, who had seen and heard and smelled it all

many times, and had, in his younger days, journeyed to and from the city by horseback, before becoming wealthy enough to afford the relative comfort of a stage coach, watched his womenfolk's excited amazement benevolently.

The coach finally jolted to a standstill, ostlers ran to hold the horses' heads, Alexander Fraser's face bobbed at the edge of the crowd in the yard, and they had arrived.

Alexander's new warehouse was a large, airy building situated conveniently near to the London Dock at Wapping, which was in the course of being enlarged in the interests of commerce. Alexander's warehouse was, his father confided to Christian a few days after arriving in London, a better choice than Alexander's wife.

Dorothy Fraser was a neat little doll of a woman with wide blue eyes and smooth brown hair and a pretty little rosebud mouth containing a vinegarish tongue that prattled of little else but the latest fashion in clothes and the latest gossip. Her guests had to endure a continual flood of tales about King George's supposed madness, and the escapades of the handsome Prince of Wales who had gone through an illegal marriage with Mrs Maria Fitzherbert, kept a string of mistresses at his Carlton House, and had lived apart from his legal wife, Princess Caroline, since the birth of their infant daughter.

Dorothy's tastes were extravagant, for her father was a rich and influential grain merchant.

'It's rumoured,' Christian told Angus with amusement, 'that Dorothy's grandfather made his money during the time when Britain was denied French brandy and it was found that an inexpensive drink called gin could be distilled from the surplus grain that could no longer be sent abroad. And, apparently, half the folk in the city were inebriated.'

He shook his head in mock reproof. 'Not one week in London, and you're tattling like all the other women. I'm sure Dorothy didn't tell you that.'

'No, it was Lady Carruthers – or perhaps Mistress Thomas Richmond. They're such gossips, Angus!'

'I suppose,' he said dryly, 'they never gossip in Paisley?'

'Well – they do,' his young wife admitted, then added with a toss of her glossy dark head: 'But only about interesting things!'

Chapter Eleven

Following on a time of stagnation a few years earlier, London was now in a period of growth.

There was a bustling air of progress about the place that Christian found agreeable, although at times, particularly those times when she was closeted with Dorothy and her chattering friends while Angus was off somewhere on business, she found it all too much, and longed for Paisley's familiar streets and loom shops.

She was disturbed, too, by Angus's insistence on buying things for her. New clothes and hats, shoes and gloves and ribbons and lace were showered on her, and her protests were waved aside.

'I have a beautiful young wife, and I want her to have only the best.'

It was as though, she thought, hating herself for her betrayal, Angus Fraser was determined to match his bride against his son's, and prove that he had made the better marriage.

For the first time since her wedding day Christian admitted something to herself that until then she had denied – she, like Rachel, was treated like a beloved little daughter. It made her feel uncomfortable, but if she tried to put a stop to her husband's extravagances he retreated into a hurt silence, and she found it easier to let him have his own way and surround her with gifts.

The purchases that gave her the most pleasure were two magnificent silk shawls from Spitalfield market. As soon as Christian saw them, she had to have them.

The finest of the two had a black centre panel and a broad, richly embroidered border. The shop-keeper, seeing the look on Christian's face, took it down from the wall where it hung and put it into her hands. It was soft and light, beautifully made.

'Try it on, lady,' the woman suggested, and Angus took it and put it about his wife's shoulders. It was feather-soft, yet warm. She ran the long fringes through her fingers, and saw the red and blue and green and gold silk threads in the border winking at her in the sunlight.

'It's like a casket of jewels!'

The shop-keeper, confident of a sale, beamed. 'It comes from a place called Kashmir, in India. There's another one here – a different style.'

The second shawl was every bit as beautiful in its own way as the first. Christian eyed them both, moving from one to the other, then back again, undecided, until Angus said firmly, 'We'll take them both.'

He was in an expansive mood. He and Alexander had just struck a good bargain with Mister Peter Dawson, who owned a fleet of ships working out of London Docks, whereby a certain percentage of the Fraser cloth would be shipped directly out to foreign buyers from the warehouse, cutting out the middlemen and making a good profit for both parties.

As they left the stall and resumed their walk, a chill wind blew down the narrow crowded street. Christian was snug in her new fur-lined pelisse, but Angus had refused to burden himself with a heavy coat, and his plum-coloured embroidered jacket with the gilt buttons was thin. He shivered, and at once she put a hand on his arm.

'I think we should go back now.'

'Nonsense, I want to see the rest of the stalls,' he insisted, and she let him have his way.

That night they went to the theatre with Angus's new business partner, Peter Dawson, and his wife. In the morning Angus was coughing, but obstinately refusing to stay in the house. By the following day his cough had flared into a fever, and Alexander's physician had to be called in.

Now it was Christian's turn to be adamant. When the fever eased a few days later she insisted that the two of them should return to Paisley.

'We intended going home by the end of the month anyway,' she pointed out. 'Your business is done, and we'd be as well leaving while the weather's mild.'

Weakened by the fever, Angus gave in. A few days later he and Christian left the capital without Rachel, who was entranced by London and far happier there than she had been in Paisley. She begged to stay over Christmas, at least, with Alexander and Dorothy. Angus, who only wanted Christian by his side, agreed.

The journey home was long and arduous. By the time they reached Paisley Angus's fever had come back, and he was happy to take to his bed.

For the next few days he tossed and perspired and muttered in the big bed where he had gently, tenderly initiated his young bride into the delights of physical love.

Christian, banished because of his restlessness to sleep on Rachel's virginal bed across the hall, watched over him and worried about the way the fever had taken hold.

'Angus isn't as young as he used to be,' her father

pointed out reasonably after visiting the patient. 'He needs more time to get over an illness than a younger man. Have patience, lassie. He'll be restored to you soon enough.'

Benjamin Selbie's support made things easier for her. While Christian spent as much time as she could spare in the warehouse or dealing with weavers, spinners and packmen he dealt briskly and calmly with the paperwork.

He took to calling in at the house in the evenings and going over the books with her. Although he knew nothing of the practical side of the business, he was ready to listen to what Christian had to say, and to talk matters out with her and advise her as best he could.

Gradually Angus improved, though at first he was weak and lethargic. Christian had assumed that he would be eager to pick up the reins again, but for a while he was simply not interested. His illness had aged him. The sheen had left his hair, and there was more grey in it.

The lines in his face had deepened and the fire had gone out of his eyes. He moved slowly, as though it was an effort, and fell into a doze easily, no matter what time of day it was. Christian and Benjamin became accustomed to these sudden naps, continuing their conversation, discussing the business while Angus slumbered in his chair, his fingers twitching now and again on the rug over his legs.

The new year came in and the months passed, and winter began to recede. Rachel's letters told of balls and theatre engagements, of visits with friends of her sister-in-law. She seemed to be in no hurry to come home, though each letter ended with a dutiful offer to return if her father and Christian needed her.

Angus was indifferent, content as long as his wife was with him.

'Rachel's as well in London, where she's happy,' Christian said, and he agreed.

'You could do with her help,' Benjamin Selbie said shrewdly. 'You never have a minute to yourself, what with the warehouse and seeing to your husband. It's not right!'

She flushed at the sharpness of his voice. 'I'm fine.'

'You're pale from want of fresh air. Come with me tomorrow,' he said impulsively, while Angus snored gently on the other side of the fireplace. 'I've to go out to Brig o' Johnstoun, to see a farmer there. I'd like your company.'

Her heart sang at the thought of a ride into the countryside. She hadn't been out of Paisley for a long time. But duty came first.

'I couldn't leave Angus with just the servants,' she replied, with an inevitable note of regret in her voice.

At that moment Angus woke with a jerk. 'Eh? What's that?'

'I'm to visit a farmer at the Brig o' Johnstoun tomorrow. I was suggesting, sir,' said Selbie, 'that Mistress Fraser should come with me, and get some fresh air.'

'A good idea. She's been fussing round me for altogether too long. Ask your Aunt Mary to come in and have a crack with me while you're away, Christian. I always enjoy her company.'

'Come with us, Angus,' she urged, but he shook his head.

'I couldn't be doing with the lurching of a carriage along that road, lassie. I'd as soon stay here. Write to Mary, and mebbe Selbie could deliver the letter and bring back her answer.'

Going to the writing desk, taking a sheet of paper out, Christian knew a moment's unease. She was a married woman; she shouldn't be so eager to spend time with a man who, until quite recently, had been a stranger to her.

But the thought of a trip through the soft greening countryside was more than she could resist. She picked up the quill, dipped it into the inkwell, and began to write.

The bay, guided by Benjamin Selbie's sure hands on the reins, clopped briskly along the track and soon left Paisley behind. Its hooves threw up dirty water from deep winter puddles and clumps of drying mud as it went.

Christian, by Benjamin's side, gave herself up to enjoying the view, nodding now and again to acquaintances as they passed on foot, on horseback, or in carriages.

The Brig o' Johnstoun lay some four or five miles west of Paisley, on land owned by the Houston family. Part of it was given over to coal mines and a quarry, and there was good arable land. The laird had recently begun to lay out a small town around the river.

The way to the house where Benjamin had business passed through the Thorn village, a handful of tiny meagre houses with hens and pigs scratching in the dust outside. Nearby, the mine workings were an alien growth in the green countryside.

As a little girl Christian had shivered over Rab's stories of the men who worked in the mines – black men who rose from the bowels of the earth, their eyes glistening white and their mouths, when they spoke, opening like red bloodless gashes in their coal-besmirched faces.

Now she knew better, but she still shivered as she went by and saw the poverty of the place, and thought of the men toiling in the earth, far below the horse's hooves and the wheels of the cart.

Much as she appreciated the coal the miners brought to the surface, it didn't seem natural to her for human beings to spend all their time beneath the skin of the earth instead of on the surface, warmed by the sun and blessed by the rain.

The village and the mines fell away behind them and they were moving down the brae to where the river – called the Black Cart, to differentiate it from the White Cart which flowed through Paisley – meandered through a pleasant valley.

Directly below them lay a small area of neat streets and houses with long backlands, the beginnings of the laird's new town. One of the larger farmhouses near the water, about a mile away from the town, was their destination.

While Benjamin talked with his client, Mistress McLelland, a round rosy smiling little woman with snowy hair and eyes like jet buttons, entertained Christian in the large stone-flagged kitchen, offering her tea and freshly made bread spread with honey made by her own bees.

The kitchen door lay open to the sunshine. Dogs and cats and hens wandered in and out at will, and a calf pushed its soft nose inquisitively through the opening, its large dark beautiful eyes staring shyly at the two women.

Then the inner door leading to the rest of the house opened, Benjamin and the farmer came through it, and the calf took fright and clattered off, back to its mother.

'You look the better for your outing,' Benjamin said as they set off on the return journey. 'There's colour in your face again.'

'It's been a pleasant day.' Christian sniffed at the little bouquet of snowdrops she held. Before letting them go, Mistress McLelland had insisted on showing them the little garden she had made in a walled area off the farm-yard. It was a place where daffodils lifted their golden trumpets in thick clusters round an old apple tree, and purple and yellow and white crocuses had massed beside the delicate snowdrops along the edges of the gravel paths.

'It was good to be out in the fresh air again. I must persuade Angus to take an outing. If only he could get well!'

Benjamin took one hand from the reins and laid it briefly on hers. His touch was warm and reassuring. 'He'll make a good recovery now that the winter's by.'

'I hope so,' Christian said, but there was fear in her heart.

Pleasant though the trip had been, it was good to see the High Church spire and the ragged outline of the ruined Abbey on the horizon shortly after they had left the Thorn mining community behind and passed through the village of Elderslie.

As the carriage entered the town streets all Benjamin's attention was given to avoiding a pair of drunken men who were trying to weave their way across the road and getting in the way of carriages, carts and horse-riders.

The topers had managed to reach the opposite foot-path. One tripped over his own feet and fell in the gutter. The other tried to pick him up, failed, and sat down heavily by his side.

Benjamin, with a short tisk of annoyance, managed to manoeuvre the carriage past without running the heavy wheels over one of the feet stretched out into the road.

Christian looked beyond the men to the doorway of the howff they had been heading for, and met Rab's eyes. He was standing with Gregor MacEwan. She waved, and he gave her a curt nod. MacEwan, turning to see what Rab had been looking at, swept off his hat and made a deep, mocking bow.

A shiver ran through Christian. She moved a little closer towards Benjamin, then moved away again as their shoulders brushed, keenly aware of the vibrant health and strength of the man by her side.

Something within her stirred with an answering thrill; it was like two hands meeting and clasping in recognition. It was a good feeling, and yet it was dangerous.

When she got home Mary was sitting in the parlour, busy with her knitting wires. Angus dozed in his chair.

'We'd a fine visit while you were gone,' her aunt told her briskly, then added in a whisper: 'What's amiss with him, Christian? He's just not the man he used to be.'

Angus opened his eyes, smiled at the sight of his wife, and reached out to take her hand.

'Did I sleep for long?' Then he looked beyond her and saw Mary. 'You should have wakened me when our visitor arrived, Christian.'

The two women exchanged glances. 'I thought I'd let you finish your sleep,' Christian said, round the sudden lump that had risen in her throat.

The day's outing was over.

'Supporting the poor by way of a tax on the townspeople,' said the Reverend Robert Ambrose, 'can only produce bad effects. I trust you don't subscribe to such opinions, sir?'

Angus, who, to Christian's relief at last seemed more like his old self than he had been for some time, took a turn about the parlour. He stopped to glance from the window before returning to the empty grate to help himself to a pinch of snuff.

'I've not made up my mind to the matter as yet.' He mopped at his face with a large handkerchief. 'But surely such a scheme would mean that the poor folk of the town could rely on a settled amount of silver, which must ease their lot?'

The minister flushed with annoyance. 'A settled maintenance would be the same as a wage – something that they'd begin to take for granted. Such a scheme can only be disruptive to the well-being of a community.'

'In what way?' Christian wanted to know.

'Why, by increasing the number of folk out of work. It would destroy the natural principles of charity.'

'But I think there's a fairness to the scheme,' she pursued. 'It would mean that the burden of keeping the poor would fall on all those who could afford to pay a tax, instead of on the church-goers entirely.'

'Very few of the decent folk of Paisley,' the minister reminded her icily, 'are not church-goers. Our three parishes have always worked together to hold weekly collections at the kirk doors. It's an arrangement which has suited everyone, and to my mind it would be foolhardy, if not downright wicked, to support a change in the system.'

'Are you certain of that, Mister Ambrose?'

'I am, Mistress Fraser. For one thing, it would lead to an increase in the unemployed, which would in turn lead to more dissatisfaction and mischief-making.'

'If you're talking of those Societies for the Friends of the People, there are as many working folk involved in them as there are unemployed folk – from what I hear,' Christian added hastily. Her information came from Mally, but she had no desire to let Robert Ambrose know that.

'A fine example of the way Satan finds mischief for

empty heads and idle hands,' he said sweepingly.

'Ach, young men were aye hot-headed.' Angus rocked from toes to heels, his hands tucked beneath the tails of his coat. 'I was wild in my own young days, and it did me no harm.'

'Mebbe so, sir, but there's more to these societies than youthful high spirits. I hear that the members call each other "Citizen", as the blood-thirsty French rebels do – aye, and they plot the downfall of decent folk like you and me, not to mention the nobility.'

'It'll not come to that, Minister.'

'No, sir, it will not – but only because they'll not be allowed to flourish much longer.'

'D'ye tell me?'

'I do, sir.' The man leaned forward and lowered his voice. 'Haven't you noticed that there's extra militia in the town these days? They're here to fall on the young men suspected of plotting against the well-being of the country.'

'Why Paisley?' Angus wanted to know, half sceptical.

'Not just in Paisley, but elsewhere. There's to be a purge, sir.'

'A purge?'

'Aye, Mistress Fraser – this very night, so the captain in charge of the men told me. The ring-leaders will be dealt with severely – and Britain will be the healthier for it, I can assure you.'

Christian's embroidery needle missed the petal of the rose she was working on – a rose very like the first flower Benjamin Selbie had presented her with some months before – and stabbed into a finger instead. She raised her hand to her mouth and sucked at the tiny wound.

The men's voices faded into the background. Her own

blood tasted sharp and coppery on her tongue as she considered the information she had just received.

Rab! His name flared into her mind to the exclusion of everything else. Rab was in danger. He must be warned.

Chapter Twelve

Fortunately for Christian's plans, Angus fell into a doze as soon as the minister left. After seeing that all was well in the kitchen she snatched up a cloak and hurried to her uncle's home in Townhead.

She was almost there when Rab himself appeared, striding towards her. His face went carefully blank when he recognised her, and his eyes skittered away from hers. He would have hurried by with a muttered greeting if she hadn't put a hand on his arm.

'Rab, I must talk with you!'

'I can't think of anything that Mistress Angus Fraser might have to say to the likes of me.'

'You're going to a meeting of the Friends of the People Society, aren't you?'

His eyes, once so open and honest, narrowed with quick suspicion. 'What business is that of yours?'

She shook the arm that she held. 'Listen to me, you daft lummox! The militia are here in the town to break up the societies. They're going to strike this very night!'

His face went slack with shock. 'You're certain?'

'As certain as I can be. They'll force their way in wherever they suspect there's a meeting. They plan to make an example of the leaders. Rab, I don't care what happens to the likes of that man MacEwan, but for God's sake stay away from him and his sort until the whole thing's over and done with!'

'I must warn them.'

Rab began to move past her, but she wound her fingers into his sleeve and held him back.

'No! You have to go back home so that your parents can honestly swear that you were with them all the night.'

'I'll not let the others be caught while I stay safe!'

'Then I'll warn them,' she said without thinking. 'Tell me where they are.'

'Christian, I can't let you—'

'For any favour, Rab Montgomery, will you stop wasting time? You're not going to them tonight, even if I have to wrap my arms about your knees and hold you back! Now tell me where they are!'

He hesitated for another few seconds, then, reading the determination in the face uplifted to his, muttered, 'In Gregor MacEwan's house, on the Old Bridge.'

'I think I know the building,' Christian said hurriedly. 'I'll see to them. Get back home and stay there till morning.'

'If anything happens to you it'll be my doing.'

'Nothing'll happen to me,' Christian told him roundly. 'I'm a respectable woman going about my own business. The soldiers have no quarrel with me. Go on with you!'

He swung away, then paused and turned back to her. 'I'm grateful, Christian.'

She reached up and touched his face. 'I've no wish to see you hurt, or taken away from us.'

His own hand came up swiftly to cover hers. For a brief moment it was as though there had never been a coolness between them.

Then Christian turned herself about and began to walk to the Cross, looking neither to left nor right, swinging confidently along as befitted the law-abiding wife of a town merchant.

There were, as the minister had said, more soldiers in the streets than usual, even at this time of busy recruitment. Like Christian, they had about them an air of innocence.

She guessed that the planned raids were to be held later in the evening, when the authorities were certain that the illegal meetings were in full swing. Stopping halfway along the Old Bridge, she took a deep breath then turned in at the close-mouth that led to the MacEwans' home.

There was no answer to her knock at first. She stared at the battered, shabby door, quite certain that she could sense the tension on the other side. She knew well enough that the society members would have a special way of knocking, and railed at herself for not having made Rab describe it.

Then, realising that there was no time to waste, she lifted her fist and thumped hard at the door.

It was finally opened, after the third time of knocking, by a slender girl the same height as Christian but several years younger. She stared at the visitor with dark hostile eyes.

'I'm looking for Gregor MacEwan.'

The girl said something in Gaelic, shook her head, and began to close the door. Christian put a determined hand on the panels.

'Never mind the pretence that you don't know what I'm saying, lassie. You understand me well enough – and I know that Gregor MacEwan's here. I must see him!'

'What's your business with my brother?' the girl wanted to know sulkily.

'I'll tell him that when I speak with him. Just tell him it's to do with Rab Montgomery.'

There was a movement in the shadows behind the girl, and the young man Christian had dismissed from the warehouse came into view. His eyes, too, bored into her with fierce antagonism. But she wasn't there to seek friendship, just to deliver a message on Rab's behalf.

'Let me in, for what I've got to say's best kept from other ears.' She glanced significantly at the other doors on the small landing.

MacEwan said something in Gaelic to the girl, who opened the door to let Christian through.

'Welcome to my home, Mistress Fraser.'

There was, as ever, silky insolence in the Highlander's voice. Ignoring it, Christian moved past him into the small room beyond.

It was like many other homes she had visited in her mother's company when she was a child – dark and airless, smelling of damp and poverty and apathy. The grate was empty, and rags had been stuffed into broken panes in the small window to keep the chill out.

There was scarcely any furniture, and no covering on the sagging wooden floor.

An old woman huddled over the cheerless grate, her knitting wires in her hands. Two young girls, still mere children, crouched close behind her, staring up at Christian with startled eyes. A lad several years younger than Gregor sat at the table, hands fisted tensely before him.

The girl who had opened the door stood back against the wall by the window, watching the visitor suspiciously as Christian spilled out her story without wasting any time.

As soon as she realised what was happening the old woman gave a frightened whimper, reaching out to clutch at her elder son's wrist tightly. He himself had eyes for nobody but Christian.

'How d'you know this?'

'Never mind that – if you're planning a meeting here, tonight, you must prevent it before it's too late.' Then, exasperated, she stamped her foot, feeling the rotting timbers give slightly. 'D'you not understand what I'm trying to tell you, man? D'you want to be taken by the militia?'

The old woman, recognising the last word, whimpered again. The younger children started to wail. MacEwan spoke to them all harshly in his native tongue, and the noise was stifled in ragged aprons and skirts. He added something else, pointing at the door, and one of the girls fled from the room, taking a threadbare cloak from a nail in one wall as she went.

'My sister will wait outside and warn any friends who try to come in.'

Christian nodded, then bent to the old woman. 'I'm sorry to fright you, but I'd little time to waste.'

'She doesn't have the English,' MacEwan said.

'Is this your mother?'

'Aye – and my sisters, and my brother. You'll forgive us, Mistress Fraser, if we don't offer you tea,' he went on mockingly. 'We have none.'

She let the sarcasm flow off her back. 'D'you think the soldiers will come to this house?'

'Surely. The Highlanders are always the first to be blamed if there is trouble.'

'Only those known to cause trouble. Just because a man's a Highlander or a Lowlander it doesn't mean that he's a saint or sinner. We're all different.'

The sneer curling his lips deepened. He began to speak, then stopped as the sound of a hubbub broke out in the street below. There was a rush of feet over the bridge, men's voices were raised, a woman screamed, someone hammered on a door further along, then came the splintering sound of wood being forced.

The old woman began to wail in earnest, the girl by her side pushed her face into her mother's lap, and the lad who had been sitting at the table jumped up and went to stand by his brother, lifting a stool to use as a weapon if need be.

'They're here!' Christian cried, flying to the window, but between rags and grime and the darkness outside there was little to be seen apart from the bobbing light of a number of torches.

She spun round to see that the older girl, who had kept her fists out of sight behind her back since coming into the room, was crouched by a cupboard, pushing something into its dank depths.

Christian held out her hands. 'They'll mebbe search the place. Give it to me.'

The girl held back, looking at her brother for guidance.

'Do as she says,' he snapped crisply, and she relinquished a small collection of books and pamphlets and letters.

After spreading them over a chair by the table Christian sat on them, carefully arranging her skirts so that they spilled out on both sides. As she did so, heavy feet came tramping up the outer stairs.

'Sit down, man, and try to look as if you're entertaining a visitor – and tell your womenfolk to stop their wailing!'

MacEwan, surprise momentarily displacing the cold dislike in his gaze, snapped out orders under his breath and the sobbing was choked back. He caught the older girl's wrist and forced her to sit at the table by his side.

As he did so a man's fist thundered on the door so hard that Christian thought it was going to give way.

The lad, obeying a jerk of his brother's head, opened the door, and suddenly the room was crowded with soldiers.

'Is this the home of the man MacEwan?'

The Highlander rose slowly and faced the sergeant before him.

'I am Gregor MacEwan,' he said with the formal dignity of his race. 'I am the man of this house. What do you want with me?'

'We've reason to believe—' The sergeant pushed the young man aside and stepped to the table. Then his voice died away and he gaped at Christian.

'Good evening to you, Sergeant. Is there something amiss?'

The man shut his mouth with an audible click, and swallowed hard before saying, 'We've got orders to search certain houses, ma'am.'

'Indeed? And what d'you hope to find here?'

'We're looking for illegal gatherings.'

'The societies I've heard my husband and his colleagues talk about?'

The edge of a book was biting into the soft flesh of Christian's backside, but she could do nothing about the discomfort. She dared not shift position in case the pamphlets she was sitting on spilled to the floor.

'The gatherings aimed at destroying the monarchy and the Government of this country, ma'am.'

'And you think I'm visiting my friends so that we can talk of destroying the monarchy?' Christian asked with cool amusement.

The man's face turned dusky red. 'We've reason to

believe that MacEwan here's a member of such a society,' he said stiffly, standing to attention before her.

'And where are the other members?' Gregor MacEwan challenged. 'Where is your proof?'

Christian looked slowly round the small, bare room. 'I must confess, Sergeant, that I can't for the life of me see where these rebels might be hiding. There's no outsider here but myself – and you and your men, of course.'

The officer muttered an order at the two men who had entered the room with him. One of them went at once to the cupboard and opened the doors.

The girl who had almost hidden the books there watched him stonily. She sat across the table from Christian, and the single candle guttering between them shone in her lovely eyes and highlighted the planes and shadows of her small face. A tangle of rich black hair framed her forehead and temples and cheeks; watching her, Christian found herself quite stunned by the girl's exquisite beauty.

Then her attention was taken by a movement by her side, where Gregor MacEwan sat. The other soldier had taken the old woman by the arm and drawn her to her feet so that he could shift the wooden chair she sat in and satisfy himself that there was nothing hidden behind it.

He treated her with rough gentleness, though with none of the deference that had been shown to Christian. As his mother was pulled upright MacEwan began to rise, opening his mouth to protest.

The sergeant swung round on him, eyes gleaming. Christian put a swift, warning hand on the young man's arm and beneath the thin material of his shirt she felt his muscles tense. She dug her fingers in hard, little caring what her nails must be doing to his skin, and to her relief felt some of the tension ease. Slowly, reluctantly, he subsided back on to the stool.

'Have you been here long, ma'am?'

'Some thirty minutes.'

'It's getting late. Should you not be safe home by your own fireside by now?'

'Sergeant' – it was Christian's turn to experience a genuine spark of anger – 'I was born and raised in this town, and I go about it as and when I please. I often visit friends in the evenings. I've never been told before that it wasn't permitted.'

He bit his lip at the obvious reprimand, then commanded his men with a jerk of his head to quit the place.

'I'll leave you to continue with your visit, ma'am. But you should go home soon, for there's men's work afoot in the town tonight.'

'I'll go home,' said Christian, 'when I'm ready, and not before.'

As the door closed behind him the girl sitting opposite turned her head and spat on the exact spot where he had been standing. Then she moved swiftly to kneel by her mother, who had begun weeping again, silently and wretchedly, without hope.

Christian got to her feet, light-headed with relief, and put a hand on the older woman's shoulder.

'Tell your mother not to distress herself. You're all safe now, though I'd advise you to watch your step until the militia are well away from Paisley.'

MacEwan's eyes flashed at her and his lips curved in a thin, mirthless smile. 'You'll be expecting my grateful thanks, Mistress Fraser.'

She didn't like the man one bit. As she had said, every race had its saints and its sinners, and there was a badness in Gregor MacEwan that would have been there whether he was a king or a beggar, Highlander or Lowlander.

'Keep your gratitude, for I've no need of it. Nor would I value it. I did what I did for my cousin, not for you,' she said coldly.

A muscle twitched in his jaw. His fingers curled and straightened and curled again, and she sensed that he would have dearly liked to have put tnem about her throat. For a moment, she almost felt their wiry strength there. It took all her control not to put protecting hands to her neck.

Then he turned his back on her, and she went out.

The streets were busy as she made her way home, but nobody stopped her or asked her business.

They were all too involved with their own concerns. Throughout the town groups of soldiers had suddenly arrived to hammer on doors, demanding entry. If it was refused, they used the butts of their muskets to smash their way in.

The next morning it was all round the town that a handful of young men had been herded away in carts to be questioned.

As time went on some of them were returned home, some retained to stand trial. A few were imprisoned, a few, it was said, sent off to Botany Bay. A few, in other towns throughout the country, were hanged.

Rab Montgomery, sitting quietly at home with his parents, went unscathed. Thanks to his cousin's warning he had survived.

The day after the raids, when she had dealt with her domestic duties and before she went down to the warehouse on Angus's business Christian saw to it that one of the servants took a basket of food and some warm clothing to the room where the MacEwans lived.

'Tell Gregor MacEwan, if he's there, that it's a gift for his mother, in return for her hospitality,' she instructed the girl, who arrived back with an empty basket and a scowl on her brow.

'He's a right cold man, that young one,' she said indignantly to her mistress. 'Looked at me all the time I was there as if I was nothing more than the dirt under his boots.'

'It's a way that he has with everyone, Greta,' Christian assured her dryly.

'Me a Paisley lassie born and bred, too, and him nothing but a Highlander! The old woman, though,' Greta said in wonder. 'She took my two hands and kissed them!'

Chapter Thirteen

When Angus Fraser came into the bedchamber the two Indian shawls he had bought in London for his wife were spread out over the big bed, and Christian was examining them both carefully.

'Angus, come and look.'

She picked up the better of the shawls.

'See – this cloth's been plain woven, and the stitching done by hand, by tambourers – except that I've never seen such tambouring before, with the border covered completely with tiny stitches. But this other shawl's been made in small pieces with the pattern woven right into the cloth, then the pieces were stitched together to make the whole.'

'Well?'

'Our weavers could do that.'

'Christian, don't talk foolish nonsense! It would take months to make something like that – even if we could find a designer to draw the pattern and a weaver skilled enough to follow it.'

'But women all over the country would be happy to wear a shawl like this, if only they could be made for less money than you paid in the market.'

'No,' said Angus firmly.

'You've got over five hundred looms. Could we not put one of them to—'

'I said no, Christian. Our looms do well enough with harness plaids and twills. I'm not letting even one of them waste time trying something like this.'

'If you don't, someone else will.'

'I doubt if anyone in Paisley would be daft enough to try it,' Angus grunted, rubbing a hand over his eyes.

Immediately, the shawls forgotten, Christian asked anxiously, 'What's amiss?'

'Nothing – my head's aching, that's all. I spent too long going over the books this morning.'

In a matter of seconds the brilliantly coloured shawls were swept from the bed and the sheet turned back. 'Rest quietly until your evening meal,' Christian ordered, and Angus, for once, obeyed without argument, giving a sigh of relief when his aching head touched the pillow.

She drew the curtains across the windows to cut out the afternoon light and went quietly out of the room, the shawls over her arm.

In the room below she stretched them over the big table and spent a long time closely examining the magnificent stitching, the brilliant colours. The predominant pattern, repeated again and again over both shawls in varying size, resembled an elaborate pine cone made up of hundreds of tiny flowers, with its tip curved to the right.

With one finger Christian traced and retraced the outline of the cone-shaped pattern, deep in thought.

Angus Fraser's health continued to follow an erratic course. On some days he was his old self, but on others he was easily tired and forgetful, and quickly stirred to irritation.

The warehouse workers and the house servants quickly learned to read his face, and to watch their step when his brow was furrowed and his eyes impatient.

The headaches that had started to trouble him continued, and sometimes he was unable to attend to business for days on end.

Irked by his own inability to fight off ill-health, he insisted on making the most of his better days, and at his urging Christian began to fill the hous? with friends again.

The next phase of Angus's ill-health showed itself for the first time one evening in early summer when Jamie Todd and his lovely Highland wife Islay were guests for dinner, together with Mary MacLeod and Benjamin Selbie. Everything was progressing well until one of the maidservants brought in a letter that had just been delivered.

'I'll take it, Florrie.' Christian held out her hand, but Angus had already taken the folded paper from the girl's fingers and opened it, his lips moving as he followed the wording.

Then, puzzled, Angus looked down the length of the table at his wife.

'It's from the warehouse overseer. Some nonsense about a delivery to Edinburgh being delayed for a further day instead of getting off this evening.'

Her heart sank. 'I know about it, Angus,' she said calmly. 'I'll deal with it tomorrow morning.'

His face began to flush. 'We'll deal with it now. What's the meaning of it? Why hasn't the order gone out?'

Uncomfortably aware of their guests, Christian explained briefly, lightly, that one of the weavers supplying a special order had fallen sick and she had had trouble in finding someone to take over his loom for the two days needed to complete the web.

'Be damned to finding someone for a short time,' her husband interrupted explosively. 'If the man's too ill to finish the cloth, then turn him off altogether and find somebody else. I'll not have the buyers kept waiting! They've never before had to wait for an order from the Fraser warehouse!'

'Angus, it's Jocky Nesbitt we're talking about. You know what a good worker he is. It would be wrong—'

Angus's face suddenly, frighteningly, began to purple. Veins stood out on his forehead. His fist thumped the table so hard that the platters on it danced. Florrie, who had returned with a bowl of potatoes, stopped by the door, afraid to advance into the room.

'Don't presume to tell me what's right and what's wrong, madam! I know my business better than you do. Finish with him tomorrow and find someone else!' Then he surveyed the empty space before him on the table and demanded of his wife: 'Where's the food? We've got guests here – d'you want them to starve to death?'

The faces round the table were blank with shock. Christian fought to keep her voice level, to maintain some sense of decorum in the face of her husband's unexpected and uncharacteristic outburst.

'Florrie, you can put the potatoes on the table now.'

The girl advanced, the bowl trembling in her hands. As she put it down before Angus a floury potato that had been balanced on the very top shook and toppled, to roll over the edge of the bowl and bounce on to the linen cloth. His eyes, bulging from his head, followed it.

'Confound it, lassie, you're not throwing swill to the pigs in a stinking farmyard, you're serving my guests!'

The girl, completely unnerved, burst into noisy sobs before fleeing from the room, hands clapped tightly over her mouth.

Angus planted his hands on the table and began to rise. Then he stopped, swaying slightly, and looked at the faces uplifted to his.

'What are you all looking at me like that for? Is there – there—'

He sat down suddenly, a puzzled look on his face, and stared at the potatoes, steaming gently before him. The heavy colour began to recede rapidly from his face. He picked up the serving spoon, then put it down and lifted a hand to his forehead.

'It's damnably hot in here, Christian.'

'It is indeed, Angus. I think,' said Mary MacLeod, 'that you should go upstairs and rest for a while.'

'Our guests—'

'Och, we're not guests, we're family, and friends. You'll not offend us by dozing for a few minutes.'

'Christian?' His eyes, as he looked down the length of the table, were puzzled, pleading with her to make the decision for him.

'I'll see to things here, Angus,' she said through lips that were dry with fear. 'You can finish your supper later.'

Relief washed over his face. 'Aye, you're right. I'd not mind a wee rest, for there's such a tiredness come over me.' He looked apologetically at his guests. 'I'll not be long.'

'Let Jamie and Mister Selbie help you, Angus,' Mary advised, and he nodded without argument.

As the two younger men eased him to his feet and led him from the room Mary began to tell the womenfolk, with brisk determination and a great deal of dry humour, about some incident she had witnessed at the market on the day before.

* * *

Somehow, Christian managed to get through the rest of the evening. Her guests left soon after rising from the table; Benjamin was the last to go, lingering in the hall, her hands clasped in his.

'I could stay here tonight, if you wish.'

'It's kind of you, but there's no need.'

He cast a worried look towards the stairs. 'If he's still in that mood when he wakes—'

Fear for Angus's well-being and exhaustion following the strain of the evening made her voice sharper than she intended. 'I see no reason to be afraid of my own husband! Good night to you, Mister Selbie!'

As soon as he had gone she regretted her harshness. He had only been thinking of her own comfort. But she had quite enough to do, worrying about Angus, without fretting over Benjamin Selbie's hurt feelings as well.

With a sigh, she bolted the street door against the night and went to the kitchen, where Greta was trying to console Florrie. The little maid's usual perkiness had disappeared. Her face was blotched with red patches, her eyes swollen and watery. At the sight of Christian she broke into fresh sobs.

'Oh, Mistress Fraser, I never meant tae spill the tatties! I never meant tae anger the master! Please, mistress, you'll n – no' turn me away?'

Florrie was a foundling, raised in the Poors' Hospital. If she lost her position in the Fraser household she would have nowhere to go, nobody to turn to.

Christian, struck to the heart by the girl's terror, and guilty because she had unthinkingly left her to suffer and fret all evening, knelt by her chair and gathered the bony little body into her arms.

'Hush now, Florrie, what's all this nonsense? Nobody's going to turn you away.'

The maid's face was hot and wet against her neck. Her body spasmed with deep exhausted sobs. 'M – Mister Fraser said—'

'Oh, tush, he didn't mean what he said. Mister Fraser's not been well, you know that. We've got no intention of putting you out, lassie!'

'And I've never fed pigs in a farmyard in my life,' Florrie wailed, totally bewildered. 'Why did he say that I had when I never have?'

When she had been soothed and calmed and reassured and both serving-women had been sent off to their beds Christian returned to the parlour and stirred up the dying fire before curling into Angus's favourite chair.

She gazed into the red-gold embers, seeing nothing but her husband's face as she had known it when she first began to work for him, when she promised to marry him, during the first happy year of their life together.

Tomorrow she would go and see her father, tell him that the fever wasn't after all, something that would pass in time.

Angus was getting worse, not better. She made herself face up to the truth, dry-eyed and refusing to let her grief get the better of her.

When he spoke her name from the shadowy doorway she jumped, then peered round the wing of the chair at him. 'Angus – how long have you been there?'

He had a robe on over his nightshirt. His hair was ruffled from the pillow, his face still flushed with sleep.

'Why aren't you in bed?'

As he stepped out of the shadows and came silently across the carpet toward her, she was shocked and horrified to feel a moment's fear. She almost cringed away from him, into the cushions of the chair. Then he moved into the firelight and she saw that his eyes were clear and calm and the hand he held out to her was steady.

Cursing herself for a nervous fool, hating herself for betraying him with wild imaginings, she put her hand in his, and as his fingers curled hers warmly into their clasp she stood up, reaching on tiptoe to kiss his cheek as she always did.

'Come to bed,' he said tenderly, and put an arm about her, drawing her close so that her head rested in the hollow of his shoulder.

Locked together, they mounted the stairs. At the top, Christian made a slight move away from Angus.

'Where are you going?'

'To Rachel's room. You know fine I've been sleeping in there so that you could get a proper rest at nights.'

'That,' said her husband huskily, 'was when I was ill. I'm fine now.'

He bent his head and his mouth brushed hers, then moved on to the hollow beneath her ear.

'Come to bed, my love,' he whispered, and drew her through the door of the room where the great double marriage bed waited for them.

When Benjamin Selbie called midway through the morning Christian, her hair tied up in a square of cloth and a large apron over her gown, was in the wash-house in the back yard, dealing with the laundry.

'Mercy – what a time to call,' she fretted when Florrie, thankfully recovered from the previous night's tears, came scuttling from the kitchen to announce the visitor. 'Florrie, you stay here and see to the sheets. And mind they're well rinsed before you put them out to dry.'

'Yes'm.' The little maid nodded eagerly. Angus had smiled at her that morning while he was breaking his fast, and had patted her on the head when she was helping him on with his coat afterwards. Florrie's world was on an even keel again. She was as happy as a lark and prepared to work herself to death to please her master and mistress.

Christian hurriedly dried her arms and hands and rolled her sleeves down. She pulled the covering from her hair and smoothed the skirt of her gown as she went through the hall.

Benjamin Selbie, pacing the parlour floor, swung round when he heard her come in. His face lit up at the sight of her.

'Mistress Fraser, you look—' he stopped, then laughed and shrugged: 'You look like one of my roses in full bloom.'

'They teach their bairns pretty manners in Falkirk, Mister Selbie. Anyone would think you'd been raised in London.'

'It's no pretty compliment, ma'am, I can assure you.' He came forward to take her hand in his and kiss it; when he straightened the laughter had gone, and his eyes scanned her closely. 'I'd thought, after last night, to find you in a different way. How's your husband?'

'Very well, and down at the warehouse this past hour.'

His brows rose. 'Is it wise to let him undertake the concerns of business when he's not well?'

'He's perfectly well, Mister Selbie.'

'But last night—'

'Last night's over and done with. Were you wanting to see Angus on business?'

The rebuff brought colour to his face and once again Christian rebuked herself for having hurt him.

'No – I only called to see how you were.'

'And you can see that I'm fine – and in the middle of attending to the washing.'

He gathered up his hat and stick. 'In that case I'll not detain you. You'll be sure to let me know if there's anything I can do for you – or Mister Fraser?'

'I will.' She held out her hand, and after a moment's hesitation he took it.

'I think,' he said, choosing his words as carefully as a kitten picking its way across a wet floor, 'that you'd be well advised to speak to a medical man about your husband.'

'I'd already decided to pay a call on my father this afternoon.' Then, just as carefully, she said: 'Mister Selbie – Benjamin – thank you for your concern, and your friendship.'

The colour in his face suddenly deepened. He dragged in a lungful of air and took a firm grip on his stick, then said in a rush of words: 'If I'm to be truly honest with you I must say that there's more to my concern than business or mere friendship. Christian, you surely know the truth of my feelings for you. Even since that first night when I came upon you with Mally Bruce you've filled my thoughts—'

'No!'

He stopped abruptly, as though she had struck him.

'You must never ever say such things to me again! I'm another man's wife – and happy to be so. You're a good friend to me, Mister Selbie, but if you presume to think that there could ever be anything more than that you're doing our friendship nothing but harm.'

The high colour had drained from his handsome young face. A muscle twitched in the angle of his grimly set jaw.

He nodded, and said formally, painfully, 'You've every right to be angered with me. I had to tell you what's in my heart, but I'll not say it again. I hope that you can still call on me if you need a friend.'

They stood awkwardly for a moment, their eyes meeting then veering away like panicky butterflies. Then Benjamin turned and blundered out of the room and across the hall. Christian followed him to the street door, closed it behind him, then leaned against it, suddenly uncertain of her ability to walk unaided across the hall floor.

Thoughts of Angus came flooding into her mind, and she seized at them, drawing them round her like a warm, sheltering cloak.

Last night, while the rest of the household slept and the town was silent outside their bedchamber windows, he had made love to her with all the tenderness and passion she had first encountered on their wedding night.

Come what may, he would always be her husband. She had wanted him fiercely long before he would admit to his own love for her. She had married him despite her parents' concern over the difference in their ages, and in the face of the town's gossiping and Rab's outright opposition. She would never ever desert him. Angus was a good and loving husband, and there could never be room for any other man in her life.

But even so, as she finally relinquished the door's support and walked slowly back to the steam and heat of the wash-house to get on with her work, Benjamin Selbie's face superimposed itself now and then over Angus's.

If she weren't already married to Angus, she admitted to herself as she twisted a tight rope of linen sheet hard between her hands to squeeze the water from it, she might well have lost her heart to Benjamin.

She shook out the linen and Florrie helped her to fold it and carry it out into the warm sunny morning to spread

173

it over the bushes to be dried and bleached. Then she went back into the wash-house to tackle the rest of the washing, working automatically, her mind filled with the two faces, Angus's and Benjamin's, Benjamin's and Angus's.

Chapter Fourteen

Rab had thought, when Christian married another man, that he knew all about loving and suffering. But Breda MacEwan's sparkling, mocking dark-blue eyes and the wealth of wild black hair about her small, lovely face taught him otherwise.

He wanted the girl. His body ached for her; his mind was filled with her to the exclusion of everything else. The love he had known for Christian crisped and vanished like a brittle autumn leaf in the furnace of his lust for Breda.

When the Friends of the People Societies melted away after the authorities had made an example of those leaders that they caught, Rab didn't mourn their going, for now his passion for Breda was far more important than his passion for any political cause.

She was aware of his interest from the first, and went out of her way to scorn it. Gregor looked on, amused, as Rab did his best to court the girl, bringing her small gifts that were accepted with the regal condescension of a queen. He smiled when he heard his friend asking and then begging Breda to go out walking with him, and being scornfully refused.

'She's wild, that one,' the Highlander said across the table of a small dim howff. 'A creature that no man can tame. You'd be better to set your cap at a quiet, biddable

wee Paisley lassie, my friend. Choose one of your own
kind and let Breda go to damnation in her own way, for
that's where she's been bound since she first drew
breath.'

Rab, overfull of ale, shook his head and stared at his
companion owlishly. 'Would you – would you give me
your blessing?'

MacEwan drew the corners of his mouth down. 'If
Breda ever weds it'll be a man of her own choosing, with
or without my blessing. Take my advice, Rab – forget
her.'

He couldn't. Her vivid red-mouthed face hung before
him in the darkness of the night and wove itself into the
cloth on the loom before him during the day.

His father warned him again and again about his lack
of attention and finally, when Rab ruined a web that was
nearing completion, the older man lost his temper.

'It was bad enough when you were out every night with
those ne'er-do-weel friends of yours – but now there's
no understanding you at all. What's got into your thick
skull, lad?'

'If you ask me,' said Rab's mother shrewdly, 'the
boy's found a lassie for himself.'

'It's never that,' Robert scoffed. 'What lassie could
set a man's brains in such a scramble that he spoils a
good web?'

Annie shook her head at him. 'I'm sure you did the
same when you were courting me. It's time the laddie was
settling down. What's her name, Rab?'

Rab went crimson. 'Breda MacEwan.'

His mother's smile faded. She looked back at him in
dismay.

'Och, Rab, you've never lost your heart to one of
those Highlanders?'

'What's wrong with them? Jamie Todd married with a Highlander and you were all pleased for him.'

'Aye, but Islay's one of the sweetest lassies you could hope to find. That MacEwan lot's different altogether,' his father said with an air of finality. 'Look elsewhere, Rab.'

'You don't know Breda!'

'I know of her,' Annie rapped back. 'And she's a strange creature, by all accounts. Not what I'd hoped for, for a son of mine.'

Furious, he slammed out of the door and let his legs carry him swiftly along to Broomlands, past the weaving shop owned by Jamie Todd, past Pit Land, the premises with the cock-fighting pit at the back, and out into the fields and braes beyond.

May was a beautiful month in that year of 1799. The fruit trees in the orchards were heavy with blossom, and the broom bushes on the braes already reflected their clustered bright yellow flowers back at the sun. The colour of the sky was held in the delicate flowers of the wild bluebells, and there were still some primroses here and there.

Rab strode past them without seeing them, climbing up and up, his boots tearing their way through thick stiff spiky clumps of grass, and crushing down a carpeting of white and purple clover.

All he could think of was the black turmoil inside him, a turmoil made up of frustrated longing for Breda and rage at his parents for daring to criticise her.

He didn't look back, so he didn't see that behind him, hanging back far enough to hide behind a bush or a tree if he should suddenly turn, was a woman's shape. Having decided that it was time to stop baiting the young weaver and find out what his next move might be, Breda had left the town and followed him.

* * *

When he had gained the peak of a hill and dropped down the other side, shutting Paisley from view, Rab threw himself on to the grass, one arm over his eyes to bar the sun that was painting the inner lining of his closed lids with gold.

It was peaceful up here on the braes, away from the clatter of looms and the noises of the town. The place was silent but for the music of the birds, the chirruping of grasshoppers, and the chuckling sound of water purling over stones in a burn a few yards downhill from where he lay.

But the storm raging in his mind wouldn't let him rest. A letter had arrived from his brother Duncan that morning. His regiment was in London again, being fêted by the people as heroes. Rab wondered briefly if he should turn his back on all he had known up till then, desert his loom and enlist as a soldier.

But soldiering wasn't the right way out of the dilemma – not for him. He knew that well enough. He had once rejected all thought of the Army because of Christian, and now he rejected it for a second time because of his burning desire for Breda. Even if she never became his, he had to stay where he could see her every day.

Breda, Breda, Breda – the name and the girl who bore it filled his mind to such an extent that when a light, teasing Highland voice said, 'You're lazy today, Rab,' he thought at first that he was only hearing it in his imagination.

Then it came again, with an undercurrent of amusement: 'Never tell me you're asleep on a grand afternoon like this?'

And he knew, with a painful, wrenching surge of the heart that it was real.

He sat up, blinking the sun's dazzle from his eyes, and stared round. A mocking, musical laugh drew his attention to the burn below.

Breda MacEwan stood in the fast-running shallow water, her hair feathering about her face in the light breeze. She wore no shawl, and her light gown was unfastened and pulled aside at the neckline to let her smooth shoulders and throat enjoy the benefit of the sun.

She held her skirts kilted to her thighs, clear of the water that rippled against her rounded knees. Her bare calves showed white beneath the surface of the burn.

Staring, unable to believe that she was really there, Rab got to his feet slowly and began to move down the slope.

'Breda?' Is it really you?'

Her teeth shone white in her small brown face. 'D'you think I'm a ghostie, then?'

'I didn't think to see you here.'

'The braes are free to all, are they not? And you've long wanted to be alone with me, Rab Montgomery. I've seen it in your eyes every time you looked at me.'

'Come out.' He stopped on the edge of the burn, holding out his hand. 'Come to me, Breda.'

She shook her head, laughing, moving backwards in the direction of the opposite bank.

'I'm not as easy to catch as all that. If you want me' – with a nimble movement she hopped on to the other bank, water droplets sparkling like diamonds as they fell from her bare feet—' you'll have to cross the burn for me.'

She let her skirts drop to swing about her ankles and her young breasts pushed at the thin material covering them. The roughly made gown, little more than a piece of cloth caught in at the waist with a sash, couldn't hide the beauty of her body, the curves and hollows and sweetness of it.

She leaned towards him, laughing, and Rab caught his breath at the sight of her bare skin as the neck of her blouse fell open. He began to retreat slowly, step by step, up the slope behind him. She watched, chin up, lips curved in a secret smile, eyes sharp and bright as the sunlight glinting on the burn.

Realising what he was about, she called to him. 'You'll never manage to jump the burn, Rab. It's too wide for you.'

It was broad at that point, and the sloping banks, clumped here and there with marigolds and exotic deep-pink marsh orchids, made it an even more difficult jump. But today, with Breda waiting for him only a few yards away, Rab Montgomery felt that he could move mountains and jump whole seas if he so chose.

He stopped, measuring the space between himself and the water.

'You'll fall in and soak your clothes,' the mocking voice called across the busy sound of the water. 'Then you'll get into trouble with your mammy!'

'I'll manage the jump fine. And when I do, what's my reward?'

Her smile broadened into a laugh. 'You wait and see, my fine braggart. Wait and see.'

Exultation swept through Rab, firing his muscles and sinews. He drew in a deep breath of the soft spring air, clenched his fists, lowered his head, and began to run down the grassy slope, faster and faster, legs pumping, feet bouncing on the grass.

His right foot landed on exactly the right spot at the lip of the bank. He rocked forward, putting all his weight on to it, and launched himself into space, his left foot reaching out before him, his arms spread to keep his balance.

For a few wonderful seconds he soared above the earth, free of its shackles. The glittering water of the burn was below him, and for a moment he thought that he was going to splash into it after all.

He urged his strong young body forward with all the energy his mind could summon up. His left foot hit the edge of the banking and almost slipped off again.

Balancing his body, he threw himself beyond it, fingers reaching for the ground now. They bit into grass, clawed deep, and held as the length of him between foot and fingers thudded down on to firm ground.

He was up at once, grinning at Breda, demanding breathlessly, 'Now – where's my reward?'

'You still have to work for it,' she said, and with a whisk of her skirts she turned and ran from him, bobbing and weaving among the broom, leaping over clumps of grass and reeds, twisting round the small trees scattered here and there.

He followed, laughing, the blood surging through his veins and his muscles singing with youth and good health.

She was like an eel; every time he thought that she was within his grasp she melted away and gained a few yards again. Around and about she led him, further away from Paisley, deeper into the untamed countryside. Her laughter floated back to him, teasing him, urging him on.

She reached a rocky outcropping, and slid round it. Rab plunged after her, only to find that instead of running on she had halted, and was waiting for him. Before he could stop himself he had tripped over a slender outstretched leg and measured his length with a resounding thud on the grass. She followed him down, wrapping herself around him, her breath warm on his throat.

'And now, my bonny lad,' she whispered, her lips and then her teeth nibbling at his ear, 'you shall have your reward.'

Her love-making was a strange mixture of demanding and rejecting. He quickly realised, by the practised way she touched him and aroused him, that he was not the first man she had lain with. And yet she managed to blend in a shyness that inflamed him further, as it was intended to do.

Once or twice at the beginning, when she suddenly began to struggle in his arms, pushing him away, scratching at him, turning her head away from his urgent mouth, Rab hesitated, puzzled. But each time her arms wrapped about him again, and she drew him back to her. He went willingly, becoming more insistent once he realised that she had no real intention of stopping him.

Their final coupling was swift, bodies joining in a dazzling searing flame of passion such as he had never thought to experience. They were well-matched; strong and lithe and youthful, free of the trappings of modesty and embarrassment, made only for pleasure. And yet it was all over so swiftly - too swiftly.

When he tried, after a while, to draw Breda into his arms again, she shook her head, getting to her feet.

'Enough, my bonny lad. I must go home now.'

He got to his knees, then said hoarsely, 'Will we meet again - like this?'

She smiled down on him, and reached out to cup his face with one hand.

'Perhaps—' she said, and he had to be content with the half-promise.

When Gavin Knox joined his daughter in the parlour his brows were drawn into a puzzled frown.

'I can't make head nor tail of the matter at all. As far as I can see Angus is well clear of the fever and as fit as ever he was. You say he doesn't remember his sudden burst of temper?'

She shook her head. 'And he forgets other things, too. D'you think there's something far wrong?'

'No, no!' He put a reassuring hand on her shoulder. 'Don't fret yourself, lass, your man'll be fine in another week or two. I must go now, for I'm due in Glasgow just after noon.'

He picked up his hat then added, as they stood at the door: 'All the same, I think I'll ask a friend of mine, a Glasgow man, to come to Paisley to visit Angus. Could you persuade him to see another physician?'

'Make the arrangements, Father. I'll see to it that Angus agrees.'

'I'll do that, this very day,' said Gavin.

Christian watched him climb into the neat little carriage he had bought to make his journeys to and from Glasgow more comfortable. He tossed a coin to the barefooted lad who had been holding the horse's head, gathered up the reins, and set off.

She closed the door and went slowly upstairs to the bedchamber where Angus was resting. He had wakened that morning with another headache, and she had seized on it as an excuse to call in her father.

The curtains were drawn and Angus, in a robe, lay on top of the bed-coverings. When Christian sat down beside him he took her hand in his.

'I trust your father scolded you for making altogether too much fuss about me?'

She forced a smile. 'He did. How's your head?'

'All the better for your nursing. Have you not realised yet,' Angus teased, 'that it's all a ploy to hold your attention?'

'No need to stoop to trickery for that. But there's one thing . . .' She hesitated, choosing her words. 'I mind my father talking once of a man he works with in Glasgow. A man who's got a great name for easing pains in the head. Let me send for him.'

'Ach, Christian!'

'Humour me, Angus.' She reached out her free hand and ran her fingers through his hair. He turned his head so that the side of his face nestled into her cool palm, and smiled up at her.

'Very well, if it'll make you happy.'

She returned the smile, but behind it she was praying desperately that her father's colleague would tell her what she wanted to hear – that Angus was fine, that the headaches and temper and forgetfulness would soon vanish. Deep inside, she was trying very hard to believe that.

Chapter Fifteen

Every day Rab made a point of tramping up the braes. Sometimes he walked alone and returned home a few hours later, tired and depressed, his body hungering for the girl who had not come to him that day.

But at other times she was there, materialising before or behind or beside him, taking his hand, drawing him into the warmth of a hollow, the shelter of a rock-face or, if the weather was unfriendly, to a small tumbledown building that had once housed a shepherd's family.

Dried grass was thick on the hard earth floor and there was a roof of sorts above; although the wind sometimes blew through gaps in the stone walls and the rain got in to chill their skin, their bodies were warmed by desire and the hot blood raced along their veins as they tumbled together.

Rab was completely besotted by the girl. She was in his thoughts day and night, waking and sleeping. When he was with her they scarcely spoke, other than with their bodies, but to him that was communication enough. He had no way of knowing how long the affair might last, and no desire to ask her, for he was afraid of the answer.

For his part, it would go on as long as Breda wished. If he was fortunate, that would be for ever.

When he visited the MacEwan house Breda stayed in the background as always. Sensing that she would be angry with him if he singled her out in front of her family he managed with an effort to keep his eyes from her, though his loins tingled every time she happened to brush past him, or if their fingers lightly kissed when she handed him a mug of ale.

Gregor's quick dark eyes soon saw what was going on. 'You should forget about our Breda,' he told his friend, his face expressionless. 'I warned you that she's not for the likes of you. She can only bring you sorrow.'

Rab swung round on him, fists doubled. 'Mind your own business!'

Gregor shrugged, a mere twitch of the shoulders, and said no more. But now and then, his face hot because of some fleeting contact with the girl, Rab looked up to see the Highlander surveying him, a mocking smile not unlike Breda's on his lips.

Rab's parents had long since given up trying to reason with him. The three of them shared the same house, but they were strangers within it. In the weaving shop Rab and his father worked in silence, the older man casting puzzled, anxious glances at his son now and again – glances that Rab scarcely saw, for his mind was fixed on Breda, and he did his work with deft, automatic precision, not really aware of the cloth shaping itself on the rollers before him.

May and June passed in a haze of happiness, July gave way to August, and MacEwan sought Rab out at home one evening, knocking on the door and indicating, with a jerk of the head when Rab himself answered, that he wanted to speak to him outside.

'I'm going out,' Rab said tersely through the kitchen door, and followed the other man to the footpath outside.

Since leaving the Fraser warehouse the Highlander

had managed to find work here and there, but nothing settled. His fiery nature always set him at loggerheads with the phlegmatic Lowlanders who controlled Paisley.

And so Gregor MacEwan moved from one employer to another, earning just enough to keep his family together.

As they walked together Rab noticed the shirt and jacket his friend wore were ragged and patched. A thin scarf was wound about his neck, and above it his face was gaunt.

'Our Breda's carrying your child,' he said without wasting time on formalities. Then, when Rab gaped at him, he added impatiently: 'You're surely not surprised? Not after what the two of you have been up to these past months.'

'She's certain?'

'Of course she's certain! The thing is, my friend – what d'you mean to do about it?'

'Marry with her,' Rab said promptly, then added with sudden concern: 'If she'll have me.'

'Oh, she'll have you all right.' MacEwan's voice was grim. 'I'll see to that. It's hard enough feeding the mouths already in our house without taking on another one. And Breda knows that.'

'Then it's arranged. I'll find a place for us to live and we'll wed as soon as the banns can be called.'

Rab held out his hand and after a moment the Highlander took it.

'I'll tell Breda you'll come to the house tomorrow after work to talk about it.'

'I'll come now.'

'Best not,' said MacEwan's soft, musical voice. 'You've got your own folk to talk to first. I'm thinking that they'll not be pleased when they hear your news.'

'Be damned to them!' said Rab.

When his friend had gone he paced the footpath for a while before going in to confront his parents. He was ablaze with happiness. It little mattered what his mother and father had to say, for tonight he, Rab Montgomery, had everything a man could ever want.

Soon he would be in his own house with Breda for his wife; his child, the child they had made together with their loving, nestling in her sweet belly, waiting to emerge into the world.

A smile curved his lips. He had never felt so strong, so invincible.

Whistling, he turned in at the street door to tell his parents the news.

The colleague that Gavin brought to Paisley suggested that Angus should visit the Infirmary in Glasgow, where he could be examined more thoroughly. The manufacturer scoffed at the idea at first, but finally agreed to his wife's urging.

Christian and her mother went with him, and waited tensely on a wooden bench in a small stuffy room for what seemed like hours.

Margaret, her worried eyes on her daughter's drawn face, tried to ease the slow passage of time with an endless flood of chatter.

Christian scarcely heard the words that winged about her head until a familiar name jolted through her thoughts.

'What was that about Rab?'

'I said, he's marrying with that Highland girl, Breda MacEwan. You mind her brother – he worked in Angus's warehouse at one time, did he not?'

Christian recalled the man's handsome, sneering face and the poverty-stricken little room where the

MacEwans lived. She recalled, too, the beautiful, wild girl who had been seated opposite her at the table when the militia came into the house to search for Society members.

'I remember him, and his sister as well. Rab's to wed with her, you say?'

'Annie's in a right taking about it but it seems that there's no reasoning with the laddie. He's found a wee place in New Street and they're being wed right away. The lassie's carrying his child, so at least Rab's doing the right thing by her.'

Margaret knew that she was twittering like a bird, but she couldn't bear the thought of sitting in silence. 'Not that that makes Annie and Robert feel any better about it. They're convinced that the lad's making a mist—'

The door opened and Christian jumped to her feet as Gavin and another man came in. She was immediately struck to the heart by the expression on their faces.

'Christian.' Her father's voice was gentle. He took her hands in his, and she stood before him, her eyes locked on his face, listening as he told her that it seemed that the fever that Angus had suffered had inflamed the lining of his brain.

'Oh, dear God!' her mother half-whispered behind her.

'What can be done for him?'

'Nothing that we know of, lass.'

'Will he . . .' She looked her father in the eye. 'Will he die of it?'

'It's likely – unless the trouble somehow manages to correct itself. It might. There are so many things we don't know yet,' he said. It was a frustrated cry that his wife and daughter had heard from him so often in the past.

'I don't want him to be told.'

'But Christian, the man has a right to know. He'll mebbe want to put his affairs in order.'

'I can do that for him. I don't want him to know,' she repeated fiercely, her hands gripping Gavin's. 'Angus has such a love of life – let him think that this will pass. Tell him that it will pass! You said yourself that it might, so why fright him for no good reason?'

The medical men looked at each other, then, to her relief, they nodded.

'If it's what you want,' her father said. 'It'll make it all the harder on you, Christian, for you'll have to bear the burden on your own. That won't be easy.'

'I can do it . . .' Her voice broke, and she took a deep breath and got it under control, turning slightly to include her ashen-faced mother in the group. 'Nobody but ourselves must know. And there's to be nothing said or done to make Angus suspicious. Nothing!'

'Very well. I'll bring Angus to you now and you can both go home. Margaret, mebbe you'd best come with me.'

Left alone, Christian paced the room, banging her heels down sharply with each step in an attempt to keep thought at bay.

After a few moments Angus came in, tired from the long and arduous examination, but beaming at the sight of his wife.

'What did I tell you, my dearest? They say the headaches will go, in time. I knew that all along. There's nothing to concern yourself over.'

She smiled and linked her arm closely in his. 'I just wanted to be certain. You must allow me a little wifely fussing, Angus. Come on, my love – let's go home.'

As Gavin had said, Christian's undertaking to bear the burden of her new and terrible knowledge alone was a difficult one.

For a week she managed to go on as though nothing was wrong. But one evening when Angus had had a difficult day and had retired to bed early, exhausted, she knew that she couldn't bear her lonely grief any longer.

As she left the silent house she hesitated on the footpath. She could cross to the Almshouse pend and go up the hill to her parents' house, but tonight she had no wish to look into their faces and see their pity.

Mally's lodgings were quite close at hand, and her first thought, when she turned to her right and began walking along the High Street, was to go and visit with him.

But when she reached the top of St Mirren Brae she stopped. Se needed to talk to someone who could help her to make the right decisions through the time ahead, someone fitted to see that Angus's business concerns were handled properly. Someone who could advise and guide her. Instead of making another turn to the right she went straight ahead, crossing the Old Bridge, following the street that began as Smithhills to the corner where it divided, with Lawn Street going off to the left and Gauze Street continuing straight ahead.

Christian walked briskly along Gauze Street, past the Union Bank where Benjamin Selbie worked and where Angus was a shareholder, then turned left into Silk Street.

After his talk of his affection for her had been firmly quelled, as much for her sake as for his if he had only known it, the young banker had managed to make it obvious by his courteous manner whenever they met that he would not speak in such a way again. Clearly, he had no wish to endanger the friendship that they shared, and Christian, who valued her friends, was grateful to him. Now that she was sorely in need of companionship and support, it was to Benjamin Selbie that she turned.

'He's out in the back yard, seeing to those roses of his,' his housekeeper said when called to the door. She stepped back to let her employer's visitor into the neat little house.

'Come away in, Mistress Fraser, I know he'll be pleased to see you. In the parlour here.' She opened a door. 'Sit yourself down and I'll away an' give the man a shout. He'll be with you in a minute.'

Pictures of flowers that Selbie had commissioned from a young Paisley man with a talent for water-colours hung on the panelled parlour walls, and some opened horticultural books lay on the big table by the window.

One or two of them displayed pictures of roses, and a few sketches lying on a small table by a fireside chair showed that somebody had been copying from the books.

She was studying the sketches when Benjamin Selbie came in, his hair hastily smoothed, his face alight with pleasure at her visit, some red roses in his hand.

'This is an unexpected and welcome pleasure.'

'Have I interrupted your work?'

'There's always work to be done in a garden. But I was almost finished. I brought these in for you.' He held them out. 'They're damask roses. My favourite flowers.'

'I thought that damask was a cloth, or a way of weaving a pattern.'

'Aye, so I've heard. I believe the word comes from Damascus, a city in the Ottoman Empire.'

'Where St Paul visited in the Bible?' Christian asked in awe.

'The same. No doubt they have their weavers there, and their roses too. During the centuries travellers – tradesmen, merchants, perhaps soldiers – have brought the weaving skills and the roses all the way

192

across the seas to Scotland. At times,' said Benjamin Selbie with deep satisfaction, 'the world's not so huge that its peoples can't mingle and exchange their talents.'

As she took the flowers from him she nodded at the sketches. 'Are these your work?'

'Aye – not as good as John Lang's pict ires, but I like to try my hand now and again.'

Then he said abruptly, his eyes searching her face. 'There's something amiss.'

'No, nothing. I just wondered what you could tell me of the arrangement Angus has made with that man in Dumfries who's buying some of our cloth now. I believe you drew up the papers for him.'

'Mister Smillie – yes, I did. But the papers are in the bank, not here.'

'I should have thought of that,' Christian said with a nervous laugh. 'I – I happened to be in the New Town, and it came to me when I was passing that I should call in and ask you about them. I'll call at the bank in the morning, if I may.'

'Of course.'

'It's time' – she heard her own voice running on and was unable to stop it— 'that I took more of an interest in Angus's business affairs. I do know something of them, of course, but I should—'

She saw Benjamin's eyes widen in quick concern, felt a coolness on her cheeks, but didn't recognise it for tears until one trickled down to her chin and dropped on to the hand holding the flowers. Her voice trailed away as she stared down at the moisture in dumb surprise.

Another tear followed, then another and another, then they were suddenly coming thick and fast, pouring down her face without any effort on her part. Her fingers uncurled, letting the crimson blossoms fall to the floor as she swayed slightly.

Benjamin gave a muffled exclamation, then he moved quickly across the room, one arm going about her to steady her. She could smell the fragrant evening air he had brought in from the garden on his clothes and his skin and his hair.

She made an effort to bring herself under control, but his comforting nearness was her undoing. At last she was able to turn and pillow her head on a broad shoulder and release the great burden of grief that she had been carrying about with her for the past seven or eight days. And that was just what she did, no longer caring that she was behaving like a weak, foolish woman.

Benjamin Selbie's other arm came up to embrace her, then he stood holding her, having the common sense to say and do nothing until her deep, shuddering sobs subsided. At last he put her gently into a chair, placed a large dry handkerchief in her hands, and crossed to a small corner cupboard.

Christian, emptied of the emotions she had been carrying around with her, stayed where she was, content to let someone look after her for a change.

This, she reflected with a trace of bitterness, was what growing up meant. Ten or even five years ago she would have pulled herself together without help. She would never have let Benjamin Selbie, or anyone else for that matter, see her give way to weak tears. But being a woman meant being vulnerable, being exposed to griefs that she hadn't even dreamed of five or ten years before.

Now, for the first time, she openly admitted to herself that the burden of Angus's illness was too much for her to carry alone.

'Take this.' Selbie came back to her and put a small

glass tumbler into her hand. She obediently raised it to her lips and took a mouthful, the glass chattering against her teeth. Then she sat up abruptly, coughing and choking as the liquid burned its way down into her stomach, bringing fresh tears to her eyes.

'For any favour – what is it?'

'Brandy. It'll not kill you – drink it all, he instructed, and she did so, but in small sips instead of the mouthful she had started with. To her relief the burning sensation that had alarmed her subsided to a pleasant, strengthening glow.

Selbie drew a chair forward and seated himself on the edge of it, elbows on knees.

'Tell me,' he said.

She told him everything that she knew herself, ending, as she began to regain her usual energy, with: 'Mind now, I'll not have anyone else knowing about this, or telling it to Angus. I have your word on it?'

'Of course.' He waved the point aside with an impatient movement of one hand. 'But are you certain you'll be able to keep the warehouse going on your own?'

'Yes – with your help, for you know all about the money side of it. Between us we can see that Angus does all he can, all he wants to do. But no more that that. I'll see to the rest.'

'What about Rachel and her brother? They surely have the right to know.'

She nibbled at her lower lip. 'I've been thinking of them. It seems that Rachel's well settled in London, with no thought of coming back to Paisley. And Alexander's busy with the warehouse. Angus would be suspicious if they both came north suddenly. Besides, it would be difficult to speak to them with him in the house. I must write to them.'

'It would be better if you went to London yourself.'

'How can I?' she asked impatiently. 'How can I leave Angus at such a time?'

He shrugged helplessly, then said with an air of triumph, 'You could tell him that you're buying new gowns for yourself.'

By now the brandy had fully restored her wits. She gave a short bark of laughter. 'Mister Selbie, my husband knows full well that I'm not one of those empty-headed women who goes all the way to London to buy silks and laces! Besides, I don't want to leave him, not for a moment.'

'Then I'll go, with your permission.'

She looked at him with dawning hope. 'Could you do that?'

'There's been talk in the bank of sending someone to London for a few days. I can easily see that the duty falls to me. Give me Alexander's address and tell me what you want me to say. I think it can be arranged within the next day or two.'

'And you'll work with me, and see that my husband's interests are properly seen to?'

'With all my heart,' said Benjamin Selbie.

'I'm more grateful to you than I can say. Now' – she stood up and handed him the empty glass – 'I must go home.'

'I'll walk with you.'

'No, I prefer to be on my own, and I'd not want folk to be wondering what we're up to. As to that, it was foolish of me to come running to your house, but I couldn't think of anyone else to turn to.'

'I'm honoured.' His hands took hers and held them for a moment. 'Your servant, Mistress Fraser – for as long as it pleases you.'

She summoned up a smile. 'You're a good friend – to Angus and me.' Then as he went to the door and she began to follow she felt something soft beneath her foot, and looked down in dismay at the broken roses, their velvety petals scattered over the carpet.

'Oh – your beautiful flowers!'

'It's no matter,' said Selbie. 'No matter at all.'

The perfume of the dying roses was strong in the room as he stood at the window, watching Christian Fraser's small straight-backed figure going along the road, moving further away from him with each step. He half lifted one hand, ready to wave when she reached the corner, but she didn't turn to look back.

Long after she had disappeared from sight the young banker stood there, his brown eyes fixed on the path she had walked along.

It was damnable, he reflected wryly, to hopelessly, desperately want a woman who was not only married, but married and utterly devoted to a sick man.

Chapter Sixteen

Rab whistled beneath his breath as he strode from Townhead along High Street, past Storie Street then past the handsome façade of Angus Fraser's house. He had had a longer day than usual, for he and his drawboy had stayed on to complete the web on the loom.

Now he was going home to Breda, and his footsteps began to speed up as he approached the corner of High Street and New Street.

Halfway down New Street he turned in at a small close-mouth, waving a cheerful hand at an acquaintance on the opposite footpath. Along the passageway he went, and lifted the latch of a low wooden door towards the back of the building. And then, with the surge of astonished pride that always accompanied him through that particular door, he stepped over the threshold of his very own house.

His nose twitched, searching for the appetising smell of food being prepared for the evening meal, but there was none. The house had a stillness about it that told him that the two small rooms were empty. The whistling died away.

'Breda? I'm home, lass.'

Even as he called, he knew she wasn't there to hear him. The kitchen was cold, for the fire had gone out. Plates and mugs used for the morning meal were still lying on the table.

The cupboard that was graced with the name of bed-chamber lay abandoned, the coverings on the bed pushed back, the pillows rumpled and still bearing the imprint of his and Breda's heads. A petticoat and a blouse sprawled carelessly over the end of the bed.

Rab swallowed hard, then took off his jacket with fingers that fumbled at the buttons. He hung it neatly behind the door, gathered up the spilled clothes from the bed, folded them as best he could and put them into the corner press, then drew the coverings straight.

After that he went into the other room and began to rake out the grey ashes and replace them with kindling wood, the happiness in him ebbing away as he worked, to be replaced by growing anger.

For the first few weeks of his marriage to Breda he had been transported to paradise. Each day when he left his loom she was waiting at home for him. They fell asleep in each other's arms, woke together at dawn to make love before he scrambled out of bed and hurried off to the weaving shop.

But soon the edge of Rab's happiness had become dulled. Breda wasn't a home-maker, and his hopes of turning her into one were beginning to fade. She was bored in the house with nobody to speak to, so she refused to stay there when he wasn't at home.

He lit the fire and then foraged in the cupboard. For a wonder, there was bread there, and a lump of cheese on a platter.

Rab cut a great slice from the loaf and another from the cheese. He investigated the ale jug, found that there was a little left, and poured it into the unwashed mug he had used that morning.

All too often this was becoming his staple evening meal. As he bit off chunks of bread and cheese, then chewed, his belly craved the hot broth and the appetising meat dishes he'd been used to sitting down to in his mother's kitchen.

He could have gone along to Townhead and been welcome to share in the evening meal there, but he would have died of hunger before he let his parents know that Breda was a less than perfect wife.

The marriage had caused a coolness between Robert and Annie and their elder son, and Rab had no desire to let them know that some of the accusations they had made against Breda were turning out to be close to the truth.

He was still alone when he finished eating. He filled the kettle with the last of the water in the stoup beside the range, set it over the fire to heat, and took the stoup out into the darkening evening. At the nearest well he waited in line, ignoring the swift curious glances of the chattering women and the more open stares of the children. It wasn't often that a young man went to the street wells to collect water.

At last Rab's turn came and he filled his stoup then tramped back up the hill to the house.

By the time Breda's quick footsteps came tapping along the street the place was put to rights, the lamp lit, and Rab had washed himself and put on clean linen.

She came sliding in through the door like a shadow, still light and graceful despite her thickening waistline.

'Where have you been?'

She lifted the shawl back from her dark hair. 'With my mother.'

'Till this time?' Relief and pleasure at seeing her warred with anger and resentment. 'Confound it, Breda, I've been home this past hour or more!'

'Have you supped?' she asked indifferently.

'I've staved off my hunger with bread and cheese, but it's not right for a man to come home from a day's work to find an empty house and ashes in the grate and not a bit of food got ready for him.'

She looked at him from under long lashes. Her eyes smouldered and her mouth took on a sulky look that was becoming all too familiar. 'My mother's getting old. She needs me.'

'Aye – and so does your man need you. You're a married woman now, Breda, and your first duty's to me.'

'I owe duty to no man, Rab Montgomery!' She almost spat the words at him, but he stood his ground.

'Mebbe that's how they see things where you come from, but it's not the way in Paisley. Every day of her life my mother has a pot of broth simmering on the range at the end of a day's work – and potatoes and meat too.'

'Then go to your mammy's and let her give you your meal. I'm not bothered.'

Without thought, Rab's fists clenched and one of them began to lift. To his horror he saw Breda brace herself for the blow, and turned from her, forcing his hand to his side. The day Rab Montgomery struck his wife would be a black day indeed. He was appalled to think how close he had come to it.

There was a short, angry silence in the little room, then: 'Rab,' she said softly, coaxingly, and her hands slid up the length of his back and over his shoulders.

He let himself be turned about, and looked down at her. She had unbuttoned the top of her gown, and the smooth firm curves of her enlarged breasts gleamed in the lamplight. Her lips were parted and her eyes half closed, the long lashes almost brushing her cheeks.

'Rab,' she said again, her hands slipping inside his shirt to flutter against his chest.

The anger drained from him. His need for her filled his entire body, rousing him to a sharp, clamouring hunger greater than the mere need for food.

With a low groan he bent to fasten his mouth on hers, then lifted her and carried her into the other room and laid her on the bed.

Alexander Fraser sent word from London to his step-mother that he couldn't travel to Paisley because his wife was expecting their first child, and was in delicate health.

But when Benjamin returned from London he brought Rachel with him. She came swiftly into the house, seeming years older than the girl who had left Paisley. Her dark hair was neatly dressed, her gown of the finest silk with lace at wrists and throat. Over it was a velvet cloak, and a lovely feathered bonnet was perched on her head.

Her once-rounded face was thinner and her grey eyes shadowed. She was, Christian noted as she greeted the girl, far too pale, and her manner was brittle, as though she was carefully controlling herself.

'Where's Father?' she asked at once.

'Down at the warehouse.'

Rachel's eyes widened. 'But surely, if he's ill—'

'He's not ill,' Christian said sharply. 'At least, not that he knows. Did Benjamin not explain the way of it to you?'

'Yes, but even so—' The girl broke off and staggered slightly. Her face had suddenly turned waxy and perspiration stood out on her brow. She lifted a hand to her head as Benjamin Selbie stepped forward to put a supporting arm about her shoulders.

'The journey unsettled her,' he explained tersely over

his shoulder. 'The coach was full, and the roads badly rutted.'

'I'm fine.' Rachel's voice was shaky. 'I just need to rest for an hour.'

'Come along, your room's ready and waiting for you.' Christian put her arm about the girl and drew her upstairs.

When she returned to the hall a few minutes later it was empty. At first, with a sense of loss, she thought that Benjamin had left the house. Then she caught sight of him through the half-open parlour door, pacing the carpet.

Like Rachel, he was travel-stained, but even so, he looked exceptionally fine in his sky-blue coat and brown breeches and high brown leather boots. She had missed him while he was away. Paisley had had an empty feeling to it.

'How is she?'

'Almost asleep when I left her. But I managed to keep her awake long enough to explain how she should behave when she sees her father.'

'You received Alexander's letter?'

She seated herself by the fireside. 'I did.'

'If you ask me,' Selbie said a trifle grimly, 'it's the prospect of seeing his father an invalid that's stopping him from coming to Paisley, rather than any concern for his wife!'

'At least Rachel came back with you. Did she take much persuading?'

'Not as much as I would have thought.' He grinned. 'From all accounts, Mistress Rachel has been having a fine time in London. She's become much sought-after, socially.'

'Indeed?'

'Indeed. But Alexander was anxious to see her on her way home. In fact, he all but welcomed me with open arms.'

'Why? What's amiss?'

He shrugged his broad shoulders and the amusement faded from his eyes. 'It seems that his sister has become altogether too enamoured of a man who's titled and very well-to-do. Unfortunately, he's also well married, and to a wealthy wife he'd not dream of deserting for any woman, even one as appealing as Rachel. Not,' added Selbie grimly, 'that that stops the gentleman in question from seeking his pleasures wherever he may find them.'

'I see. Mebbe it's as well that Rachel came home.'

'Alexander certainly thinks so.' Then he came to sit on the chair opposite, eyeing her keenly. 'How have you been during my absence?'

'Well enough. And Angus has been well too.'

'No more outbreaks of rage?'

'Nothing worth the mention.' No sense in telling him about the porcelain statuette, one of her favourite pieces, which had been hurled against the wall and smashed into a hundred shards when Angus flew into a temper over some trivial matter.

Christian had grown accustomed to these outbursts now; she knew that they offered no physical threat to her, and that she could cope with them and with Angus. After each one he slept deeply and woke with no knowledge of what had happened. For that, for his sake, she was grateful.

The brown eyes set in the square face opposite bored into her and she looked back calmly, refusing to lower her gaze.

'I'm not certain that I believe you,' he said at last.

She opened her mouth to argue, then stopped as the door opened and Angus came into the parlour.

'So – we have a visitor.'

'Mister Fraser.' Selbie got up and held out his hand. 'How have things been with you, sir?'

'Well enough. How was London? Did you see my son there?'

'Indeed I did, and dined at his house on two occasions.' As well as the deference due to an older man and a valued customer of the bank, Selbie's manner towards Angus held genuine liking. 'He and his wife are well, and send their respects to you. He hopes to come north to visit you soon.'

'Good. And what of Rachel?'

'As to that matter,' Christian told him smilingly, 'you can ask her yourself when she's wakened from her sleep.'

Quick pleasure flared in her husband's eyes. 'She's here?'

'She travelled home with me, sir. She's had enough of London for the moment, and decided that it was time to think of home.'

The older man rubbed his hands together. 'It'll be grand to see her. You'll have a glass of claret, Selbie?'

The golden-brown head was shaken decisively. 'With your permission I'll make my own way home. I sent my luggage ahead, with word to the housekeeper that I'd not be long.'

'And no doubt,' Christian put in, 'you'll be anxious to see how your roses are faring.'

He laughed. 'You know my weaknesses, Mistress Fraser. The roses in the London gardens were very fine indeed, and I'm eager to see my own bushes and compare them.'

'You'll come tonight then, for your supper.'

'I'd be honoured, Mister Fraser.'

When the younger man had gone Angus said thoughtfully: 'He's a fine lad, Selbie. He'll go far in his profession, mark my words.'

Then he added, his shoulders slumping a little: 'I wish to God that Alexander had half his brains, and half his ambition.'

Although summer was now easing towards autumn the boxes of pinks in the weaving shop windows were still in full flower, and the bee-skeps kept in wall-niches in most gardens were busy with comings and goings as their residents gathered pollen from the fragrant bushes specially grown for them.

The garden behind Benjamin Selbie's house was a mass of perfumed colour. Roses clung to the walls, tumbled over and around trellises, and massed the bushes and trees between the paved paths.

Mally Bruce had long since overcome his suspicious antagonism towards Benjamin and he, like Christian, was a frequent visitor to Silk Street. On more than one occasion she had found the two of them among the flowers, Benjamin weeding or pruning while Mally sprawled on a bench, long legs stuck out in front of him and pipe in hand. Always, the two of them were arguing over something.

Angus's health continued to be unstable, but it didn't seem to Christian to be any worse than before. Sometimes she allowed herself to hope that the inflammation her father had spoken of had gone away, and Angus was better.

At first she had been nervous in case Rachel betrayed the truth to Angus, but the girl had managed to behave normally when he was around, although she continued to look ill and strained, and when Angus wasn't in the house she often gave way to storms of tears and sometimes took to her bed for days at a time, pleading headaches.

'I know that Angus is the happier for having her at home, but sometimes it's like having two invalids in the house,' Christian confessed to her mother. 'It only takes a word too much or too little to set Rachel into a crying fit.

'I don't know what's amiss with the lassie at all. And she'll scarcely go out of the house, let alone take up with her old friends. I've asked her if she'd prefer to go back to London, but that just sets the tears off again.'

'Has she lost weight?'

'Not that I've noticed,' said Christian with naive innocence. 'If anything she's gained it – yet she scarcely eats a thing.'

Her mother eyed her, then said carefully 'Have you thought, Christian, that mebbe . . .'

'Mebbe what?' Then, as the older woman said nothing, but raised an eyebrow, Christian said with horror, 'You don't mean a child? She can't! Not Rachel!'

'Why not Rachel? She's a very pretty lassie. And it would explain the bouts of tears and the refusal to go out and about.'

'Mercy!' Christian felt as though the cares of the world were descending on her shoulders. 'What'll Angus say if you're right? I couldn't bring myself to tell him!'

'That,' said Margaret gently, 'is something you'd have to talk to Rachel about. If I'm right, that is. It may well be that worry over her father's illness is all that's wrong with her.'

'I hope so. But somehow I think your first suspicion's more likely to be the right one,' Christian said with gloomy resignation.

Chapter Seventeen

As her feet carried her downhill towards the High Street a half-hour later she became aware of a reluctance to face up to yet another problem. She had enough on her hands without worrying about Rachel as well.

Angus was still busying himself about the warehouse, but of late he had almost made one or two bad, money-losing blunders. Fortunately Benjamin Selbie had detected them in time, and he and Christian between them had managed to put things right without Angus being any the wiser.

Thinking of Benjamin made her long to see him, to sit among his roses and tell him about the latest worry and ask him to advise her.

But as she emerged on to the busy High Street she made herself cross the road towards the house, taking advantage of a gap between a packman on horseback, his saddlebags slung across his saddle, and a cart loaded with linen for the bleachfields.

Rachel's business wasn't for Benjamin Selbie's ears. And besides, Christian sometimes felt that she relied on the young banker altogether too much. She must stand on her own feet, she told herself firmly.

To her relief Angus was out, and Rachel sitting in the parlour with her embroidery tambours in her hand.

Without stopping to take her cloak off Christian closed

the door behind her and said, 'Rachel, are you with child?'

The girl's head jerked back. Colour flooded into her face and her eyes went huge with shock.

'How could you think such a—'

'Lassie, I've got too much on my mind just now to choose my words carefully. Now tell me the truth of it. Is that what's been wrong with you since you came home, or is it not?'

The flush faded from Rachel's cheeks. She bit her pale lower lip, then a flood of tears set her eyes sparkling before they overflowed. The embroidery fell from her hands to her lap, then slid to the floor.

'Oh, Christian,' she wailed. 'What am I to do?'

'Dear God!' said Christian. It was only when she knelt to take her weeping step-daughter into her arms that she realised how passionately she had wanted her mother to be wrong.

Once she calmed Rachel down and got her to tell the whole sad story Christian found that things were even worse than she had first thought.

The child was, Rachel admitted shame-facedly, the result of a secret liaison between herself and the married man Benjamin Selbie had spoken of.

'Rachel, Rachel! Did you not have the sense to realise that you were doing wrong?'

The girl shook her head, swallowing back fresh tears. 'I only knew that he was kind and – and loving. I thought . . .' Then she looked up, her pretty face blotched and drawn. 'Nobody ever told me about – about . . .'

Christian sat back on her heels, the skirts of her yellow gown spread about her on the carpet, and damned herself for a stupid woman. Rachel had been motherless from childhood. There had been, as she so rightly said, nobody to tell her about men and women and loving as she grew into womanhood.

Angus had made such a pet of his daughter that Christian herself had tended to forget that Rachel was fast becoming an adult. She had assumed, somehow, that the girl would know how to conduct herself. She, who had once in Lancashire accused Angus Fraser of treating Rachel like a child, had fallen into the same trap.

'Does Alexander know about this?'

Rachel looked horrified. 'Oh no – I could never have told him! I was at my wit's end when I began to realise about the child. Then Benjamin came to London and I was able to pretend that I wanted to return home for a while with him.'

'Alexander and Dorothy should have taken better care of you!' Christian said hotly, then added with a resigned shrug of the shoulders: 'But there's no sense in saying that now. What's done is done, and we must decide what to do about it.'

'You'll not tell my father?' Rachel seized hold of her step-mother's wrist with two determined hands. 'I couldn't bear it if he knew! And what would it do to him, the way he is just now?'

'Aye, you're right. You could go away somewhere.' Christian's mind was twisting and turning. 'We could find some discreet lady willing to accompany you on a trip, and then pay a decent couple to raise the child as their own.'

'But that would take time to arrange.'

'A month or two at most.'

'Christian' – the tears began to flow again – 'the child's due in eight weeks' time – it will soon be obvious to everyone!'

Horrified, Christian gaped at her step-daughter for a speechless moment, then she said weakly, 'You've kept your secret all this time?'

The girl was crying freely now. 'I laced myself tightly, and I was c-careful as to the gowns I wore. And I n-never went out unless I h-had to.'

'And what were you going to do when the bairn arrived?'

Rachel shook her head and her dark curls danced. 'I h-hadn't thought of that y-yet. Oh, Christian!'

Mistress Christian Fraser wanted to throw herself on the ground and hammer her fists and heels on the carpet and bawl like a child. She wanted someone else – her mother, her father, Angus, anyone – to come to her aid and take care of everything and tell her that she had nothing more to worry about in the whole world.

But nobody was going to do that. Angus and Rachel depended on her, Alexander had sensibly decided to keep away from all the problems that had suddenly beset the Frasers, and, for the time being at least, she, Christian, was the only one in the household who could make decisions and sort things out.

'Rachel, listen to me.' She wiped the girl's face and tilted her chin up. Rachel sniffed, and did as she was told.

'Now – you're right about your father. We can't tell him. I'm going to call on my Aunt Mary MacLeod. Mebbe you could go to her house to have the child, and then afterwards we'll see about finding a foster mother for it. Will you agree to that?'

Rachel nodded, and a faint relieved smile began to touch the corners of her mouth. Then it vanished and she asked anxiously, 'But will Mistress MacLeod agree to it?'

'I think so. She's never let any of us down yet,' Christian said vigorously. 'Now go on upstairs and wash your face and have a rest, so that you'll look well enough at the supper table.'

Although the truth about Angus's condition was being kept secret Mary MacLeod knew about it.

Christian and her parents had realised almost immediately that there was no sense in trying to withhold the news from her, for somehow Mary managed to ferret out everything in the end. And, as Christian had said to Rachel, Mary never let her family down when they turned to her for help.

'It seems to me,' she said with a certain smug satisfaction when her great-niece had poured out her story, 'that whenever there's a worry in the family, I'm the one that's supposed to deal with it.'

'That's because you're the one with all the money and the fine big empty house.'

'Tuts, Christian, you're as sharp-tongued as your mother. Why could you not have inherited your father's manner instead of Margaret's? I never could best her in an argument.'

'Aunt Mary, will you do it? Will you help me?'

Mary looked at her niece over the edge of her spectacles and decided that the lassie was altogether too thin these days. There were shadows beneath Christian's eyes, and the first lines to touch her pretty face were shading themselves prematurely about her mouth. It wasn't right that the girl should have to take on so much trouble at her age.

But then, trouble never did take account of age, only of ability. And Christian was able enough to shoulder responsibilities, not like that wife of Daniel's, who did nothing but produce one child after another as if she was plucking apples from a tree.

'How many bairns has Daniel fathered?' she asked absently.

'Four. Aunt Mary, what has that got to do with Rachel?'

Mary came back to the matter in hand with a start. 'Nothing at all. Can an old body not let her mind wander now and again? The Lord knows I've worked hard enough in my time to earn the right. Of course the lassie can come here. I'll see that it's all taken care of, and nobody any the wiser. I'll have to call in the midwife, but Mistress Bain's a close-mouthed creature and I've silver enough to put an extra lock on her tongue – and on the servants' tongues as well.'

'We'll have to think of a reason that Angus'll accept.'

'Ahem!' Mary gave a dry peck of a cough then said serenely. 'I think I feel my bronchitis coming on. And if I should have a wee bit of a fall on the stairs and turn my ankle into the bargain, I'd need someone here to keep me company for some considerable time. I'd look on it as a kindness if you were to send Rachel along this very day to help me out. Now your only worry's the bairn itself, poor wee fatherless morsel.'

'As to that, we can think about it when the time comes.'

Mary's sharp ears took account of the 'we', but she only said: 'It'll be pleasant having a bairn about the place for a while.'

Christian's arms went about her, and her niece's soft cheek was pressed against her own. 'Thank you, Aunt Mary!'

'Och, think nothing of it, lass. You've got more than enough to carry at the moment without fretting your head about Rachel.'

As she left the MacLeod house Christian felt light-headed with relief. She sped down the hill to tell Rachel the good news. At least that was one worry off her shoulders. If everything went according to plan Angus need never know about his daughter's pregnancy.

She wasn't to know, as she hurried along the High Street with a smile on her lips, that Angus would find out the truth for himself.

'Aye, well, it'll give the lassie something to do,' Angus said that evening when he heard that his daughter had gone to Mary's house. 'I've been a wee bit worried about her, Christian. She's been keeping to her own room too much. Your aunt will take her mind off herself.'

And as the weeks wore on and Rachel's time came nearer she kept away from the town, contenting herself with occasional walks near Mary's house, well muffled in a voluminous cloak. Fortunately, she remained quite slender, and those who happened to meet her on these walks had no notion of her condition.

A week before her child was due to be born a restlessness seized Rachel. She paced the house until Mary, for the sake of peace, suggested a stroll round the garden.

'I've heard that women can get right fidgety at your stage,' she said. 'I know that there was no stopping Margaret or her mother when they were carrying bairns.'

As Rachel walked on the neat gravel paths her mind busily checked over a list of all that she would need for her confinement. She recalled with annoyance that her favourite shawl had been left at her father's house. She would have to send word to Christian to bring it on her next visit.

The shawl became fixed in her mind as she patrolled the garden. The more she thought of it the more she wanted it. Her need for it became a craving that couldn't wait. She must have the comfort of that particular shawl about her shoulders.

She looked down at the folds of the cloak that concealed her body. Her father's health had improved lately and he spent each day at the warehouse again. If she went quickly down the hill and along the High Street without stopping to talk to anybody she could reach his house, obtain the shawl, and be back before Mary realised that she had left the garden.

Even while she was thinking about it her feet were carrying her swiftly down the path towards the gate. She lifted the latch and slipped out.

As she stepped in to her father's house, Florrie, who was working in the parlour, was brought to the door by the sound of footsteps in the hall.

'It's yourself, Miss Rachel.'

Rachel drew the cloak more closely about her. 'Is Mistress Fraser not at home?'

'She's gone to the market, and the master's at the warehouse.'

'I've just come to fetch something. You can get back to your work.'

'Yes, miss,' the little maid said obediently, and Rachel crossed the hall and began to climb the stairs. There were more of them than she had realised, and by the time she reached her own small room her back was aching fiercely.

She dropped the cloak on to the bed and sank down on to a chair for a moment to rest. The walk from Oakshaw-hill had tired her more than she had thought it would. And she had the hill to climb on the return journey. But the house was quiet and peaceful.

There was time to sit quietly for a few moments, gathering her strength. Rachel leaned her head back and closed her eyes.

* * *

Angus Fraser had had a nagging headache since noon. His temper deteriorated as the pain in his temples grew, until finally he left the warehouse earlier than usual and stamped home in a foul mood, ignoring friends and acquaintances, pushing his way through a group of chattering drawboys with a few surly words, slamming the house door behind him when he finally arrived.

Florrie met her master in the hall, her face whitening as she recognised the choleric flush on his cheeks.

'Where's your mistress, girl?'

With trembling hands Florrie helped him off with his coat and put it into the hall press. 'Gone to the market, sir.'

Angus grunted, then said 'Well? What are you standing gawping at me for? Get to the kitchen.'

Florrie hesitated, thinking of Rachel, who was still upstairs. She and Greta were no fools – they had known the way of things regarding their master's daughter long before Christian found out. Loyalty had kept their tongues still.

'I was just going to see to something—' she said through dry lips and made for the stairs. Rachel had to be warned to stay where she was until it was safe for her to leave unseen.

Angus Fraser's face purpled. 'Confound you, girl, am I the master of this house or am I not? Get back to the kitchen when I tell you, or get out through that street door and stay out!'

Terrified, Florrie scuttled to the kitchen. She had scarcely had time to tell Greta what was happening before the parlour bell began to jerk frantically on the kitchen wall, dancing to the impatient tugging of the connecting cord.

The two serving-women looked at each other with frightened eyes.

'You go,' pleaded Florrie, but Greta shook her head.

'It's no' me that's supposed tae answer the bells, it's you, He'll ken somethin's wrong if I go.'

'I wish the mistress was here!'

The bell jangled again, almost spinning right off its perch.

'God help me,' said Florrie, and went tremblingly to find out what was amiss.

Her employer was storming round the parlour, dragging drawers out and tossing their contents around.

'Where the devil have you put my spectacles, woman?'

'Are they not in your pocket, sir?' The maidservant's voice quavered.

Without putting a hand to his pocket Angus Fraser barked, 'If they were there would I not know it, you empty-headed fool? You've cleared them away somewhere!'

'No sir, I—'

He brushed past her to cross the hallway to the dining room. She got there in time to find him burrowing impatiently through the cutlery drawer, tossing spoons and knives aside with a jangling sound that set Florrie's teeth on edge.

'They'd not be in there, Mister Fraser.'

'Confound it, they must be somewhere! Look in the kitchen,' he commanded, and made for the stairs. Appalled, Florrie ignored her orders and followed him.

With some idea of warning Rachel the maid tried to dart past Angus once he had gained the top step.

He swatted at her as though she was a fly, sending her reeling against the wall.

'Do as you're told, damn you! Go down and search in the kitchen!'

Then he opened the nearest door, the door to his daughter's room, and walked in before Florrie could stop him.

Rachel, roused from her rest by the sound of her father's raised voice, had jumped to her feet, and was

218

reaching for her cloak when the door suddenly slammed back on its hinges.

'Rachel, I'm looking for—' Angus Fraser began, then stopped suddenly, staring at his daughter's swollen belly. Then he said in a whisper. 'What's this?'

'Father—' She began to move towards him, her face ashen but determined.

A trembling, accusing finger was pointed at her like a sword. 'You're with child! Don't deny it, I'm not a fool to be hoodwinked!' His voice began to rise. 'My daughter – my own child, shaming me before the world!' Then he said between his teeth: 'Tell me who the man is!'

She put a hand on his arm, but it was thrown aside. 'Listen to me, father. Sit down with me and I'll explain.'

She was bone-white to the lips now, her voice shaking. For the first time in her life she was aware of barely controlled violence emanating from her father.

'Explain? What is there to explain when I can see what the situation is with my own eyes? Confound it,' his voice rose to a bellow, 'tell me who the man is and I'll horsewhip him. Then, my lady, I'll deal with you!'

'He's far away, in London.'

Angus's eyes were still fixed on her belly. His face had purpled ominously. 'In London, is he? If he's in London, slut, what are you doing here under my roof, instead of being with him as his wife?'

Florrie had melted away, fleeing downstairs and out of the front door, taking to her heels in a desperate bid to fetch Christian home before murder was done.

Rachel swallowed hard, and without thinking, placed protective hands over her unborn child. 'He already has a wife.'

'And, it seems,' said Angus with a sneer, 'a Scottish whore as well.'

'Father!'

219

He advanced across the room towards her. She held her ground, then cried out sharply as his palm slammed across her face.

She almost fell, but caught at the bed-post and managed to keep herself upright. Angus, foam flecking his lips, blundered after her.

Clumsy as she was, she managed to duck beneath the hands outstretched and fingering the air in search of her throat.

Then, in an agony of terror, she ran across the room and out into the corridor, her face smarting and her head spinning from the violent blow she had received. From behind her came a stream of abuse, laced with words that she had never in her life heard her gentle father use.

Whimpering, Rachel staggered towards the top of the stairs, her only thought to get away from him, even if she had to run out into the street in her thin gown. She was dimly aware of the child she carried moving against the confining walls of her womb as though urging her on in her bid for safety. For the first time she realised that she had two souls to look after now, not just one.

She gained the top of the stairs, but behind her Angus Fraser's steady stream of profanity was louder and she knew that he was there, just at her back, and that her chances of escape were slim.

She felt him clutching at her, and turned, trying to fend him off with one upraised arm. He drew his hand back and hit out at her, a blow that had all the strength he could muster behind it.

Rachel's sweat-slicked fingers lost their grip on the banisters. One ankle turned beneath her, and with a scream of terror she felt herself overbalance and start to fall.

* * *

Chapter Eighteen

Christian was almost home when she saw Florrie, her carrot-coloured hair flying out beneath her cap, scurrying along the footpath towards her. At the sight of the girl's bulging, frightened eyes her heart seemed to stop in her breast.

'Dear heavens, lassie, what's amiss?'

The maidservant clutched frantically at her. 'It's Miss Rachel – and the master' – she sucked air in with an audible wheeze, then said – 'I'm feared he'll kill her—'

Christian didn't wait to hear any more. For the second time in a few minutes poor Florrie was pushed impatiently against a wall as her mistress started to run the last few yards to the house.

She burst into the hall just in time to hear Rachel's wrenching scream of despair and fear, followed by a sickening series of thuds as the girl's body crashed from stair to stair. She finally came to rest in the hall, and lay still.

For a moment there was utter silence. Greta, who had run from the kitchen, stood with her hands pressed tightly to her mouth, staring at Rachel. Christian felt as though her own feet were rooted to the spot.

Her gaze lifted from the bulky, huddled body on the floor and travelled up the staircase to where Angus stood on the top step, silent now, and gasping for breath.

221

As she looked at him he lifted both arms to his head, grinding the heels of his hands into his temples as though trying to contain a sudden fierce burst of pain. His eyes closed and his face was contorted. Slowly, he sank to his knees.

Florrie, stumbling behind her mistress, coming up short at Christian's side and giving a cry of horror when she took in the still, crumpled body at the foot of the stairs, broke the spell that held Christian.

She dragged her gaze away from Angus and ran forward to kneel beside his daughter. Rachel's eyes were closed and one side of her face bore the glowing red imprint of a hand, the fingers outspread, each clearly seen.

'Greta, bring as many cloaks as you can find – quickly!' Even in the midst of her panic Christian realised that the women would refuse to go upstairs, where Angus was, to get blankets. 'Florrie, run and fetch Mistress Bain. Tell her she's needed at once.'

As the servants scattered in different directions Rachel's body twisted in a sudden contraction and she uttered a sharp cry, then opened dazed eyes.

'Christian—'

'Lie quiet for a minute. We'll lift you into the parlour in a wee while, when we've got some help.'

'Oh Christian, I'm glad to see you!' Rachel said, then convulsed again and gave a grunt of pain. Her teeth bit into her lower lip, drawing blood. Her fingers tightened over Christian's, then slowly eased.

'I'm thinking,' she whispered, summoning up the ghost of a smile, 'that it'll be too late to go into the parlour. My bairn's going to be birthed right here.'

The pain came again and Christian, smoothing the

hair back from the girl's forehead, took time to glance up at the top of the stairs.

To her relief, she saw that Angus was no longer there.

Mistress Bain the midwife came along the street at a run, escorted by Florrie. Passers-by watched with interest, and more than one pair of brows lifted when the woman was seen to hurry into the Fraser house.

'You don't think it's young Mistress Fraser?' a plump woman on the opposite pavement speculated, stopping for a moment to rest her basket against her ample belly.

Her friend looked down her long thin nose at her. 'I scarce think so, for we'd all have heard the news by this time. If you ask me, it's thon daughter of his, home from London and never over the doorstep. There's carryings-on in London the like of which you've never heard before.'

They pursed their lips, nodded significantly at each other, then proceeded on their way.

On the other side of the closed door Christian and Mistress Bain were kneeling over Rachel while the two servants ran here and there in a flurry of activity, fetching things for the midwife.

The woman examined Rachel with firm, experienced hands, then looked up and shook her head slowly. 'We'll mebbe save the lassie,' she whispered. 'But I'm feared it's ower late for the bairn.'

It was a short but difficult birthing for Rachel. At the end of it her daughter was still-born. Even the skills Mistress Bain had amassed over the years failed to save her.

The midwife put the limp little body aside and dealt

with the living, then she wrapped the still-born child in some cloths and pushed the bundle into her copious bag.

Christian's eyes lingered on the bag. 'What are you going to do with it?'

'Leave that tae me, lassie. Best no' tae ask questions.'

'Should there not be some form of burial?'

The woman's face was expressionless, her voice brisk and matter-of-fact. 'Mistress Fraser, the bairn never lived. An' I'm thinking that the fewer folk that ken aboot this, the better for you an' yer man. The lassie'll recover, an' she'll bear more bairns – alive an' well, God willin'. Best tae put the past oot o' yer mind an' tend tae the present. Noo – call yer servin'-women an' we'll get the lass intae her ain bed.'

Once Rachel was settled the midwife said: 'I'll be back the morn tae see how she is. She'll no' be comfortable for a while, for there's milk ready in her breasts an' she'll need tae be bound wi' sheets tae make it go awa'. But she'll be right in a week or so.'

She departed, and Rachel fell into a deep sleep. Christian, free to leave the girl at last, went into Angus's room.

He, too, was sleeping, sprawled across his bed, fully dressed. Gently, she stooped and drew the coverlet over him. He opened his eyes, blinked up at her, then smiled and took her hand.

'Christian, you're home.' Then he asked in sudden concern. 'Is Rachel all right?'

'She's fine.'

He nodded, relaxing back against the pillows, his hand still clasping hers. 'I'd such a bad dream, Christian – about Rachel . . .'

She smoothed a lock of hair back from his forehead.

'It was only a dream, Angus. Sleep now, and I'll waken you when your supper's ready.'

He smiled up at her, and fell asleep almost at once.

A few days later Breda Montgomery, about to turn from the footpath into the doorway of her home, caught her breath sharply and dropped the basket she carried. Its contents spilled out and rolled over the path as she leaned against the wall of the building, both hands clutching her back, her face twisted in pain.

A neighbour who had been following her along the path hastened to reach her and put a supporting hand beneath her elbow. The spasm eased, and Breda drew a long shuddering breath.

'It looks as though yer time's come, lass,' the woman said calmly. 'I'll help ye intae the hoose an' send the laddie runnin' for the midwife an' yer man.'

Christian put the story about that Rachel, arriving back from her stay at Mary's house, had taken a severe chill.

Little more than a week after losing her baby the girl was up and about again. She had made a good recovery, but even so she was pale and listless, eating little, uninterested in life.

'It happens when a bairn's lost,' Mistress Bain said consolingly when Christian questioned her. 'Ye'll hae tae gie the lass time tae get ower her grief.'

It was some comfort to know that Angus, at least, seemed to be back to his old self after the outburst that had cost the life of his grandchild. Mercifully, he had no memory of what had happened, though once or twice Christian saw him looking at his daughter with puzzled, concerned eyes.

He was particularly attentive to Rachel, and she, after

225

an instinctive shrinking back when they first met again, had the sense to realise that the stranger who had terrified her was gone.

Now, she responded to him as affectionately as she always had, although Christian knew that neither of them would ever be free of the worry of wondering when his sudden temper might be unleashed again.

Annie Montgomery, Rab's mother, brought some of her home-made tartlets to tempt the invalid's appetite, and stayed to pour out all her worries about her daughter-in-law.

'The birth of the bairn's left Breda with a terrible sickness. The midwife and Gavin both say that it happens to some women, but there's no knowing why it should, or what to do about it.'

The woman's face was lined with worry. 'It seems that Breda must just be cared for until she gets better, poor lass. Rab's fair out of his mind with worry about her. And as for the bairn . . .'

Christian cast a swift glance at her step-daughter, ready to think of some pretext that would get Rachel out of the room if it appeared that talk of a living child upset her. But the girl was working diligently at her sewing, head bent, apparently not even listening to the woman's chatter.

'. . . as bonny a laddie as ever you'd hope to see,' Annie's voice flowed on. 'Poor wee soul, he might as well be motherless for all the notice Breda takes of him at the moment.'

'He'll have a wet-nurse?'

'Aye, but if you ask me she's a shiftless sort of a creature. The poor lamb's not gaining ground at all. Rab's talking of asking the woman to take wee Adam into her own house just now, for when she's not there he's just left to lie in his crib. But I'm not for that. The Lord only knows what sort of ailments the bairn might get if he's taken into a stranger's house where his own folk can't keep an eye on him.' Annie shook her head, and sighed. 'I'm trying to find a wet-nurse that'll do better, but it's awful hard. Poor wee soul - what sort of a start is that for any bairn?'

When Annie Montgomery had gone bustling back to her own house and Christian was busy in the kitchen Rachel put down her sewing and went quietly upstairs to her own chamber.

Slowly but deliberately she took off her gown and unfastened the lengths of milk-stained sheeting that had been wrapped about the upper part of her body.

She set her teeth in her bottom lip as the material came free, but even so a whimper of pain forced its way out as her hard, heavy, milk-laden breasts were released from their imprisonment, sending lancing shafts of agony through her body.

Very gently, she put her cool hands against the sore breasts for a moment in an attempt to ease their burning pain, then dressed again in a plain blouse and skirt. She put a shawl about her shoulders and went downstairs and out of the house, opening and closing the door so quietly that neither Christian nor the servants heard her going.

Along the footpath she went, her face calm and set; round the corner of New Street and down the steep slope between the buildings. She found the doorway she was looking for, and went in and along the passageway, the thin fretful cry of a very small child guiding her.

Without hesitation Rachel Fraser lifted the latch, and walked into the Montgomery house.

She turned away from the cries at first, going to the

tiny bedroom where Breda slept, her black hair tumbled over the pillow, her lovely face sharp and gaunt, the bones seeming to strain at the skin that had tightened over them.

Rachel looked down at her sleeping, then moved into the kitchen.

There, everything was neat enough and warm enough. The fire was on and a kettle puffed steam gently into the air; but all the same there was a hollow chill about the place, an atmosphere that told of a house without a heart.

The thready, hopeless wailing went on, a weak cry without much expectation of being heard or answered. Rachel stooped over the crib by the range and the baby's dark head, the hair plastered damply to the tiny, perfect skull, turned on the mattress as he became aware that at last he was not alone.

Huge, dark blue eyes, too young as yet to focus, strained upwards in a desperate search for the new-comer. A tiny fist, free of the coverlet, waved feebly.

Gently, Rachel Fraser turned the blanket back and lifted the little boy into her arms. She carried him to a chair by the fire and sat down, settling him into the crook of one elbow. His body was as light, she thought with tender compassion, as an empty eggshell.

His head turned, butting into her breast, mouth opening like a flower, finger-spread hands beating against her with all the force of moth wings. Angry frustration sharpened the edge of his wailing.

'Hush now, Adam!' She unfastened her blouse with her free hand, pushing the material aside, cupping one sore milk-laden breast and offering it to him.

The wailing stopped abruptly as the seeking mouth found her nipple and clung to it. His hands fastened securely on her, at rest at last. He began to suck, his cheeks hollowing then filling regularly as he settled to his work.

Above his head Rachel smiled through tears of relief as the milk her own child hadn't needed began to flow, easing the pain in her heart as well as in her body.

'Mister Montgomery.' The woman who had been employed to wet-nurse Rab's son burst into his father's loom shop, a slimy-nosed toddler clutching at her skirts, a small squalling baby in her arms. 'Am I or am I no' nursin' your bairn?'

Rab gaped at her from his loom, then said, 'Aye, you are – and why are you here, and not doing just that?'

The nurse's round face was blotched with indignation. 'How can I, when there's someone else already there?'

'Eh?' Rab turned to his father, who was equally dumbfounded. 'Did my mother take matters into her own hands?' His face reddened with anger. 'If she did—'

'No, no! She'd never do that without consulting with you first.'

'Howsoever's the way o' it,' the woman squawked, in competition with her own baby, 'I was employed tae see tae the laddie, an' I've more tae dae than tae go traipsing along tae your house jist tae find that I'm no' wanted.'

'Woman, who told you you werenae wanted?'

'There's other folk'd be glad enough o' my services.'

Rab stood up and reached for his jacket. 'I'll have to go to the house to see what's going on.'

'You've got a web that's been promised for Thursday, man!'

'I'll work late on it tonight.' Rab, already on his way out, threw the words over his shoulder.

'And what about me? Am I tae nurse the bairn or am I

no'? Mister Montgomery! Ach, Jockie, get oot o' my way, ye wee scoondrel!' The nurse, in her haste to follow Rab, almost fell over the toddler, who set up a furious screaming. Determined to take on the newcomer and win, the baby redoubled its own noise.

'Here.' Robert Montgomery dug into his pocket and held out some coins. 'Take that for your trouble, woman, and get yourself and your bairns out of my weaving shop!'

She swooped on the money and scooped it into a hand that was none too clean. After it was safely stowed into some hiding place among her clothing she spat on the floor and said, 'There's nae sense in tryin' tae dae a good turn for some folk! Ye can tell him I'll no' be back. Come on, Jockie!'

As the wailing faded into the distance and he was left alone in the peace of his own weaving shop, apart from Rab's wide-eyed drawboy, Robert Montgomery took out a handkerchief and mopped his forehead.

He wished, not for the first time, that Rab had had the sense to find himself a sturdy Lowland wife instead of Breda MacEwan, who always reminded her father-in-law of a lovely, but dangerous, wild animal, never meant for captivity.

Rab ran all the way home, pushing his way impatiently through the busy footpaths, almost beside himself with worry.

There had been nothing but trouble since Adam's birth. He had no way of knowing if Breda would ever come back to him from the far distant place her mind seemed to be inhabiting at the moment; he knew that the wet-nurse wasn't the most suitable of women, and even his unpractised eyes could see that the child wasn't gaining ground.

But Breda's mother was in poor health, and eager though his own mother was to do all she could Rab refused to ask her for help, knowing full well that his parents had never approved of his marriage. The humiliation of having to depend on them now was something he couldn't swallow.

And now, it seemed, there was some other worry awaiting him at home. Despair took hold of him. It seemed that his life was never again going to be a matter of comfort and ease and freedom from worry.

He skidded in at the close-mouth, his shoulder hitting off the damp stone wall of the passage with a painful thump that he didn't even notice.

Throwing open the house door, he burst into the kitchen then stopped short, staring at the scene before him.

The crib was empty, the coverlet folded back. The room was warm and serene. Rachel Fraser sat in a low chair by the fire, her head bent over the baby in her arms. Her blouse was open and drawn aside to expose one full, blue-veined breast; the baby was fastened to it like a leech, and Rab could hear the sound of his strong sucking.

Rachel had been intent on the child. Now she lifted her head and smiled at Rab, a smile of utter joy and contentment that illuminated not only her face, but the whole room.

In that moment Rab Montgomery, gaping speechlessly, thought that he had never seen anything as beautiful as the sight of Rachel, her face flushed by the fire's glow, her eyes bright, his son nestled contentedly against her round white breast.

Chapter Nineteen

'It's foolish to let him go on working when the man's not well,' Alexander Fraser said curtly.

Christian looked up at her step-son and wondered why a man like Angus should have been blessed with such an empty-headed heir.

'Your father's well enough – at the moment. How can I stop him working when the business belongs to him? Besides, what would he do with himself all day if he didn't have the warehouse?'

'He could rest.'

'It would make no difference, Alexander.'

'The business should be made over to me now. Then I could see to things for him properly.'

'Mister Fraser's doing well enough,' Benjamin Selbie said quietly but firmly. Christian shot him a quick smile, glad that he had called at that particular time.

Ever since he had arrived from London, Alexander had been pressuring her behind his father's back to use her influence on Angus and persuade him to relinquish the firm he had built up from nothing. Clearly, that was the sole reason for the younger Fraser's visit to Paisley.

'And Mistress Fraser's always there to give me instructions if her husband's poorly,' Selbie went on blandly.

Alexander scowled at the banker, who looked back at him calmly, quite unruffled.

Alexander had put on weight since Christian had last seen him, and there was a sulkiness about the set of his lips that she didn't care for.

'My step-mother, sir, has enough on her hands,' he informed Benjamin stiffly. 'Besides, it's not seemly for a woman to be fretting over business.'

'That's nonsense!' Christian's temper, never far from the surface since Alexander's arrival, flared up. 'I ran the warehouse long before I became your father's wife, and I'm as capable as you are when it comes to knowing what's best for the Fraser company!'

'I fully agree,' said Selbie, and Alexander, thwarted, scowled from one to the other of them.

'He must be told.'

'Told what?'

'The truth about his condition.'

'No!' Cold fear caught at Christian.

'He has the right to know and to make up his own mind about the disposal of the company.'

'I said no!' She was on her feet now, advancing upon the elegantly dressed young man who sprawled in a tapestry chair by the window. 'Alexander, if you dare to say a word to the man – if you even mention such a plan to me again – I'll wring your neck as though you were a chicken!'

Surprise and apprehension flitted across his face as she moved across the room towards him. With a scrambling of the legs that had been stretched over the carpet he got up and backed away, his hands coming up in swift defence.

'I . . . I . . .' he spluttered, and almost fell over a footstool.

Christian wondered, later, what would have transpired between them if Benjamin Selbie hadn't been there. She was certainly angry enough to try to carry out her threat, and she saw by the look in her step-son's eyes that he believed her.

But in one movement Selbie was by her side, facing Alexander, and laying a calming hand on Christian's arm.

'While I'm not putting it as strongly as Mistress Fraser, sir, I'm warning you against making any foolish moves.' His voice was serene, but there was an undertone of sharp steel beneath it that made Alexander's eyes widen in further startled apprehension.

'There's no knowing how Mister Fraser might respond to such terrible news. And the man brave enough to blurt it out to him may well be the man who suffers for it. Have you never heard of those folk long ago who believed in killing the poor messenger who brought bad news to them? It made no sense – but I believe that it gave them some kind of satisfaction.' He paused for a moment before adding silkily: 'I can understand that. I'd not be surprised if your father felt the same way.'

Alexander hesitated, the tip of his tongue running nervously along dry lips. He glared at the couple before him.

Christian, her head up, the gold flecks dancing in her angry eyes, seemed to him to be ready to fight with every weapon she had; Benjamin Selbie stood firmly by her side, his mouth grim, his hand still resting on Christian's arm.

With his gaze lingering on that protective touch Alexander drawled slowly, deliberately: 'It must be of great comfort to my step-mother to have such a hot-blooded protector close at hand at all times.'

Christian pulled away from Selbie as though his fingers had suddenly burned her. The banker took a step towards the other man, hands curling into fists, then stopped short as the street door opened.

'You'll hold your tongue, Alexander!' It was an order from his step-mother rather than a request. Alexander's top lip curled slightly in a sneer.

'It seems that I've little choice in the natter – at the moment,' he said, then his father came into the room.

'Ah – you're here before me, Selbie. I stopped on the way to talk to Jamie Todd. He tells me that trade's getting worse instead of better. Poor wretches.' Angus shook his head. 'It's bad when a man with a good trade to his hand isn't able to make his own way in the world.'

'There's a lot of fine weavers out of work,' Christian agreed.

'Aye. But gentlemen,' her husband's voice took on a brisk note, 'it falls to us to see that the weavers we employ are kept in work, instead of spending time talking of the others. Come into the other room, both of you.'

They went, and Christian was left alone with her knitting wires and her embroidery. She glared at the closed door for a moment, railing silently against Angus's frequently aired views that a wife should not bother her pretty little noddle about business matters. Even the way she coped during his bouts of illness couldn't persuade him to include her in his meetings once the reins were back into his own hands again.

She was glad that Alexander was returning to London in a few days' time. Although it had done Angus good to see his son, the younger Fraser's presence made Christian uneasy, particularly after the scene that had just taken place.

236

She went into the hall and looked at the handsome grandfather clock that stood by the stairs, then went to the kitchen to see that the midday meal was well in hand.

At least Alexander didn't know of the terrible tragedy that had befallen his sister. That was one blessing, for Christian would never have heard the end of it – although the girl's pregnancy had come about when she was supposed to be in her brother's care.

As far as Alexander and his father were concerned Rachel's long and frequent absences were explained away as visits with her many friends. Alexander accepted the reason without comment; Angus, relieved to see the improvement in his daughter's health and her new air of purpose and contentment, was happy for her, and asked no questions.

As for Christian – she was only too glad that since becoming wet-nurse to Rab's son, the girl had got over her own loss.

At least one member of the Fraser family was happy, and for that, Christian was thankful.

Rab Montgomery's spirits rose as he strode down New Street.

In the close leading to his home his nostrils flared to the fragrant smell of meat cooking. It was almost like the old days, at home. It was the way he had hoped it would be when he and Breda first married.

But he knew that it was Rachel Fraser, not Breda, who would be setting the table for the evening meal and stirring the pots on the range; Rachel, not Breda, smiling in at the crib as she passed it on her journeyings from range to table.

Even so, there was a spring to Rab's step as he went along the stone-flagged passage and in at the house door.

As he opened it Rachel came from the bedchamber, a half-empty bowl in her hand, a strand of shining hair adrift across her brow.

She smiled at him. 'The supper'll not be a minute. I was just giving Breda hers first.'

'How is she?'

'She took most of her broth. Mister Knox looked in this afternoon, and he was pleased with her.'

Rab's brow knotted with worry. 'He's looking in a lot these days. D'you think it means that—'

'No, no.' She put a quick hand on his arm as she passed on her way to the range. 'He just wanted to make certain everything's all right. She's on the mend, Rab. You'll want to see her before you sit down to your meat.'

'Aye.' He shrugged out of his jacket, put it over the back of a chair, and went to look in the crib. 'No need to ask how Master Adam's doing.'

Rachel's voice was warm with amused tenderness. 'Aye, he's a bright wee button already. You and Breda'll have your hands full when that one gets on to his feet.'

In the ten days since she had come to the rescue the baby had improved beyond Rab's wildest hopes. His face and body had rounded out and he had begun to gain weight steadily. He lay contentedly in his cradle, dark-blue eyes wide.

When his father put a tentative finger into his open hand, his own tiny fingers curled round it in a surprisingly strong grip.

'Aye, he'll do,' Rab said, and went to see his wife.

Breda's crisis had come and gone, and the fever that had gripped her spasmodically was over; but it had left her in the grip of an apathy that refused to go away. Her face was almost grey, her cheeks fallen in. Her eyes were huge, with little life in them.

She slept most of the time, but she was awake when he went into the room, turning her head towards him when he took her hand in his.

'Rachel says you ate most of your supper.'

With his free hand he took up a cloth that lay on the chair by the bed and wiped away the sweat that glistened at her temples. Her hair was lank and lifeless.

'The wee one's doing fine. Rachel's looking after him, so don't you fret yourself, lass.'

Her eyes closed, her fingers slipped from his, and she turned her head away from him. He got up and stood looking down at her for a moment, then went back to the other room, where Rachel was ladling broth into a bowl.

She put it on the table before his chair and picked up her cloak.

'I'll be back later to see to the bairn.'

'Could you not stop and eat with me?' Rab asked on an impulse. Then as she hesitated, he added awkwardly: 'It's lonely, eating alone, and I'm sure there's enough food for us both.'

She bit her lip in indecision, then smiled. 'I'll stay, gladly.'

Moving gracefully, she put the cloak down, brought out another bowl and filled it, then carried it over to the stool opposite Rab – Breda's usual place at the table.

He took a deep breath, smiled shyly at her, and lifted his spoon.

Once the first awkwardness between them eased they talked low-voiced across the table so that Breda wasn't disturbed. Rab discovered that he felt comfortable with Rachel, more at ease than he had been with anyone for a long time. More at ease, he realised guiltily, that he had been since before his marriage.

Later, with a full stomach, his feet comfortably settled on the rug before the range, tobacco smoke from his pipe creating a grey-blue halo about his dark head, he watched Rachel move about the room, seeing to the dishes.

When she had finished her work she searched the dresser until she found the little woven basket where Breda kept her sewing needles and threads. Then she took Rab's jacket down from its hook and settled herself in the chair opposite his.

'What are you doing?'

'One of your buttons is almost off. I saw it when you came home. I'll make it fast for you.'

'No need for you to do that. I can see to my own buttons.'

She held up the jacket, eyeing a button held in place by a great clumsy clump of thread. Then she looked across at him, her mouth solemn but her grey eyes alight with laughter. 'So I see.'

He grinned widely. 'It's not bad – for a man.'

'Not at all bad – for a man. But all the same, I'll put it right.'

During the meal he had told her about his work, and gone on to talk about his concern for the weavers leaving the town because they could find no employment. Rachel had proved to be a good listener.

Now, as she stitched and he smoked, she told him about London, painting a vivid picture of a world he had never seen, but really didn't long for, although he enjoyed hearing about it.

'Will you be going back there?'

The needle paused for a moment then made a swift flashing downward movement, centring with perfect precision on the eye of the button. 'No, I don't think so,' she said, her head bent and her voice serene.

As she finished her work and bit through the thread with neat white teeth Adam stirred and uttered a sleepy murmur, the prelude to a request for food. Rab knocked his pipe out against the range and got to his feet.

'I'll take a turn outside.'

Rachel handed the jacket to him then went to lift the baby into her arms, murmuring soothing words.

At the door he paused. 'I'm grateful to you, Rachel,' he said awkwardly. She smiled at him, her chin nestled against the baby's head.

'Not as grateful as I am to you, Rab.'

'Aye – well . . .' said Rab, confused, and left the house.

As he walked the night streets he pondered over her final words, then slowly the thought came to him, for the first time, that in order to have milk for Adam, Rachel Fraser must have birthed a child of her own.

The shock of it hit him so hard that it stopped him in his tracks. Fool that he was – he had never once given a thought to the girl's situation. He walked on, his mind racing, gathering up what few facts he knew and fitting them into place.

It didn't take him long to decide that Rachel's child had probably been conceived in London, and that the baby must have died – or been taken away from her at birth.

His feet carried him along, turning corners when he reached them without any thought of where he was going. 'Poor lassie,' he murmured to himself, his mind full of the girl who had, in his view, saved his son's life. The girl who had undoubtedly saved his own sanity and brought comfort and order and meaning back to his existence.

'Poor lassie,' thought Rab again, and pondered savagely over the man who had fathered a child on Rachel and not carried his obligations through. She deserved better than that, did Rachel. She deserved a lot better than that, Rab thought warmly.

Breda had been awake for a long time, listening to the comfortable buzz of voices in the other room. She heard the door close behind Rab, heard Rachel talking and crooning to the baby.

A frown flickered across the Highland girl's forehead. Her mouth compressed slightly, opened to call out, closed again. She lay in the darkness, listening.

When Rachel Fraser came quietly in to look at her she closed her eyes and listened to the rustle of skirts as Rachel moved away, and to the soft click of the latch as the girl left the house.

Then, slowly, she eased herself up in the bed, pushed the blanket aside and put her thin white feet on the floor.

The room circled round her and she clung to the edge of the bed, setting her teeth deeply into her lip until the walls steadied and stilled and she was able to lift her head, then get to her feet.

Step by step, holding on to a chair-back, the doorframe, the kitchen dresser, she made her way through to the other room. There, she sank down on to a stool at the table, looking about the place.

She had been in her bed for almost four weeks, and already her own kitchen felt like an alien land, a place where she was a stranger. She rested for a moment, then got up again and shuffled over to the crib.

Small Adam had fallen asleep, his belly comfortably full, his world at peace. He woke with a start as his mother's groping hands curled around him, lifting him awkwardly up into the air. He gave a protesting squawk, his arms sawing about in search of security.

'Shhh!' Breda commanded, gathering him into her embrace. She started on the long journey back to her bed, finally collapsing on to it with a grunt of relief. Then she drew the blanket about herself and her baby and fell into an exhausted sleep.

For a little while Adam, disturbed from his sleep and close to a presence he didn't recognise, grizzled gently to himself. Then the warmth of the thin body against his and the darkness of the room prevailed, and he too fell asleep.

Chapter Twenty

Rab ended his walk with an enjoyable half-hour in a howff with Gregor MacEwan and some other friends. Towards the close of the evening, the cheerful gathering almost came to blows.

In company with many of the men who had formed the exiled and now disbanded Friends of the People Societies, Gregor had set up a new society, the United Scotsmen, and he had constantly urged Rab to join, without success.

'Why not?' he wanted to know angrily when his sister's husband declined yet again.

'I got enough of a fright when I was near lifted by the militia thon night. I'd've thought you'd learned your lesson too.'

'But nothing's changed! The working men are as ill thought of as before. If we let them go on bullying us and frighting us into subjection, if we don't speak up for our rights, who'll do it for us?' Gregor's fist thumped on the rough wooden table for emphasis. 'And those in work are sent to the jail for trying to get a minimum legal wage, Rab. How can a man get an assurance on what he's worth when the employers have all the rights – and the power to cut wages to boost their own profits when they show signs of falling?'

'I'm not arguing with that, man, and if there's anything

I can do in a more legal way to help the cause of the ordinary man I'll do it.'

'The legal way!' Gregor sneered. 'Where's the sense in asking the British courts to bring their precious justice to bear on the workers' behalf, when the judges are the employers as well? We'll get nothing done by appealing to the likes of them!'

'Gregor, I've a wife and bairn to think of now. I'm not free to go fleeing all over the country talking of revolution and putting myself into danger.'

'Aye – and you've got work in plenty, and silver in your pocket,' Gregor sneered. 'What need has the likes of Rab Montgomery for justice, lads? He's got all he wants already, and be damned to his fellow men.'

Anger welled up in Rab. He could tell by the gleam in the other man's eyes that he knew it, and welcomed it. MacEwan was spoiling for a fight – and he was also on the lookout for a convert for his group.

He almost had both, then Rab recalled the peaceful evening he had just spent with Rachel, the good meal they had enjoyed together. He thought of the days and nights he and Breda and their son would share in the future when Breda got better. And with a great effort he smiled, and got to his feet.

'Find someone else, Gregor. I've other things to do with my time now,' he said, and sauntered from the howff, nodding to Mally Bruce, who was huddled over a mug of ale at a table by the door.

Once outside he had a last tramp round the streets to work off the rage Gregor's taunts had fired. Then, calm again, he made for home – only to find that the baby's crib was empty, and the tumbled blankets cold to the touch.

He stared round the room in growing panic then picked

up the lamp and darted into the little bedchamber. The light in his upraised hand showed his wife's dark head on the pillow.

'Breda?' Beside himself with worry, Rab pulled the blanket from her shoulders. Blinking in the light, she turned on to her back, one white arm lifting to shade her eyes. It was then that Rab saw the tiny dark head nestled close to her.

Heart thudding, fearful of what he might find, he put the lamp down and lifted his son for only the second or third time. Rab was mortally afraid of babies; their fragility terrified him.

To his great relief Adam's eyelids flickered and his mouth opened to squeak faint protest at being disturbed yet again.

'Give him to me!' Breda snatched the little bundle from Rab and it uttered another squeak. Protectively she wrapped her arms about the baby and glared up at her husband.

'What the devil d'you think you're doing, woman? You could've smothered him, taking him into your bed like that!'

'He's mine!' There was new strength in her voice. 'I'll not have that woman you've brought around the place taking him away from me!'

Bewildered, confused, he stared at her, then said slowly, 'Breda, you've been poorly. Rachel's been a good friend to us. She's tended you and fed the bairn because you weren't able to see to him yourself.'

'I heard you laughing with her. You're not giving her my bairn!'

'There's no question of that.' Rab tried to sound calm and reasonable. 'As soon as you're back on your feet Rachel will stay away. Now' – he held out his hands –

'give the wee one to me and I'll put him back into his crib.'

Her arms tightened about the baby. 'No!'

Rab's mouth was suddenly dry. 'Breda, it's not safe, keeping him in the big bed. I've heard of bairns being stifled—'

'He's safer with me that he is with her. I'm his mother!'

Nothing he said would move her. Finally he undressed and got into bed, lying tensely at the very edge, terrified in case he dropped into a doze and rolled over and smothered or crushed his little son.

After a while he heard Breda's breathing deepen and knew that she had fallen into an exhausted sleep.

Gently, he tried to ease the child from her arms, but she woke at once, turning over in the bed so fiercely that he thought for a minute that she might dash the baby's little skull against the wall. She fell asleep again, but this time he knew better than to disturb her.

Instead he lay by her side, waiting for morning to come, fretting over what new troubles it was to bring with it.

At ease in body as well as in mind now, Rachel Fraser slept well and rose early in the morning, before the servants were about.

By the time Florrie and Greta had emerged from the bed they shared in a tiny room hard by the kitchen, yawning and scratching and knuckling sleep from their eyes, Rachel had stirred the glowing embers in the range, built up the fire for the day, and made tea.

She sat at the kitchen table, elbows propped on the scrubbed boards, and smiled at them over the rim of her cup.

'I've left enough in the pot for the two of you. Drink it quick, before you start on your work. I'll be back by the time my father rises.'

'Mistress Rachel,' Florrie warned as she lifted the pot, 'if your father knew that you were up and out at this hour . . .'

'I know.' Rachel opened the door that led through the garden to a side entrance to the street. 'So not a word to him about this – from either of you.'

'It's not seemly,' Greta grumbled when they were alone, 'for a young lady like herself to be up and about and away on secretive business at this time in the morning.'

'Specially,' Florrie agreed, scratching a tousled head with one hand and pouring tea with the other, 'when she's fortunate enough to be able to lie abed if she wants to.'

The streets were almost empty as Rachel sped through them. The few folk who were out early scarcely gave her a look, for she was dressed plainly, with a shawl about her head.

She rapped lightly on the door of the Montgomery house, opened it and went in. Just inside the kitchen she stopped short.

'Rachel—' Rab, on his knees by the range, coaxing the kindling wood into flame, got up hurriedly. His shirt was unbuttoned, his hair a mop of curls about a pale, strained face.

He was interrupted by his wife, who was huddled in a chair, a blanket about her. Within its folds Rachel glimpsed a tiny dark head pressed against Breda's small breast.

'I'm on my feet again, so there's no need for you to come about my house now,' Breda told her visitor bluntly.

The baby whimpered, a muffled sound within the blanket that bound him to his mother. Rachel recognised that sound – Adam was hungry.

She linked her hands together to keep them from

reaching for him. 'But you'll not be able to feed him properly – not for a day or two, until you get your strength back. I can—'

'We'll manage, him and me.' Breda's voice was hostile. 'I can see to my own bairn and my own home – and my own man,' she added venomously. 'You're not wanted here.'

Rachel's cheeks, bright from her walk in the cold morning air, flamed even more. Without another word she turned and walked out.

She had only gone a few steps along the road when a hand fell on her arm and Rab swung her round. He looked distraught.

'I'm sorry, lass. She'll not heed a word I say.'

Rachel eyed him stonily, refusing to allow the tears crowding to the backs of her eyes to show. 'Adam's hers, as she says – and so are you, Rab. You'd best go back to them,' she said, and left him standing on the path, staring after her.

A few moments later she slipped into the Fraser kitchen the way she had left.

'You're back early this morning,' Greta said from the range, where she was stirring the big pot of porridge.

'Mind your tongue and get on with your work,' Rachel snapped, and marched on through to the hall, leaving the serving-lassies to stare at each other in astonishment.

Upstairs, she stripped off her blouse and skirt, recovered the discarded strips of sheeting and bound them tightly about her breasts. As sounds of people rousing themselves and preparing to face another day filtered through the adjoining walls she dressed in a clean morning gown, moving slowly and stiffly like an old woman, all the vitality gone from her.

Then she left her room to descend the stairs and wait for her family in the dining room.

Chapter Twenty-One

As the century came to its close the trade slump among the silk weavers showed no signs of easing.

It began to seem to Christian that the town had taken on the very smell of hopeless poverty. Oatmeal, the staple diet of many folk, became scarce. Women and children – and men, too – queued at shops every time rumours flew that a consignment of meal was due in.

The price rose to four shillings the peck, and more than once the militia were called out to put down minor riots as people fought with each other to be served first in the shops or ran in groups through the streets, noisily protesting at the price increases.

Meetings were held, funds raised to alleviate the sufferings of the families who found themselves penniless, the bread-winners turned away from their looms.

Christian and Rachel volunteered their services at one of the public kitchens that opened up to provide the needy with food. Gallons of soup were handed out every day and John Love, a local landowner, donated four acres of potatoes to the kitchens.

Young men, unable to find work within their trade, emigrated or became soldiers or sailors and Paisley itself raised a Volunteer Corps of three hundred men.

'It's sad to see weavers and carpenters and masons taking up arms,' Christian said to Benjamin Selbie as they stood at the window of her little upstairs sitting room, watching the men march in the street below to martial music from fife and drum, their new colours billowing above their heads.

'Mebbe, but it's surely good to see Paisley men stepping forward in defence of their King and their country.'

She gave him a withering glance. 'The half of them at least are only wearing the colours because it's a way of putting food in their bellies and keeping their families alive.'

Then as a roar of laughter rose from the crowd in the street below she looked down again and a smile curved her mouth. 'Look at that – it's true what they've been saying about the other volunteer regiment – look at the bellies on them. There's the folk that are going to fight for King and country – God help us!'

Selbie looked, and grinned. Two regiments had been established in the town; the first was made up of working-class men, all of them lean and wiry, all of them needing the King's money. The second group had been recruited from the middle class, and was assembled from men who were volunteering to fight for their country, with no need of the payment to keep themselves alive.

Each time they drilled, the second regiment excited interest and amusement, and a crowd always gathered to watch these volunteers, some of them carrying more weight than was good for them, puffing and panting through their paces.

It was said in the town that watching the volunteers drill was more entertaining than going to the theatre.

'Besides,' Christian said as they marched past, red-faced, trying hard to ignore the jeers that assailed their ears from both sides, 'it's not force that'll have the last word between men, it's commerce.'

'You think so?'

'I know so.' Enthusiasm crept into her voice. She turned away from the sight of the people flocking below.

'Money means power, and folk who deal in business have the ability to use that power the right way. Not the landowners,' she added scathingly, 'for they inherited their silver and the most of them haven't got the brains to know how to use it. But those that have had to deal with others all their lives and know about the ways of the world have the knowledge and the good sense that's sorely lacking among the leaders of the country these days.'

He dropped the curtain back into place and followed her. There was admiration in the dark eyes that surveyed her, but apprehension too.

'You speak as though you're in love with commerce.'

She raised an amused eyebrow at him. 'D'you think so?'

'I've never heard a man talk of it in that way, let alone a woman. You use fine words.'

'And they're not empty words, either, so don't think that. I know what I'm saying.'

Catching sight of herself in the mantelshelf mirror she saw that her face was alight with the force of her thinking.

'Times I wish I was a man, so that I could turn my words into action!'

'Never wish that. I for one wouldn't have you any different, not for all the gold in the world.' Benjamin's voice was suddenly soft, intimate.

She flushed, and picked up an ornament, fiddling with it. 'Take care, Mister Selbie. You're turning your steps along the wrong road again.'

'It's a road I was meant to walk, like it or not. And I like it fine.'

'Even though you'll have to walk it alone, and it'll never lead anywhere?'

'I can hope,' he said, and moved towards her.

She put down the little figurine and took a hurried step back. 'Now Benjamin—'

'Christian,' he said, just as the door opened and Angus came into the room.

'This is where you are.'

Christian went to him at once, her eyes searching his face as always. For some time past he had been free of the headaches and confusion. She had begun to hope again. 'We were watching the volunteers from the window.'

Angus grimaced. 'And I, for my sins, was out in the street trying to make my way home. I'd have been here half an hour since if it hadn't been for the crowds. The delay's fairly sharpened my appetite. You're eating with us, Selbie?'

'Mistress Fraser was kind enough to invite me.'

'Good,' said Angus, and led his wife from the room.

Going downstairs, her hand linked through his arm, Christian was keenly aware of Benjamin Selbie just a few steps behind and above her. Lately she had come to realise that she was always keenly aware of his presence if he happened to be in the vicinity.

It was an intuition that was developing fast. Only a few evenings before, when she and Angus had attended a gathering at a large house, she had known the moment she set foot in the crowded drawing room that Selbie was there. The blood had bustled faster through her veins, her skin had tingled, and her whole being seemed to tauten and take on new life.

The feeling had been so strong that she had craned her neck to look for him. And found him, in a far corner, his own head turned alertly to where she stood as though he, too, shared the same extra sense.

Her growing physical awareness of the man troubled her. Not that it was unpleasant – on the contrary, it was altogether so warming and thrilling that it frightened her.

She had never in her life been so affected by anyone, even Angus.

At first, the baby had fretted for Rachel. Breda's thin flow of milk didn't satisfy him, and Rab grew used to coming home to the sound of the child's wailing, and to finding Breda trying to give him extra nourishment from a rag dipped in cow's milk, pushed into his mouth so that he could suck at it.

His suggestion that they ask Rachel to come back was met with such fury on his wife's part that he didn't make it again, deciding that his son would just have to make the best of the world he had been born into.

Although she couldn't give her baby the rich nourishment he had been receiving from Rachel Fraser, Breda made up for it by lavishing all her love on him.

Gone were the passionate nights that, in Rab's eyes, had gone a long way to making up for his wife's lack of prowess as a housekeeper. The child was scarcely out of her arms, and in the night, when he slept soundly in his crib, Breda as often as not pushed Rab's groping hands and eager body away, protesting, 'You'll wake the bairn!'

'Ach, it'll take more than a bit of loving to wake him.'

But she slapped at him then turned her back. 'Let me be! D'you not think you made me suffer enough with the last bairn without forcing more on me?'

Rab, wounded to the quick by the jibe, racked with guilt and with his need of her, would draw away from her and lie silent, staring into the darkness overhead long

after Breda slept, thinking bitterly of the days of court-
ship and the early joys of marriage.

More and more he found himself remembering Rachel
Fraser and her lively smile, her quiet soothing presence,
her loving ways with Adam.

Mebbe his mother was right, he thought in the long
dark lonely nights. Mebbe he should have married with a
Paisley lassie. If only Christian hadn't met Angus
Fraser! Perhaps then . . .

He tossed and turned, and mental images of Christian
and Rachel and Breda as she had been before marriage
changed her whirled through his alert, yet exhausted
mind.

Things were to get worse. As time went on and Adam
learned to sit up, then to crawl, then to toddle about after
his mother, a handful of her skirt clutched firmly in his
little fist, Breda Montgomery turned into a nag.

Soon her husband's face began to take on a bitter,
ageing look. He began to frequent the howffs at night,
spending more time with Gregor MacEwan and his
friends.

But when he spoke of joining the secret United
Scotsmen Society that her brother had set up Breda put
her foot down.

'D'ye want Gregor to think I'm frighted?' Discontent
with his home life had changed Rab's way of thinking.
He longed now for a cause, for the chance to hit back at
someone – anyone. 'D'ye want him to see me content to
sit by my fireside and smoke my pipe and leave the
work of trying for a better life for us all just to
him?'

'Let Gregor go his own way. I'll not risk you being put
into the jail or transported or hanged for any of his
causes. What would Adam and me do then?'

'It seems to me that you'd both manage fine with me out of the way.'

'We'd miss the silver you bring in,' she said, her mouth hard, her eyes hooded against him.

He kept out of the society as she wanted him to, but the plight of the unemployed weavers was beginning to strike at his heart. When collections were made round the loom shops Rab put more into the proferred cap than he could afford and worked long hours to make it up again.

The sight of men he knew well hanging round the street corners, their faces gaunt, their eyes desperate, were added to the thoughts and images that kept him sleepless at night.

There was a strange air about Paisley these days – a coiled-spring feeling, as though something was about to erupt. When it did, Rab learned about it from a woman who lived in the house above his.

Breda wasn't popular with her neighbours, being looked on as too high and mighty for her own good; but even so, the gossip who was taking the news from door to door couldn't stop herself from calling in on the Montgomerys, her eyes bulging from her head, her tongue so laden with the news of the crowd that was gathering in the High Street that she stuttered over the words.

Rab tossed aside the paper he was reading and looked up. 'What are you telling us, mistress?'

'Did you n-not hear me? There's word gone round that the C-Council's been storing potatoes in a cellar d-down by the Abbey – waiting until the price goes up before they sell them. And folk in the t-town starving!' She looked from husband to wife. 'The mob's off to force the cellar open!'

'Where are you going?' Breda wanted to know as Rab snatched up his coat. 'We don't need their potatoes.'

'Plenty do. And they'll need every pair of hands they can get to clear those potatoes away before the militia arrive.'

'Rab!' Her voice was shrill. 'Keep out of it – it's no business of yours or mine!'

'I've kept my hand still for long enough,' her husband said grimly. 'It's time I stood shoulder to shoulder with the rest of them!'

By the time he reached the Cross the crowd had grown to a few hundred, with folk hurrying to swell it from all directions. Rab fell into step on the fringe, marching with them over the Old Bridge towards the Abbey ruins.

Anger at folk who could store food in order to make a profit while others starved within a mile away blazed up in him. When a hand plucked at his sleeve he swung himself about, fists doubled, ready to strike down anyone who might try to hold him back from helping the crowd.

'What brings a full-bellied man out on an errand such as this?' Gregor MacEwan wanted to know. His face was more gaunt than ever, his eyes coldly bright, his mouth stretched in the thin, mirthless grin of the hunter who's scented his quarry.

In his shabby clothing, with a wolfish air of hunger about him, he was a sight to chill any fat merchant's blood.

'I'm not here for my own gain. I've come to help to get the potatoes out – if they're there.'

'Oh, they're there, all right. And I know who put them there. Are you game for firing his house once the cellar's cleared – or are you frighted?' Gregor asked, his eyes narrowing into icy slits.

Rab gave a brief moment's thought to Breda, waiting at home. He knew that there would be a violent quarrel when he finally got back.

'I'm your man,' he said.

'Good.' MacEwan gave a quick nod of the head. 'We'll have some fine sport tonight, Rab, I promise you. As for now – come with me.'

His lithe figure eeled its way through the mob and Rab went with him, dragged along by a firm grip of his sleeve. All about them people pressed forward, faces grim with purpose.

The two young men fetched up at the front of the crowd just as it reached the church by the Abbey. Someone had had the foresight to bring a stout piece of timber to act as a battering ram.

Rab and Gregor fell in with the team that was forming to operate it, the Highlander naturally taking his place at the front, Rab at the back.

'Come on lads,' Gregor yelled. 'One . . . two . . . three . . .'

The timber swung back, then forwards, and bounced off the door with a hollow thump. The crowd cheered at the noise, and the ram swung again, this time with more weight behind it. The door shook under the impact.

'It'll give. One . . . two . . . three . . .'

This time the door timbers creaked. Heartened by the sound, the team swung harder and there came the sound of splintering wood.

'One more,' Gregor bawled, and the crowd behind them suddenly fell silent, waiting. Back went the ram, then forward, the eight or ten young men holding it running full tilt at the door.

Excitement tingled through Rab's veins and gave added strength to his muscles. He threw all his weight behind the ram and felt the shock of the impact shudder through him. The splintering sound came again, louder than before.

'We've got it – again, lads!' Gregor's voice soared in a breathless screech of triumph. The timber crashed against the door with a force that wouldn't be denied.

As the broken door swung open, canting on its lower hinge, the crowd heaved a great sigh. Someone raised a cheer, but it wasn't taken up.

Gregor jumped up on to a convenient mounting block, cupping his hands to his mouth. 'Stand back – let us in so that we can see what's here.'

They obeyed him, holding their trembling eagerness in check. Someone in the forefront was carrying a blazing torch; Gregor and two others took it and disappeared into the cellar's dark jaws. They were back within seconds, faces triumphant.

There was no need for the Highlander to make an announcement. The crowd swayed and rippled and murmured as the message, 'They're in there, all right!' was carried to its outer edges.

MacEwan leapt back on to the mounting block for a moment. 'Quick now, citizens – the militia'll not be far away. Let some of us bring the potatoes out and others divide them up. When you've got your share, make for home as fast as you can!'

The battering ram was discarded and the team immediately formed themselves into a chain, passing sacks of potatoes from the cellar to the people waiting outside.

A few men and women established themselves into a second team. Each sack that came out was lifted on to the mounting block and the coarse hessian slashed with a blade.

Then the workers thrust their hands in through the hole and scooped the contents of the sack into the caps and aprons outstretched before them.

Once the precious bounty had been received the folk slipped away like shadows so that those pressing forward anxiously behind them could be served.

The feverish excitement of the mob that had pushed its way across the Old Bridge was gone, replaced by an air of urgency. They all knew that time was running out.

Sack after sack came through the dark cellar entrance. Rab's back and shoulders and thighs ached from the task of manhandling each of them from the man before him, swinging round, and passing them to the man who stood on his other side. And still they came. A never-ending store of potatoes, and a never-ending line of hungry people.

Then suddenly there was a flurry and a commotion near the bridge, and a woman on the edge of the mob screamed, high-pitched: 'The militia! God help us, they're here!'

Chapter Twenty-two

An agitated bustling spread through the crowd. Some pressed forwards towards the cellar, determined to get their share of the potatoes while there was still time, while others broke and ran for shelter, scattering throughout the New Town because retreat across the bridge was cut off by the oncoming soldiers.

'They're late, but none the more welcome for all that,' Gregor appeared from the cellar at the first call, grimy and gasping for breath, but as dauntless as ever. 'Come on, lads – the folk must see to their own harvesting now. We're off to confound the soldiers and delay them as much as we can!'

Without stopping to think Rab plunged into the crowd at his friend's back. The sight of all those sacks of potatoes locked away so that they might bring in a fine profit to the man who owned them had fanned his anger into white-hot fury.

As the crowd stampeded away from the militia he followed MacEwan in the other direction, heading towards the soldiers. As they ran they picked up any weapons they could. Without knowing where it came from Rab found himself clutching a piece of thick wooden fencing in one hand and a fair-sized stone in the other.

The militia, advancing at a purposeful trot across the bridge, halted then reeled back as they were met by a rain of stones. Then, while the young men confronting them were scrabbling on the ground for more missiles, an officer barked a command and the soldiers regrouped and lunged forward.

There was a brief skirmish, during which Rab received a painful blow on one shoulder, got in a retaliatory smack with his piece of fencing, and tripped up a uniformed figure, hearing a satisfactory grunt of pain as it crashed to the road.

Then like the others he turned and ran down a side-street, drawing the soldiers away from the cellar and the hungry people milling around it, still frantically snatching up whatever they could carry before it was too late.

He caught a glimpse of a handful of militia converging on MacEwan, who whirled to meet them, swinging a stick round his head. The Highlander knocked two men flying then went down himself beneath the others. With a howl of rage Rab went to his rescue, throwing himself into the struggling, kicking mass.

One soldier, stunned by a blow from his stick, went limp and fell away. Rab dragged the other off his friend and threw him back against the wall. The man rebounded and came at him, murder in his eyes, his musket raised as a club. Rab ducked beneath it and managed to ram his shoulder into the man's midriff.

As the soldier doubled up Rab's fist met his chin with a solid, satisfying thump. The soldier's head jerked back, his eyes glazed and his knees gave way.

'Good man! Now run, for there's more of the bastards coming.' Gregor jerked the words out breathlessly, then vanished down a convenient lane as a crowd of militia suddenly appeared at the end of the street.

Rab blew on his broken, bruised knuckles, sized up the group advancing towards him, and decided that discretion was the best policy for the moment. Besides, the longer the militia could be kept away from the cellar the better. He turned and ran, hearing the thud of booted feet behind him. Windows were being thrown open all through the town, and heads poked out to watch the goings-on.

Rab skidded round a corner into a lane, ran to the end, and shinned over a wall, landing on his feet with a thud that jarred all the way from his heels to the top of his skull. He found himself in a small back yard connected to the street by a pend.

Without stopping he ran through the pend and out into the street, then recognising where he was he proceeded to slip through closes, backlands and alleyways, getting nearer and nearer to the Old Bridge. The noise of the crowd, shouting and screaming, was behind him.

It was getting dark. Taking advantage of the gloom he dropped his stick and rested for a moment to get his breath back, bent over with hands locked on knees.

'Is it yourself, Rab Montgomery?' The quiet voice jolted him upright, fists doubling and every hair at the nape of his neck standing on edge.

'Nae need tae hit oot at me, lad,' Mally Bruce said mildly. 'Ye've been wi' the mob, hae ye?'

'Aye. What are you doing out at a time like this, ye daft old fool? Get to your house and stay there, where it's safe. When the militia get it into their heads to put down a riot they're careless about who they hurt.'

'I'm no' afraid o' the sojers,' said Mally. 'But I'm thinkin' that you should be. Come on wi' me, lad. Ye can shelter in my room 'til the stramash is a' by.'

'Leave me be and go along yourself,' Rab told him gruffly. 'I'll be all right.'

'Mistress Christian'd never forgive me if I went aff an'

left ye. Come on, now,' Mally insisted, tugging at his arm. Rab pulled back, and for a moment the two of them tussled together.

All at once there was a shout from the bridge and running figures swept down on them out of the gathering darkness. Rab caught a glimpse of Gregor MacEwan among them.

As bad luck would have it, they turned and faced the militia just at that point, and in an instant the quiet path where he and Mally argued had become a battle-ground.

With one hand Rab pushed the old knife grinder back against the wall, and with the other he snatched up his piece of fencing and threw himself into the fray. Out of the corner of his eye he saw Mally lunge forward to trip up a soldier who was passing. The man went sprawling on the footpath, and the old man let out a cackle of glee that was cut short as another soldier, chasing after someone who had pulled away from his grasp, pushed him violently out of the way.

Mally staggered back, arms wheeling as he struggled to regain his balance. He tripped over a still body lying on the ground behind him, then fell.

Even over the noise of the struggle going on around him Rab heard the sickening thud as the old man's head hit against the stone wall. He pushed away the soldier he was grappling with and stood frozen with horror for a moment. In the glow of a torch he watched helplessly as Mally slid slowly down the wall, the light dying from his eyes.

'Mally!' he yelled with all the force left in his lungs, and leapt across to the path to kneel over the old man's body. 'Oh God – Mally!'

An officer shouted an order.

'Come on, Rab, run for your life!' Gregor yelled. Rab,

dazed with the shock of Mally's sudden death, turned his head and saw three soldiers who had just arrived stand back and raise their muskets to their shoulders.

One of them, he realised, was a man he knew. They had been drawboys together. They had served their apprenticeships at the same time. Johnny, like Rab's brother Duncan, had been a silk weaver, and had lost his place when the depression started.

Now, eyes wide and disbelieving, Rab watched his old friend, in the King's uniform, point a musket at him.

'Johnny! Johnny Dunlop!'

The man heard him, recognised him, and hesitated, lowering the musket. The officer screamed at him and slowly the muzzle lifted once again.

'Run, you fool!' Gregor MacEwan yelled as he fled into the night shadows. The others had already scattered, leaving soldiers and one of their own number on the ground – and Mally Bruce sitting on the pavement, his legs stretched out before him, his head lolling on one shoulder, his eyes rolled up so that only the whites showed beneath half-closed lids.

Rab dragged himself to his feet and fled blindly, not knowing whether he was heading back into the New Town or into the older district where he lived.

There was a dry rattle of musketry behind him, like the cracking of sticks underfoot on an autumn day, and the feeling suddenly went out of one of his legs. He staggered, lurched, almost fell, then kept going somehow.

Dragging himself round the corner, he ran into Gregor and another man. They caught at his arms and pulled him with them into a close, through into the back yard. As they went, pain began to flower in his injured leg.

By the time they had lowered him to the ground and crouched beside him, listening for sounds of pursuit, the pain had become a steady pouring of molten lead from thigh to toes.

They stayed there for a long time, Gregor's hand pressed tightly to Rab Montgomery's mouth to muffle the screams that wanted, more and more, to burst from his throat.

Breda and Gregor tried for almost twenty-four hours to tend Rab's leg injury on their own. The wound got worse, and their patient became delirious.

'It's no use,' the young woman said on Sunday evening. 'I'm at my wit's end. I'll have to fetch a physician to him.'

Her brother's hand shot out and caught her wrist, his fingers squeezing painfully. 'You'll bring no physician here! As soon as the militia hear of Rab's injury they'll guess that one of their bullets found its mark.'

Rab mumbled something, but neither or them paid him any heed. 'They'll have him in the jail by morning. And the way he is' – MacEwan glanced down at his fevered, babbling brother-in-law – 'he'll name names and we'll all be taken! Is that what you want?'

She wrenched herself free, glaring at him. 'And if I don't get help for him he'll be dead by this time tomorrow, and how do I explain that away? Forbye, I've no wish to be left a widow with a bairn to support and little hope of any help from the likes of you!'

'I tell you you'll not bring a physician in here, to run tattling to the authorities! God knows they've been after me for years. But they've never had their proof. That's all they need, Breda – proof.' MacEwan's teeth gleamed in a savage grin. 'But I'll make certain that they never get it!'

Rab tossed and turned and muttered and burned with the fever while over his head brother and sister faced each other, so intent on their quarrel that for the moment he was forgotten.

'Are you a fool entirely?' Breda demanded. 'Come the morn his father's going to want to know why he's not at his loom. It's his father I'm going to now, for the man's got a sister that's married to a surgeon. There's no need for the matter to go outside Rab's own family – and they'll be as anxious as you are to keep matters quiet.'

MacEwan scowled over the proposal, gnawing at his lower lip. Then he nodded. 'Tell his father, then, and let him fetch this surgeon. But if I'm brought into it, Breda, you'll regret it. That's a promise, for I'll do whatever I must to prevent them from taking me.'

'No need to fret for your own skin. They'll not take you,' she said contemptuously, pushing past him and going to the kitchen to glance into the cradle. The baby was sound asleep. She nodded to herself and took her shawl from behind the door, winding it over her head so that her face was in shadow.

'You'd best go home,' she ordered her brother as she turned the lamp down low.

Together they slipped out of the close-mouth on to the footpath, where they separated without a word, MacEwan flitting into the gathering twilight in the direction of the Old Bridge, Breda turning towards Townhead.

News of the riot had been the sole topic of conversation in the town that day. After church the congregations flocked to inspect the broken cellar door hanging loose on one hinge, the fencing and causey-stones that had been torn up when the mob looked for weapons, the slimy scatter of crushed rotting potatoes on the ground.

Throughout breakfast in the Fraser household Angus, given the news by Florrie, ranted against the folk who had flocked in their hundreds to the Abbey to steal the potatoes: seed potatoes, it was now believed, being stored for use in the fields.

If this was true, it meant that the poor souls that had taken them had filled their bellies briefly at the cost of next year's crop. Not that Angus was in the mood to waste his sympathy and compassion on them. He was sorry for the town's poor, but he had no time for stupidity or for theft of another man's property. And in his opinion, he said for the tenth time, the raid on the cellar was a fine example of both.

Christian and Rachel listened in patient silence for a while, until Christian was finally unable to keep her tongue between her teeth any longer.

'I'd not call it theft, Angus,' she said, setting down her knife. The folk were hungry – they needed the food.'

'Taking something that doesn't belong to you is theft!'

'If you ask me, putting folk out of work and into the constant fear of starvation is more criminal than anything those poor souls did!'

Husband and wife scowled at each other, neither about to give way.

Finally Angus muttered, 'It's views like those that show why women are useless in business!' and stumped from the room.

'Sometimes,' Christian said icily to Rachel, 'your father talks terrible nonsense!'

At church the minister preached a fiery sermon on the twin sins of theft and rioting. Christian, her eyes fixed firmly on the pulpit, was nonetheless aware of her husband's triumphant sidelong glances, the twitch of lips that longed to say aloud, 'I told you so!'

Instead of returning home with his womenfolk Angus went off to the warehouse to make certain that it hadn't come to any harm during the rioting. Rachel, who at last seemed to have recovered from the loss of her child and the further loss of young Adam Montgomery, and had in the process completely shed the spoiled temperament of the girl she had once been, announced that she would pay a visit to a friend.

So Christian walked back to the house on her own, to find Benjamin Selbie pacing the drawing room.

The sight of him lifted her spirits. 'Angus is at the warehouse, but he'll not be long.'

'It's not your husband I've come to see.'

His face, Christian noted, was pale, his eyes shadowed. A tiny thrill of apprehension came into being deep in the centre of her body. 'What's happened?'

'You'll have heard of the rioting.'

'Who hasn't, by now? The whole town's seething with it. And from what I hear there'll be many a family enjoying a hot dinner today for the first time in weeks, and God's blessing on the poor souls.'

'Christian' – he paid no heed to what she was saying – 'there was an – an accident, in the midst of the running and fighting. It seems that Mally Bruce was still out with his turney lay.'

She stared at him, the apprehension growing. 'He's hurt?'

'He's dead, Christian.'

Her body was suddenly encased in ice. It didn't seem to belong with her brain any more.

'What happened?' Her voice, too, sounded like that of a stranger.

'He fell against a wall and broke his skull. Mebbe he was pushed, and mebbe he was trying to get out of the way. Nobody knows for certain, for there was so much going on.'

'Where is he?'

'They took him to the Poors' House.'

'I must go to him.'

'Better not.'

'I must!'

'Then I'll take you, when you're ready. Sit down for a minute.'

Christian shook her head. He was watching her anxiously. She took her bonnet off, laid it down and wandered about the room, unable to settle.

Mally, who had opened so many doors for her eager, hungry mind. Mally, with his sharp tongue and his fondness for drink. Mally, her closest friend. The thought of the world going calmly on as usual when Mally was no longer in it seemed ridiculous.

'Christian?'

She waved a hand impatiently, her back to him. 'I'm fine. Leave me be. It's hard to—'

She stopped abruptly, then said: 'All my adult years I've known him.' She was talking without listening to what she was saying. 'What'll the townsfolk do without him? He was the best knife grinder in the town, Mally. Did I ever tell you of how I came to buy the turney lay for him?'

'Christian,' said Benjamin Selbie from just behind her, and his voice was deep with such feeling that for the second time in her life she turned blindly and went into his arms, put her head on his chest and wept, this time for Mally.

Yet even through her grief she was aware of how right his embrace was and how well she fitted into it, as though they had been made for each other. She knew how much Mally would disapprove of such unseemly thoughts on the part of a married woman.

And the thought only made her cry all the harder.

Chapter Twenty-Three

Throughout the rest of that terrible Sunday Christian's mind went over every memory of Mally Bruce.

Benjamin Selbie, true to his word, had taken her to the Poors' Hospital, to the small bare room where Mally, his head bandaged, lay beneath a sheet on a wooden table.

Christian had stood for a long moment, looking down on him. In one way he looked so like himself that she was certain that the touch of a hand on his shoulder would bring him back to the land of the living, back to her.

In another way, the way that mattered, he was frighteningly unlike himself. There was a faintly stern, withdrawn look about the closed eyes and mouth that didn't belong to Mally Bruce. It was that remote sternness that told her, uncompromisingly, that he had gone from her for ever.

She turned away, dry-eyed, and Benjamin stepped forward, put a supporting hand beneath her elbow, and took her home. As they went, she wished fruitlessly that the clock could be turned back and the old man scooped from the streets and put safely into his house before the mob began their advance on the cellar.

'What was he thinking of, staying out so late at such a time?' she asked over and over again as the day wore on.

'There's no sense in thinking like that,' Angus said gently. The news had shocked him, and there was no more thundering about rioting and theft. 'What's done's done, Christian, and all we can do now is to make certain that the old man's decently laid to rest. I'll see to it.'

'You're a kind man, Angus Fraser.' Touched by his generosity towards someone he scarcely knew, she went to him and he put his arms about her. Christian laid her head on his shoulder for a moment – and to her horror found herself wishing that it was Benjamin Selbie who held her.

That evening, unable to sit calmly at her sewing, she put on her cloak. 'I'm going to visit with my mother for a wee while.'

Angus, who had settled down for a quiet evening with a book, put it aside at once. 'I'll come with you to make certain you're safe.'

'You'll do nothing of the kind. The streets are quiet tonight. Everyone's staying indoors, and besides, the militia are everywhere. I'll not be long,' said Christian.

To her relief it didn't take much persuasion to convince him that she was right. She needed the short walk on her own, with nobody to distract her thoughts.

When she rose to leave her parents' home her father said casually, 'I'll just walk down to the High Street with you.'

'Tuts – you're as fussy as Angus. I'm well able to go on my lone, as usual.'

'Gavin shall escort you home,' her mother said firmly.

'But I—'

'Christian, the town's still in turmoil after what happened last night. And it's getting late. I'll not let you walk down the brae on your lone – not tonight.'

'Anybody'd think the place was alive with thieves and murderers and vagabonds,' Christian grumbled as she and her father left the house.

'I'd not go so far as to say that, but nobody knows what

might happen under cover of darkness. There are trouble-makers in plenty in every town just now. Folk aren't accepting hardship quietly, the way they used to. They're speaking out about it and taking action – and I can't say I blame the poor souls,' Gavin said. 'But more often that not it's innocent by-standers like old Mally that get hurt.'

Christian thought fleetingly of Gregor MacEwan and wondered how much he had had to do with the assault on the cellar and the running skirmishes with the militia afterwards.

'How's Angus?'

'Very well, apart from bouts of tiredness. Scarcely a sore head these last few months, and not a single burst of temper. D'you not think that the inflammation might have passed over?'

'We know little about these things, Christian. He's mebbe—'

Gavin stopped and put a cautioning hand on her wrist, drawing her to a halt. They were about to enter the Almshouse pend, and someone else had come into it from the High Street side, a man whose booted feet clattered hastily over the cobblestones.

As he burst out of the pend's darkness and almost collided with them father and daughter recognised Robert Montgomery.

The weaver muttered a swift apology without even looking up, and was about to go on when Gavin said cheerfully 'You're in a rare hurry, Robert.'

The man stopped and surveyed the couple before him. 'Gavin! You're well met tonight, man – I was on my way to fetch you.'

Gavin's voice sharpened. 'Is something wrong at home?'

'Not at my home.' Robert glanced round, but there was nobody close enough to hear. 'It's our Rab.' He dropped his voice and spoke in a half-whisper. 'The lad was in that crowd down by the Abbey yesterday and he took a musket ball in the leg. He's in a bad way.'

'Yesterday? Why did you not send for me before this?'

'I knew nothing of it 'til that wife of his came knocking at my door a half-hour since. They didn't want anyone to know in case the militia got to hear of it and came for him.'

'The daft fools,' Gavin snapped.

'He's . . .' Robert Montgomery gulped air then said again, his voice taut with anxiety: 'He's in a bad way, Gavin.'

'Come on – but don't run, for we don't want to attract attention from the wrong folk.' Gavin took hold of Robert's arm and set off at a brisk, purposeful walk, asking questions and assessing the answers as he led the way through the pend and across the High Street, forced to wait impatiently for some rich man's carriage to go by before gaining the other footpath.

'Christian, it's only a step or two to your own door from here. Off with you.'

'And spend the night wondering what's happening with Rab? I'm coming with you.'

Gavin wasted no more time in arguing. The three of them went down New Street, Christian hurrying to keep up with the men's long strides, then turned in at the close.

In the tiny bedchamber Annie was bending over her son, who was half-conscious and delirious. Breda stood behind her, the baby in her arms.

Gavin took charge at once, dragging his jacket off, unfastening his shirt sleeves and rolling them up.

'Annie, I'll have a basin of hot water, if you please, and a good sharp knife, and as many clean rags as you can find. And some cold water and cloths for his head, to try to ease the fever. Robert, go to my house and tell Margaret to give you my bag. You can tell her the truth, she'll not babble to anyone.'

He turned to his patient, then said as an afterthought: 'Oh – and mind and instruct her particularly to stay at home and wait for me, for there's more than enough folk in here as it is without her coming down as well.'

The weaver ducked his head in understanding and left at once.

'Christian, since you're here you can help me.'

She nodded. Now and again before her marriage she had gone with her father when he visited his patients, and had been allowed to help him because of her ability to keep a cool head and follow instructions. It was the only time, her father used to remark dryly, when she did as she was told without asking questions.

'The rest of you can wait in the kitchen, for there's little enough room in here as it is,' Gavin finished, and waited until he and his daughter were alone with their patient before he drew back the coverlet.

Rab's right leg was swathed from thigh to ankle in blood-splotched bindings. There was blood on the sheet beneath him and on the blanket over him. His foot was red and swollen. Gavin touched it lightly with the back of one hand and Rab moaned.

'He's burning up with fever. By the looks of it he'll be lucky if he keeps this leg. Why in damnation didn't they have the sense to send for me at once? Did they think I'd betray my own wife's kin to the militia?'

Annie came in with everything he had asked for. He took it from her and brusquely ordered her out, then

277

took the knife, carefully slit the bandages, and peeled them back.

At first sight of her cousin's injured leg Christian caught her breath sharply. The wound was festering, the skin badly discoloured and swollen.

'If you're going to faint, have the good sense to do it in the kitchen,' her father said tensely, without looking up at her.

'I'm not going to faint!'

'Good. Hold his leg still.'

She did as she was told. The limb was burning hot beneath her hands. Rab groaned and rolled his head on the pillow, his lips drawn back from set teeth.

Annie brought in a second lamp so that Gavin could see what he was doing. Robert came back, handed in the medical bag, and retired to the kitchen.

Father and daughter worked over the injured man, Christian fetching and carrying, wringing out cloths in cold water and laying them on Rab's head, watching anxiously as her father worked on the mass of broken skin and bone that had once been a strong healthy limb.

Finally Gavin Knox straightened his back and stretched cramped muscles. 'We've done all we can do for the moment, lass,' he said, and went into the kitchen where Rab's wife and parents waited.

'The ball went into his leg just below the knee,' he told them bluntly, washing his bloody hands in the bowl of water Annie had prepared for him. 'It's damaged the bone. If I'd been called in right away I could have saved him a lot of suffering – and mebbe some further injury.'

'We – I thought it best to tell nobody.' Breda's voice was sullen.

'Surely Rab knew that I could be trusted,' the surgeon said dryly, then added astutely: 'Or was the decision made by someone else? Someone afraid of what Rab might say?'

Breda's face closed and she turned away, bending over the cradle. Gavin watched her for moment, then shrugged.

'Whatever the reason, the damage is done now.'

'Gavin, he's not going to die?'

'I don't think so, Annie. He's young, and he's strong. But it'll be a long hard struggle for him. My worry at the moment is that the leg might have to be amputated.'

Annie Montgomery gasped, then put her hands to her face. Robert's arm went tightly about her shoulders. Breda swung round, her small face tense with shock.

'You mean he could be crippled?'

'I hope it doesn't come to that,' Gavin told her. 'It depends on how well he fights the infection that's settled in. I'll stay here for the night to watch over him. Robert, mebbe you'd go back to the house and tell Margaret she'll not see me before morning. Christian, you've done all you can here. Off you go to your own house.'

'And what's to become of me?' Breda asked shrilly.

'You'll make me some tea,' Gavin said, 'then rest while I see to your man during the night. He'll be in need of your nursing tomorrow.'

His voice was mild, but Christian knew him well enough to recognise the undertone of distaste and dislike.

'I'm not talking of now!' said Breda impatiently. She was as lovely as ever, Christian thought, but there was a hardness to her now, the first flaw in her vivid beauty. 'What about me and my bairn if Rab loses his leg? How will we live if he can't bring in the silver to pay for food? We'll be paupers!'

With a muffled exclamation Robert Montgomery

blundered out of the house, going on his errand to Oakshawhill before his control gave way and he found himself lifting a hand to his daughter-in-law. Annie turned away, her hands clenched on her apron.

Gavin ignored Breda's question, and it was left to Christian to say: 'You've no need to worry about that, Breda. There's none of us going to let Rab and his family want while he's ill.'

'I've your word on it?'

Bile rose suddenly in Christian's throat. She had controlled her stomach while working with Rab's injuries, but his wife's indifference to his suffering, her greed during his time of trial, was more than Christian could bear.

She opened the small purse fastened to her waist, pulled out a few coins, and tossed them on to the table. Breda promptly gathered them up and tucked them into the front of her gown, pushing them well down into the valley between her small breasts without a word of gratitude.

As Christian set off for home the bitter taste of disgust was still choking her. She breathed the night air deep into her lungs as she went, but it was no use.

As she reached the side entrance to her own house she turned down it, her steps hastening until she was running to the privy in the back yard.

Fortunately it was unoccupied. She threw the door open, plunged inside, and vomited until her whole body felt hollow and light and scoured clean.

Then she wiped her mouth, shaped it into a smile, and went back along the side entrance so that she could step calmly through the street door as though nothing was amiss.

*   *   *

By the time Mally Bruce was laid to rest, with Christian, Angus, Rachel and Benjamin Selbie as his mourners, Gavin knew that he wouldn't have to amputate Rab's leg.

'But I doubt if you'll be able to ply your trade again, lad,' he told the young weaver as gently as he could. 'The bone's damaged, and you're going to be left with a stiff leg once it heals.'

The fever had broken, and Rab's face was as pale as the pillow behind his head. He tried to summon up a smile. 'At least I've held on to my life.'

Gavin nodded, and put a hand on his shoulder. 'There are other ways to earn a living.'

Breda stood at the foot of the bed, her face like stone. When the surgeon left she went into the kitchen and Rab heard her talking to the baby. He called to her, and after a long while she came to him.

'What is it?'

'Breda.' He stretched out his hand, but she was too far away for him to reach, and she didn't move forward or lift her own fingers to meet his. 'Breda,' he said again, 'don't fret yourself. We'll manage, lass.'

'Aye – on the charity of your fine relations, like Mistress Christian Fraser with her nose in the air!'

'We'll only need their help until I can get back on my feet and find other work.'

'You're a fool, Rab Montgomery,' she said viciously. 'You had to be the one to get hurt – not Gregor, not any of the others, just you!'

'I didnae ask the soldiers to fire their muskets at me!' A bitter edge came to his voice as he recalled Johnny Dunlop's face beneath his cap, the way the man he had called friend had aimed the musket when ordered. He had no way of knowing if it was Johnny who had shot him, but he did know that the man must have fired along with the others.

'You should never have been there! I wish to God,' said Breda passionately, 'that it had been Gregor that had been hit, not you.'

'You'd wish that on your own brother?'

'Why not? What's he ever done for me – or for you?'

Then she went away, taking the lamp with her, leaving him alone in the dark.

Chapter Twenty-Four

Benjamin Selbie erupted into the Fraser household without ceremony, almost knocking Florrie backwards as he came through the door.

'Is your mistress at home?'

'Aye, sir. If you'll just go into the par—'

'Where is she?'

Florrie gaped at him. Then as he said with rising impatience, 'Lassie, have you swallowed your tongue? Where is she?' she found her voice.

'In the kitchen.'

'Through here?'

'Aye, but ye cannae—'

But he had already crossed the hall and opened the door in the back wall. It led, through a short passageway, to a large warm kitchen, filled with the fragrant aroma of newly baked bread and fruit pies and oatcakes.

The mistress of the house was standing at the big wooden table, rolling out dough. Greta, the other maidservant, was measuring currants from a large earthenware container.

When Selbie burst in both women jumped. A cloud of flour rose to powder the front of Christian's apron, while the jar slipped from Greta's fingers and fell on to the table, spilling currants over the pastry.

'Now look what you've done!' Christian turned on the banker, her own fright taking refuge in anger.

Florrie's face bobbed round his arm. 'I couldnae stop him, ma'am. I telt him tae wait in the—'

'Christian, I must speak with you.' The urgency in Selbie's voice was unmistakable, and Christian's anger evaporated in fear.

'Angus—'

'Don't fret yourself, he's fine as far as I know. It's . . .' He glanced at the pop-eyed maids. 'It's a matter of business.'

Without further questioning she began to unfasten her apron swiftly. 'Greta, see that you pick up every one of those currants. And you, Florrie – finish the pastry and put the tart into the oven. Don't forget the bread'll soon be ready.'

'Where is Angus?' Selbie asked as he followed her to the parlour. 'I'd not want him to know why I've called.'

'At the warehouse – or mebbe in the Coffee House.' The Coffee House at the Cross had become a favourite meeting place for all the town's businessmen. Christian closed the parlour door and turned to the banker. 'What's amiss?'

'This.' He produced some papers from his pocket. 'A letter from Alexander. It arrived at the bank less than an hour ago. I came here as soon as I had read it. He says—'

Irked by his air of command she held her hand out for the letter. 'I'd as soon read it for myself. I may only be a woman, but I can read, Mister Selbie.'

Benjamin Selbie had the grace to colour. 'Your pardon, ma'am. I'm in such a taking that . . .' He shrugged, handed the pages over, then waited as patiently as he could while Christian scanned them.

She read her step-son's letter once, then went back to

the beginning and read it again with growing amazement. The words tumbled over themselves, the lines sloped down the pages.

Alexander, normally a meticulously exact penman, had been in such a state of alarm and confusion when he wrote this letter that he hadn't taken any care with its preparation whatsoever.

Finally Christian looked up at the banker. 'I don't understand.'

'Neither does Alexander,' he said grimly. 'Did you know that your husband had severed all connections with one of his most important London buyers?'

'I'd no idea of it. I was with him in London when he first met Peter Dawson, and they got on well together.'

'Did you know that he'd written the man a . . .' He paused.

' "A scurrilous letter?" ' she continued, quoting Alexander's letter.

'Exactly.'

'I did not. He's said nothing to me about being displeased with Mister Dawson as a business colleague.'

'And I don't suppose,' Benjamin Selbie said glumly, 'that you knew he'd summoned his son back from London to take charge of his warehouse here?'

'D'you think I'd have idly stood by and let any of these things happen? You're his banker – did you not know yourself?'

'Not about this.' He gestured towards the letter, then admitted: 'Oh, there have been a few strange happenings lately, but they were easily smoothed over and put right, and I didn't want to worry you with them. Twice he decided to invest his money in some foolish scheme but I managed to dissuade him. And I understood from Alexander that a few weeks ago his father wrote to him with some firebrand idea to do with the London side of the business, but again he was dissuaded. But he didn't consult me about this business at all. Naturally I would have talked him into a different frame of mind, if that was possible.'

'And I thought that he was so well! I'd begun to think that—' Christian stopped short, biting her lip in an effort to hold back the tears.

Benjamin Selbie made a move towards her, but she shook her head, backing away from him. 'Leave me be, Benjamin. One word of sympathy and I'll no doubt resort to being a weak woman and take an attack of the vapours. And that's the last thing I want. What'll be the result of this thing Angus has done?'

Denied the right to comfort her, he paced the floor, thinking hard. 'For one thing, he's got a warehouse in London filled with cloth that was made specially for Mister Dawson.'

'Surely Dawson must take that cloth, at least?'

'Not,' said Selbie grimly, 'after receiving a letter like the letter your husband wrote to him. Now that Angus has seen fit to tell the man that he'll not deal with him again under any circumstances, Alexander must try to sell the cloth elsewhere, probably for less than it cost to make, thus losing money for the company.'

He reached the fireplace, swung round, and started pacing towards the window. 'For another thing, if he insists on closing down his office in London and bringing Alexander back here to be the warehouse overseer, Angus will lose all the English and overseas contacts that he and his son have built up.'

'Not to mention terrifying poor Alexander with the suggestion that his life in London is over,' Christian put in with the ghost of a laugh. Selbie glanced at her, then permitted himself a faint smile.

'As you say, Alexander's in a terrible taking at the prospect of bringing his English wife up here and becoming a mere warehouse overseer instead of his own master.'

Christian indicated the letter clutched in her hand. 'And to make matters worse, this new ploy of Angus's has given Alexander the perfect excuse to say that we should have joined him in persuading his father to sign the business over to him.'

'At the moment, I can't blame him for his anger. If your husband goes on like this, there'll be no company left for Alexander to inherit. To be honest with you, this latest business could mean the end to everything right now.'

She looked at him, aghast. 'Surely it's not as bad as all that?'

'Dawson's a powerful man, and an honest man too, well respected everywhere. Slighting and insulting him was a bad move. He could see to it that the Frasers never trade in London again. And no man cares to be accused, however untruthful the accusations might be, of being a traitor to his King.'

'If only Alexander had had the wit to talk to the man!'

'Unfortunately, Alexander Fraser doesn't have half the imagination and intelligence his father . . .' Benjamin stopped short, then continued carefully: '. . . his father had at his age.'

'D'you think that if I persuaded Angus to travel to London himself he could put things right?'

'I'd not rely on it. He may well make things worse. You must go in his stead.'

'Me? But my place is here, with my husband.'

'Rachel and the servants can look after him well enough for a few days, surely. It seems to me that your presence is more urgently needed in London at this moment.'

'But what could I do?'

'Talk to Mister Dawson,' Benjamin Selbie said. 'Explain that the letter was a misunderstanding. Ask him to forgive your husband's lapse and to take up trading with the Fraser house again.'

He ran his fingers through his thick bright hair then burst out: 'Confound it, Christian, you're a woman – you could charm the birds from the trees if you wanted to. Persuade the man to change his mind.'

Anger sparked within her. 'I'd as soon persuade him with my tongue and my brain.'

'If that would do it,' said Selbie wryly, 'I'd go down to see him myself. I'm sorry if my words have offended you, but I do truly believe that gentle persuasion would sway the man more than logic. And there's no doubt in my mind that you could do it.'

He came to a standstill before her. 'Will you, Christian – for your husband's sake?'

'If it's for his sake, then I must.'

'Good,' he said crisply, then held out his hand 'I'd best keep the letters with me. And I'd best go now, before Angus comes home and wonders what I'm doing here.'

In the hall he paused, lifted his hand to her cheek. His fingers touched her so lightly that she wondered if she had imagined the caress, then fell away.

'I wish to God,' said Benjamin Selbie hoarsely, his eyes suddenly lost and lonely as they took and held hers, 'that I was this man Dawson. I envy him, being sought out by you.'

Then he opened the door and went out without another word.

Christian discovered that she was shaking. Upstairs in her sitting room she looked at her reflection in the mantel mirror and touched her face, just where his fingers had rested. And meeting her own gaze in the glass she knew that there was no sense in continuing to deny something she had denied for a long time.

She loved Benjamin Selbie, loved him with a passion she had never known before, even in her happiest moments with Angus.

She had fallen romantically in love with Angus when she was emerging from childhood to maturity. She still loved him dearly, but over the past few years she had changed and matured. Now she loved Benjamin Selbie as well, in a different way, a stronger way.

But this wondrous second love had come too late.

Her mouth softened, trembled, then firmed. There was nothing she could do about her feelings for Benjamin – other than to hope that in time they would fade and die and take the pain of wanting him with them.

She bit hard on the inside of her lip in order to ease that pain by creating a more immediate hurt, then straightened her shoulders and picked up the embroidery tambours that waited on a small table. Five minutes later, when Angus arrived home and came to the sitting room in search of her, she was stitching calmly, as though she hadn't a care in the world.

He blundered against the door as he came in, and moved across the room in a clumsy, jerky way that spoke of a bout of irritability.

'I saw that man Selbie on my way home,' he said abruptly. 'He was fleeing along the road as if the hounds of hell were after him, with a face like thunder and not a word to say for himself apart from a greeting as he went past.'

He paused, then asked: 'Was he here?'

She opened her mouth to deny it, then decided that Angus deserved better than dishonesty.

'He looked in for a moment. He'd heard of your decision to stop supplying cloth to Dawson and Pettifer.'

'Indeed I have. A man who has spoken kindly of the French in my company. I've no time for traitors.'

'I'm sure that Mister Dawson didn't mean his remarks to be traitorous,' Christian said lightly, and his face hardened.

'I'll not trade with a lover of the King's enemies.'

'But it seems that in return for your action Mister Dawson now refuses to honour the contract his company holds with yours.'

'You see?' said her husband triumphantly. 'I was right not to trust the man.'

'But ending the contract at this stage means that Alexander's left with a warehouse full of unwanted cloth.'

'If the lad's worth a penny of the silver I give him he'll find another buyer. Besides,' Angus said with sudden irritation, 'I see no need to keep on the warehouse in London. Alexander would be better suited here, where he belongs.'

'Mister Selbie's concerned that—'

Her husband interrupted her with a short bark of laughter. 'Mister Selbie's not concerned at all! I know full well why he was here, Christian, and it wasnae about the cloth for Dawson.'

'But – what other reason could there be?'

'Why would a bumble bee buzz round a flower? The man's besotted with you!'

For a moment her heart seemed to stand still. She laid the embroidery aside and got to her feet with a rustle of skirts. 'What foolish nonsense is this you've got into your head?'

'You've not seen it for yourself?'

'I have not,' Christian said firmly. 'And what's more,

I've never heard the like. Now – you'll be hungry, and Rachel's expected in at any moment. I'll away and see if the food's ready.'

He put out a hand to detain her. His mouth was pursed in a way that she hadn't seen for some time, and had hoped never to see again.

'I know what I'm talking about!' Angus said angrily. 'I'm a man and I know when a man hungers for a woman. I see it in the way he looks at you and I hear it in his voice when he speaks to you!'

He strode towards her, and for a moment she almost flinched back, remembering what had happened to Rachel when he had been in the grip of one of his rages. It took all her courage to stand still.

But he threw himself past her, his outstretched arm swinging back, his hand catching a bowl of roses that Benjamin had brought two days earlier. The delicate china vessel flew from the corner cupboard where it stood and smashed against the back of a chair. The carpet was showered with water, and as the roses – the damask roses that were Benjamin's favourites – fell to the ground Angus kicked them out of the way.

'Angus!'

Now he swung round on her, catching her shoulders in his big hands. 'Promise me, Christian, that you're mine!'

'How could you think that I—'

'Promise me!' He began to shake her, his fingers digging into her arms. She bit her lip against the pain, determined that no matter what happened she would not call out and bring the servants running. She wouldn't humiliate Angus by letting anyone else witness this scene.

'I – I promise.' The words shuddered out of her throat. 'Angus!'

He blinked, then frowned down on her, puzzled. His hands fell from her arms.

'What was I saying?' he asked in confusion.

Below, the street door opened. 'Nothing of importance,' Christian said gently, watching the anger fade away. Once again he was the man she had so joyously married. 'Nothing at all. That's Rachel back – you'll be ready for your supper.'

'Aye, I am.' He turned towards the door, then stopped, seeing the spilled flowers, the broken vase.

'What happened here?'

'My arm caught the vase and knocked it over. Florrie can see to it once we sit down to our meal.'

'Aye,' he said, adding 'It's a pity about that bowl. I bought it for you in London, did I not?'

'You did.' As they left the room, her hand tucked into the crook of his elbow, she added casually: 'Mebbe I could buy another like it. I was just thinking of going to London for a short while.'

'What would you want to do that for?' Angus asked, but mildly.

'I thought to buy myself some fine gowns, and spend time with Alexander's wife and the bairn. And I can visit Daniel too, now that he's moved to London.'

Angus indulgently patted the hand resting on his arm as they began to descend the stairs side by side. 'Aye, lassie, mebbe it would do you good to have a change of scene. You go to London – but don't stay away from me for too long.'

'I never would,' Christian promised him as they went into the dining room where Florrie was placing the big soup tureen carefully on the table.

Chapter Twenty-Five

When the stage coach finally arrived at its destination Alexander was waiting to claim Christian and see to her baggage.

'I've got a hackney waiting – confound the driver, where's the man off to now?'

He looked round, scowling, then beckoned. A small man dressed in rusty black and with his face shadowed by a three-cornered hat that was far too large for him came darting out of a chattering group and somehow managed to gather up all Christian's luggage under his short, thin arms.

Then he led the way with a bent, sideways, crablike gait to where the cab waited on the corner, out of the way of the coaches that were coming into London all the time, from all over the country.

Christian thought that Alexander, clearly younger, stronger, and more able, should take his share of the burden. But her elegant step-son strutted, empty-handed, after the driver, leaving her to follow in his wake.

He didn't ask after his father until they were seated opposite each other in the cab, jolting through the streets. When he did mention Angus, it was with an air of distaste, as though he was making the enquiry against his will.

'In his body he's well enough. As to his state of mind
– I thought that he'd greatly improved until Benjamin
Selbie brought me your letter. Alexander—'

'If you please, Christian, I'd as soon wait until we're
settled in the house before we discuss business,'
Alexander interrupted, the fingers drumming ceaselessly
on his knee.

The rest of the journey was passed in silence, during
which Christian took stock of her husband's son with a
series of swift glances from beneath her lashes.

His resemblance to Angus had increased with the
years, but even so he still lacked, and always would lack,
his father's upright bearing, his warmth and his ability to
command any gathering he entered.

Alexander was handsome in a foppish way, his fine
fair hair powdered and tied with a black velvet ribbon.
He wore pantaloons instead of breeches, and a rust-
coloured silk-embroidered coat over a white ruffled
shirt. His shoes sported fine silver buckles and he had
taken off a smart beaver hat in order to climb into the
cab's small interior.

He raised his eyes and met hers. Embarrassed at being
caught gaping, Christian looked hurriedly away, and her
attention was at once held by a group of vivid figures
lounging round the doorway of a coffee house.

They wore tiny feathered hats perched absurdly on
high, over-elaborate wigs. Their clothes were bright,
with great lacy ruffles at throat and cuff and huge buttons down the front of their coats, as well as on their
pockets and coat-tails. They wore tight-fitting breeches
and hose, and their shoes were decorated with flounces
of ribbon. Two of them carried elegant canes; a third
flourished a large lace handkerchief.

Christian stared, then asked, 'Who are they?'

The hackney was caught up in a string of carriages and carts waiting to turn a corner, so there was time for Alexander to lean forward and see the group of young men for himself.

'Macaronis,' he said laconically.

'Macaronis?' Her brow furrowed. 'Which part of the world do they come from?'

She knew at once by the pitying lift of his brow that she had blundered.

'From London, my dear step-mama. They're followers of fashion. Although now Brummell and the Prince favour less elaborate styles, so no doubt these fine gentlemen will soon be running back to their tailors.'

'Indeed,' Christian said faintly, and sank back into her corner, suddenly homesick for Paisley.

Dorothy Fraser was waiting at the door to receive her visitor, every bit as elegant as her husband in a blue muslin gown cut low in the front and waisted beneath her breasts to accommodate the swelling evidence of her second pregnancy. Some of her dark hair was piled high on her head while the rest fell down to her shoulders in ringlets.

Alexander's house had become much grander than his father's, with a number of servants in attendance. When Christian, keenly aware of the fact that it was Angus's money that kept his son in such comfort, complimented the younger Frasers on their fine home, the faint sarcasm wasn't wasted on Alexander, who flushed slightly.

'We must keep up appearances if I'm to impress buyers. We do a great deal of entertaining here.'

'I'll take you to your room,' his wife interrupted hastily. 'You'll want to rest after your journey.'

'I'd like to change out of my travelling clothes, but resting can wait until I've spoken to you about the way things are going at the warehouse, Alexander. And' – she smiled at Dorothy to soften the business-like crispness she heard in her own voice – 'I'd like fine to see the bairn.'

Oliver Fraser, Angus's grandchild, had his mother's green eyes and his father's fair hair. He was a handsome, sturdy little boy, spoiled by his doting parents, self-willed, yet endearing in his babyish assumption that the entire world had been created solely for his benefit.

Christian could have spent hours playing with him in his nursery, but Alexander was waiting downstairs, and there was a lot to be discussed.

'Well?' he asked as soon as she had settled herself in the drawing room. 'What's my father got to say for himself?'

She wished, not for the first time, that Benjamin had been able to travel to London with her. She could have done with his common sense as well as his comforting presence. But in view of Angus's sudden jealousy such a notion had been out of the question.

'If you're referring to Mister Dawson, all he has to say on that subject was said in his letter.'

'Did you not point out—'

'Alexander, you surely know your father well enough to realise that he doesn't take kindly to being told that he's in the wrong – even when he is.'

'But—'

'He's not well. He's not responsible for what he did.'

'Then for any favour take the running of the business out of his hands and turn it over to me!'

His total disregard for his father's feelings began to anger her. 'Being deprived of the business he set up himself would break his heart. Not that he'd give it up without a struggle.'

'The man's ill!'

'He doesn't know that. Mebbe you should come back

to Paisley with me and see for yourself how he is, then perhaps you'd understand the way of it.'

'I've no intention of returning to Paisley,' said Alexander huffily. 'And I've certainly no intention of becoming his warehouse overseer there.'

Some imp of mischief made Christian say blandly, 'It's an honourable occupation. I held it myself for a number of years and I liked the work fine.'

With inward amusement she watched Alexander's eyes bulge and his face change colour. 'You're surely not serious?'

'It's what Angus wants.'

The young man's tongue moistened dry lips. 'It was all very well for you,' he burst out in panic. 'You were content with the position. I'm settled in London. I've a place in society, a family to consider, a son!'

'Your son would do just as well in Scotland. Better, perhaps,' she added blandly, thinking of the colourful Macaronis she had seen earlier.

'Confound it, Christian, you're making a mock of me! Are you or are you not here to put right the damage my father's done?'

'I'm here because you didn't manage to put it right yourself,' she snapped back at him, and he subsided, red-faced.

'I did what I could,' he muttered in feeble self-defence. 'But Dawson's not an easy man to deal with when his pride's hurt.'

Dorothy appeared in the doorway and announced firmly that supper was on the table and mustn't be allowed to spoil. Alexander got to his feet immediately, the very picture of an obedient husband.

'We're going to a gathering tomorrow night,' he said as he led his guest from the room. 'You'll meet Dawson there. And you'll do what you can to make him change his mind?'

'I'll try,' Christian promised, nostrils twitching as they met the fragrant aroma of the first decent meal she had had since leaving home.

When she came face to face with Peter Dawson on the following evening she saw at once that Alexander was right – Mister Dawson wasn't easy to deal with once his pride was hurt.

She recalled the man and his wife as an affable couple, but this time his eyes, as they met hers, were cold. His wife's mouth tightened, and she did her best to look down a nose that was, unfortunately for her, snub rather than long and thin.

Recalling Mister Dawson's eye for a handsome woman, Christian had dressed in her best gown for the occasion, a green silk with low-cut bodice, and had allowed Dorothy's maidservant to dress her hair in a becoming style with ribbons through it, and soft dark ringlets resting on her white shoulders.

But there was no beguiling Peter Dawson. When Christian began, 'Mister Dawson, I hope that we can find time to talk to each other while I'm in London,' he replied at once:

'If you're here to try to persuade me to change my mind about dealing with the Fraser company, ma'am, you've had a wasted journey.'

'I'd like to explain why Angus—'

'You'll excuse us, Mistress Fraser. I must have a word with my host,' he interrupted, and walked off, his wife on his arm.

Vexed, but unable to do anything to stop them, Christian watched them go.

Alexander had been hovering on the fringe of a nearby group, tension in every line of his body. He bustled over to Christian as soon as he saw that she was alone.

'What did he say?'

'Very little.'

'Follow him, Christian – talk to him again.'

She shook her head. 'I think Mister Dawson's a fish that must be played.'

'What are you talking about?'

'I'm saying, Alexander, that I must be free to take my own good time with the man,' his step-mother told him tartly, and he had to leave it at that.

Daniel Knox had been gentle and quiet even in childhood, content to stay in the background, and quite unlike his extrovert sister.

As an adult he was still quiet, but with a quick, shrewd brain that had stood him in good stead in his chosen profession as a lawyer.

He lived with his wife and continually growing family in a large comfortable house in a less fashionable district of the city than Alexander.

Once Christian had been introduced to all her nephews and nieces, her brother and his wife handed their family over to a plump, cheerful nursemaid and drew their visitor into another room where they could hear all the news of home.

'Rab's leg's mending, thank God, but he'll never be able to follow his trade again.'

'How's he taking it?'

'Better than I first thought he would. Breda's not much help to him, though. There's talk,' said Christian miserably, 'of her being seen about the town with other men.'

'It can't be easy for her,' Anne Knox pointed out compassionately, 'with her husband half-crippled and not able to – to be a real man for her just now.'

Christian nodded. 'Aye, but even so, it's not right. He should never have married with her, and that's the truth of it.'

'But he did, so they'll have to sort out their own problems,' Daniel commented briskly. 'Now – what about Angus?'

It was a relief to be able to talk properly about Angus. Alexander and Dorothy, she had quickly discovered, disliked hearing her worries. They were only concerned about the effect Angus's illness would have on them, whereas Daniel and Anne listened sympathetically and joined together in trying to help Christian to find a way out of the morass her husband had landed his company in.

Daniel stroked his chin thoughtfully. 'I know Dawson well. He's a fair man, but self-made and a trifle thin-skinned because of it. You could take him to court and demand that he buy the cloth he contracted for, but you'd still lose his future custom as well as any goodwill he might have towards the Fraser business, and besides, it'd not help you if the truth about Angus was spread all over the city.'

'I think,' said Anne suddenly 'I might have the answer.'

Her husband grinned affectionately at her. 'I thought you might come up with something. I've learned, Christian, that where the law falls short, a shrewd woman can aye reach further!'

During the next week it seemed to Peter Dawson that he encountered Christian Fraser all over London.

When he went riding in the park she was certain to pass by in an open carriage, pretty as a picture, bowing and smiling to him when his eyes met hers.

When he went to the theatre she was in the opposite box, and when he visited friends Christian was always among the other guests, either with her step-son and his wife, or with her brother.

At first, he shied away from her, but once he realised that she had no intention of talking about her husband's business after all he began to enjoy her company and her quick wit.

Under Anne Knox's wing Christian quickly became a member of Amelia Dawson's social circle, which meant that when she wasn't actually present, Dawson became used to hearing his wife, who had soon been won over, chattering on about the Scotswoman's kindness, her warmth – and her concern over her husband's indifferent health.

Dawson, a fair man when all was said and done, listened without comment, and considered what he heard.

Chapter Twenty-Six

A brisk wind was scouring the Paisley streets, tweaking at the women's skirts and trying, in great strong gusts, to free the red cloth canopies over the market stalls at the Cross.

Several times as he strode along the walk by the river Benjamin Selbie had to clap a hand to his head to prevent his tall hat from being whisked away. He nodded to an acquaintance here and there, but didn't stop to talk. His mind was on Christian, and he hated to be diverted when he was thinking about her.

She had been in London for a week now. Benjamin had received a letter that morning, telling him of Peter Dawson's initial hostility and of the need to take time to bring the man round.

The letter was optimistic; Christian had no doubt that she would succeed in the end, although she would have to stay on in London for several more days at least.

Benjamin had read the letter over and over again. At that moment it was tucked into a small pocket in his waistcoat, resting against his heart.

His mouth was grim as he walked, for he missed Christian more than he had thought possible. Without her, the town was bleak and empty. He cursed himself for a lovesick fool, a dolt-head, an idiot. He thought wildly of leaving Paisley, of settling somewhere else – and knew at once that he couldn't live in a town that didn't offer him the chance of meeting Christian each time he turned a corner.

An extra-strong gust of wind managed to dislodge his hat, sending it bowling along the path in front of him, dangerously close to tumbling over the edge into the river below.

A lad who had been crouched on the river bank trying to coax passing flotsam from the water with a long stick skipped up to the footpath and intercepted the tall hat, managing to insert the end of his stick inside it as it flew past him.

Grinning, he took a firm hold of it and brought it back to its owner, presenting it with a cheeky bow.

Benjamin tossed him a coin, which was caught in mid-air, then smoothed his thick, wind-tousled hair and clamped the hat securely on top of it as he took the lane to the right. He was going to visit the Fraser warehouse, partly because he had taken to calling in now and again to see Angus, but mainly because the warehouse was a link with Christian.

A cart was being loaded with bales of cloth in the yard. The horse had tired of waiting and was tossing its head and stamping its big hooves, made nervous by the wind that was funnelled by buildings on both sides and forced to roar through the narrow conduit offered by the yard.

As Benjamin crossed to the warehouse door a piece of rag went flapping like a tattered bird past the animal, which reared up, eyes rolling and iron-shod hooves striking sparks from the cobblestones. The carter's lad jumped to the horse's head to take the reins, talking soothingly to the great beast.

Inside the warehouse the sound of the wind was muted to an eerie howling, and the hems of the warehouse girls fluttered in the draughts that came in through gaps in the wooden walls.

As Selbie had expected, Angus Fraser was standing at the high desk, a big ledger open before him.

'I'd word from Christian this morning,' he said when a few small matters of business between himself and the banker were over.

'How is she?' Benjamin had more sense than to let the man know that he too had received a letter.

'Well enough – and having a pleasant time by the sound of it.' Angus's fingers twiddled with the buttons on his coat as he talked. He was restless this morning, fidgeting with the papers on the desk, the quill, the inkwell.

He reminded Benjamin of a volcano trembling on the verge of eruption. The workers nearby were watching him uneasily from the corners of their eyes. His sudden tempers were well known now.

'I wish she would come home,' he said, a fretful note creeping into his voice.

'I was about to go to the Coffee House. Come along with me and we'll see who's there,' the young man suggested.

'I will, I will – when that confounded cart's finished loading and gone on its way. Devil take them, they should have finished loading a good ten minutes since!'

He took out his silver watch and studied it, then bellowed, 'Maxwell!' without warning into the dim depths of the warehouse. Despite himself, the banker jumped, taken aback by the suddenness of the roar. 'Maxwell!'

A nervous young man came scurrying at once to explain that the overseer was out in the yard. 'I'll fetch him, Mister Fraser.'

'I'll fetch him myself,' his master snapped, his face beginning to redden ominously. 'And I'll have something to say to him, too! I'll not have deliveries from this warehouse made late because of his laziness!'

The cautioning hand Benjamin laid on his arm was thrown off. Angus Fraser stormed out of the warehouse door, thrusting his way through a group of weavers who had just arrived to see him, and marched into the yard. As he went, his unbuttoned coat, caught by the wind, flew out on each side like giant wings. From the back, head thrust into his shoulders, he resembled a huge bird of doom.

'Maxwell!' he bellowed and, spotting the overseer, who was helping to carry out a bale of cloth, he went charging towards the man, across the open space and past the great carthorse.

As he reached the animal, Angus, with eyes for nothing but the tardy overseer, yelled out the man's name again and lifted his arms, shaking both fists.

The wind flapped his open coat beneath the very nose of the horse, which reared in terror, dragging the reins from the hands of the carter's lad.

'Fraser!' Benjamin Selbie, who had been watching from the warehouse door, threw himself forward in an attempt to push the man out of the way. The carter and overseer on the other side of the yard did the same, but they were all too far away. Benjamin measured his length on the ground, feeling pain jolt through his forearm to his hand as his elbow cracked against the cobbles. He began to scramble to his feet then froze, horrified, as one of the flailing hooves caught Angus Fraser's temple and sent him spinning like a rag doll across the yard to crash sickeningly into the stone wall of the loading shed.

From there he fell into a puddle almost at the feet of his overseer, and lay still.

It was during the interval at the concert hall that Peter Dawson excused himself, left his wife and the group of friends she chatted to, and crossed the parquet ante-room to where Mistress Christian Fraser happened to be standing alone, within sight of him as usual, and looking extremely young and pretty.

She glanced up as he approached, and smiled at him. He wondered, briefly and with a twinge of envy, how on earth Angus Fraser, who was his own age, had ever managed to catch such a prize as this second wife of his.

'Mistress Fraser.'

She inclined her head, and the brilliant light from the overhead chandelier sparkled on the gems that swung from her neat ear lobes. 'Good evening to you, Mister Dawson. I trust you're enjoying the recital?'

'It suits me well enough,' he said vaguely, and plunged into the matter in hand. 'Mistress Fraser, I'd like to talk business with you for a moment, if you've no objection . . .'

Christian could scarcely keep from bouncing like an excited child on the carriage seat as she and Alexander and Dorothy left the thronged concert hall behind.

'It was Mister Dawson who approached you, when all was said and done – not the other way around,' Alexander said at last, a trifle sourly. 'He'd had time to think things over and he'd decided that he'd acted hastily in cancelling the contract. It's as simple as that.'

Having summoned Christian to London to put matters right, he was put out because she had managed to do just that without his help.

'Perhaps,' she agreed sweetly, too elated to argue, or to point out that she had, as she had said she would at the beginning, been playing the merchant like a fish on a line until he came quietly to the shallows to be taken.

Now, she couldn't wait to give Benjamin the good news.

'I must go home as soon as possible,' she announced as the carriage bumped its way to the Fraser house. 'Tomorrow, if I can.'

'But we've all been invited to Lady Carruther's house tomorrow night,' Dorothy protested.

Christian gave a flap of an arm. 'Tuts, I'm sure her ladyship can manage very well without me. And I've got important business to see to at home. Alexander, you must find out how soon I can travel back. Don't forget,' she added cunningly as Dorothy began to protest, 'that your father's still of a mind to close down the warehouse and summon you back to Paisley. Now that Mister Dawson's taken up the contract again we must do all we can to keep you here, where you're needed.'

As she had expected, Alexander and Dorothy immediately gave their full support to her return to Paisley.

The thought of going home made Christian feel lightheaded with happiness. When the cab stopped she scarcely gave Alexander time to get out and help her to the ground.

She skipped to the footpath while he was in the process of reaching his hand up to her, ran lightly up the stairs to where the housekeeper, who had been watching for the carriage, stood at the open door.

'There's a gentleman called to see you, Mistress Fraser,' the woman said as soon as Christian was in the hall. 'I told him that you'd be late, but he—'

The drawing room door was thrown open and

Benjamin Selbie appeared, hatless and dust-stained, still in his travelling clothes. In the lamplight his hair, combed time and time again by distraught fingers during his wait, stood up in a tumbled mass of gleaming curls about a face that was drawn with exhaustion.

'Christian – I couldn't leave it until the morning . . .'

The triumph and joy drained from her as he advanced across the hall, hands outstretched. She knew in one glance that her journey to London had been made for nothing.

She knew, before his lips had begun to shape the words, what he had come hurrying from Paisley to tell her.

Chapter Twenty-Seven

It came as a considerable shock to Christian when Alexander Fraser announced after his father's elaborate funeral that he intended to sell the business Angus had built up from nothing.

'You can't do that!'

Alexander faced her across the High Street parlour, his face set and stubborn. 'I can and I will.'

'But Angus—'

'Is dead and buried, and I've no intention of toiling all my days the way he did,' Alexander said crisply. 'I've got my own son to consider, and the children yet to come. Dorothy and I have discussed the whole matter, and we're in agreement. If I sell the Fraser company and invest the money well we can live comfortably on the proceeds.'

Christian clenched her fists impotently. 'And you care nothing for what your father would have wanted?'

'He lived his life – I intend to live mine. As to this house,' Alexander went on relentlessly, 'it shall, of course, be a home for you and Rachel for as long as you both need it. Then it will be sold, for I've no intention of ever returning to Paisley.'

For the first time he looked and sounded like his father. For the first time he was doing what he wanted, not what he was bid, and she knew by the heartbreakingly familiar set of his mouth, his Fraser mouth, that there was nothing she could do to stop him.

Furious, but helpless, she shrugged and said quietly: 'Very well, if your mind's set on it you must do as you think best. But for my part, Alexander, I think you're betraying your father.'

'That,' said her step-son, 'is of no concern to me.'

Her fingers itched to slap his self-righteous face. She could tell by the slight flaring of his nostrils, the nervousness that flashed in his eyes, the way he took an involuntary step back that he was aware of her rage, and afraid of it.

But for his dead father's sake she kept her temper under control until she was at last free to retire to the room she had shared with Angus.

There, she threw herself on to the big bed and wept angry tears, her clenched fists hammering into the high soft pillows.

After a while, the tears spent, she sat up, dried her eyes, and began to think about her own future.

On the following day Christian, dressed from head to toe in the mourning black that she would wear for at least a year, walked to the Union Bank in Gauze Street and asked for Benjamin Selbie.

He came to her at once and led her into a small private room. 'How are you, Christian?' His brown eyes studied her face.

'I'll be all the better when Alexander and his wife leave for England,' she said tartly. 'Oh, they've been kind enough in their own way, but Rachel and I need to have the house to ourselves again.' Then she added flatly, 'Alexander's selling the firm.'

'What?' Selbie looked dumbfounded. 'He's not said anything to me about it.'

'Oh, he'll be along to see you today, mark my words. I thought I'd get to you before he did.' She smoothed her skirt, then looked up at him. 'Benjamin, I want to buy the Fraser company from Alexander.'

When he had found his voice again he said cautiously: 'And who would run it?'

'I would – who else is there?'

'But you're a woman!'

'A woman's as well able as a man to run a business. Plenty of women in Paisley earn their own living very well.'

'But they run sweetie shops and glove shops, or employ tambourers or girls to knit garments.'

'And I'm talking of becoming a manufacturer – a cork. And corks are always men. That doesn't mean to say that things can't change,' Christian said with passion. 'I ran my own tambouring business when I was a slip of a lassie – and I was a warehouse overseer for Angus. I've just won back our most important buyer in London – does that not say something for my ability?'

She leaned forward, gloved hands unconsciously fisting in her lap. 'I can do it, Benjamin! I can run the Fraser business. But I need your help to buy it from Alexander, for I've no money to speak of. What do I have to do?'

He gnawed his lower lip for a moment, eyeing her with a mixture of disbelief, exasperation and admiration, then said, 'If you're serious, then you must ask the bank to lend you the money you need.'

'Will they give it to me?'

'I can't tell. You're well known in the town, and so's your family, but you don't have anything of your own to put against the loan. How much is Alexander asking for the company?'

'I don't know as yet. No doubt he'll tell you himself before the day's out.'

Benjamin nodded. 'I'll see what I can do about raising a loan for you, but it would help if you could put forward some money yourself.'

It was Christian's turn to nibble on her lip. 'There's mebbe one way,' she said after a moment's intense thought, and got to her feet. 'I'll go this very day and see what I can do. Thank you for not making a mock of my idea, Benjamin.'

'I know better than to mock any of your ideas,' he said wryly.

As she walked along Smithhills five minutes later her step-son came marching purposefully towards her, almost certainly on his way to the bank. He stopped, puzzled to see her there, and raised his hat.

Christian inclined her head, gave him a dry 'good morning' and walked on. She had just crossed the Old Bridge when she remembered that she had promised Rachel that she would pay a visit to Rab. She made for New Street and went in at the close where her cousin lived.

Rab was alone, sitting by the grate in the kitchen, his bandaged leg stiff and straight before him and a roughly made crutch by his side. Christian drew her gloves off and took a seat opposite him.

'How are you?'

'Damned well useless to everyone, including myself.' His voice was sullen, his eyes lifeless.

'Tuts, Rab Montgomery, that's not the way to talk!'

'Don't try to raise my spirits with empty words, Christian. I thought that you of all folk would have more sense.'

She noted with concern that the bitter lines on his face had come to stay. The cheerful, sturdy young man who had once been her best friend had gone as surely as Angus Fraser. Rab had been forced to mature, and in that maturing he had changed almost beyond recognition.

'Rachel tells me that she visits from time to time.'

'Aye. She's a kindly soul, Rachel.'

'She's fond of you,' Christian said quietly, then: 'How's Adam?'

For the first time a smile touched his lips. 'Coming on well. It's grand to have a bairn, Christian.'

'Aye.' For a moment it was her turn to feel bleak. If she and Angus had only had a son, she thought, she would have had someone to fight for, someone to go on building the Fraser business for. A Fraser who would have been raised to carry on the duty that Alexander had refused to accept.

Rab, struck to the heart by the expression on her face, startled for once out of his self-pity, reached across the little rag rug and touched her hand. 'I'm sorry, Christian, I didnae mean anything by it.'

She blinked back the thought of what might have been and smiled at him. 'I know that.' Then after a moment's silence she asked: 'D'you mind the night I made you swim with me in the Hammills and you had to drag me ashore when I near drowned?'

He grinned, and the old carefree Rab looked at her out of his eyes for a few seconds. 'I mind it well. We've both walked a long road since then.' Then the grin faded and the bitterness came back. 'And I mind telling you that I wanted to marry you, and being turned away. Now you're widowed – and I'm tied to Breda.'

'Ach, we'd never have made a success of it! You and me – we're too alike to be happy together!'

'I'd not have minded giving it a try,' he said, low-voiced.

They were moving on to dangerous ground now. Christian smoothed her gloves in her lap and said briskly: 'Angus's son's got a mind to sell the business, and I'm thinking of buying it.'

'You – a cork?'

'And why not? It's not certain, so don't speak about it to anyone. I'm trying to raise the silver. If I do,' said Christian without stopping to think, 'will you come in as my warehouse overseer?'

'D'you mean it?'

'Would I say it if I didn't mean it? I thought it was your leg that got in the way of the musket shot, not your brain! You know all about the trade, and you know most of the weavers that work for Frasers. I'd not want anyone else – unless you refuse me.'

She saw a faint spark of hope begin to glow in his eyes. 'I'll not do that!'

'Mind, it's not certain. But if I get the warehouse, you're the man I need to run it,' said Christian.

A few minutes later her brow was furrowed in thought as she gained the top of New Street, crossed over, and went through the pend that led to Oakshawhill.

She had fully intended to run the warehouse herself if she managed to buy Alexander out. Finding wages for her cousin would be an added financial drain, but in the face of his misery the offer of work had popped out, and it was too late to go back on it. Now Rab was eagerly relying on a good outcome to her negotiations. She couldn't let him down.

Christian told herself grimly, as she began the uphill walk, that now she must work twice as hard to get what she wanted, for Rab's sake as well as Angus's.

* * *

'Lassie, you've not been widowed two minutes and here you are tossing high-falutin' ideas about the future at me!' Mary MacLeod's voice was dry.

'They're not high-falutin' at all. They're perfectly sound. What would you have me do – sit around in my widow's weeds for my year's mourning then hope to find another man to take me on?'

'Other women do. You're not a nebby wee lass now, Christian. You'd have no trouble finding another man.'

'Angus was a good man, and I want to see to it that his business is kept on, not sold to some stranger who won't give a fig about all the hard work that's gone into building it.'

'I thought I'd played my part when you came to me for the silver for a turney lay for Mally Bruce all those years ago.'

'I paid back the price of it, did I not?'

'You did – within the year.'

'Just so. And I'll settle this loan too. You've got my word on it. I'll not take a penny to myself, except what I need for food for me and Rachel, until the money I borrow's paid back, to you and to the bank.'

For a moment Mary's fingers drummed thoughtfully on the table by her chair. 'Are you certain you're doing the right thing, Christian? It'll not be easy. The corks'll not take kindly to a woman in their midst.'

'Then they must get used to it or look the other way. I'm certain, Aunt Mary. But Benjamin says that I must have some money behind me or the bank won't even consider a loan.'

There was another pause.

'I'll tell you what I'll do,' said Mary MacLeod. 'I'm an old woman now—'

'Away! You'll live for years yet, Aunt Mary.'

'Stop flattering me, Christian, you know fine it irritates my skin as bad as lice.'

'If it's the repayment you're worrying about I'll make it as soon as I can.' The corners of Christian's mouth suddenly quirked. That'll keep you alive – waiting for it all to be given back to you.'

'Cheeky besom!' her aunt snapped, and put a beringed hand to her mouth to hide her own smile. 'I was about to say before you interrupted me – as usual – that I'm not getting any younger and I've been giving a lot of thought lately to what I'm going to do with my silver, not having any bairns of my own to pass it to. I was going to make an equal division among you and Daniel and your cousins, but it seems daft to me to make folk wait until I'm under the ground if the money's going to be of use to them while I'm still here to see them enjoy it.'

She stopped to draw breath, then leaned forward in her chair. 'I'll not lend anything to you, Christian. But I'll give you the silver I was going to leave to you.'

'I couldn't take it!'

'You can accept my offer or wait empty-handed until I'm gone,' her aunt told her firmly. 'That way, if things go the wrong way for you it's your money you've lost, not mine. But mind – when I die there's no more silver for you. You'll be fortunate if you get a pair of gloves from my will.'

'If I do I'll treasure them always. Thank you, Aunt Mary!' Christian hugged the old lady, who submitted to the caress for a moment before pushing her away.

'Tuts! Mind you're a grown woman, and a widow at that. It's not seemly, skipping round the room like a bairn. That's just the way you behaved when I gave you the money for the turney lay.'

She blew her nose vigorously into a delicate, lacy little handkerchief then added: 'And now you've set your bonnet all awry.'

Christian laughed, looked into the handsome gilt-edged mirror, and put her bonnet straight.

'I'll let you know as soon as I get word from the bank.'

She paused in the doorway on her way out. 'Aunt Mary, since you say you'd as soon see your money put to use when it's needed – Rab's in sore need of silver just now.'

'I've already thought of that,' her great-aunt said. 'But not a penny of his inheritance will he get from me while that wife of his is there to get her hands on it. Once I'm gone she can do as she pleases, but not until then. Rab's made his own bed, and hard and lumpy though it might be, he'll have to lie on it, poor lad.'

'There's one more thing – could you mebbe let me know of anyone looking for maidservants? I'll have to let Florrie and Greta go, for I'll not be able to pay their wages. I want to find good places for them.'

'Who's to see to the house if you turn your serving-lassies off?'

'I can cook a plain meal and bake bread and scrub a floor. And Rachel won't be averse to doing her share of the work.'

'She'd be better marrying well. I could look about for a man for her an' all,' Mary offered, bright-eyed.

Christian recalled the flush that came to her step-daughter's cheeks whenever Rab Montgomery's name was mentioned, and the habit Rachel had got into of calling on Rab when she knew Breda was out of the house.

'I think Rachel's got her own views on marriage, Aunt Mary.'

Her aunt sniffed. 'It must be a gey strange household that, with two self-willed women in it!'

As she went along the High Street Christian skirted a group of people watching a man paste a notice to a wall. She stopped to crane her neck, and saw that it offered a reward to anyone who could give the authorities the names of local men who belonged to the outlawed United Scotsmen Societies.

'I'd die in the gutter with my ribs sticking to my backbone afore I'd sell a man to the courts for flogging or hanging or transportation!' a gaunt middle-aged woman was saying loudly, indignantly, to all about her.

Christian nodded agreement and went on to the house, where she found Florrie in her bedchamber, packing away the bright clothes that could not be worn until the period of mourning was over.

She sent the girl off to clean out the parlour and got on with the work herself, carefully folding and putting away the silks and muslins that Angus had delighted to see her in.

When she got to the two beautiful shawls he had bought for her at Spitalfield market she hesitated, then put them aside to be studied later.

An idea that had been loitering at the back of her mind for a long time was beginning to take shape.

Chapter Twenty-Eight

Rab Montgomery shifted in his chair and eased his aching leg.

Adam, playing on the floor by the window with a wooden dog Rachel had given him, looked up at the movement, his blue eyes round with apprehension. Long-dried tears had made a dirty path down each of the child's plump little cheeks. Seeing them, and the anxious look on his son's face, Rob cursed his own bad temper.

He held out a hand. 'Come on and show me the wee dog, son.'

Adam came slowly but obediently, hoisting himself from the floor to waddle towards his father on feet set well apart so that they would support his body on the journey across the floor. Rab took the toy from him, then clumsily hoisted the little boy on to his knee. Pain jolted through his leg as he did so, making him wince, but he gritted his teeth and ignored it.

'Mam?'

'Your mammy'll be home soon,' Rab assured the child. He gave the toy back to Adam, gathered him into his arms, and rocked him to and fro, crooning a song he remembered his mother singing to him when he was a toddler.

He'd been a fool to strike Breda. God knew the woman had driven him to the point of madness more than once, but until that day he had managed to control himself, getting away from her constant nagging by limping into the other room or going outside to lean against the house wall.

Rab knew that a lot of men thought that wives needed to be kept in their place. He knew men who were over-quick to lift their hands when their womenfolk needed to be disciplined. But it had never been his way, and until recently he had thought that it never would be.

At times he had worried about Breda's possessive love for Adam, and the effect it would have on the child as he grew to manhood, but even then he had kept quiet, held back, promised himself that once he was up and about again things would be different. He would earn good money again, give Breda the things she wanted, see to it that Adam wasn't ruined by her attentions.

But all that must wait until later, when he was his own man again. Until then he would keep his tongue between his teeth and not cause further trouble between himself and his wife.

That afternoon, however, when her tongue had been particularly virulent, his temper had snapped. He had given her a hefty open-handed slap across the face that rocked her back against the table and set Adam to screaming with fear.

Breda had said not a word. She had glared at him with murderous hate, then snatched her shawl from its nail at the back of the door and stormed from the house, not even stopping to gather up the child. And she hadn't come back.

Worry nagged at Rab more than the pain of his bad leg. What if she stayed away? What if she had gone off with someone and he was left to look after the bairn?

How could a man who was, for the moment, a cripple,

care for a child the way a mother could?

He knew, although he wouldn't even admit it to himself, about the men Breda sometimes met when she went out alone at night after the evening meal was over and Adam settled in his crib. She refused to say where she was going, but she always came back bright-eyed, moving as languorously as a sated cat, and with a smell of ale about her.

Gregor had told him that she visited the howffs. Gregor had taken her to task more than once, Rab knew, but she had ignored him. There was little love between brother and sister, and now that Breda had a husband Gregor no longer had any right to tell her what to do.

'You want to take your belt to that one,' the Highlander had told his friend on more than one occasion. But Rab always shook his head. Once he was able to walk without a stick, once he was earning his own money and not dependent on charity from his family, things would improve. He and Breda might even be happy together again, as they had been in the early days.

Adam, almost asleep on his lap, suddenly withdrew a thumb from his mouth and said joyfully, 'Mam!'

He had begun to scramble from his father's lap, setting the bad leg into a jangle of pain, before Rab heard the rattle of the latch.

Breda scooped the little boy into her arms, kissing and petting him, then put him down again and took off her shawl and set about making the evening meal without a word to Rab.

He watched as she skilfully peeled and sliced vegetables and put them with a meat bone into a pot of water. There was high colour in her face, and an air of subdued excitement about her that made him uneasy.

As she set the pot on the range he said awkwardly,

'Breda lass – I'm vexed with myself. I should never have struck you as I did.'

'You'll not do it again, Rab Montgomery,' she said with frightening calmness.

'I never would! I was just – you drove me to madness with your talk. Breda—'

She looked at him, then looked away.

They ate their meal in silence. Adam, aware of the tension between his parents, was tearful and difficult, refusing to drink the milk his mother had brought in specially for him. Finally she took him on her knee and held the cup to his lips.

'Drink it for me,' she coaxed, then, when he turned his head away: 'Drink it, I said!'

'Breda, there's no sense in forcing him.'

She ignored him, tipping the liquid down Adam's throat until he choked and swallowed, making him drink until the cup was drained. Then she wiped his face and kissed him and nursed him in her arms, singing a Gaelic song to him, until soon his lids drooped and he slept.

'I'll put him into his nightshirt later,' Breda said, and laid him in his crib. Then she sat down with her knitting wires.

Rab tried to read the book on his lap but his mind couldn't concentrate on it. Finally he said, 'Come to bed, lass.'

'When I've finished this. You go on ahead of me.'

Clumsily, he undressed and washed and put on his nightshirt. He climbed thankfully into bed and lay listening to her movements in the next room, waiting for her to join him.

He dozed, and woke with a start as he heard the outer door close quietly.

With a feeling of sick dread, he called her name.

There was a waiting silence in the next room, as though someone was motionless, holding their breath. Then Rab's straining ears heard swift, mysterious rustlings, and the baby gave a sleepy whimper of protest.

He scrambled out of bed as quickly as he could and, seizing the crutch that leaned by the bed, limped over the cold floor to the doorway.

Breda hadn't gone out after all. She was in the kitchen, in the act of wrapping Adam tightly against her body with a blanket, so that she could carry him. A small cloth bag was close by her hand.

'What are you doing, woman?'

She looked at him as though he was a stranger, then said: 'I'm taking my bairn and going away to some place better than here.'

'Who with?' Rage at the faceless man who was stealing his wife and child from him rose up and almost choked the words in his throat.

She laughed at him. 'D'ye think I'd be so daft as to go from the griddle into the fire? I can see to myself.'

'You'll not take Adam from me!'

'He's mine,' Breda said coldly. 'I carried him and I birthed him and I'll not leave him behind.'

'But how can you feed him? What about putting a roof over his head?'

Her eyes met his, then slithered away. 'I've got silver enough to see to the two of us.'

'You're havering! There's no money in this house, and who'd give silver to—'

He stopped, reading the truth in her face, not wanting to believe it, yet knowing that it had to be right. He thought of the sound that had wakened him, the sound that he had thought to be her going out. She had been coming in – coming back to gather up her child and a few of her belongings before fleeing from a town she could no longer live in.

He recalled the posters that had been pasted up all over the town. And he knew.

'God, Breda, you've been to the militia,' Rab said, the words as heavy as stones in his mouth. 'You've told on Gregor – your own flesh and blood. You've taken their money—'

'What's Gregor MacEwan to you?' she spat at him like a cornered wildcat. 'He's done nothing for us but cause us trouble!'

As she made for the door Rab tried to reach it first to bar her way, cursing the bad leg that held him back. 'You're not leaving this house. You're not taking my son!'

She hit out with the arm that was free of the blanket. The bag she was carrying caught the side of his head and he lost his balance and fell to the floor, his crutch clattering off into a corner. A great gout of fire ran the length of his bad leg, licking out along the veins and muscles from knee to ankle, taking the breath from him.

By the time he had struggled to a sitting position she was gone.

Rab's urgency only made him clumsier. He fell twice before finally managing to get to his feet, sick and dizzy with pain. Holding on to the furniture, he managed to reach his crutch, then got the door opened and limped out to the street. There was no sign of Breda.

He knew where Gregor would be. There was a meeting of the United Scotsmen that evening. Breda knew of it too – and by now, so did the militia.

Realising that he had little chance of reaching the howff before the soldiers got there Rab turned back into the close and hammered on the door opposite his own.

When Mistress Stewart opened it he asked urgently: 'Is your laddie at home?'

'Aye, he's jist havin' his supper. Lachie, you're wanted,' she skirled into the dark stuffy interior of the house, and the boy came scampering to the door.

Rab dug into his pocket and, by the grace of God, found a coin. 'Here, lad – get down to Becky MacBride's howff as fast as you can and tell Becky you've to be let into the backroom. Gregor MacEwan's there. Tell him – tell him the militia are coming for him. Tell him and the men he's with to get out of there! And you be careful, mind.'

His eyes like saucers, the boy nodded, eeled round his mother, and ran.

'Don't you worry about him. If onyone can get tae the howff afore the sojers it's my Lachie,' Mistress Stewart said proudly, then added in concern, 'Mister Montgomery, ye look awful ill. Come away in, son, an' hae a sup o' ale tae ease ye.'

He thanked her and made some excuse, wanting only to get back to his own house, to be alone.

Fifteen minutes dragged slowly by before he heard the boy's swift, light footsteps returning, together with a heavier tread. Rab pressed back in his chair, his heart in his mouth.

Outside the door the two pairs of feet stopped and there was the sound of a man's voice, low-pitched. Then the door latch lifted and Gregor MacEwan came into the room.

At the sight of him Rab's pent-up breath was expelled in a long sigh of relief. 'You got away in time!'

'I got away because I was held back, and late in getting to the howff.'

MacEwan dropped his tall thin body into a chair. His

face was even more wolf-like tonight, the skin drawn back tightly against the bones. 'But it was too late for the other six poor souls. I saw the soldiers running in at the door as I came along the road so I ducked into a doorway and watched. Then the laddie you sent came running, and found me there. We watched the rest of them being taken away.'

His eyes swept round the room 'Where's Breda?'

'She's gone, and taken Adam with her.'

'Sold us for silver, did she?'

There was no sense in denying it. Rab nodded wretchedly, and Gregor took a moment to curse his sister fluently, viciously, in Gaelic. Then he said 'Where has she gone?'

'I don't know. She's been away this past half-hour.'

'There's a coach leaves the Waingaitend just about now,' the Highlander said, and got to his feet. 'She'll not dare to board it there, just in case her wee plan goes wrong. She'll have gone outside the town, to stop the coach on the road where there's nobody to see her.'

'Gregor – don't hurt her!'

The brilliant blue eyes looking down on Rab were cold and blank. They struck fear deep into his heart.

'Don't – hurt her,' he repeated, pleadingly.

'This matter's between me and my sister,' the man said, his voice empty of all feeling, and slipped out of the door.

The next sixty minutes or so crawled by one after another. The clock on the wall that Breda had been so proud of when they first set up house ticked off each second with a sound that rang in Rab's ears like the knell of doom.

He waited and worried, pacing the floor with a

monotonous thump of the crutch and a hop of his good foot. When he finally heard steps at the window, then in the close, he turned to the door, his mouth dry.

Gregor MacEwan carried a small still bundle wrapped in the blanket Breda had wrapped herself and Adam in before leaving.

'Here,' he said, and Rab took the bundle from him, pushing the material back to see his son's slumbering face. 'She must have given the bairn something to make him sleep. He's not stirred – mercifully for him.'

'And Breda?' Rab looked at his friend's face and saw a grey-white death-mask. Suddenly his whole body was icy cold with terror.

'Dear God, Gregor MacEwan,' he whispered through rigid lips, 'what have you done to my wife?'

'My sister betrayed me, and my friends are suffering for it. D'ye think I'd let her away with that?'

There was a great lump in Rab's throat. He wanted to run at the other man, to close his hands round his neck and make him spit out the truth of what had happened to Breda, but the weight of the sleeping child burdened him.

'You're best not to know things ahead of time, for your own sake,' the expressionless voice went on. 'Breda went out and left you to mind the bairn, as she's done many a night before this. You've not seen me tonight, and you'll never see me again.'

Everything swam before Rab's eyes as they filled with frightened, helpless tears. 'Damn you, Gregor MacEwan!' he said thickly.

'I'm damned already,' said Gregor, and slipped like a wraith into the night.

There was nothing for Rab to do but rub the moisture from his eyes with a corner of Adam's blanket, then lay the little boy down in his crib and wait for whatever transpired next.

As Gregor had said, the child must be drugged. Rab recalled the way Breda had forced the cup of milk down his throat, determined to make him drink it all. She must have put something into it to ensure that he would sleep during their flight. He was unconscious, but there was good colour in his face, and his breathing was easy and regular.

Rab covered him warmly, poked the fire into a blaze, and huddled in a chair to wait the night out.

A soldier came early in the morning to tell him that Breda had been found on the banks of the River Cart, among the debris that the river cast on to its banks every day, half a mile from the outskirts of the town. She had been strangled.

The soldier wanted to know if Rab knew the whereabouts of one Gregor MacEwan, brother to the dead woman. There was neither hide nor hair of him to be found, he said, and nobody seemed to know where he had gone. Rab shook his head hopelessly, and returned, dazed, to his sleeping child.

Chapter Twenty-Nine

Mary MacLeod's money and the loan that Benjamin Selbie had arranged from the bank made up the sum Christian needed.

On her first visit to the warehouse after the Fraser business became hers she stopped short before entering the building, looking it over with satisfaction.

Now that it belonged to her and to nobody else the place had taken on a new look. She thrilled to the thought that she was her own mistress.

'What happens now?' asked Benjamin Selbie, who stood beside her.

'Rab's taking over here next week. Poor man, he needs something to occupy his mind after all the trouble he's had. As for myself,' said Christian, 'I must get the other corks accustomed to doing business with a woman.'

'You'll not be able to do so much by yourself,' the banker protested. 'It was foolish of you to find other places for your maidservants and take on the task of running the house as well.'

'Tuts, man, I'm as strong as you are – and as able. It'll fall to Rachel to see to most of the housework, but she's willing enough. We'll manage!'

He looked down at the vivid face uplifted to his, saw the steely determination there, and sighed. 'Yes, Christian,' he said, 'I suppose you will. But it'll not be easy.'

'Nothing ever is,' said Christian, a bleak note suddenly coming into her voice.

Since his wife's murder Rab had worked tirelessly at exercising and strengthening his injured leg, driving himself on when the pain of stiff and healing muscles took the breath from him and sent sweat rolling down his face. Four weeks later, when he became overseer at the Fraser warehouse, he had discarded his crutch and was walking well enough with the aid of a stick.

He was spurred on by the knowledge that young Adam was now entirely dependent on him. And in order to be both mother and father to the child, Rab must be fit and well.

His parents, who had taken their son and grandson into their own house at Townhead after the tragedy, wanted Rab to make his home with them, but he resisted the idea fiercely.

'I've got my own place, and I'll raise my own child.'

'But how are you going to see to a bairn and earn your keep as well?' his mother asked reasonably.

'I'll find a way. Now that Duncan's coming home from the Army to take up the loom again you'll not have room for me and Adam as well.'

'We managed with the two of you at home before, and a wee bairn doesn't take up much space,' Annie persisted, but her elder son shook his head obstinately. He couldn't bear the thought of being under the same roof as Duncan, who had spent years in the Army, travelled all over, faced the dangers of battle – and was returning to Paisley a whole man, a hero, while he, Rab, the stay-at-home, had been hurt badly enough to lose his trade.

When he finally returned to the house in order to get it ready for Adam's return he found the kitchen cold and lonely, the ash grey in the grate as he had left it the day Breda had died, food decaying in the pots on the range.

Mice scattered and scampered off the table and over the floor as he went in, and there were spiders' webs at the window and high in the corners.

In the other room the bed was rumpled, its covers thrust back as he had left them when he clambered out to confront Breda for the last time.

As Rab looked about the place the resolve to stand on his own feet ebbed out of him. Suddenly he felt lost and lonely, weighed down by his responsibilities and his confounded bitter pride. He would have given everything he had, even Adam himself at that moment, to turn the clock back to the carefree days when he and Christian had roamed the braes together without a care in the world and a fine future at their feet.

He sat down at the table, pushed a mug and a plate aside, and put his face into his hands.

Then he lifted it swiftly, scrubbing a fist over stinging eyes, as Rachel Fraser pushed open the door and walked in.

'I went to your mother's house and she said I'd find you here.'

'Aye – I'm getting the place ready so that I can bring the bairn back tomorrow.'

She looked round the room in silence for a moment. Her nose wrinkled at the smell of rotten food, then she shivered and said, 'It's awful cheerless, is it not?'

He glared. 'It's not been lived in for this past month! Once I get the fire going and the dust off the surfaces it'll be fine.'

'Who's going to see to Adam while you're at the

warehouse?' Rachel's soft voice wanted to know.

'I'll find some woman to take him in when I'm working.'

'It's to be hoped you find someone trustworthy.'

'Beggars can't be choosers,' he rapped, wishing her a thousand miles away. 'But I'll not have my mother troubled by him, for she's done her share of rearing bairns, and she's past the time to be bothered by another one.'

He picked up a pot, put it down again, ran a hand over the dresser then rubbed the dust from his fingers, not certain where to begin. He had never felt so helpless in his life.

'I'll see to him,' Rachel said.

'You'll have that big house to tend now that the serving-lassies are away. How could you find time to come here and care for a bairn as well?'

Colour was high in the girl's cheeks, and her fingers fluttered round each other. 'I could look after Adam and the house if they were together – if you and the bairn moved to the High Street. There's plenty of room.'

'I couldnae do that!'

'Now there's just me and Christian we're rattling round the place like peas in a drum,' Rachel argued, her voice strengthening as the idea grew in her mind. 'There's the garden, too – the bairn could run about outside and no harm come to him. You could pay rent to Christian.'

Hope flowered in him for a moment, but nevertheless he said irritably, 'It wouldnae work out!'

'It would. I'll talk to Christian about it when I go home. Please, Rab,' Rachel said, 'I want to look after . . .' – she stopped, and bit her lip, then looked down at her hands – '. . . after Adam.'

There was silence in the musty, chilled, stinking room. A mouse scuttered behind the wall.

Then Rab said gruffly, 'Mebbe you're right. Mebbe it'd

be for the best – for all of us. Aye, see what Christian thinks.'

'Are you certain,' said Benjamin Selbie, 'that you're doing the right thing?'

Christian stopped short on the Plainstanes, the paved section at the Cross where folk gathered for a gossip with friends and acquaintances on Sundays and Fair days, and looked sternly up at him.

'What d'you mean, doing the right thing? I'm a manu-facturer – a cork, the same as the men in there.' She nod-ded in the direction of the Coffee House. 'And I've proved it too, these past six months, whether they like it or not.'

For the hundredth time Benjamin thought that wid-ow's weeds suited Christian. Against the sombre clothing her lovely face was a jewel in a black velvet case. She had refused to don the close-fitting cambric cap and black silk hood worn by most widows, and her dark hair shone beneath the fine veiling on her bonnet. The gold lights in her hazel eyes sparkled up at him, and her skin was soft and smooth, with a glow to it that made the banker's heart turn over beneath his ribs.

He didn't want her to be hurt – and he had a feeling that that was just what was going to happen.

'Aye, but there's never been a woman in the Coffee House.'

'As to that,' said Christian, giving an extra tug to her gloves, 'mebbe it's a time for change.'

'But—'

'Don't fash me with your buts, Benjamin Selbie. I'm tired of the way the other corks try to pretend that I'm not there whenever they see me in my own warehouse. I must be accepted into the Coffee House if I've to have any standing in Paisley at all!'

'I suppose you're right.'

'I know I'm right,' said Christian Fraser, and led the way purposefully to the fine wooden door set between stone pillars.

The Coffee House at Paisley Cross, hard by the Paisley Inn, was the favourite meeting place of the local manufacturers and merchants. On this day, as on all other days except the Sabbath, it was abuzz with activity and servants hurried up and down between the long tables, carrying laden trays.

Men stretched over the wooden boards, comfortably propped on their elbows, and talked confidentially to each other, or leaned back in their chairs, booted legs stretched out, bawling news and business offers, refusals and acceptances, across the room. On one wall a huge expanse of slate carried crayoned messages and intimations.

There wasn't a woman to be seen in the place, for the Coffee House wasn't for recreation, but business. Here, the merchants met their friends and enemies, their partners and rivals, their customers and debtors and creditors.

For an annual fee of one guinea they had full use of the premises, and welcomed it too, for it was better to do their most important business over food and drink in the comfort of the Coffee House than at the doors of their warehouses or in small cramped offices with every passer-by able to eavesdrop.

When Christian walked in through the door a hush fell over the place. Head after head turned. A man's deep, baying laugh faltered and then died. The servants stopped short, gaping.

They were all aware, and had discussed it as thoroughly as any woman at the market or on the street corners, that Angus Fraser's young widow had bought her step-son out of the business and become a cork in her own right.

Many of them traded with the company as they had traded with it in Angus Fraser's day, for the Fraser warehouse was still a place to be trusted. Some of them had even admitted in the privacy of the Coffee House that the lassie had a fine brain in that pretty head of hers. A few of them secretly wished her well.

But even so, they couldn't go so far as to accept a woman openly into their midst, and it had never occurred to any of them that Christian might one day have the effrontery to step through the portals of the Coffee House itself.

As she looked at the rows of astonished faces upturned to hers Christian's nerve almost failed her. She took a swift step back and came up against Selbie's strong body. His hand curled about her elbow, his fingers tightening briefly in comfort.

Slowly, she stepped away from him and walked into the middle of the room, through the ranks of staring men.

'Gentlemen.' For a wonder, her voice hadn't deserted her completely, though it sounded to her own ears to be a trifle reedy. She cleared her throat and tried again, deepening it. 'Good day to you, gentlemen. You all know me. My name's Christian Fraser, and I own the Fraser warehouse and the Fraser looms.'

She turned to make sure that the men behind her could hear, and saw Selbie standing by the door where she had left him, his dark eyes fixed on her face, a slight smile touching the corners of his firm mouth. Gratefully, she felt the man's strength and support reach out and touch her and enfold her.

'I've come to take my place among you as a Paisley cork,' she said, turning from him to survey the others.

There was a short silence, then Patrick King, thread manufacturer, got to his feet. His eyes met hers, then slid away.

'Mistress Fraser, we all of us know that you're keeping your man's business going.'

'It's my business now, Mister King,' she corrected him crisply.

'Aye – well . . .' Disconcerted, he huffed deep in his throat, then said: 'But even so, lassie – you're a woman, and women dinnae come into the Coffee House.'

There was an embarrassed rumble of agreement, a shifting of feet.

'Best go back to your home,' Mister King urged. There was a second murmur of agreement, then almost all of the men turned their backs on the young woman who stood in their midst and returned to their talk.

Colour burned in Christian's face. The man's voice, his manner, drew the years from her, sending her back to the days when she first began to work for Angus Fraser and he insisted on treating her as though she was still a child.

For a moment she almost gave in, almost walked from the place with as much dignity as she could muster; then her self-respect took over.

The flush receded from her face, all except for a splash of angry bright colour along each cheekbone. She picked up an empty pewter tankard that stood nearby and thumped it hard on the table.

The noise brought all the heads jerking back in her direction and stilled the buzz of conversation for the second time.

'Listen to me!' Her voice rang out clearly now, with no nervousness in it, only anger. 'You know me, and you knew my husband, rest his soul. I've taken over where he left off and, if you ask me, gentlemen, he'd turn in his grave if he knew how his wife was being treated today by the lot of you!'

'He'd turn in his grave if he saw a woman standing in the Coffee House,' someone said, and there was a general snigger. From the corner of her eye Christian saw Benjamin Selbie start forward angrily. She gave him one glance, and he subsided.

'I think he'd be proud of me, as you should be proud of me for trying to keep his warehouse – my warehouse – open and keeping Paisley folk in work.' She glared round the assembly, then demanded: 'How am I to do business if the Coffee House is closed to me? Tell me that if you can, gentlemen.'

It fell to Mister King, again, to answer her. 'Your cousin Rab Montgomery can surely handle any business that needs doing in here. Let him put forward his guinea and it'll be accepted with good heart, I can assure you, for there's none of us want to stand in the way of the Fraser warehouse.'

Heads – grey, white, fair and dark, bewigged, balding, powdered and unpowdered – wagged vigorously all over the big room.

'No!' Christian thundered. 'I will not have my cousin speaking for me. I'll speak for myself!'

Patrick King's kindly face was wrinkled with concern. 'But lassie, you know fine that women—'

The pewter mug was slammed on the table again. 'I'm not a woman, I'm a cork – a manufacturer! I've worked my way through the warehouse. I know as much as Angus knew of the business, and there's not a man among you can stand up and deny that!'

She turned in a half-circle, fixing first one then the other with her gaze.

'I've entertained almost every one of you in my

house – aye, and listened to your talk of markets and buyers and sellers and silks and linen and damask. When Angus died I was in London seeing to the business in his place.'

She paused, and the long room was so silent that when a servant put a mug down on the table the click of it rang out loudly.

'And why did I buy the business?' Christian demanded into that silence. 'Because my step-son – a man, gentlemen, one of your own – was of a mind to sell it from the moment he inherited it. I couldn't stand by and see that happen, for all that I'm only a woman.'

'Aye, but . . .' said King, looking round for support and meeting only averted eyes, and an angry glare from the doorway where Benjamin Selbie stood, arms folded.

'I'm not just a woman and I'll not thank any man here who tries to treat me as one,' Christian swept on. 'I'm a cork, and before God, gentlemen, I'm claiming my rights as a cork no matter how long it takes the lot of you to come round to my way of thinking!'

She dug into her pocket then tossed a coin on to the table. It spun across the board and came to rest before Patrick King, the sound of its passage echoing through the room.

'I believe that the fee is one guinea, gentlemen,' said Christian stonily.

The silence went on for two seconds, three, four.

Mister King looked round the room, meeting eyes, communing silently with them.

Then his hand reached out and pushed the guinea back towards Christian.

'Mistress Fraser, we'll do business with your company, but we'll not have a woman inside the Coffee House,' he said, and turned away from her.

340

Someone said 'Hear, hear!' Someone else called for ale, and the servants, who had been standing like statues throughout the room while the battle raged about them, began their ceaseless hurrying to and fro once more.

The men at the tables began to talk again, nobody looking at Christian. Her fingers curled about the pewter mug, then Selbie's hand cupped itself under her arm.

'There's no use in arguing with them, Christian,' he murmured.

He was right, she knew that even in her anger. Further protest at this stage would just be looked on as a womanly temper tantrum.

Christian released the mug and walked out, head high.

Benjamin's handsome face was dark with anger when they regained the street. 'You should have let me do the talking.'

'What would be the sense of that?' she wanted to know shortly. 'If – when – I'm accepted into the Coffee House it'll be for myself, not for what someone else says for me.'

'The trouble with them is that they're rooted in tradition, every one of them.'

She glared at him, her hazel eyes hot and bright with humiliation and anger. 'Traditions can be broken. I'll change their way of thinking – you'll see!'

Her anger sparked off his. 'For God's sake, Christian! Will you never learn? This town's not ready to accept you as a manufacturer and that's all there is to it. You're a woman, a beautiful woman at that. Be content with what you are, what you've achieved already, and leave the rest to the men.'

'I'll do nothing of the kind. Before I'm done,' Christian said, as intensely as if she was making a vow, 'I'll have those men in there acknowledging me. And I'll not rest until the day that happens!'

'Christian.' He put a hand on her arm, little caring who was watching. 'It's early days for me to say again what's in my heart, but—'

'I think,' said Christian, 'that it's time I paid a visit to Edinburgh.'

The sudden change in the conversation caught Selbie off-balance. 'Where?'

'Edinburgh. They're weaving shawls there, I hear. I want to see the men at work on the looms. I'll not be away long – Rab can manage things very well while I'm gone. It was a good day when I asked him to take over the warehouse.'

'You can't travel alone.'

'I'm a grown woman, I can see to myself.'

'Take Rachel with you for company.'

'Rachel has enough to do looking after the house and young Adam,' said Christian, her anger swept away in the excitement of seeing the plan she had been turning over in her mind for a long time beginning to reach fruition. 'Besides, if she's half the woman I think she is she'll make the most of the time she'll have Rab to herself without me around to get in the way.'

She wheeled about and began to march off towards the warehouse, then spun back to ask: 'Benjamin, thon man who did the paintings of the roses for you – what's his name?'

'John Lang. He lives in Lawn Street.'

Christian nodded. 'I'll pay him a visit,' she said, and went on her way.

Later that day, Mister King's clerk returned the guinea, wrapped in a screw of paper. Christian put it away carefully in a small drawer of the desk, so that she would know where it was when she next visited the Coffee House.

Chapter Thirty

Up until the last thirty years of the eighteenth century Edinburgh had grown up around the Castle that rose from a sheer cliff, dominating the land for many miles around.

Because the Edinburgh folk thought nothing of building up rather than out, the old city covered a fairly small area, with the streets flanked by tenement buildings of twelve or more floors. But, as had happened in Paisley, the continual growth of the place finally required the building of a New Town.

Both Edinburgh and Paisley built their extensions in the last quarter of the century. Paisley's New Town had been built on the opposite bank of the River Cart from the original town, on the former site of Abbey gardens and parks. Edinburgh's New Town was built on the high ground that had once been the far bank of the loch which protected the Castle cliff on one side.

The loch had long since been drained, and when Christian came alone to Edinburgh in search of the shawl weavers most of the affluent citizens had uprooted their families and servants, bag and baggage, and re-settled in the elegant streets and squares and terraces of the New Town.

The handsome old houses they left behind across the bridge built over the old loch had already become slums, rabbit-warrens of single-room homes for the most part, seething with working-class and lower-class humanity.

During her ten days in Scotland's capital city Christian lodged with a merchant who had been friend as well as colleague to Angus. The man lived in a fine house in George Square, a handsomely laid out area of elegant homes.

From here, young Mistress Fraser sallied forth each morning to spend the day in the old town's weaving shops, studying the work done on the looms, asking countless questions.

Her hostess, a middle-aged woman who had once been beautiful and was now forced to rely on her maid's skill with paints and powders to retain the illusion of what she'd lost, was most put out when the theatre outings and the gatherings and the carriage drives she had arranged for her guest were either turned aside politely or attended with the minimum of interest.

'The only time she ever shows a spark of liveliness is when she's talking business,' the lady complained to her husband in the privacy of their bedchamber. 'The rest of the time she's sitting around thinking. A fine-looking lassie like that, too. She could get any man she wanted if she just put her mind to it.'

She looked dolefully into her mirror, remembering the days when she, too, had been a beauty.

'If you ask me, she'd not be the least put out if she had a hare-lip and three warts on her chin. It's a terrible waste!'

'It is that,' agreed her husband, his tone carefully non-committal.

It came as a great shock to the lady when Christian Fraser finally left Edinburgh bound for home – with a man by her side.

And it came as a further shock to find out that he was nothing but a common weaver.

'I want both of you to have a good look at these.'

As Rab and Benjamin watched, Christian spread the Kashmir shawls on the big table in the dining room. Beside them she laid other shawls that she had ordered from London and Edinburgh over the past few months.

Then she moved to the window, out of the way, and left the two men to study the materials.

It had been raining outside, although the month was July. The carriages passing the window splashed through pockets of muddy water, and the sun, showing itself at last through the clouds, made the drops falling from the house roofs opposite glitter like jewels. The red damask roses Benjamin had brought with him from his garden had been wet with rain, cool and fresh and velvety, they were in a white jug in the parlour, filling the whole room with their perfume.

Christian turned from the view outside and fiddled with the seam of the curtain, watching the men, waiting for their reaction. She had been back from Edinburgh for almost a month, but she had had a lot of work to do and a lot of people to see before telling her overseer and her financial adviser what she intended to do. Now, at last, she was ready.

Excitement gripped her as she waited. A pulse throbbed in her throat, her stomach fluttered, and her fingers couldn't stay at peace.

Rab moved from shawl to shawl, running the material through practised hands, carrying some of the pieces to where Christian stood at the window so that he could examine the fine colours in a better light.

'They're bonny, but what of them?' he said at last, his

brow knotted with puzzlement. He had long since discarded his stick and walked unaided now, though with a limp that would stay with him for the rest of his life.

A sense of purpose and a mind that was easy at last had smoothed some of the bitterness from his face, but not all. There were still grooves cut deeply between his eyes, and a hardness about the mouth that had once grinned readily. The easy, friendly youth Christian had known was gone for ever, and she grieved for his passing.

'I want to make shawls like that.'

Both men looked astounded, then Benjamin Selbie said, 'You're not serious!'

'Why not?'

For a moment he floundered, looking from one to the other of the cousins, then he said, 'The Paisley folk don't weave materials like that.'

'This one' – Rab touched the beautiful Kashmir shawl – 'was embroidered. It would be hard to find women with such skills, Christian.'

'I'm not suggesting that we should manufacture anything as perfect as that – not immediately. Or use tambourers. Look at this one, Rab.'

She picked up another shawl and held it out for his inspection. 'This is a damask pattern; it's all woven into the cloth, not darned. Woven in pieces and stitched together. Our draw-looms could do that. We could weave a patterned border and sew it on to a plain centre, could we not?'

'Aye, we could, but do we have any weavers with the skills needed? Our people are good, but they're not used to this sort of thing.'

It was time to play her trump card. 'That's why I brought Lochrie MacNeil home with me from Edinburgh.'

Understanding dawned on Rab's face, but Benjamin was still in the dark. 'Who's Lochrie MacNeil?'

'He was a silk weaver in Paisley – a good man at his loom too – until trade got bad a few years ago,' Rab explained. 'He went to Edinburgh to seek work, like many Paisley weavers.'

'And that's where he learned how to weave damask shawls with the pattern put on in the loom, not tamboured on afterwards,' Christian broke in. 'Bonny shawls, but not as bonny as the shawls we could make. That's why I brought him back to work for us.'

'And here was me thinking it was for the sake of the old days,' her cousin said ironically.

'Oh, he was willing enough, for he wanted to come back home. But the real reason I brought him back with me is because we need him.'

Christian went to a wall-cupboard, brought out a sheet of paper, and laid it on top of the brilliant silky shawls.

'Before I went away I asked John Lang to have a good look at these shawls of mine and try his hand at that sort of pattern.'

Both men bent over the neatly executed, colourful design.

'Our draw-looms could carry out that pattern, couldn't they?'

'Aye,' Rab said. 'Aye, they could.'

It was Benjamin who raised the objections. 'Christian, you're doing fine as you are. Let things be and don't go rushing into something that might cost you a deal of money for no return.'

'It makes sense to try out new things.'

He started to say something else, but Rab cut in with, 'How many looms would you think of using? They'd be kept busy for months, mind, bringing in no return.'

'Only the one loom at first, and the one shawl until we find out if we can do it. If we can, I'll bring in other weavers from Edinburgh to show our own folk the way of it. And mebbe we'll end up with all the looms turning out work like this.'

She smiled at her cousin and saw an answering glint of excitement in his eyes – a light that wasn't often seen in Rab's eyes these days.

'I don't think it's worth the work entailed,' Benjamin said stubbornly.

'That's because you're a banker, not a weaver,' Rab shot back at him, his fingers caressing the shawl.

'Benjamin, from what I hear all the women in London are wearing these shawls. And in Edinburgh too. Soon women'll be wearing them all over the country – and mebbe abroad as well. Why shouldn't we be the ones to provide them? Fashions change,' said Christian, afire with her own idea. 'We must change with them and give the folk what they want.'

'And if it doesn't work? You might well lose everything.'

Christian, impatient to be started on her fine new plan, wanted to bounce her hand off Benjamin Selbie's ear. But she resisted the impulse, and said carefully, 'I don't think that'll happen. If anything goes wrong I'll lose some money, but not everything. Not if we've only got one loom working on a shawl.' She turned back to her cousin. 'I've already made arrangements to have the warp dyed.'

Rab caressed the mass of colourful intertwined flowers and leaves again, then glanced up and said, 'It'd be worth the trying.'

Selbie shot him an angry look. 'I don't agree!'

'It's only a matter of time before another Paisley cork comes up with the idea of trying a shawl. I want to be the first!'

'Just so that you can gain entry to the Coffee House?'

It wasn't often that Benjamin Selbie was on the receiving end of the cool, crisp voice Christian used when she wanted to put folk in their places. She used it now, to good effect.

'When I was a bairn my father went against my mother's wishes and vaccinated me and Daniel against the smallpox. I've got the mark on my arm to this day. We didn't go down with the disease, though my father was taking a terrible risk, exposing us to the danger.'

She took the shawl from Rab and ran it through her hands, her fingertips relishing the cool firm feel of woven silk. 'I heard the other day that in Glasgow they've decided to vaccinate all the poor folk's bairns to try to prevent them sickening and dying.'

The banker looked mystified. 'What's that got to do with this notion you've got into your head?'

'I'm my father's daughter, Benjamin, and I'm not afraid to take risks. In five or ten or twenty years,' said Christian, stabbing the air with a slender forefinger for emphasis, 'someone right here in Paisley'll be making a lot of silver out of weaving those shawls. I want it to be me.'

Benjamin Selbie's eyes widened, then his face became expressionless, apart from a muscle that jumped in his jawline.

Christian, intent on what she wanted to say, didn't notice his reaction. 'So I'm going to set Lochrie to weaving a shawl for me,' she swept on, 'whatever you might think about it.'

He went crimson to the tips of his ears, then bowed

and said stiffly. 'Very well. I can see that there's no sense in saying anything further.'

'You were over-hard on him, Christian,' Rab said when the banker had stalked from the house.

'I'll not have him or anyone else telling me what I should do with my own looms.'

'Except me,' said Rab.

She gave him a level look. 'Including you.'

The ghost of a smile touched a mouth that these days was more often than not down-turned. 'You're hard, Christian Fraser.'

'In business you have to be hard,' his cousin said, her eyes turning to the door that had closed behind Benjamin Selbie's broad back five minutes earlier.

Rachel was ironing in the kitchen, her face flushed with heat and wisps of dark hair escaping from beneath her cap. At her feet young Adam galloped a brightly painted wooden horse across the floor, making it jump over a soup ladle.

When his father came in the little boy's face brightened, but he stayed where he was. Since the night of Breda's death and Gregor MacEwan's disappearance Rab had found it hard to show natural affection towards anyone, including his son, and young as he was, Adam had somehow grasped the fact that it embarrassed his father to be openly claimed and loved.

As a result, the relationship between them was one of wary acceptance and cautious recognition. It was one that Rachel was intent on improving.

'Christian's decided that we should become shawl-manufacturers.' Rab pulled out a chair and sat at the table.

'And what do you think?' Rachel put a finger to her

mouth then touched it lightly to the iron she held. Finding that it was too cool she put it on the range to reheat.

'I think it's a fine notion,' he said, then added with a half-smile: 'But Selbie's not happy at all. He's worried about the money she might lose on it.'

Instead of taking up the other iron, Rachel sat down opposite Rab, picking up Adam and cuddling him.

'If you ask me, he's worried in case Christian gets so deep into this shawl-making that he loses her.'

'Loses her?'

'Have you no eyes in your head, Rab Montgomery? The man's daft about her. He's hoping that she'll grow tired of being a cork. Then he might persuade her to marry with him.'

'Has he told you this?'

'He didnae need to tell me.' Rachel's voice was scathing.

'But Christian's only just buried her husband – it's not seemly for another man to be thinking already of making her his wife!'

'It's been seven months since my father died.'

'As long as that?'

Rachel gave him a sidelong glance. 'Are you still in love with her?' her soft voice asked, and Rab coloured, taken aback.

'I – care about what happens to her. I'll always care.'

'So will I. But we must let Christian go her own way.' Rachel relinquished Adam, who was struggling on her lap, demanding to go back to his toy horse. 'We've all got our own paths to lead, and if Christian's path is destined to meet with Benjamin Selbie's it'll happen whether you want it or not. So think on your own happiness first.'

He looked at her, at the rounded arms easing his son to the ground, the dark head lowered over the child, the soft curve of her breasts just visible, as she bent forward, beneath the open top of the blouse she had unbuttoned because of the kitchen's heat.

His heart warmed, and he sensed a tingle, like the return of life, in his loins. He wished that he could express himself properly, unlock the door that, when his marriage soured, had begun to close between him and the rest of the world and, after Breda's death, had locked itself completely.

Rachel lifted her head and smiled at him, and Rab remembered that his own bereavement, like Christian's, was slipping away into the past, and that in time he would be free to plan his own future. If he had the courage to do it.

Clumsily, he bent to the child crouched between himself and Rachel. 'That's as bonny a nag as ever I did see,' he said with grave appreciation. 'Let me see it going through its paces.'

The little boy beamed and began to bounce the toy along the flagstones, clicking his tongue vigorously.

'Aye – a good piece of horseflesh. You've got yourself a bargain there,' his father said solemnly as Rachel, well pleased to see the two of them together, returned to her ironing.

Chapter Thirty-One

Over the next few weeks Lochrie MacNeil studied and approved John Lang's fine design for a broad border, incorporating the colours of the shawls Christian had shown him, and following the Indian motif of the curved pine cone, picked out in tiny flowers.

John then began work on an enlarged version of the pattern on squared paper, meticulously putting in each crossing of the warp and weft, so that Lochrie could pin the pattern to his loom and follow it.

Christian then took the approved design to the flower-lasher, a man skilled in reading the pattern and preparing the web for the loom. It was his task to set the threads on to a frame and carefully tie them up in groups of individual colours with strong cotton thread. Each group was controlled by a cord, or 'lash' so that once they were in place on the loom they could be raised in the right order by Lochrie's drawboy to let the shuttles pass through and so complete the pattern.

After that, the web – the set of warp threads that would be wound on to the loom to act as the base of the cloth – had to be made up. Then came the intricate task of dying it so that it could play its part in forming the pattern.

'Once the yarn's dyed every thread'll have to be in its exact place as I weave,' Lochrie explained cheerfully. 'A mistake'll mean that the pattern's all out of place and all the money you've put into the shawl's been wasted.'

Christian listened to the placid, sturdy weaver, and bit her lip, praying that there wouldn't be a mistake.

The preparation was a long business, at times exasperating. There were moments when she wondered why on earth she had ever thought of manufacturing a shawl; and then there were times when everything seemed to be working out, and she knew that she had set her foot on the right road.

At long last the loom was set up in a small weaving shop in Storie Street and Lochrie took his place on the saytree, nodded to his drawboy, and began work.

After that there was nothing to do but wait. Christian did this with bad grace, paying frequent visits to the loom shop to see the border grow. Not that there was much to see, for the pattern was on the underside of the cloth and all that was on view was a mass of colourful thread ends that would be trimmed off once the shawl was completed.

'I know fine what's going on,' Lochrie assured his young employer confidently, and she had to be content with that.

She had known all along that it would be impossible to keep her new venture a secret from the other manufacturers, but by working swiftly she managed to get the project well under way before anyone found out about it.

When they did, Christian found first one cork then another, then more, dropping in at the warehouse to pass the time of day, intent on finding out more about the new shawl she was attempting.

She dealt with them all cheerfully, refusing to bear any grudges for the day she had been refused entry to the

Coffee House. The past was past, and the future was what mattered.

And, as she herself had predicted, other Paisley manufacturers had found the Kashmir and Cantonese shawls in the London markets and brought them home to study them. Other silk weavers who, like Lochrie, had gone to Edinburgh when trade was bad, returned to Paisley, bringing with them the seeds of the shawl-making art.

'But God willing,' said Christian to Benjamin Selbie, her chin tilted in a way that set him into a turmoil, with half of him wanting to shake her for her single-mindedness, the other half wanting to take her into his arms, 'I'll be the first!'

Under Lochrie's expert hands the Fraser shawl began to take shape. The grey-haired weaver, happy to be back in Paisley again, put his heart and soul into his work, often toiling on, much to Christian's approval and his drawboy's annoyance, when the other two weavers in the loom shop had completed their quota of work for the day.

'The day'll come,' Lochrie told the drawboy one dull wet day when the others had left, complaining that there wasn't enough light coming in through the windows for them to see what they were about, 'when you'll be proud to boast to your grandweans that you helped to make the first Paisley shawl. Now stop girning at me and bring a light over here so that I can see what I'm doing.'

The boy had the sense to shut his mouth and do as he was told. Drawboys were at the mercy of their masters, and many of them were ill-treated. If Lochrie was roused to anger he was quite capable of using his iron-hard fists as well as his sharp tongue, but on the whole he was a considerate master, and his drawboy knew better than to persist with his complaining.

So, while the weaver checked the pattern on the loom to make certain that everything was as it should be, the lad lit one of the little oil-burning 'crusies' stored on the window-sill and carried it carefully across the room to the small shelf fixed to the wall by the loom.

He had almost reached his goal when there was a sharp crack as one of the taut harness threads suddenly gave way. As man and boy looked up in surprise at the unexpected noise the freed end of the thread flew into the air then fell across the lamp, which ignited it at once.

With a yell of fear the boy dropped the crusie, sending burning oil scattering across the floor. It could have been stamped out quickly enough, but the real damage was done by the single strand that had caught light.

The flame darted along the length of the thread, following it back to the loom. There, it found a feast of dry inflammable material at its mercy.

Before Lochrie had time to do more than yell a warning, before he could even complete his leap from the saytree, the cloth on the loom before him had exploded into a mass of flame that shot the height of the harness towering above, and sent man and boy reeling back, their hands thrown over their faces to protect their eyes.

One of Christian's prime objectives after buying the business from Alexander had been to raise the money to buy the High Street house as well. She hated to think that, while she and Rachel were living in the place, they were dependent on her step-son's generosity, and vulnerable to any whim he might have to sell the house from under their very feet.

On the dark, wet day when she came into possession of the documents acknowledging her as full and sole owner of the house Angus had brought her to as his bride, she locked them away carefully in the writing desk. Then she went out into the hall and stood with her hand resting on the polished newel post at the foot of the stairs, thinking of the years she had spent in the place as Angus's wife.

Rachel, bustling in from the kitchen, stopped and eyed her with an understanding smile.

'You're pleased about owning the house.'

'I'm pleased that we don't have to feel that we're living on your brother's charity any more,' her step-mother said with satisfaction. 'And no doubt Alexander'll be happy to have more silver in his pocket.'

'He always did prefer silver to anything else. But I still think you'd have been as well buying something smaller and letting him sell this place off.'

Christian ran the palm of her hand down the banister. 'But this is a bonny house. Thanks to your father we've both of us been happy here. It's only right that we keep it. It's yours as much as mine.'

Rachel's smile faded slightly. She bit her lip, then said: 'Christian, I'm not likely to be staying here much longer.'

'Why not?' Then, as the younger woman's cheeks suddenly glowed a soft rose-pink, Christian's eyes widened. 'It's never you and Rab?'

Now that the secret was out Rachel allowed the glow to reach her eyes. 'Aye, it is. You're not angered, are you?'

'Angered? Why should I be?'

'I know that you've always been close to each other – and he's got a great fondness for you.'

'Ach, we'd never have made a good marriage, if that's what you mean. You're just the right wife for the man – and the right mother for Adam too. When's the marriage to be?'

'It's early days yet, Christian,' her step-daughter

protested, the blush deepening. 'It's not a full year since Breda went. But I thought you'd best know that there was an understanding between us.'

'Take my advice, Rachel, and marry the man as soon as the year's out. The Lord knows he deserves happiness. The only thing I'm wondering about . . .' Christian hesitated, then said carefully: 'Rachel, the man's changed in the past few years. There's a bitterness to him, and he never used to have such a quick temper. Are you certain that you'll be happy with him?'

'I can manage Rab,' his future wife said with serene confidence, then added, the blush deepening: 'And he's the only man I'll ever want.'

'As long as you're certain, I'm happy for you – for the two of you!' Christian hugged the girl, then said briskly: 'Now, as to you and Rab finding a home of your own, why don't the two of you stay on here? There's plenty of—'

Fists and boots thudded on the sturdy street door, and they both jumped. A shrill childish voice screamed through the thick panels: 'Mistress Fraser – are ye in? Mistress Fraser!'

Christian flew across the hall, Rachel close behind her. When the door opened they found themselves looking down on a rough-headed ragged little boy who was hopping up and down on the doorstep, oblivious to the rain that poured down on him from a heavy grey sky, his eyes huge with excitement and importance.

'Mistress,' he gabbled, 'there's a fire in the loom shop in Storie Street. The weaver said for me tae tell ye.'

For a moment the blood stopped in Christian's veins, then it started bustling along twice as fast as before.

'Get down to my warehouse as fast as you can, laddie, and tell Mister Montgomery. Rachel . . .'

As she turned, her cloak was pushed into her hands. 'On you go,' Rachel ordered. 'I'll have to stay here with Adam.'

Passers-by, already alerted by the boy's assault on the door, stared as Christian erupted from the house and ran in one direction, splashing heedlessly through puddles, while the messenger boy ran in the other.

There was a small knot of onlookers clustered outside the weaving shop when she got there, some of them peering in through the windows of the apartment where the looms were kept.

As soon as Christian entered the passageway the acrid smell of burned cloth surrounded her. The weaving shop was smoky and filled with men; the earthen floor underfoot was soaking wet and littered with the empty buckets they had brought to extinguish the fire.

All the voices stopped when she entered, and the men drew back to form a pathway for her. She moved between their ranks, heedless of the faces watching her, past the loom that held a stretch of good sound cloth between its rollers. Then she stopped by Lochrie's loom.

It was a mass of wet, charred wood. The beams overhead were blackened, the treadle pit, dug in the earth floor to make room for the wooden treadles the weaver worked with his feet, was awash.

The half-finished silk shawl had gone, disappeared in a blaze of flame.

'Mistress Fraser.' Lochrie, his face a map of lobster-pink and soot-black, his eyes red-rimmed, was almost unrecognisable. 'Mistress Fraser, I'm mortally vexed,' he said wretchedly, his teeth gleaming white as he spoke.

'What happened?'

'One of the harness threads broke and fell on to a

crusie. It was my fault,' the weaver said. 'If I'd left the loom until tomorrow the way I should have – but I wanted to get some more work done, and we needed the light—'

'Let me see your hands,' Christian interrupted. He held them out, sucking in his breath with a sharp hiss as she touched the puffed, reddened flesh.

'You'll have to get them seen to.'

She heard the sound of feet running along the stone-flagged passage, then Rab burst into the room, his eyes wide with horror as he took in the situation.

'The shawl—'

'Never mind the shawl,' his cousin told him crisply. 'There's nothing that can be done about it. You tend to this place, Rab, while I get Lochrie's hands bandaged. Come on, now.'

She took the weaver by the elbow and steered him out of the loom shop and in through the door on the other side of the passageway, where she and the woman of the house tended and bandaged his hands.

After that Christian sent Lochrie and the shaken drawboy home and walked back to the High Street.

Rab and Rachel were in the kitchen when she went in.

'Is Lochrie all right?' Rab asked.

'Aye, he'll be fine.' Christian heard the depression in her own voice, but she could do nothing about it. 'You gave something to the men who helped to put the fire out, Rab?'

'Aye.' He looked as wretched as Lochrie had. 'Christian . . .'

She felt the tears welling into her eyes. 'We'll talk about it in the morning, Rab. I'm away to my bed,' she said, and walked out, unable to face the pity in the two faces before her.

Chapter Thirty-Two

When Benjamin Selbie returned from Glasgow that evening and heard the news he went straight to the Fraser house.

'Where is she?' he demanded as soon as Rachel opened the door.

'In her bedchamber. She's not wanting to see any—'

He passed her and strode across the hall, divesting himself of hat, stick and coat as he went. Tossing the coat over the banisters, leaning the stick against a convenient small table, and dropping the hat over the newel post, he began to take the stairs two at a time.

'Mister Selbie, you can't go into her bedchamber!' said Rachel, scandalised. He ignored her.

She started to follow him, then stopped, a faint smile curving the corners of her mouth. Turning, she went back into the parlour, where she settled into a chair, picked up her knitting wires and went on with her work, casting a glance now and again at the ceiling.

Christian had sobbed out all her anger and disappointment, then washed her tear-streaked face, changed into her nightshift and brushed her hair out, letting it fall over her shoulders.

Then she got into bed and lay awake, watching the lamplight casting shadows on the wall, her mind filled with the sight of the blackened loom, the ruined shawl.

The house was well made and its walls thick; lost in her own thoughts, Christian scarcely heard the front door opening and closing and footsteps coming up the staircase and along the corridor.

When the door opened she sat up with a start, then said: 'Benjamin!'

He stepped into the room and closed the door behind him. 'I've been in Glasgow all day. I've just heard the news.'

'You shouldn't be in here.' She scrambled out of bed and reached for the robe that hung over a chair.

'Christian – my dear—'

'Never mind that,' said Christian as sharply as she could. 'What do you think you're—' To her horror her voice broke, and Benjamin's handsome face suddenly shimmered before her as her eyes filled again. Before she could blink the tears away he was by her side, gathering her into his arms, his cheek against her hair.

'I'm always weeping on your shoulder,' she said indistinctly into his waistcoat. 'You must think I'm a very weak woman.'

Her voice wobbled, and his arms tightened about her. 'Hush, my love,' he said tenderly. 'Hush.'

She had wondered, in the deep darkness of the lonely nights, what it would be like to be kissed by Benjamin Selbie.

As his mouth brushed hers once, twice, as gently as the touch of a butterfly's wing, then came a third time to settle and stay and mould itself to her own lips, claiming them with passionate arrogance, she knew that her imagination had only hinted at the pleasures she would find in his arms.

She clung to him, heedless of the fact that they were

alone together in her bedchamber, and that her opened robe was slipping from her shoulders.

When his lips finally left hers they traced a path along the line of her jaw to her ear then moved lower, to tease and tantalise the soft hollow beneath her lobe before travelling to the base of her throat.

She whispered his name and let her fingers sink into his rich, thick gold hair. He lifted his head, eyes dazed with the strength of his feelings for her, and took her mouth again in a kiss that parted her lips and brought the tip of her tongue stealing eagerly between her teeth to meet his.

The small clock on the mantelshelf ticked the seconds away and, in the room below, Rachel Fraser knitted her way along more than one row of the work in her deft hands before Christian, all at once aware of the bed just behind them, its coverlet invitingly turned back, found the strength to put her palms against Benjamin's chest and ease him away from her.

He stepped back, but only a small step, still close enough to keep his hands curved round her shoulders. Flushed, dishevelled, dazed, joyful, they looked at each other for a long moment before Christian gave a shaky laugh.

'This is most improper, Mister Selbie. We might well have the whole town talking about us by dawn.'

'Let them.' said Benjamin. 'Christian, when I told you about my feelings a long time ago I gave my word that I would say no more. But I can't be silent any longer. I won't be silent, because I love you, Christian. I love you.'

She put a hand to his mouth as he bent towards her again. 'One more kiss and I'll be lost for ever. You must go. Benjamin!'

'Not until I have your word that you'll be my wife.'

Then, before she could say anything, he went on: 'Christian, I'm leaving Paisley.'

She stared up at him in dismay. 'When?'

'Very soon. I'm going to live and work in London. You've been so busy with this precious shawl of yours that I couldn't tell you. But now that the shawl's gone there's nothing to stop you coming with me.'

'What are you talking about? I can't leave Paisley just now!'

'But don't you see, my love, as my wife you'll have no more need to keep the warehouse. You've done all you could – you can't do any more.'

'Benjamin.' She lifted her hand to stop the flow of words. The movement pulled her arm free of his grasp, and both his hands fell to his side. 'What about the shawl?'

He stared at her, not understanding. Then he said gently, as though reasoning with a child, 'The shawl's gone, Christian.'

'The first shawl, yes – but by the time Lochrie's hands are better we'll have another draw-loom set up, another web dyed . . .'

As she watched, the blaze of happiness faded from his eyes. 'Christian—'

'I'll wed you willingly – once the first Fraser shawl comes off the loom.'

'For God's sake, woman, enough of this nonsense! It's time to put your own happiness first, and your happiness lies with me!'

'All I need,' she said as reasonably as she could, 'is a few more months here.'

'And then,' he said in a cold, hard voice, 'there'll be the next shawl – and the next. When you and Rab were talking about the shawl that first day, you said that in five or ten years a Paisley manufacturer would be making a fortune from the shawls. You said' – he wrenched the words out as though each one tasted bitter—' that you wanted to be that manufacturer. I hoped then that I'd be able to make you change your mind, but it seems that I was wrong.'

'Benjamin, I love you. But I must prove to the town that I'm a manufacturer!'

'No!' Benjamin's voice was suddenly very quiet. 'Prove your love for me instead by turning your back on this place and coming to London as my wife.'

Time stopped as they faced each other. She wanted to throw herself into his arms, to promise everything that he wanted, to be with him for the rest of her life.

But at the same time she wanted to see a Paisley-woven shawl come off the loom, whole and beautiful. She wanted to be accepted as a cork, to reach the end of the road she had set her foot on when Angus died.

The woman and the manufacturer in her fought together, almost tearing her into shreds between them. It would only have taken a touch of Benjamin's hand, the right words, to give victory to the woman.

Instead he said coldly, 'I warn you – I will not take second place to a confounded shawl. For God's sake, Christian, give up this nonsense once and for all!'

'I'll not be scolded like a child!'

'You want to have everything, don't you? Me and the warehouse and the shawls – everything, letting nothing go. That's not possible. Not as far as I'm concerned. Why, in God's name,' said Benjamin Selbie bitterly, 'did I have to lose my heart to such a stubborn creature?'

Then he turned and blundered from the room, leaving her alone.

*   *   *

The new shawl blossomed on the loom under Lochrie's careful ministrations.

This time there was no mishap, and Christian was there when the last piece of the brilliantly coloured border was completed and cut off the loom.

Lochrie handed it to her, and she took it as a young mother would take her new-born child into her arms, stroking the soft silk.

There was still work to be done before the garment was completed. The borders had to be trimmed and clipped and fringed, then stitched on to a plain white centre. Then the shawl had to be washed.

Because of the fire that had destroyed the work on Lochrie's loom this shawl wasn't the first to come off a Paisley loom, but it was the most beautiful. A host of manufacturers came to the warehouse to see it when it was finished.

'Aye, you've done a grand job there,' Mister King commented after a close study of the shawl.

Christian gave him a brisk nod. 'I'm pleased with it.'

'You've every right to be,' he said.

When he had gone she folded the shawl into a triangle and put it over her shoulders. It was light but warm, and in the sunlight coming through the warehouse door the coloured threads of the border shimmered.

Benjamin had been gone from Paisley for three months. In his letters Daniel, who saw him occasionally, told her about the small house he had bought for himself, with a fine back yard for his roses. Benjamin himself hadn't written to her, or asked her brother to convey any messages to her.

Christian had convinced herself that before he left he would come to her, and somehow, everything would be put right between them.

But he hadn't come near the warehouse or the High Street house, and she had been too proud to go to him. He had left her without another word. It was over.

She took the shawl off and folded it carefully. She had made her choice. She had elected to stay in Paisley, and that was an end to it.

And to her surprise, her heart hadn't broken in the weeks after his going, though more than once she had thought it might.

Two weeks later a London merchant visiting Paisley bought the shawl for a good price that still enabled him to sell it for far less than those brought from India, and make a handsome profit. He left orders for further work, and Christian and Rab decided to turn more of the Fraser looms over to shawl-weaving.

They took on trimmers and clippers and fringers and finishers and needlewomen. By the end of the summer the new line was well established.

Christian was exultant with the success of the new shawls. She had proved herself as a cork and she had given new life to the Fraser warehouse.

Whenever thoughts of Benjamin Selbie filled her mind, usually in the night when she lay alone in bed, she pushed them away. She had surely proved that her rightful place was here, in Paisley. Her life, she told herself firmly, was following the path she had mapped out for it and she was well content.

On their way back from a visit to a silk weaver who had fallen ill Christian and Rachel found themselves strolling along Silk Street.

As soon as she realised that they were approaching the house where Benjamin Selbie had lived Christian felt a knotting sensation deep in the pit of her belly.

She hadn't once passed the house since he had left it, preferring, when alone, to make a detour along Lawn Street if she happened to be in the area.

But this time she wasn't alone, and Adam, running along ahead of the two women, was already peering inquisitively through the open gate into the back yard. There was no turning back, no time to think of an excuse.

A cart stood outside the gate, and men were loading it with hessian-wrapped bundles. Christian and Rachel peeped over the high wooden side and saw what looked like a forest of dead, dry twigs, carefully wrapped in clumps.

'Good day to you, Mistress Fraser – Mistress Montgomery.'

The housekeeper, who had been standing watching the men, hands folded beneath her apron, greeted the newcomers warmly. Rachel, who had only been wearing Rab's wedding ring for two weeks and was still getting used to her new title, glowed with pleasure at the sound of it.

'What's happening here?' she wanted to know, stepping through the gate. Adam had already gone into the yard and was skipping up and down the little gravel paths.

Following Rachel, Christian saw to her dismay that the trim, colourful garden where she had spent so many happy hours was a wilderness of overturned earth.

The housekeeper nodded at the wrapped bundles still waiting to go and at a great pile of dead leaves and dying flower heads heaped in one corner. 'Mister Selbie's sent for everything from the garden, so the men have been preparing the bushes for the journey. It seems that he's found a house in London with a back yard, so he can keep growing his roses.'

Rachel called to Adam, who came trotting obediently

back to her with several late roses culled from the rubbish heap clutched in his small fat fist. Solemnly he presented one to each of the women, then went outside and tried to feed the rest to the cart horse.

While Rachel was busy dissuading him Christian stared down at the wilting blossom in her fingers. Its fragrance brought back so many memories that her throat constricted.

She hurried from the garden, and didn't realise until Patrick King hailed her as she and Rachel went through the Cross that she still carried the flower.

She pushed it into her pocket as the man came across the street towards her, beaming.

'We're well met, Mistress Fraser. I'd had it in mind to go down to the warehouse in search of you. The fact is, I've bought an interest in a silk-twisting company in Glasgow, and I think we might be able to do business together.'

'Indeed? Will you walk down to the warehouse with me, Mister King?'

He looked slightly embarrassed, then said gruffly: 'I'd as soon we stepped across to the Coffee House, for my throat's dry with the talking I've done today.'

'The Coffee House?'

A wide beam almost split his face in two. 'Mistress Fraser, you've given us all a great deal to think about over the past year. And it seems that you were right after all. A cork's a cork, whether it be a man or a woman. So' – he offered her his arm—' will we have our talk in comfort?'

Rachel squeezed Christian's arm, then gave her a slight push in the thread-manufacturer's direction. 'You go on, Christian.' Her voice rang with pleasure for her step-mother. 'I'll take Adam home.'

Her cheeks suddenly as red as the rose she had taken from Benjamin Selbie's garden, her chin tilting proudly, Christian Fraser accepted the manufacturer's proffered arm, crossed the street, and walked in through the door of the Coffee House.

Chapter Thirty-Three

The Coffee House interior was just as it had been the last time she had stepped into it – busy, noisy, bustling, the air thick with the smoke from the men's pipes, richly loaded with the smell of ale and cooking meat.

But this time it was Patrick King, and not Benjamin Selbie, who escorted her in. And this time the faces that turned towards her were friendly, not astonished and hostile.

Once again a silence fell as Christian, urged by the thread-manufacturer's hand on her arm, walked into the middle of the room. A man stood up, then another and another. To her horror, someone began to tap a tankard gently on the table, and the sound was taken up until they were all standing, beaming at her, applauding her in their own way.

Head high, she painted a smile on her lips to stop them from quivering. She could feel her face glowing like a hot coal. Deep inside, a thrill fired her entire body, tingling through her fingers and toes and the hair on her head.

She had done it. She had proved herself to these hard-bitten men of business, had managed to make them acknowledge her as a cork like themselves, instead of a mere woman. She wished that Angus and Mally could have been there to see the way she had finally been accepted.

371

By her side, King held up a large hand for silence. 'Gentlemen – since Mistress Fraser was one of the first folk among us to bring the damask shawl to Paisley where, in my opinion, it will prosper, I submit to you that she should be accepted as a Paisley cork and invited to join us here in the Coffee House.'

Voices buzzed in agreement.

'If you care to pay the entry fee of one guinea, Mistress Fraser, we'd be happy to accept you as a member of the Coffee House,' King was saying.

Christian had been carrying the paper-wrapped guinea ever since her first shawl was completed, preparing for the day when she would once again beard the other corks in their secluded den.

She thrust her hand into her pocket in search of it, but instead of the tiny hard parcel she felt her fingers closing round something soft and fragile.

She knew at once that it was the damask rose that had been tossed aside in Benjamin's garden, left to wither and die while the bush that had given it life travelled to London.

She felt the thrill of triumph ebb away, leaving in its place a great deep loneliness and the realisation that, now she had reached the summit she had been striving towards, there was nothing left for her in Paisley.

Her eyes sought the door, where once Benjamin Selbie had stood, arms folded, his eyes holding hers, willing the other men to accept her, angry for her sake when they denied her – as she had later denied him.

But the doorway was empty. He was far away, in London. And just as the rose in her pocket was dying without the roots and stems that had given it life, Christian herself knew she was nothing without the man she loved.

For a strange, brief moment she felt as though she was falling through space, with only emptiness beneath her feet. Then her mind cleared and suddenly she knew what she must do.

'Mistress Fraser?' Patrick King prompted her gently.

The exultation came sweeping, soaring back. She smiled at him, a dazzling smile that lit up the room as she withdrew the guinea from her pocket, unwrapped the paper around it, and put the coin down gently on the wooden table before her.

'Gentlemen' – her voice rang out clear and true and a hush fell on the room as they all craned to listen – 'I thank you for the honour you've done me today. This guinea is paid in the name of Rab Montgomery who, I trust, will be taking over the Fraser warehouse in my place.'

There was a flutter of movement as men turned to stare at each other, a furry buzzing of undertones and whispers.

Patrick King gaped at his young companion. 'But—'

'You must have your business talk with Rab, Mister King, not with me,' said Christian kindly.

She gathered up her skirts and left the Coffee House for the last time, pausing at the door to look at the sea of puzzled faces she was leaving behind.

'For me, gentlemen,' she said 'the damask days are over.'

As the coach rattled away from Paisley three days later some of Christian's fellow travellers peered out through the windows, but she herself looked straight ahead. The decision had been made. There was to be no turning back, no last sight of the town that had birthed and raised her. In her mind she heard the decisive click of a door closing, shutting out the past, leaving her with only the future to look to. A future that might or might not hold Benjamin Selbie.

She hadn't written to him or to Daniel to let them know that she was on her way south. She was quite aware that Benjamin's anger might still be too deep for him to forgive her for her earlier rejection. If so, Christian decided calmly, she would have to accept it and make her future elsewhere, alone. She wouldn't beg or plead. She wouldn't let him know, if he looked at her coldly, how much she loved him, wanted him. She would manage on her own. She would build a new life for herself without him.

But by the time she arrived in London several weary days later she was in such a ferment of longing to see him, to know her fate, that she couldn't take the time to go to Daniel's house and change her dusty, travel-stained clothing.

Instead, she hired a cab and went straight to the address that Daniel had given her in one of his letters.

The final part of her journey had been made by night. It was early morning when she arrived at the house.

'He's at his breakfast,' the elderly maidservant who opened the door told the caller, eyeing her crumpled clothes and her pale tired face with disapproval. 'I'm not certain if he'll want to be disturbed.'

Christian swept past the woman. 'Which room is he in?'

'That one, but—'

'If he can burst into my bedchamber, then I can walk into his breakfast room,' said the newcomer, and threw the door open before the scandalised woman could stop her.

When Benjamin, in shirt sleeves and with his fair hair

ungroomed, looked up at her, Christian's courage failed her. Instead of going across the room to him as she had intended she faltered, her fingers tightening on the door-handle, her heart suddenly racing.

It was only then, seeing him for the first time in months, that she realised how much she needed him. If he should reject her . . .

He got to his feet so swiftly that his chair fell over.

'Christian!' He spoke her name in a whisper, as though unsure whether he was seeing a living breathing woman before him, or a ghost conjured up by his own thoughts.

And when he came towards her, his face alight, she knew, with a blazing surge of happiness, that there was another door opening in her life.

He reached her and drew her into his arms without a word.

Returning kiss for kiss, her lips hungry beneath his, Christian joyously passed across the threshold, and into her future.